By the same author

Recherché: A Tale of Memories and Murder

Scherzo
A Venetian Entertainment

Jim Williams

Scribner

First published in Great Britain by Scribner, 1999
An imprint of Simon & Schuster UK Ltd
A Viacom Company

1 3 5 7 9 10 8 6 4 2

Simon & Schuster UK Ltd
Africa House
64-78 Kingsway
London WC2B 6AH

Simon & Schuster Australia
Sydney

A CIP catalogue record for this book is available from the British Library

ISBN 0-684-84012-X

Printed and bound in Great Britain by
The Bath Press, Bath

If you steal from one author, it's plagiarism; if you steal from many, it's research.

Wilson Mizner

And what of this new book the whole world makes such a rout about? – Oh, 'tis all out of plumb, my Lord – quite an irregular thing! – not one of the angles at the four corners was a right angle.

Laurence Sterne: *Tristram Shandy*

Je suis fou. Voilà toute ma sagesse.

M Arouet: *Philosophie et autres mensonges*

DEDICATION TO THE
TWENTIETH EDITION

To Monsieur VOLTAIRE

Alcázar en España
1st April 17—

Monsieur,

In this Degenerate Age, as my friend Signor Gucci has observed, a man may not buy his carriage, his watch, his baggage or his stockings upon their intrinsic Quality but only by the name or Reputation clapped on them like so many labels. So it is with Books: that they may as well be left to a drunken midwife as brought into the World without either the encomia of the tribe of Critics or a dedication to a Personage of Distinction. In this latter case the vicious practice has arisen of printing only the Dedication and not the Reply; so that an unscrupulous Author may foist his offspring upon Alexander the Great without risk of enquiry whether that poor booby was in a situation to decline the Honour; and thus a man may find himself God-father to a child of whose parents he is ignorant. Yet, Monsieur, such is my Confidence in you that I am certain that, should any Reader apply to you directly, he shall receive no reply depreciating this Work.

Monsieur, despite the remarkable Success of the first nineteen editions of the present Book (in the eyes of those

whom I Esteem), I find myself accused of Plagiarism,
Pastiche and the production of a mere Conceit spatchcocked
together from bits and pieces of Inferior Learning. As
to Plagiarism, I assure you that I eschew it as a vile
Crime which snatches bread from the mouths of Authors
and gin from the lips of Publishers (who should not be
forgotten since they take the greater risk in the Venture
— to say nothing of Editors, as, indeed, one does). As to
Pastiche: while an Author may be praised for his Mastery
of another's idiom, it seems to me probable that he will
be so constrained thereby that his Work will necessarily
be trivial and inconsequential — an achievement to which
no true Artist aspires. And, finally, as to Conceit: if the
Reader fulfils his duty by co-operating with the Author,
why then we shall both be Conceited together! The supposed
shallowness of my Learning matters not; for one must get
Wisdom where one may, and to this end I refer you to the
noble and learned Cicero, who said: 'Magis magnos clericos
non sunt magis magnos sapientes.'*

Therefore, Monsieur, I entrust this Child of mine
to your Generosity and challenge my Critics to produce
any observations of the Great Voltaire disparaging this
Book. In such a case they will promptly receive a fulsome
Apology from

Your fellow Philosopher and Author

---

* Them most biggest clerks ain't the most wisest. Editor's note: The author is in error in attributing this remark to Cicero; the source is Rabelais.

CHAPTER ONE

Overture

Take a country – let us say Italy. And a city – let us say Venice. The year was 17—. And there was a murder.

Be warned that my Italy may not be your Italy, nor my Venice yours. They may be the Italy and Venice of my imagination or indeed not Italy or Venice at all but a mere pretext or subterfuge, a literary fiction more plausible than Arcadia or Hyperborea. There is a fashion for these realms of the imagination. Do we suppose that Candide's Bulgaria or the territories of the Grand Turk have any existence outside the fancies of Monsieur Voltaire, even though we may locate them on the map? As for the year 17—, I have a notoriously poor memory for dates and perhaps I have allowed myself to juggle with events in the interest of dramatic effect and because, if things were not in fact just so, then, at least, they should have been. You will therefore understand from my elaborate deceit that this story must be true.

Your narrator is called Ludovico il Tedesco, and despite his undoubted corporeal reality he is just as much an equivocation, a doubtful essay at truth, as the date and place of his tale. He was not born with the name Ludovico, nor is he Italian. He is rather one Ludwig Bauer, an insignificant subject of the Electoral Prince of Bavaria in the Holy Roman Empire of the German Nation. Nor is he a man as the World understands these things.

Believe me when I tell you that I sing like an angel. As a child in my village of Kleinkleckersdorf and in its little church with an onion-dome and paintings of female saints in states of dubious ecstasy, I was famous. Indeed, I was so famous and my voice so clear and sweet, that my master the Elector packed me off to His Holiness the Pope. I sang in front of him, and the Pontiff and his Cardinals pronounced themselves delighted, praised me and showered me with sweetmeats; and my head was so turned with vanity that I scarcely noticed when they cut off my tender parts. In short, I was debollocked.

So who am I? Like the angels I sing and I do not age as others age, yet I am not an angel. Like a man I strut in breeches and powdered hair, yet in those things that make a man I am not a man. Am I a woman? Ah, well, I have my dreams! Let us leave it thus.

They call me Lewis the German and also Lewis the Eunuch, and sometimes Lewis the Liar.

In one thing I am not lying. The murder was real enough. And that excuses all my fakement. I have knowledge that I should like to share. But I have no desire to end my days at the bottom of a canal with a knife in my back.

During the seven years of my adolescence spent in Rome, I perfected my training as a singer. My build was slight and to this day I have never developed the massive chest and pendulous breasts of the mature castrato. It seemed that my destiny was to play young female parts in the opera. In the territories of the Holy Father women are not allowed on the stage. Their appearance would be indecent. By contrast it is entirely proper to emasculate young boys. In Rome I met Beppino della Mammana, who was one of the most famous in our profession and a person of great charm.

The close company of priests and de-natured boys is not likely to lead to the salvation of either. At the age of seventeen I grew tired of Rome and had a mind to go to Venice which was, even more than the Holy City, the goal of every visitor to Italy and the locus of every vice and frivolity in our vicious and frivolous age. I thought that my talents were more likely to be rewarded there.

I had managed to make some little savings from the allowance paid to me by my master, the Elector, and from the presents given to me for certain favours by my admirers. With these I made a contract with a *vetturino* who was going north and, by stages, in his coach and those of other *vetturini* I reached Padua.

There I spent some time enjoying myself with students at the Bo, which is their name for the university. Then, realising that I must sooner or later go to Venice, I took the *burchiello* which sails regularly up and down the Brenta canal between the two cities, and by this means at last reached my destination.

I was seventeen years old. I had no relatives or protector, no letter of recommendation or money, and no abilities other than the ones I have described. I soon discovered that my voice was not especially remarkable and that singing in the opera was a crowded and jealous occupation. I was unable to find work in that direction and therefore turned my talents to the only other job for which I was cut out.

Those next two years, which I spent, so to speak, servicing the needs of the Navy were the most miserable of my existence. I lodged in poor quarters near the Arsenal and earned my bread as Man – if not God – apparently intended. The brightest spot of that dismal period was the six months I lived as catamite to a Turkish merchant of a tolerable and generous disposition. The worst was a three-month spell as a slave, more or less, to a Slavonian captain in Venetian service who believed buggery to be the continuation of war by other means, as I was later to remark to a German officer who became a military historian of some repute.

I was relieved from my torment when, during a moment of intimate discourse with Signor Annibale Bulgarone, who will be remembered as the owner of the Teatro San Samuele for a time, I mentioned to him that I had once attracted the notice of Beppino della Mammana. It was made apparent to me that Signor Bulgarone had himself known Beppino both professionally and personally. Pleased with me, the *impresario* treated this connection as enough to give me an audition – though, in truth, it was no recommendation at all since he had only my word for it – and I was fortunate enough to satisfy him on the point of being able to sing competently.

At the Teatro San Samuele, I was put to the task of singing in the chorus or small female parts of no distinction. I have no pretension to being a great singer, and I have already mentioned that, for some reason, I did not acquire in the same degree the physical attributes of the famous castrati. Frankly, I had been lucky and it was enough that I could feed and clothe myself. Then, one night, I attracted the attention of Signorina Angelica Morosini.

The Morosini are an ancient, patrician family who have furnished Venice with several Doges and other dignitaries. Angelica's father, Signor Tomasso Morosini, was a member of the highest body of the state, the Council of Ten. He was cultivated and easy-going in manner, and mildly anti-clerical and enlightened in outlook. By way of disadvantage, he had a fierce family pride and also a kind of vanity, not so much of appearance as the intellectual kind, which he masked by his manners. Indeed he was the perfect dissembler of emotions. This branch of the Morosini lived in the Ca' di Spagna, so called to distinguish it from the family's other palazzi.

On her sixteenth birthday, Signor Morosini brought Angelica to the theatre. He did not consider the spectacle too indecent for a young mind. She was entranced. The piece was a slight one, of the kind that run briefly and are never revived, but it contained the role of a maidservant which I had the honour to play. Such roles earned my daily bread, but in this case the librettist's treatment of the young mistress was insipid and the servant, by contrast, was all the more fetching. It was this that my darling Angelica found so entrancing.

She turned to her father and proclaimed, 'Isn't she wonderful, Papa! And she even has my name, Angelica!'

'Certainly she sings her part with vigour,' replied her father.

'More than that! Don't be mean! She *is* Angelica to the life.'

'Yes, if you like.'

'I insist on it.'

'Very well, my dear child.'

Angelica – that is to say the real Angelica – applauded so enthusiastically that I, the *fausse* Angelica, took notice and began to sing for her benefit to bring out of the role those turns of humour that delighted her. And in the end, the two Angelicas, genuine and *fausse*, were pretty pleased one with the other.

The matter of *my* Angelica, was not, however, over with the performance. While I was removing my make-up, the other Angelica was disturbing her father. She told him, 'I

5

should like a servant just like that one. She's so witty and gay that I'm sure I'd become so too.'

'Possibly. However, my child, that particular maidservant isn't a maidservant at all, but a singer.'

'Pah! I have servants to do the things that servants do, but a companion who was always mine and who would be sweet and cheerful only for me, now that would be a treasure!'

'I can see that,' Signor Morosini agreed circumspectly, and at that point another of his guests came to his rescue by whispering something in Angelica's ear which caused some blushes but achieved the effect of cutting the flow of her demands.

Embarrassment was spared, but the matter was not over. Signor Morosini had himself enjoyed my performance, having had his attention forced on to it by his daughter. The latter was disappointed that it would be indecent for me to fulfil the role destined by her imagination, but the former had the idea that he could gratify her by inviting me to the Ca' di Spagna to give a recital in the proper form.

In due course that is what happened. I attended the Morosini family and sang to order; and, afterwards, as my patron condescended to talk to me, he discovered that I was not a mere clown. In addition to gatherings of a formal character and great respectability, Signor Morosini held regular suppers for his more liberal acquaintances, and at these I was even allowed to dine and join afterwards in the more general conversation. I do not wish to sound peevish. His liberality was genuine and I appreciated it.

My story, therefore, begins with my presence acknowledged in the Palazzo Morosini. I was the *faux* man, the *faux* Italian, the *fausse* maidservant, the *fausse* Angelica, and I was on the point of meeting the man whose brilliant and enigmatic character was to overthrow my judgment so that even after all these years I think of him with love and admiration.

And, of course, I must deal with the murder. Everything written above is essential, but is a mere prelude or overture to this last-named matter.

CHAPTER TWO

A Letter from an Uncle to a Niece

*Geneva
15th January 17—*

Dearest,

*Your last letter – like all your letters – ravished my
Heart. The Sweetness of your Endearments brings Tears to
my eyes and I could rush to your side, fall at your feet and
bathe them in those same Tears.*

*You say that you admire my Books. Flatterer! To
me they seem now to be no more than the prattlings of a
spirit oppressed by Tedium. I disdain all praise for their
supposed Wisdom. He only is wise who can earn the Love
of another. But, if it please you to receive my Affection in
the base coinage of my Writings, then so be it. You wish
to divine the Secret of their Creation. Truly you go to the
Marrow of the thing, for what writer knows his Muse by
her true name? If you had asked me about my poetic history
of Henri Quatre, I could perhaps have answered you
plainly. That Monarch brought Peace to France after the
Religious Wars, and, from an inspired Cynicism, exchanged*

Protestant Bigotry for Catholic Idolatry and instituted harmony between the two communities. Was his Cynicism reprehensible? No, it was Glorious! For only a man of Free and Courageous Spirit could pay those Fraudulent Priests with his own Fraudulent Confession of Faith. By treating both those Creeds with deserved Contempt, he pointed the way to the Worship of the Divine Being in true Simplicity of Soul. May I do likewise!

As to the other Book you mention, what shall I say? Shall you admire me less if I say that it was the creature of Chance, an inspired Joke? That I wrote it in the spirit of Levity and that such Wisdom as it may possess came simply from the writing of it, like the dung-cart following the parade? In truth that is how it often is. I tell a tale for the simple telling of it, wondering where it will lead me and who will be my Companions on the Journey. And they turn out to be the usual motley Pilgrims, each seeking Salvation in his own way. You will find them all in my Book: the Philosopher and the Charlatan, the Honest Fellow and the Huckster, the Lecher and the innocent Virgin. All of them myself, alas!

I am told – I do not know if it is true – that Monsieur Mozart, while on a journey to Vienna, had occasion to steal an orange and that, inspired by its associations with Italy, he proceeded to write a Work of great Sublimity on themes of that country. Does not this indicate the operations of Fortune or the Divine Humour? Who can prescribe for such eventualities and predict where they will lead? The orange inspired the music of Monsieur Mozart and perhaps (such are the workings of the Muse) that tale in itself will inspire another to write about it, though I shall not.

Now away with preliminaries, and I shall tell you a story about a story for whatever enlightenment it provides you. Some years ago I found myself in the city of Venice

10

and recommended to the attention of a great Nobleman of that place. He was pleased to extend to me his Society and the Hospitality of his Palazzo and I chanced to be in his company on that night, the night of the infamous Murder of which we have often spoken.

Now my Venetian Friend had many retainers in his household, and among their number was one Monsieur Louis. He was singing-master to the daughter of my friend and, to his Misfortune, was a member of that neutered race whom it pleases the Pope to employ in the singing of female and soprano parts. As to his person, being twenty years of age, he still possessed a certain physical Delicacy; indeed, let it be said, certain charms of the Gentle Sex which might have fooled the eye or beguiled the Heart of one who was not aware of his Vile Condition. As to manner he was light-hearted and kept frivolous company; but withal he had a native Wit. He was unaffected and honest in his dealings with his friends. He was, in short, Candid.

That night of the Murder we walked together to our respective lodgings for company and Safety. It was that season when Venice is full of Mists and Stinks, oppressive to the Spirit, gloomy and Dangerous. Monsieur Louis entertained me with his insouciant conversation. He came, he said, from Bavaria, and had been apprenticed in Rome. Fleeing the unnatural Vices of the Priests, he had taken a carriage to Padua, disguising himself as a student in case his unfortunate condition should cause him to be ejected by his fellow-passengers.

Now the custom is that, if the vetturino *is to provide food and accommodation for the journey, he dines with his passengers. I know these fellows and they have a rude Intelligence and a vulgar Curiosity. This one was of that tribe and he proceeded to interrogate his passengers.*

Among them was a German, a meat-fed Beer-guzzler

11

*with a great Belly covered in a snuff-coloured suit, heavy
snuff-coloured jowls overhung by a snuff-coloured Nose
like a sprouting Potato, and the ensemble topped by a
snuff-coloured wig. He took snuff.*

'And who may you be?' asked the solid vetturino.

*'I am Professor Doctor Allewörter,' returned our snuff-
coloured friend in Italian that was barely comprehensible
beneath a thick Swabian accent.*

'Indeed!' quoth the vetturino, *who in his own
estimation was a match for any Professor and who would,
no doubt, tell anyone who cared to know that he had
studied at the* università della vita. *'And of what, pray,
are you a Professor?'*

*'Of Philosophy, the purest and noblest of the Sciences. I
am a follower of the Great Leibniz.'*

*'Aha!' replied his host, undeterred. 'And what, Signore,
are the opinions of this Great Laidezza that should trouble
a working-man?'*

*'He believed and demonstrated that we live in the Best of
All Possible Worlds.'*

'Vero?' said the vetturino, *and for a while he was
silent. (I mention these silences because they are important in
any story-telling.)*

At length spake the good vetturino, *'No, Signore! It
can't be so. We Starve, we Suffer, we grow Ill, and we
Die. The Great Laidezza is mistaken. This world is
No Good.'*

*'On the contrary, my friend,' answered the Professor
contentedly. 'We are provided with Sun and Rain, Fruit
and Seed, Birds and Beasts aplenty. If we were only Wise,
this Earth would be a Paradise.'*

'B——cks!' said the vetturino *(in Italian, naturally)
and fell silent again. (And in this silence, my dear, while
the* vetturino *racks his brains for a Riposte, shall we*

*remember our many pleasant evenings by the fireside while
you read to me? Ah! Too late! He is quick, this fellow,
and has thought of something!)*

'What about Earthquakes? or Floods? or Plague? Don't
tell me that us poor devils are responsible for those!'

'Nevertheless, we live in the Best of all Possible Worlds.'

'How so?'

*A pinch of snuff. (Imagine this gesture – slow, delicate,
the very image of Complacency.)*

'Tell me, my good fellow – are you a good Catholic?'

'God willing, baptized and confirmed, Signore.'

'Then, I assume, you accept that God is Good?'

*A grunt. Tricky, these Philosophers. They can get you
burned. The* vetturino *remembers he is from Rome, where
the Inquisition plies its trade.*

'And is He omnipotent – that is to say, can He do
anything He wishes to do within the limits of the Possible?'

'Most likely He can do anything He damn well chooses,'
affirms our good Catholic.

'I don't ask you to go so far. He cannot make two plus
two equal five or black be the same as white, since these are
Absurdities, but He can do anything else that is Possible.
Do you agree?'

'I suppose so.'

'Very well,' *says the Professor.* 'If, then, God is both
Good and capable of doing anything that is Possible, it
follows necessarily that this must be the Best of all Possible
Worlds. To conclude otherwise is to assert that God is not
Good, or not Omnipotent, or not either.'

*And there we have it, my dearest! Optimism in all its
beautiful Simplicity, and who can attack the impeccable
Logic? Certainly not my young friend Monsieur Louis.*

*However, with the innocent Percipience for which I
admired him, he asked the learned Professor,* 'Professore,

what is your opinion concerning Murder and Murderers within the scheme of this World?'

'They are necessary,' came the firm answer.

'And are they good?'

Yes indeed! Is this not the veriest Touchstone? Let us hear the reply.

'A Murderer may damn his Soul to Hellfire by his act, but within the scheme of this World the same act must be as Necessary and Good as any other.' A pause. 'Yes, in this Best of All Possible Worlds, Murder is Good.'

Thus said Professor Doctor Allewörter, and he passed into Obscurity. Except that his shadow fell upon my young friend and then upon me. And now it falls upon you, darling Child.

So that is the tale of my candid friend and it allows me to answer your question. Where do Books come from? From trifles heard and seen.

Write to me soon. Better still, come to see

Your affectionate Uncle

CHAPTER THREE

Signor Ludovico's Narrative

Signor Morosini's private entertainments were given for a dozen or so persons. Their form was generally the same: a good meal to an instrumental accompaniment, followed by a song recital or other performance, and ending in a game of faro played by the gentlemen. My patron was a widower but he kept a faithful mistress, the Contessa della Torre da S——. She was an educated and witty woman and she held conversation with those gentlemen who had neither the mind nor the pocket for cards.

The guests were for the most part persons like my patron: that is to say, members of the patrician families who serve the Republic. In addition, I recall Cardinal Francesco Aldobrandini, who had once been the Contessa's lover and also the Comte de la Ferté who fought for the Austrian Empress in the Silesian war and ended his days in the service of the Turks. They, however, were in the nature of visitors and not of the regular company.

I dined with the gentlemen, and I fancy that my prettiness – I was only twenty – confused one or two of them. After dinner I took my accustomed position at the harpsichord and sang half a dozen songs. These were of my patron's composition to poems by Guidi. Frankly, Signor Morosini was an execrable composer, but, as I have said, he was a vain man where his intellectual or artistic productions were concerned. To satisfy my own pride, I embellished this rubbish with some elegant *fioriture* of my own which pleased both my patron and his guests. And afterwards they fell to playing cards.

I had not the money to indulge in cards and I was not expected to join the party. Instead I placed myself in the vicinity of the Contessa, who was engaging two gentlemen in conversation. It would have embarrassed my host had it appeared that I was a mere hired lackey, but my inferior position did not allow me to seize the reins of conversation, and I was content to wait in case they deigned to pay me some attention.

I doubt that the younger of the two men was my age, but he had the assurance of one much older. He was neatly made, handsome, and wore his own hair curled, lightly powdered and smelling faintly of ambergris. His clothes were modest but superbly tailored. There was something about him that suggested he was a priest in minor orders, an *abate* such as Italy is full of, and he might have been a companion to the Cardinal. However, I saw no sign of a cross. Instead I saw that his rings, of which he wore several, and his fob were engraved with curious symbols which I did not recognise. His complexion was attractively smooth and dark, which made me think of the Oriental. And, to add to this confusion of signals, there was his voice. He was cultivating a fine, literary Tuscan manner, with a few words of Veneziano appropriate to being in that city. But beneath this sophistication I detected the dialect of Sicily which he was at pains to mask.

For obvious reasons it was this good-looking young man

who attracted my attention. When I turned to the other, my impressions were quite different. Frankly, on this initial acquaintance, I found him unprepossessing. He was aged above fifty, perhaps even sixty. His clothes were of good, plain English cloth such as any respectable bourgeois might have worn. He wore a wig, very smart and powdered, but unfashionably long at the sides, which told me that his tastes had been fixed in the 'twenties or even earlier. As to his features, I was subsequently to change my mind, but this was my first impression. His nose was long and jutted out straight to a point. His eyes were small and glittered with malice or irony. His mouth was thin-lipped, a sharp slit that complemented nose and eyes. When all this assembly was in motion, it suggested slyness and deep intelligence. I shuddered when he spoke to me.

'Signor Ludovico, may I compliment you on your singing.'

'I am deeply obliged to you, Signore – forgive me, but I have not been granted the honour of knowing your name?'

'I am Monsieur Arouet, a Frenchman as you see.'

'I am grateful, Monsieur Arouet, that you enjoyed the songs.'

'Ah, yes' – he hesitated and studied me for the first time with that sharp yet equivocal gaze – 'the songs. I find that, on first hearing a song, one struggles to take in both words and music. I don't doubt that these songs will also improve with repetition. I note, however, that you introduced certain flowery notes which I think were of your own invention.'

'I hope they did not distract you from the beauties of Signor Morosini's composition?'

Monsieur Arouet smiled. 'No,' he said. 'They did not do that.'

His young companion now spoke to me. His tone was gracious, indeed irresistible. He had the ability to put others at ease with his perfect manners and yet, at the same time, retain an air of reserve.

'Your surname, "il Tedesco", is not, I fancy, a family name but designates your country of origin?'

'Indeed, I am a German, a subject of His Highness the Elector of Bavaria.'

This answer might have provoked an enquiry into my history and unfortunate condition, but my interlocutor's instincts were too delicate to press me as to matters that were both shameful and self-evident. Instead he began a digression for the benefit of the Contessa.

'We were speaking earlier of languages, Contessa. My friend's name, il Tedesco, reminds me. In the speech of the Copts, whose tongue is derived from that of the ancient Egyptians, "tedescah" signifies a song or perhaps a singer of the Temple. "Ludovico" may be taken as a compound of several words, the sense of which is that the person is noble or, at least, well-born. Signor Ludovico is to be complimented on a name that is both just and flattering – when viewed from the Coptic, of course.'

The Contessa giggled prettily at this pleasantry. 'I am never certain how much of what you say to believe, Signor Balsamo. You seem at the same time to be learned and frivolous. Do you really speak Egyptian?'

'Not perfectly, but I learned the tongue while travelling in that country for the purpose of my studies.'

'What were those?'

'I had studied the works of Hermes Trismegistus in the Greek, but I wished to confirm my understanding from the uncorrupted Egyptian.'

'I thought that the Egyptian characters remained undeciphered,' intervened Monsieur Arouet, making his point both accurately and mildly, and seasoning it with his sly smile.

Unperturbed, Signor Balsamo answered, 'It is true that they resist any literal or vulgar understanding. Their nature is to describe pictures or symbols which have to be interpreted metaphysically or metaphorically. As I say, I was using them merely as a check against the Greek.'

'Ah, yes,' mused Monsieur Arouet in apparent agreement. 'So much may be understood if one looks beneath the surface and reads it metaphysically or metaphorically, even life itself. Indeed, it may perhaps be possible to read even our friend Signor Ludovico as a metaphor for something else.'

Fortunately, the subject of myself – metaphorical or otherwise – was dropped and the party shortly broke up. Those who had come by boat went to their gondolas, while those who had brought servants returned home with them. My own intention was to return to my lodging on foot and accept the risk of being waylaid and robbed by the *bravi* who infested the darkened streets; but for more fortunate guests, who included Monsieur Arouet, our host summoned his own people, who would accompany them with lanterns and cudgels.

'Where are you bound?' Monsieur Arouet asked me. I told him.

'It seems that Signor Morosini cannot spare servants for all his guests, but your way lies with mine, Signor Ludovico. I should be honoured if you would accompany me and, in this way, we may each protect the other.'

'I am infinitely obliged,' I said with a well-judged bow. It was no less than the truth. Despite his appearance, Monsieur Arouet had shown me true kindness and done so with the most delicate regard for my situation. So far as appearances go, perhaps his, too, was a metaphor for something else – I do not know. However, this small attention on his part began the transformation of my impression of him. What my feelings became will be discovered in the rest of this history.

*   *   *

It was the cold season. The night was pitch-dark. The time was about six o'clock, counting from the evening angelus. The canals were almost empty, but we had our faithful link-boy, who jogged along a few paces behind us with his lantern wavering and casting an erratic light. Unquestionably there were strangers about, dark figures haunting alleys and doorways, but three men in obvious good health could walk in security.

The notion that the lodgings of myself and Monsieur Arouet lay along the same route now appeared to me fanciful. Despite my appearance of prosperity, I was living in a garret in the Calle Malipiero and my companions in slumber (since I could not afford a whole room) were my lover and fellow castrato, Tosello, and sundry actresses and whores. I imagined that the Frenchman had a room in an hotel or with a decent family. Still he made no suggestion that our path was other than convenient for him. He seemed inclined to talk. He asked me my history and, in view of his kindnesses, I could not refuse him. However, since I have already stated my history in the overture to this work, I do not propose to elaborate it with variations and counterpoint.

At the story of Professor Doctor Allewörter my companion burst into laughter of the most open and agreeable character, which confirmed my growing good opinion of him.

'You think with me, then, that he is mistaken? That we do not live in the best of all possible worlds?' I said.

Monsieur Arouet shook his head. 'On the contrary. His premisses are sound; God is good and He is, indeed, omnipotent. Ergo it follows, as the Professor so aptly demonstrated, that we live in the best of all possible worlds – plagues, famines, volcanoes and murders notwithstanding.'

'Then I have done a good man an injustice,' I admitted reluctantly.

Monsieur Arouet detected my disappointment and placed a hand on mine. 'No, my young friend. You have done an injustice to a sound logician. But you have identified a perfect fool.' He then recited a poem to me in English, which he translated for my benefit. It went thus:

> *All Nature is but Art, unknown to thee;*
> *All Chance, Direction, which thou canst not see;*
> *All Discord, Harmony not understood;*
> *All partial Evil, universal Good:*
> *And, spite of Pride, in erring Reason's spite,*
> *One truth is clear, 'Whatever is, is Right.'*

At the end he said, 'The author of that piece is Alexander Pope, who in this particular is also a fool. Do not be puzzled by folly and wisdom occupying the same mind, like a woman with a fine bosom and an ugly face. I am often a fool, but I think nothing of it.'

'You are too subtle for me,' I said.

'And you are too candid,' he answered. 'But, come, we'll speak of it again; and perhaps in one of my literary excursions I shall make something of this fellow Allewörter.'

The remark concerning my new friend's literary excursions seemed an invitation to satisfy my curiosity concerning his own circumstances. I asked, 'Monsieur, forgive me, but you seem, also, to be of a philosophical turn of mind.'

'That is true, though I have little to do with building great systems of thought in the manner of Leibniz. I should be content if superstition were removed from Religion and if Reason were applied to the acquisition of knowledge and the ordering of human affairs. Whatever I have written is directed at those simple goals.'

21

'Would I know your works, Monsieur?'

'No. Your education has been in Rome, and my writings are all on the Index of Forbidden Books. In the mind of His Holiness I am an atheist, though I fancy he would find more atheists among his Cardinals or his predecessors.'

'You frighten me.'

'I frighten myself. Anyone must, who sets up his private confections of wisdom and folly against Revealed Truth. Still, one does what one must.'

The last remark was delivered in a melancholy tone. We were both tired and a little cold, and the light from the lantern, feeble at best, was fading because the lazy fellow who carried it had not replaced the candle before venturing into the night.

To revive our spirits, if only by the sound of my own voice, I asked, 'What is it that has brought you to Venice? And how do you come to know Signor Morosini?'

'I was not previously acquainted with your patron' was the answer. 'However, I bear a letter of introduction from a nobleman who is pleased to consider me his friend – I speak of the Duc de Richelieu. As to my purpose here in Venice, I have come to publish a book. In France I am, for the time-being, out of favour with His Majesty. In Venice, on the other hand, it is not a question of favour. For the appropriate fee one can find a printer who will print anything.'

'But won't such an illegal publication simply aggravate your problems in France?'

'No. Rather there is a considerable advantage. I can claim that the work was published without my authority or that the printers have introduced offensive material in order to increase the sales. Both practices are well known. Where publishing is concerned, one can say anything and expect to be believed. Now,' my companion said, 'are we not near the Calle de le Ostregha? I believe I recognise my way.' In fact, we were in the square beyond, near the church.

I was glad that my friend apparently lived at some little distance from my lodging, since I did not want Monsieur Arouet to see the squalor and low company that lay behind my appearance. In any case, there was no advantage, since the lantern was quite gone out and we should have had to proceed in the dark. I began to make my thanks and farewells, which he returned while still accompanying me a few paces to where a lane led from the square and divided to cross a dark, narrow canal by two bridges hard by one another. As if recollecting himself and our respective positions, the tones of slyness and irony were returning to his voice, though his words were generous enough. Alas, I thought, he will never be a true friend. I was conscious that there was a gulf of intelligence and education between us and that I was in all probability no more than a toy which a superior mind handles and then discards.

Just then my companion said, 'Have you any notion what it is that is hanging under the other bridge?'

I should explain that I was on the steps at an angle of the church which led to the bridge on the right hand. This would take me into the Campiello de la Feltrina. The bridge to the left was somewhat smaller and darker and crossed to a short length of embankment that served only as access to the buildings on that side of the canal. I say this from knowledge, not observation on that night when this corner of the city was black as pitch.

And, indeed, at first I could see nothing, but, by degrees, I made out the shape of what appeared to be a white bat, and around it something fluttering. To my mind the spectacle was nothing. I was inclined to ignore it. Monsieur Arouet, however, as I should have learned, was a person of considerable curiosity and, having dismissed the possibility that it was a seagull (as I inclined to think), he told the servant to hold his cudgel at the ready since he intended to investigate. I was dragged along by the simple power of suggestion.

We took the few steps towards the bridge. I kept an eye out for the *bravi* whose presence might account for an untoward event. I saw none. The night remained dark and chill and a salt mist rose from the water.

As we came closer, the shape began to resolve itself without enlightening me except that the white object was only part of some greater thing that hung under the bridge. It was this latter, the thing as a whole, a perfect blackness, that was fluttering against a lesser blackness.

'It is a man,' announced my companion. At once I could see he was right. No sooner was I told so than I saw that it could be no other. The body of a man was suspended from the bridge. It was clad in a full black cloak and a plumed hat, and the face was covered by a white mask. A dagger was embedded in the chest and protruded through the cloak.

CHAPTER FOUR

An Extract from A History of My Life
by Jacques de Seingalt

My return from Venice occurred shortly before the famous
murder to which I have referred. This was a curious crime.
Its very existence was denied, and yet all the world knew
of it. The secrecy was because of the character of the victim
and the interests of the State. But in the end the solution
showed it to be a mundane affair. The deceased was killed by
one Fosca or Foschia, a carpenter, who strangled him in the
course of a robbery. This Foschia was duly executed, though
in secret.

To my discomfort I was suffering again from the *chaudepisse*,
which for the time-being put an end to any thought of
amorous adventures – or at least to their consummation.
While remedying this condition, I tried to live modestly
and mend my fortune and reputation. I earned a modest
competence as clerk to a notary and reminded the world of
my diplomatic service in Constantinople and of my military
service in Corfu.

Yet I was still young and infirm of purpose. My courses
could always be swayed by the impulses of friendship or

sentiment. Always in intent, my behaviour towards the gentle sex has been inspired by chivalry. My infidelities have occurred because a cruel fate has pulled me away from my mistress. I reproach myself, but not for any evil motive.

Walking in the street one day I came across some old companions, Signori Ludovico and Tosello. These gentlemen were young like myself, but unfortunate creatures who had been made eunuchs for the sake of art. Nevertheless, they were as jolly as any other *bravi* and inclined to present pleasure since the joys of family, respect in this life, and external bliss in the next were all denied to them.

'La!' piped Ludovico. 'Am I deceived in seeing my friend Signor Giacomo?'

'It is indeed I,' I replied, and we repaired to a tavern where, over a jug of wine, we explained our present circumstances. Tosello was engaged to play the King of Ethiopia in some opera or other, and Ludovico was a singing-master.

When we were fuddled with wine, Tosello (who had the most money) proposed, 'Why do we not go to the Ridotto?' This was a foolish suggestion, since we were none of us in a position to gamble our non-existent fortunes, but we all agreed. After returning to our lodgings to dress, we gathered in the Piazza San Marco, which is hard by the Ridotto, and duly masked we entered the premises. However, I soon forsook the society of my companions. It seemed to me that they were intent on filling their purses by the pursuit of an ancient and dishonourable trade (alas, too common in their condition) and I did not wish my own reputation to be affected. Indeed, I saw each of them later in the company of some decrepit roués more pox-ridden than a camp whore.

For my part, I went to the room where faro was played, and there I watched the cards with the air of one who is merely bored. As I have stated, my preference is to hold the bank and satisfy myself with the advantage given to the house. I decline the punt itself since, though exciting enough, one can make no play or calculations which will influence the result. In the immediate case, however, circumstances did not permit me to hold the bank. Firstly, I had no funds to risk against an unlucky run of cards; and, secondly, in the public gaming-houses only patricians are permitted to act as bankers. Except for the latter and the servants, everyone was masked.

The custom of going masked adds a spice to the amorous arts. Every encounter is a risk, when she of the seductive voice may not be as fair as she seems. Yet it gives opportunity for wit and education to shine, and more ladies have been won by fine words than by a fine leg. And, of course, it is a game which can be played by two. An encounter of two masks is an encounter of illusions, and each is who it says it is until a more intimate conversation shall, perhaps, reveal the truth. I have been at times soldier, cleric, notary, necromancer and nobleman: Italian, French, Austrian and Turk – all as fancy and my own skill took me. And, although I should decline to enter upon a serious engagement under such false colours (which would not be the conduct of a gentleman or man of true sentiment), still they are good for casual sport with some fair deceiver.

Having little to do but observe my fellow-gamblers, my eyes lighted upon the form of a lady. In common with others she was wearing a hat, a black half-mask, and a *bautta* of silk which extended as a hood and mantle over a dress of *gros-de-Tours*. Hidden in this *maschera nobile* it was impossible to discern the lineaments of her person, but this is the very challenge and enchantment of the mask. Was she a crone or a beauty? A turn of her head, a glimpse of a foot, a delicate wrist, her lips, a flash of white teeth convinced me of the latter. There seemed no reason why I should not address her.

'Signora, it seems that you have dropped a coin.'

Her reply seemed more nervous than the occasion demanded. 'I thank you, Signore, but you are mistaken.'

Her accent was not Venetian but I could not place it. Certainly it was beautiful. Her voice was light and limpid.

'Then, if I may keep it in good fortune, I may in the same fortune chance it with her who gave it to me.' So saying, I matched her wager with a small stake of my own.

'You may do as you wish, though you are mistaken to regard your fortune as a gift from me and the occasion is no reason for you to press your attentions on me.'

There was acid in the reply. I looked around to see if I could recognise a male companion, but it seemed that she had come alone – interesting in itself. I decided to show my own steel.

'You do me wrong, Signora. In this place a lady may expect to receive the addresses of admiring strangers. I shall not forgo the prerogatives which both pleasure and custom afford me.'

She nodded in assent to my common right. I did not pursue my advantage. Many a siege is spoiled by a premature assault. Instead I continued to wager with her – not every time, since I must be sparing with my money, but enough to accustom her to my presence and to indicate a certain intimacy between us. Fortunately I won; but, for once, I did not let it turn my head.

'You have brought me luck,' I said.

'Indeed, Signore, it is you who have brought me luck. And for that I am grateful. Lately I have lost more than is convenient. Now seems the time to pause for wine or a cordial.' It was understood without invitation that we should seek our refreshment together.

'You are restrained in your pleasures,' she said. She was too delicate to say outright that my stakes were small. I had a choice: to claim poverty in order to excite her sympathy, or to be the man of prudence in order to attract her confidence. She appeared vulnerable to me: her pleasures fragile. I decided to be the rock who would shelter her from the blast.

'I weigh each pleasure and pay a just price for it and no more.'

'La!' she replied with the first note of gaiety. 'That is not a quality one expects to find at the Ridotto. Surely the pleasure of gaming is precisely to risk that which one cannot afford – in short, to pay too high a price?'

'One can gamble with more than coin. One may hazard one's reputation.'

Her eyes closed and her tongue passed thoughtfully along her lips.

'And what do you risk instead of coin?' she asked at last.

'I speak to you, Signora, and risk contempt and humiliation.'

She gave no answer. We resumed our play. The cards were with me but I stuck to my chosen role of prudence, though I all but choked to see the winnings I could have made. She was now gay, having continued to bet heavily and successfully.

'Truly,' she said, 'you exercise an iron control to limit yourself when from your winnings you might have doubled your stake.'

'My plan of life and purposes are constant,' I answered her. 'As are my faith and feelings. I can be no other.' Lest I be accused of hypocrisy, let me say that, in spirit at least, every word of this was true. I confess to my failings in practice. I mention this because successful love-making depends upon sincerity.

I was content that I had won the interest of the fair stranger and that, to some degree, she was in my power, since her visits to the Ridotto were evidently clandestine or, at best, disapproved of. However, it is not enough to reconnoitre the weaknesses of the opposing army; one must bring it to the appropriate field of battle. As to the latter, I was, as yet, ignorant of the terrain. However, I was in no hurry. The bodily affliction I had received from Cupid was still waiting on a cure and must delay the conflict *corps à corps*; but, happily, this necessary restraint fitted my character of honest gentleman. Both character and circumstance dictated that I reduce Love's citadel by a siege in regular form, and I was resolved to enjoy the pleasures of a leisurely campaign.

'Correct me, if I am mistaken,' I said. 'It seems to me that you are unescorted this evening. I make no enquiry as to the reasons, but feel obliged to offer my services.'

'My people are waiting for me,' she answered cautiously.

'I do not doubt it. But, in the event of a disturbance, a paid lackey may value his skin more than his honour.'

The last point gave me an idea. Given my suspicion that she might on this occasion decline my aid, it occurred to me that for a small sum I could persuade Ludovico and Tosello to play the part of rowdies and give my fair one a fright, so that on the next occasion she would look favourably on my suggestion. However, this stratagem proved unnecessary. I had wrought better than I knew. In her lovely eyes I saw a moist film of gratitude and, taking my fingers in hers, she accepted.

I confess that, as we stepped into the night, I felt a profound contentment. My purse was modestly full and I was on the way to a conquest fairly won. Although I did not know my companion's name nor, indeed, very much else about her, I was convinced that she was a creature of refinement and sensibility. Moreover, I had behaved honourably and could justly regard myself as free from reproach. Granted I must anticipate, from my fair one's caution, that there was a husband or father in the background. But, since he did not deign to attend or perhaps was ignorant of her pleasures, he was evidently a bully or a buffoon, wholly undeserving of such an exquisite woman. Honour does not confer rights on such as those. A gentleman may cuckold them with a clear conscience.

Emerging from the Ridotto, we were met by a bow-legged, squint-eyed homunculus who barely reached the height of my chest. He was my lady's servant. We followed his lantern to a gondola, where he took the oar and cast us off.

My charmer said, 'I must beg you, Signore, to wear a blindfold.' She removed one of the fichus in which she had wrapped herself and tendered it to me. I had not expected this but my honourable character would not suffer me to do aught but accept it. I began to wish that I had chosen the guise of a poor *abate* and appealed to my lady's charity. It seemed that I was to be denied both her name and any knowledge of where she lived. However, I cheered myself with the thought that this avoidance of the battleground was testament to the weakness of the forces marshalled against me, and that once I brought her to the field I should have short work in accomplishing the tender victory.

We travelled some little time and with little sound except the lapping of the water and, now and again, snatches of song as other revellers made their way home. At length, my eyes were unbound and I found myself in the darkness of a narrow canal flanked on one side by the high wall of a palazzo which gave on to the canal by a water-gate. There we duly moored.

'Now we must part,' said my lady. She pressed my hand in hers. 'You are my good and gentle cavalier.' I saw at once that she was of the melancholy kind and responded in the same vein.

'I, too, have suffered,' I said, and prayed that she would not enquire as to the nature of my pain. I could think only of the discomfort within my breeches.

'Yes, I can tell.'

'Indeed?'

'Truly. Your high regard for our sex can come only from one who has loved too well and, dare I say, been loved.'

'You cut me to the quick.'

She hesitated. 'You have not asked to see beneath my mask,' she said.

The languor in her voice made plain to me that this was a prize she desired to bestow – and the sigh that concluded her remark told me it was a prize she must deny me. No matter: I was firmly resolved to take no advantages on that night. The surprising of a sentry may alert the garrison. I would proceed as planned, by sap and mine, until I was certain the entire fortress would fall.

'Chivalry forbids,' I said. 'I will take only what is given out of affection and nothing out of gratitude. I could do no more than offer my humble service, and it was trivial enough.'

'In the Ridotto I was . . . lonely.'

'I know,' I said.

'How could you?'

'You answered your own question. I have loved too well.'

At that I saw a tear, and I knew how to value it. Rather than shame it away by staring, I turned and signalled to the homunculus that he should return whence we came. I even put on the blindfold.

It is well never to do these things by halves.

It was understood that we should meet again at the Ridotto. I was certain that I could, in time, persuade my melancholy mistress to reveal herself, but it seemed to me that, in her gambling, she was bent on such dangerous courses that the brute who had her under his roof must needs soon discover her conduct. Then chance would take away my lady, perhaps before I could enjoy her favours. This seemed an unnecessary risk.

I remembered my idea concerning Ludovico and Tosello and saw how they might still be turned to my purpose. If I could learn the name of the mysterious palazzo, the identity of my lady would follow. I was reluctant to discard my blindfold or remove the fair one's mask until I was fully equipped for the fight (which my doctor said would be some weeks yet). In the meantime, what could be simpler than for my two friends to follow our gondola? Nay, I would go further. They should waylay us and between them, I had no doubt, pitch the homunculus into the water. With a show of bravery, I would beat off their attack. Thus, at a stroke I should have the means to discover my mistress's identity and show myself in a light that would earn not only her gratitude but her admiration. I was dizzy at the perfection of my plan! I put it at once to my friends.

'I have seen the dwarf loitering in the piazza,' said Tosello doubtfully. 'He may be small but he appears powerful. It may be that he will pitch *us* into the canal.'

'Have courage!' I told him.

'It is not a question of courage,' lisped Tosello. 'I have to consider my voice. A good soaking might ruin it.'

Ludovico had more spirit and intelligence. 'I don't see that it is necessary to trade blows with the fellow,' he said. 'Tosello could hold him at pistol-point while you and I, Giacomo, exchange some passes with the sword. We have enacted enough mock-fights on stage to give a passable performance in the darkness.'

This seemed sensible to me and so it was resolved upon.

My second evening at the Ridotto in the society of my lovely companion was much as the first: that is to say that my infernal good luck was still with me and I could not exploit it without betraying myself as a profligate. I wondered if the game was worth the candle. It might be better to take the money and lose the lady. However, I reflected that Fortune is herself a fickle mistress and, like as not, if I abandoned my charmer my luck at cards would also change. At least I had the reward of seeing that my restraint increased her regard for me, for my modesty and firmness.

Her good fortune following mine, she was melancholy merry. Like many gamblers she took no pleasure in it. Indeed, I myself take little pleasure in gambling for its own sake. It is being a generous, open-handed fellow that I esteem, which is far the more gentlemanly part. Your calculating gamester is contemptible.

Tonight, with many sidelong glances, flickering smiles and accidental touchings as we placed our wagers, my lady confirmed to me that, increasingly, I enjoyed not merely the cool regard of her intellect but a share of the tender passions of her heart. This was, I fancied, a faculty not much exercised by her present guardian; in fact, it passed through my mind that she might be a virgin, so unpractised did she seem. So be it. Though maidens are in general to be avoided, both for the difficulties in winning them and for the unpredictable and often unsatisfactory results, I am not averse to the attempt. Indeed, if it may be done without injury to reputation, it is a charity and a duty to prepare such gentle creatures for the world. I have been thanked on this account: I can say it without boasting.

I am myself a creature of the heart. I possess sensibilities almost feminine in their delicacy. I cannot bear to see a fellow-soul suffer. Maiden or not, my sad lady was suffering and I was encouraged to redouble my efforts in the knowledge of the Paradise of feeling to which I should in time introduce her. My addresses to her that evening were so touching in their refinement, in the nice consideration they showed for every nuance of emotion that stirred her breast, that I shun committing them to paper. It is enough that by the end of the evening I was convinced that I had engaged her sentiments entirely. Rather, my concern was that the advance of my forces was too sudden: the enemy was defeated before the field of battle was prepared. I feared I might be unable to maintain her heightened state of receptivity until I was ready to assault the breach.

We left the Ridotto as before, under the eye of the watchful homunculus (he was, she told me, a retainer of her own family and slavishly bound to her). We took the gondola and I suffered myself to be blindfolded without a murmur. First, however, I caught sight of Ludovico and Tosello, who followed us into the night, giggling with drink and making sport of us by kissing and fondling. Still, fools have their uses.

Again the quiet darkness accompanied us through the twists and turns of the canals until we reached the dark shadow of the palazzo. There I was released from blindness.

'You may kiss me,' said my lady. 'Here, upon the cheek. A kiss of friendship.'

I did not refuse what was so freely offered, and I breathed in the scents of ambergris and styrax. At the same time I caught a glimpse of another gondola, black and bearing no lantern, which came gliding from behind us. Ludovico and Tosello! I put my hand upon my sword in preparation for the fight. Then I noticed that only one masked and hooded figure occupied the vessel. He stood at the prow and held in both hands a pistol, which seemed directed not at the homunculus as we had agreed but at me. Confusion! Had I been betrayed? What was I to make of this? I had no choice but to carry through my part with courage, and turning to face my enemy I covered my lady's body with my own and drew my blade.

The pistol ignited with a blinding flash and I fell headlong into the water.

CHAPTER FIVE

Signor Ludovico's Narrative

At the sight of the body under the bridge, Monsieur Arouet said, 'You must return to the palazzo while I remain here with this fellow. Rouse the Watch and return with some of Signor Morosini's people.'

He spoke so authoritatively that I felt I had no option but to obey. By the time I reached the Ca' di Spagna, however, the house was barred and in darkness and I had to bang and shout before I could attract attention. The person who answered the door was not a servant but Signor Feltrinelli, who was factor or man of business to Signor Morosini.

He said to me, abruptly, 'What are you doing back here at this time of night?'

I was not cast down by his manner. We were both no more than superior lackeys and he owed me no particular deference, but rather the opposite.

'A thousand apologies for disturbing you, Signor Feltrinelli,' I blurted out breathlessly. 'Your master's guest, Monsieur Arouet, and I have just discovered a body hanging from the Duodo bridge. I've been sent to rouse the Watch and return with some of your people to recover the body.'

Grudgingly, the factor led me into the kitchen and gave me a glass of spirits, and at once began to wake up the servants and issue orders. He also put on his own coat and said he would himself rouse the Watch and leave a message at the house of the Avogadore, so that the prosecutor might take charge of the case first thing in the morning. Although I was exhausted and, as I now realised, shaken by the discovery of the corpse, I insisted that I go with the party of servants to the bridge.

So, for the second time, I ventured into the night. Half a dozen of us, lanterns and cudgels swinging, trotted along the dark and misty *calli*, hooting and calling at the noise of every scurrying rat and generally making a fine racket in our excitement and self-importance.

I was surprised when, as we approached the bridge, Monsieur Arouet sprang up and whispered loudly and furiously, 'Will you all be quiet! This is not a gypsy show or the Commedia. This poor fellow whose body we have found was a gentleman. Until we know who he is and have informed the authorities, we do not know if this death happened as we believe or whether in some other fashion – or, indeed, not at all. Do you louts and stockfish understand me?'

I cannot swear they understood, but my companions were cowed by Monsieur Arouet's wrath and show of authority. Meantime he knelt on the ground by a bundle and I saw that he and the first servant had, in my absence, hauled the poor dead creature from under the bridge and laid him as decently as might be. Though I said nothing, it seemed to me that the Frenchman had been rifling the corpse when we arrived.

No-one had thought to bring the wherewithal to carry the body – if such an object existed in the Ca' di Spagna – and we therefore had to wait on the arrival of the Watch, who were used to dragging bodies from the canals and no doubt equipped for the task. In a short time they arrived, four *sbirri* in the company of the respectable Signor Feltrinelli. The latter stared down at the body and then looked at Monsieur Arouet.

He said, 'I note, Monsieur, that you have not removed the mask. I find that curious.'

Monsieur Arouet replied coolly, 'As you rightly guess, I have removed the mask and replaced it. Need I explain?'

Feltrinelli stepped forward. He called for a lantern, knelt and lifted the white mask so that only he could see the face. He emitted a gasp but otherwise said not a word. He turned to the *sbirri*.

'You shall take this poor soul's remains to the Ca' di Spagna. One of my people will go with you and none of you shall lift the mask or look on the face. Is that clear?' Looking now at myself and the Frenchman he asked us, 'Do you intend to return to the palazzo, Signori, or go to your lodgings? Monsieur Arouet, I should appreciate an account of what you have seen and done tonight, but Signor Ludovico is . . . not so important.' For a while he paused as if overcome, and then he whispered some orders to another of his people. To the rest of us he said, 'I have sent a second message to the Avogadore, pressing him to attend on us tonight instead of in the morning. In the circumstances, I propose that we all return to the palazzo.'

That being said, there was no choice in the matter, except perhaps for Monsieur Arouet, friend of the Duc de Richelieu. The rest of us, mere creatures like myself, followed in the wake of the great and could only ask ourselves: who is this dead man, that the very fact of his death may have to be kept secret?

We returned to the kitchen of the Ca' di Spagna and the body of the murdered man, masked and clothed except for his wig and plumed hat, was laid on a table. It was now eight o'clock by the angelus, still dark but the scullions were stirring and wished to be at their preparations for breakfast. Signor Feltrinelli bade them to prepare a cold collation and go, and he also told Signor Morosini's valet to waken his master and summon him to the kitchen.

I was impressed by Signor Feltrinelli's quiet command of the situation and ought, I suppose, to say something about him. He was, I should guess, in his thirty-fifth year or thereabouts, a well-made man whose features ought to have been handsome, yet were not. This failure was attributable to a lack of animation in his demeanour. He was self-controlled and his behaviour was invariably restrained and proper. As to character, his quick response to the murder says something of his level-headedness. I found him neither friendly nor condescending. He was not in the strict sense, responsible for the household, which was in the hands of a steward, but more for the family's business and financial affairs generally. I had known him for about twelve months. He had been engaged after his predecessor was dismissed for theft.

While the three of us waited for Signor Morosini and the Avogadore, Signor Feltrinelli posed some questions.

He asked me, 'Did you remove the mask and view the face?'

'No, upon my honour.'

'Why do I doubt you?'

'You doubt my honour, Signore?' I answered indignantly.

He replied, 'Come, do not be so tender. The language of honour does not suit your state.'

Monsieur Arouet came to my aid. I could see that he had respect for the factor, but no particular liking.

'I can vouch for Signor Ludovico, as can your own man. The corpse was hanging beneath the bridge when he left us. No-one could remove the mask save myself.'

Signor Feltrinelli necessarily accepted the implied rebuke. He turned his questions against his critic. 'I know, Monsieur, that you removed the mask. Did you recognise the face?'

'I did not.'

'Then why did you cover it again? Your manner made clear to me that you recognised a certain necessity for secrecy.'

Monsieur Arouet acknowledged the point with a brief nod. 'From the clothes I judged the dead man to be a person of quality. The death of any such person is a matter of some delicacy. And here in Venice, where so many of the nobility are concerned in governing the State, a private matter may easily become a public one.' The justice and shrewdness of this answer were impressive.

At this point Signor Morosini came into the room. He was wearing a night-shirt over which he had put on a heavy quilted gown of an embroidered material. On his head was a turban tied hastily to hide his shaven scalp and his feet were covered in Turkish slippers. Alfonso, his valet, had briefly told him that there was a cadaver in his kitchen and that the Avogadore had been summoned. It was an inadequate preparation.

'Dearest God!' exclaimed my patron. The dead man was indeed a pitiful sight. The dagger protruded from his chest, and the cloak and what I could see of his fine clothes were soaked in blood. Signor Feltrinelli stepped forward to offer a glass of spirits to his master. The latter asked, 'Do we know who it is?'

Monsieur Arouet and I shook our heads. The factor gave no sign. Signor Morosini swallowed his drink in one gulp, removed the mask so that all could see the face and gasped one word, '*Alessandro!*' before collapsing on to a stool.

I have some knowledge of the theatre and recognise a moment that should be one of high drama. But the truth is that the Great Ones of this earth have an exaggerated sense of their own fame, and I must confess that neither the face nor the name was of any significance to me.

Evidently my French friend was in the same state of ignorance, for he asked gravely, 'Do you know this gentleman, Signore?'

Not observing a cautious signal from his man of business, Signor Morosini answered with emotion, 'It is my friend Signor Alessandro Molin. He is a great nobleman and a member of the Council of Ten.'

I was now somewhat the wiser. Though this Alessandro Molin was unknown to me, I had a notion that some other Alessandro Molin had been an Admiral of the Republic in a long-past war against the Turk.* This intelligence was of interest but of no great moment. The mention of the Council of Ten was, however, a wholly different matter: for it had a sinister and terrible reputation. If I say that I quaked at the thought of the retribution it would visit upon the murderer, I may be believed. And not only upon the murderer. The wrath of the State did not make fine distinctions of person.

Some minutes later, Signor Dolfin arrived in response to Signor Feltrinelli's summons. He was a friend of my patron, a regular companion at his supper-parties and indeed he had attended earlier on that same evening. He was also one of the three Avogadori who handled the legal affairs of the Republic: in appearance a small man, fleshy-faced and serious of manner. Like the other nobles I had encountered, he had a fine opinion of himself. In his case that meant conveying at all times and places the air of judiciousness.

His attention was first directed to Signor Morosini, who

---

* Alessandro Molin, Captain-General of the Venetian forces, won several victories over the Ottomans in the years 1696–1698.

was still showing evident signs of distress. But, as he opened his mouth to speak to his friend, so his eyes had already passed on to the corpse and he, too, registered recognition and shock.

'Good God! Alessandro! What terrible accident is this?'

The answer came from Monsieur Arouet. 'The matter is no accident, Signore. There has been a murder. I myself discovered the body.'

The calm note of command in his voice seemed to stir Signor Morosini who raised his head and, regarding the lawyer, said, 'Alas, Monsieur Arouet speaks the truth. I am at a loss . . . I cannot . . .'

Signor Feltrinelli assisted his master by explaining, 'The gentlemen present are aware of the identity of the person in question and the delicacy of the circumstances. They are men of honour and can be trusted to wait on the decision of Your Excellency and the Council.' He went on to give some particulars of Monsieur Arouet and myself beyond what Signor Dolfin already knew. I was described as 'someone who has obligations to the family and knows his duty'. More interestingly he said of Monsieur Arouet, 'Your Excellency has seen the letter of introduction from the Duc.' The remark made me curious. It showed, on the part of Signor Feltrinelli, a degree of intimacy in his master's affairs that I had not expected. And secondly it raised a question. Who was Monsieur Arouet that he should own the friendship of a Duke? He had claimed to be a mere scribbler. However, I had no time to consider the point. The Avogadore seemed desirous of minimising the significance of the incident.

He said, 'Doubtless we are dealing with a matter of robbery. I shall call the *sbirri* and have the body removed. The Watch will be put on alert and we may discuss the subject further in the morning.'

With that he would have given orders to bring in his men

and, perhaps, I should have heard no more. But Monsieur Arouet, always respectful yet seeming to care for no other man's opinion, said, 'I cannot recommend your proposed course of action, Excellency. This is not a case of robbery, as I shall demonstrate. If the body is moved, much that might be observed may be lost.'

The Avogadore bridled at the challenge but remembered that he needed the other man's secrecy. 'You have a suggestion, Monsieur?'

'With Your Excellency's permission, I propose that the body be examined here and now, and that Your Excellency decide on his actions in the light of what is revealed.'

'You have some skill in the matter?'

Monsieur Arouet shook his head. 'I have only what plain observation and reason tell me. But we may put these to the test and lose nothing. May I proceed?'

The Avogadore was filled with visible doubt. I could see his reasons since the face of my friend (as I choose now to call him) displayed the unpleasant expression of cunning that I had remarked on first meeting him. And who knows what else passed through Signor Dolfin's mind? Fear of what might be revealed? Knowledge of the 'claims' put forward by Monsieur Arouet at which Signor Feltrinelli had mysteriously hinted?

In the end he grudgingly assented.

'I can see that you have some skill. You may do as you please, provided that you proceed with decency.'

Monsieur Arouet acknowledged the other man's condescension and then turned to the body. He began his examination, speaking all the while.

'Signori, we have here the corpse of a poor creature who has been murdered. There are visible signs that he has been both stabbed and hanged, and either could have caused his death. We shall now discover which.'

Gently, indeed almost reverently, he raised the dead man's head and cut through the remains of the ligature with his pocket-knife. He studied the rope, which to me was ordinary enough, and also briefly touched the victim's wrist.

'It is normal, when hanging a man,' he said, 'to employ a knot which will slip and tighten the noose as the body falls. This knot is of the simplest character and has achieved no such result. It suggests that the murderer was not familiar with knots and was not, therefore, a sailor, fisherman, porter, Arsenal worker or a member of any trade in which the tying of knots is required.'

He looked at the neck more closely.

'There is no bruising under the ligature, even though the rope has bitten into the victim's neck. From the wrists you will see that his hands were not bound. I have witnessed executions in London and been granted sight of the bodies, which are handed over for dissection by medical students. The eyes protrude, the face is swollen with blood, and the tongue is bitten and sticks . . .' As he spoke, Monsieur Arouet forced the dead man's jaw open with a little pressure. And at that, his confident demonstration ceased. As everyone could see, with what horror can only be imagined, the body lacked a tongue. Where that organ should have been was only a raw stump like butcher's meat.

Monsieur Arouet called for the candle to be brought closer. With admirable *sang-froid* he continued, 'The tongue has been cut off, not bitten through. The edges of the cut are clean and there are no teeth-marks. My example holds true. Signor Molin was already dead when he was hanged.'

A babble of voices covered his last remark as, in various degrees of agony, the spectators tried to understand the reason for this desecration.

Monsieur Arouet, however, merely proceeded to take each of the dead man's feet in his hand and then go on. 'There are two means by which the body may have been hanged. Either it was brought to the bridge by boat, a rope was thrown over the bridge, and the corpse hauled into the position in which it was found. Alternatively, it was taken on to the bridge, the rope tied to a fixed point, and the body cast over. The first case, in my opinion, necessarily requires two murderers: one to throw the rope and hold the boat steady, and the other to pull the body clear. The second case admits the possibility of a single murderer, though two or more are not excluded.'

Signor Dolfin no longer affected to hide his interest. 'Are you able to tell us which method was used?' he asked.

Monsieur Arouet smiled and moved the candle to the feet where, I confess, I saw nothing but a pair of red-heeled shoes of excellent quality. He answered, 'I have no doubt that the second method was used. It would, to my mind, be exceedingly difficult to hold a boat exactly under the bridge and to manoeuvre the body without there being some slack in the rope. As the body was lifted from the boat, it would swing slightly and, before the rope was tautened, the feet of the dead man would touch the water. As you can see, Signor Molin's shoes and stockings are dry. Therefore he was not lifted from a boat.

'I turn to the knife,' he went on without pause, and coolly pulled it out of the chest wound. Even I could see that the blow had been struck with great force: the blade had buried itself to the hilt. 'This weapon is not a true dagger. The handle is bound in string to improve the grip and there is neither a pommel nor a ricasso. The blade is single-edged and the edged side curves slightly to the point. In short, this is a knife such as any cook, butcher or fishmonger might have, and may be purchased from any cutler in Venice.' He passed it to the Avogadore, who looked at it with disgust. 'You should keep it safe, though I doubt we shall learn any more from it.'

After these intellectual exertions, Monsieur Arouet asked for a pause and refreshment. Indeed we all needed it. I helped Signor Feltrinelli to bring wine and water and a little stale bread. By now the dawn was beginning to break, but the window was shuttered and the candles guttered. We trimmed those that had some time to burn and replaced others. Monsieur Arouet was insistent that he must have light for his task and this was done so that – in my mind now, I see the kitchen on that terrible evening – he moved in a pool of light that matched his intellect, while we, mere ignorant creatures, sat in a darkness that felt like guilt, and saw as in a glass darkly.

'Signor Molin knew his killer,' said Monsieur Arouet, and we, too, knew that this was so, though not the reasons.

'A robber will normally attack his victim from behind. Also, even if he intends to kill his man, he will normally strike him a blow first, since this is more certain to disable him than an uncertain knife-thrust through the folds of a cloak. I find no evidence of such a blow.

'Signor Molin was, I imagine, a cautious man. Being out alone at night – in itself an interesting feature – he carried for his protection a small-sword which he would undoubtedly have drawn had he had notice of the attack. Even so, let us assume that his assassin was prepared and offered him no time to use the sword. Still, a man may raise his hands as quickly as another can strike a blow, if that first man has the slightest suspicion of the other. I have examined Signor Molin's hands and they show no cuts or other signs that he tried to defend himself against the fatal stroke. Therefore, taking these circumstances together, I say that Signor Molin knew his killer.'

'Bravo!' I murmured and was promptly stared out of countenance by Signor Dolfin. However, I made no apology. I was a young man used to the vapours and emotions of actors and harlots, and I was astonished to see how the human brain might be put to such ordered and rational effect. I saw then – more clearly, perhaps, than the others – that we were all naked before this man and that he would turn on each of us and, with no sentiment but a desire for truth, uncover those things that we did not wish to have known.

However, for the present he was not finished with the corpse.

'With your permission, Excellency, I wish to open or remove some of the clothing to see if we may learn more.'

Signor Dolfin nodded reluctantly. Monsieur Arouet pulled open the drapes of the cloak and exposed a waistcoat of yellow silk embroidered with sprigs of flowers and silver brandenbourgs, all heavily stained with blood. Deftly he undid the fastenings and opened the garment. I could not see what he saw, but, with a cry of sudden pain, he recoiled and turned away from the table. The surprise was extreme and we were all put to saving the candles from being knocked over. Monsieur Arouet paid us no attention but staggered to a stool, murmuring, 'I can do no more tonight . . . It is enough . . . In God's name this is an awful world!'

I was too busy attending to him to venture closer to the corpse, though I could hear moans from my companions as they viewed the horror. From a broken-down chair that had been relegated to this room I took a pinch of horse-hair which I put to a candle-flame and then doused so that it smouldered. This I put under Monsieur Arouet's nose to revive him.

Yet I needed to satisfy my curiosity. While my friend sat in a sort of stupor, I returned to the corpse lying on the table in order to see the cause of his distress. From the faces of Signor Feltrinelli and the Avogadore I could tell that they had seen, and my patron, whose dear friend Signor Molin had been, was on his knees, praying silently.

'It is not necessary,' said the Avogadore softly and he placed a hand on mine.

'With your permission, Excellency,' I insisted. My hand was released. I forced myself to stare down upon the dead man who, God help us all, had been a Christian and deserving of mercy. And I saw the desecration that had been inflicted upon him. I saw the wound that gaped in his abdomen. I saw the cavity where the organs of life had been. And I understood that the monster had not been satisfied with killing this man, but must needs tear out his liver.

CHAPTER SIX

A Letter from a Dutiful Brother to his Sister

Venice
11th December 17—

Dear Sister

Your letter of the 7th arrived by the carrier who brought
wine and cheeses for My Lord. I have examined the account
and enclose a copy which you must present to him. The
sum of five ducati correnti is excessive and I shall expect
Recompense. Regarding this present letter, you must not pay
the bearer, since he is under an Obligation to me. You must
inform me if he demands anything from you beyond some
refreshment for his journey.

I am pleased to learn that you are well, as are my
Father and Brother. Extend my Respect and Affection
to my Father. Regarding my Mother, I am aware that
the anniversary of her Death will take place next month.
Please speak to the Priest and ask him to say Mass. Do
not pay him more than ten soldi — the exact amount to
depend upon the number of candles, which you must count.
Give two soldi to the choir, unless they will accept cheese,

*in which case give cheese. One ducato may be given to
Charity.*

*I am in need of clothing for winter. Please send me a
cloak, the one with the indigo lining not the green. The
latter may be sold, but you must not (as has been your way)
give it to a beggar. To do so would encourage Improvidence.*

*With this letter you will find one half of a bill of
exchange. The other half will be sent separately. You may
draw upon my account with the goldsmith. He will offer to
pay at a Discount of ten per cent, but you will agree only
to five, which he will accept since he knows my Banker
in Venice. You may use this sum to provide for your
wants. In this I rely upon you to be Prudent and to give
money sparingly to my Father and Brother. My Father is
becoming silly with age and may be taken for a fool. As
for Tognolo, he has neither Discretion nor Judgment and I
maintain him only from Duty.*

*For yourself, I am pleased at the report of your
Engagement to the younger Rachitico. I have written to the
Notary so that steps may be taken to secure his Inheritance.
Once this is resolved, I shall decide upon your Dowry. Have
no regard for the Gossip of neighbours. Being bandy-legged
and one-eyed, Rachitico will never beat you or give cause for
Scandal. With possession of a fine cascina you will be able
to defy the World.*

*Lord, but the calls upon my purse are almost more than
a man of Honour can stand! This place is a city given
wholly to Money, Frivolity and Vice, where everyone is
a sharper and no-one is to be trusted. It wears a smiling
face but is steeped in the blackest Villainy. Everything is
surface. Everything is Illusion. Despite all talk of Science
and Reason, every charlatan can find a hearing.*

*My Lord is a fool. He is at the same time vulgar in
his liberality and indulgence, arrogant in his family*

Pride, vain as to his appearance, manners and tastes, and negligent in the conduct of his daily affairs. Yet this Great Man is a power in the State; and humbler men of Knowledge and Ability must dance attendance on him. In consequence, the house is run to the schemes of a Harlot with pretensions to Nobility, and the whims of a girl so light-headed that one doubts she is in her senses. And, therefore, naturally we must bear with our share of Mountebanks. I refer to Signor L———, a poor specimen of a singing-master and an effeminate fop; Signor B———, a Sicillian, who plays the part of Magus and Sage; and Monsieur A———, a pretended Frenchman and Philosopher, who combines monstrous Vanity with cool Calculation. Each of them has an eye only to his own interests and, without my oversight, they would rob His Lordship blind.

Thus it is with me, dear Sister. Beset by troubles in a world of Hypocrisy, yet determined not to play the Hypocrite myself.

When you write next, remember to send the cloak.

Salutations and kisses from your loving Brother,

Giangiacomo

CHAPTER SEVEN

Signor Ludovico's Narrative

It was my twenty-first birthday, and I was lying in bed with the King of Persia, when Gianni announced that the fishmonger had called.

The improvident nature of a young man's life, especially that of a castrato opera-singer who must display himself to please his patron, means that choices must be made between paying tailors or fishmongers. My decision to pay my tailor had allowed me to earn an income and therefore, on occasion, to satisfy my fishmonger, but the latter could not be expected to understand the finer points of political economy. It was my custom to resolve the matter by the use of my feet.

The sum of my wealth that morning amounted to a couple of copper *gazzete* and so I decided to escape an embarrassing encounter with the honest tradesman by taking to the window and across the roofs by a well-worn path. My friend Tosello, the temporary King of Persia, had no patron and a greater concern for his stomach, and he was in better standing with our visitor. Also in the room, in various states of undress, were several harlots, some of whom I even knew. As I scurried to safety I heard Signor Muazzo abusing poor Tosello as a 'chestnut-eater', meaning pimp in the local dialect.

I should say something of the location of my lodgings. The Calle Malipiero is a narrow alleyway which in Venice passes for a street. It is close by the San Samuele theatre in the parish of that name and hence a haunt of actors and strumpets: indeed, its women are noted as the most lewd in the city, a fact to which I bear testimony.

I arrived in this filthy alley amid a shower of loose tiles, clad only in my shirt and drawers, and so intended to hide myself until Signor Muazzo had left. I was in good spirits after a restful morning's sleep and because of my birthday and my escape from the fishmonger, and the horrors of the previous night were forgotten. But then, walking along the *calle*, from the direction of the archway, with his old-fashioned wig and sly smile, I saw Monsieur Arouet and there came back all at once both my memories of those events and my nervous admiration of the enigmatic Frenchman.

Seeing me, he cried, 'Signor Ludovico, I pray you not to disappear!'

I explained that I was somewhat discommoded and the reason, but he considered it nothing. He accompanied me to my lodgings and paid Signor Muazzo a few soldi on account of his bill, and the latter went away. Only then did I reflect on the indecency of my appearance and I invited my guest to wait while I dressed.

'Now you must come with me,' said Monsieur Arouet, affably. 'If I am to be rid of this business I shall need your assistance.'

Puzzled, I answered, 'I am your servant, Monsieur, but surely this affair is one for Signor Morosini and the Avogadore? Why should you concern yourself?'

'Because it is a distraction and because a satisfactory

solution will encourage the Venetian nobility to subscribe to the publication of my book. I have a certain reputation . . .' He hesitated. 'Well, never mind.'

I saw then that even Monsieur Arouet was a victim of a degree of vanity, for all his philosophy.

As we walked along, I asked, 'Truly, Monsieur, have you no previous experience in solving such mysteries?'

'No, Ludovico. Last night I did merely what I promised: I used my eyes and my reason. And also my tongue. If you reflect on my conclusions, you will see that they did no more than confirm your own. Any fool could tell that Signor Molin had been stabbed and not hanged. I merely expressed with reasons the conclusions others had reached by dumb common sense. You will learn in time that half the appearance of wisdom is to state eloquently those same obvious notions that people hold by virtue of simple experience.'

I was much taken by this display of confidence in me. 'You did not tell the Avogadore when the murder occurred. Do you know?' I asked him.

'The body was not stiff and did not stink, and the circumstances of its being hanged from the bridge required that it be done at night. Beyond that I cannot say. There are changes that occur to the condition of the muscles and skin, the heat of a body departs, and the contents of the stomach and organs should also be informative. But if there has been any study of these matters, I am not aware of it.'

I had one last point to raise, which had puzzled me. 'Monsieur, I observed that the knife that inflicted the fatal blow was still in the wound. And yet the tongue had been cut off and the body opened to remove the liver. Surely this was also done with a knife?'

'Certainly.'

'Then where is that knife? Was that instrument of death used and then replaced in the wound, which seems an absurdity? Or was there a second knife? – in which case where is it? Does not this suggest that there were two assassins?'

Monsieur Arouet halted and looked at me very seriously. 'You are an astute fellow,' he said. 'I agree that there could have been a second murderer. I gave proof that the murder was capable of being committed by one person, but I did not exclude the possibility of two, or, indeed, more.'

'Is that, then, your opinion?'

'I have no opinion. There is insufficient information. However, I have some further thoughts for which I have reasons but not proofs. Consider this: the desecration of that poor soul's body was not necessary to cause his death; it was even dangerous and inconvenient for his killer. If, therefore, it was necessary, for other reasons, to abuse the corpse, might it also not also have been necessary to do it in a particular way and with a particular instrument?'

'I understand your reasons, but cannot imagine . . .'

'No – and, as I say, I have no proofs. However, if the mutilation were a necessary part of the crime, the instrument might be of a kind that would inevitably identify the murderer.'

I was surprised when we arrived at Monsieur Arouet's lodgings. They consisted of a garret no larger than mine and smelling equally of piss-pots and cooking. Admittedly, the house was more respectable and he occupied the room alone, but a garret remains what it is and is not the chambers of a gentleman. Monsieur Arouet seemed unconcerned.

As we removed our cloaks I took in the sum of his possessions. These consisted in the main of two well-used travelling-trunks and a portable writing-desk of walnut bound in brass, which was open and displayed the usual accoutrements of pens, ink-pots, sand and sealing-wax. He had also come well supplied with paper. Of books he had few and they dealt mostly with the English mathematician Newton and the history of the French king, Louis le Grand. I saw several shirts and other clothes, all kept tidily and of decent quality. There was in everything a modesty, but whether this was because of lack of means or the demands of my friend's philosophy I could not tell.

'I have a task for you,' said Monsieur Arouet. 'I must go out a little while. I have some bills of exchange which I must turn to cash to supply my wants. In the meantime I should be obliged if you would make a fair copy of the document I am about to show you.'

He produced from about his person a small bag of waxed cloth, closed with a draw-string.

Before accepting it from him I asked, 'Did you find this in the possession of Signor Molin?'

'It was in his hand.' He acknowledged my concern and explained, as if he wanted my consent, 'I was not prepared to give it to the Avogadore without first making a copy. Knowing what you know, you will grant that I was prudent.'

'But surely you could copy it yourself?'

'Very true. However, as you will see, the content is obscure and I do not yet see its meaning. You may understand something which I do not.'

He opened the bag and withdrew a single sheet of paper. He explained, 'The hand is Italian, written with great care and in regular form according to the copy-books. It may be that it can be identified, but I tell you, Ludovico, we are dealing with a great intelligence who will not be caught by so simple a thing as handwriting.'

He gave me the paper. This is what it said:

I speak of the First and the Second of the First and the Ten that are First.

My First is the Third of the First.
My Second is the First of the Seventh.
My Third is the First of the Fourth.
My Fourth is the Third of the Second.
My Fifth is the Sixth of the Fifth.
My Sixth is the Seventh of the Sixth.
My Seventh is the Third of the Eighth.
My Eighth is the Fourth of the Fourth.
My Ninth is the First of the Fourth.
My Tenth is the First of the Seventh.
My Eleventh is the Second of the Seventh.
My Twelfth is the First of the First.
My Thirteenth is the First of the Third.
My Fourteenth is the Third of the Fifth.
My Fifteenth is the Twelfth of the Ninth.
My Sixteenth is the Seventh of the Fourth.
My Seventeenth is the Fifth of the Eighth.
My Eighteenth is the Ninth of the Tenth.
My Nineteenth is the First of the Fourth.
Thus are nineteen contained in ten that are in the First who is
the Greatest.

As I read this strange message, I found myself murmuring the lines, such was their mesmeric force. The rhythms reminded me of poetry; the numbers of mnemonics such as I had used at school to call dates and other facts to mind. Yet again I thought of notes, intervals and bars of music. The message suggested all and none of these.

'Do these lines convey any impression to you, Ludovico?' asked Monsieur Arouet.

Feeling foolish, I muttered something of poetry, mnemonics and music.

'That is very interesting. None of those ideas had occurred to me,' he confessed generously. 'I must consider them.'

'Does the message indeed mean nothing to you?'

'Nothing or next to nothing. My mind is less impression-able than yours. I thought in direct terms that the message was in a simple code substituting numbers for letters in some fashion I have not the wit to understand.'

'Surely the substitution is not of letters for numbers, but of numbers one for another?' I read out the line "My First is the Third of the First". 'Does this not signify that the number One is to be substituted by another number compounded of Three and One?'

'Or perhaps the answer is metaphysical!' my friend snapped impatiently. 'The Three in One is the Holy Trinity, of which the Third is the Paraclete or Holy Spirit. *Bien*, but what has God the Father to do with the number Nineteen, which is the final line of the stanza? No, this will not do!'

'I apologise.'

'No, on the contrary you must forgive me. This fellow challenges me to reason and I shall do it. I shall consider your idea,' he added, but his consideration was only momentary. 'No, it will not do,' he repeated. 'The terms in each line are to be read not as numbers, but as sequences. Note, he says, "My First is the Third of the First", not "My One is the Three of the One". The nineteen lines of the stanza are to be read in that definite order. They constitute a sequence of letters, of that I am sure. The other numbers also refer to sequences. The "Third" is the third in a sequence of something contained within the "First", and that final "First" is itself the first of a sequence, but I have no idea of its nature.'

'Is there no other way to resolve this conundrum?'

'I do not know. I claim no particular skill in ciphers.' Again my friend was distracted, and I considered the cause of his distraction. It seemed to me more evidence of his vanity. He dared not admit that the murderer could defeat his power of reasoning with a cipher. Perhaps because he saw my doubting expression, he revealed more of his thoughts.

He said with more moderation, 'In any language the frequency of letters is not evenly distributed. Some letters are more common than others. A cipher which substitutes one letter for another can be broken by applying the natural distribution of letters.'

'Can that be done here?' I asked.

He shook his head. 'The second and tenth lines are the "First of the Seventh". The third and nineteenth are the "First of the Fourth". By my calculations, these lines should represent the letters "i" and "a" if the principle of substitution is correct. If we assume an alphabet of twenty-three letters (supposing the language to be Italian), of which two are known, the remaining seventeen lines of the stanza contain whichever of the other twenty-one letters of that alphabet the writer has used. Yet each of the other lines is unique! Do you follow me? How is it possible to write a message of seventeen letters and never use the same letter twice?'

'I have heard that this may be done.'

'Games for children! Mere contrivance! One may avoid repetition if one does not care for the meaning of the message, but that is not our case. Great risks have been taken to convey this message. It has a meaning for someone!'

Monsieur Arouet left about his business. He was still angry, but not, I think, with me. I sat down at the walnut writing-desk and made a fair copy of the enciphered writing. This was not easy for me, since I write naturally in a German hand which others cannot read. As I finished, one of Signor Morosini's people came with a letter for my friend. I gave the bearer my last few coppers for his trouble and put the letter aside until Monsieur Arouet should return. Having nothing else to do, and being curious as to his true nature and the mysterious 'claims' he had made (if I understood what Signor Feltrinelli had said and the Avogadore's deference), I began to read his correspondence, God forgive me.

There were four letters, each of them written in French. I speak no French, but there are sufficient resemblances to Italian for me to understand the sense of something written in that language.

The seal on the first letter had crumbled on being opened. The paper bore various impresses of the Imperial posts and a date some months before. I read a message full of fondness and reproach. The writer claimed to be the soul of generosity and love. My friend, on the other hand, was flint-hearted and arrogant and had treated the writer's ideas and finer feelings with contempt, as if he alone knew the truth. Still, my friend was forgiven. Was it not possible for them to be reconciled? If so the writer would fly to my friend's bosom and bathe his face in kisses.

The letter was signed 'Frédéric' and contained the following verse:

> Mon âme sent le prix de vos divins appas;
> Mais ne présumez point qu'elle soit satisfaite.
> Traître, vous me quittez, pour suivre une coquette,
> Moi je ne vous quitterais pas.

I found a draft response, penned by Monsieur Arouet. It contained only a verse in reply to the above. The verse read.

> Je vous quitte, il est vrai; mais mon coeur déchiré
> Vers vous révolera sans cesse;
> Depuis quatre ans vous êtes ma maîtresse

It was incomplete.

Without stopping to consider the implications of this exchange (fearing the return of my friend at any moment), I picked up the third letter. It bore an intact seal whose arms I did not recognise, and several impressions of the French posts. The contents showed that the writer was on terms of intimacy with Monsieur Arouet such that it was worthwhile to describe the events of daily life and send greetings from mutual acquaintances. In addition, it contained expressions of longing and affection that would have been indecent but for the delicacy of the language. This letter was signed with a woman's name: Marie.

Again the response was in draft, but it was more nearly complete than the first. It said little of Monsieur Arouet's stay in Venice, but it returned the expressions of endearment in language even finer than that of his correspondent, so that I was much moved.

And there they were, an exchange of four letters between Monsieur Arouet and two other persons, one male and one female. Each pair comprised love letters. Was one to be understood in a purely spiritual sense, and, if so, which? I have come to no final conclusions concerning my friend's character, and so I cannot say. The reality was enciphered by his manners and intelligence. With him everything was mysterious and — as I was to discover in the end — illusory.

When Monsieur Arouet returned, he was in a mood for business. He praised me for my fair copy of the manuscript and told his news, or, rather, lack of it.

'I have been through the city and talked to various men of affairs who might be expected to know these things, but there are no reports of the murder of Signor Molin. Indeed, he might be at home and eating his dinner. It is as I expected: the Avogadore and the Council of Ten have decided to suppress all knowledge of the affair until it can be revealed in the way most pleasing to them.' Sombrely, he added, 'This is not a time to be an innocent man.'

'A message has come from Signor Morosini,' I said, and gave him the letter. He opened it and grunted.

'This is no surprise. We are both invited to the Ca' di Spagna this evening. Our investigation must continue, but under colour of a meal and a game of cards among friends. Until then I have things to do and letters to write. I must go to the San Casciano bridge to deliver them to the Flanders post.'

'You must have many correspondents,' I hazarded. 'To whom do you write?'

'To the King of the Bulgarians,' answered my friend with what I thought was a note of bitterness. Yet I may be mistaken and the answer may have been a joke, since there is no King in Bulgaria. The country is ruled by Pashas appointed by the Grand Turk.

CHAPTER EIGHT

A Letter from a Philosopher to the King of Bulgaria

Venice
2nd February 17—

Sire,

Forgive me if I write in Haste and Anger, but a subject
must follow the Dictates of his Monarch, and your last
letter to me, which I received by the Flanders post, was
not in your wonted tone. Or is my memory faulty? Does
Age creep upon me with murderous Stealth? In short, was
there ever a time when we corresponded student to teacher,
Philosopher to Philosopher — nay! Friend to Friend?
What? Even closer? Fickle memory! It tells me that we
wrote to each other with a Freedom and using such terms of
Endearment and Tenderness that a stranger, not knowing
us, might blush with shame.

I mistake myself. As you remind me, you were ever a
King and I . . . what? Your pet? Your toad-eater? Your
minion? Clearly language, when used by Your Majesty,
has a different meaning from that used by mere Mortals.
What? say you. Language? May I remind Your Majesty

of the expressions with which you used to address me: 'My dearest' — 'My darling one' — 'I burn until I hear from your own sweet lips.' Modesty forbids that I go further. The World would not understand that these expressions come from the language of Kings and mean precisely . . . Nothing.

You reproach me. For what? Because you passed to me, thinking to receive my Approbation, some trifling thing you had written? Alas, I thought that you desired my True Opinion. I had not understood that you wished me to cast aside the garb of Philosopher and assume the servile splendour of a Courtier. However, it seems the noble Seneca spoke truly when he said, 'Maximum hoc regni bonum est, quod facta domini cogitur populus sui quam ferre tam laudare.'* I, on the other hand, had thought to discuss and criticise the thoughts of a Man, not praise the spittle of a Tyrant and call it nectar.

Your Majesty is gracious enough to suggest that I was motivated to criticise Your Majesty's writings because you had dealt harshly with something of my own. In short, that I was a mere creature of emotion, spouting Bile because of my own wounded Vanity. I? Vain? Even if this foul allegation were true, would a true Friend not have been more forgiving? Would Youth not have shown more respect for Age? I could weep with Vexation that you should so misprise me. What you call Vanity is no more than a proper Pride in works that have been tested and found true in the general estimation of the World. Am I to be permitted no Joy in this? Is Your Majesty, like some Eastern potentate, to hold the patent on all Praise? Am I to be denied the regard of others for the products of my

---

* The greatest advantage of being a king is that his people are not only forced to bear with whatever their master does: they must praise it.

own Mind because such regard is not addressed to Your Majesty? Fie! I had thought you greater.

Far from being vain, I aver that a Humbler man does not exist than Your Majesty's servant. My Intelligence is the product of Nature, and I am no more vain of it than I am of my height or weight or having two legs to walk upon. Only a spirit of Envy could prompt such a Calumny. I beg you, Sire: set aside the Majesty of Kingship and examine yourself in the true mirror of Philosophy not the distorted glass of Sycophancy. Then, perhaps, shall we resume the Love and Friendship of like minds and the fond Companionship of Souls that are one.

Until Your Majesty shall write to me again, I remain Your Majesty's humble, dutiful and obedient servant,

    et cetera

CHAPTER NINE

Signor Ludovico's Narrative

Monsieur Arouet returned to my lodgings that evening in company with a link-boy, a grinning Friulian who would bear a torch or cut a throat for a few soldi. Venice is full of them. The link-boy carried a knife and a cudgel. Cloaked and masked, as is usual in the theatre season and because of the secrecy of our business, we went forth into the winter night, which smelled of mist, brine and sewage.

The narrow lanes were dark. We followed the bobbing torch of our guide. For other lights to mark our path we had only lanterns swaying from such boats as passed along the canals and the occasional rush torch over the canal-gate of a palazzo which dripped gobbets of flaming tar with a hiss into the water. We encountered no-one except a party of drunken *bravi* and their jolly harlots, masked like ourselves, who sang to the accompaniment of a mandolin and demanded that we sing a verse with them as the price of our passage.

I could not read the face behind my companion's mask. His voice, like the rest of him, had strange qualities, at once attractive and repellent. So he seemed cheerful, but scornful. He sought my opinion and then seemed to dismiss it. His words, even when sensible in the literal sense, seemed to veil another meaning. I say 'seemed' because everything with him was a 'seeming' and I did not know – I do not know – what was true and what was false.

He asked me, 'What did you make of Signor Morosini's grief at the death of Signor Molin?'

'I thought it was sincere and unaffected,' I answered.

'They were friends?'

'So we were told.'

'Indeed – so we were told.'

We paused at a crossing by a bridge, trying to make out our way in the fog. The link-boy called to a passing gondola and a voice returned an answer from the darkness.

'This is where Signor Molin was killed,' said my companion. 'Is it not strange that we did not recognise it?'

'There are many bridges and the night is dark.'

'True – and yet no sense of infamy attaches to it. One feels that it should.' A pause. 'Do you believe in ghosts?'

'I have never seen one.'

Monsieur Arouet laughed. 'Spoken like a sceptic! I come to think that I am dealing with a rational man.'

'I use my wits to live,' I said, and added modestly, 'though they are not as great as yours.'

My companion accepted this compliment as his due. We forgot the subject of ghosts and passed on.

'How often do you visit the Palazzo Morosini?' he asked.

'Once or twice each week. In the evening I entertain my patron's friends, and during the day I give singing-lessons to Signorina Angelica.'

'Then you have met Signor Morosini's most intimate friends as well as occasional visitors such as Signor Balsamo and the Cardinal?'

'I believe that to be so.'

'And yet you did not know Signor Molin – strange, isn't it?'

On consideration I admitted the point was just.

Monsieur Arouet asked, 'How do we explain it? The operation of Chance? I do not like "Chance". Like "God" it explains everything and nothing. We must find a reason why Signor Molin was not known to you; and I can think of only two. Either Signor Molin was not a close friend of your patron – in which case Signor Morosini and the Avogadore have been less than truthful. Or – as seems to me more probable – Signor Molin did not attend the suppers at which you might have met him, because there was something in the character of those suppers or of the guests that required his exclusion.'

'I find that difficult to believe,' I answered. 'The conversation at supper may be considered a little liberal for some tastes, but it is not improper. And the guests are men of the highest reputation, members of the Council of Ten and the Senate. You yourself met Cardinal Aldobrandini.'

'And Signor Balsamo – a puzzling young man. Still, perhaps you are right and I am vexing my brain for nothing. Nevertheless, I should be obliged if you would make me a list of Signor Morosini's dinner guests. We may find something of interest. And one final matter: do not mention the paper found on Signor Molin's body. I should like to reveal that after my own fashion.'

At length we arrived at the Ca' di Spagna and dismissed our link-boy. A servant admitted us and took our cloaks and masks. Signor Feltrinelli, severe in a black suit and plain white neck-band, was waiting. He informed us that this evening both the dinner and the entertainment would take place in the great salon and not in the more intimate music-room to which I was used. No reason was given for this change.

On the staircase I encountered my pupil, Angelica. With more excitement in her voice than the subject could account for, she said gaily, 'Signor Ludovico, I should like to discuss some songs with you.'

'At your pleasure, Signorina.'

'I mean now, this very instant.'

Signor Feltrinelli nodded. 'You may join us once you have finished your conversation.' He continued up the staircase with Monsieur Arouet.

Angelica placed a hand confidingly in mine. Ah! If she had been a boy or if I had been of a different persuasion, I swear I could have fallen in love with her. She had a dangerous attraction – all flashing eyes and pertness – that made even her banalities of speech seductive. Her face was small and mobile, heart-shaped and with the sweetest of lips which formed an imploring moue at the least pause or hesitation. Her eyes were large, brown, and long-lashed and fixed the speaker (perhaps because of a little short-sightedness) with innocent directness. As to her neck and bosom, these were modestly veiled by a lace fichu, but their curve and swell held a promise that no whole man could resist. She would, I may fancy in my detached way, turn in due course into a stout matron whose girlish wiles would become mere flutterings and vapours of an annoying kind, but at eighteen she could ravish even this poor eunuch. I was, as always, flattered and flustered by her attentions. In her naivety, her manner went always beyond the proper distance between mistress and servant, as if I were a brother or, indeed, sister; the false Angelica who had first appealed to her.

'Which songs do you wish to discuss?' I asked.

'Songs? Oh, that was just an excuse!' she whispered. 'I want to know what is happening.'

'Happening?'

'You know very well! The *murder* of Signor Molin!' She spoke the word 'murder' with a delicious frisson. 'I'm told that it was most bloody and horrible. You must give me all the particulars.'

'Those would be improper to tell without your father's permission.'

'Oh!' she answered crossly. Then, 'At least you can tell me about this conspiracy that you and my father and that foul Frenchman are engaged in.'

'There is no conspiracy,' I said with such appearance of frankness as I could muster. 'Monsieur Arouet is simply a visiting gentleman.'

'I hear that he is a wizard.'

'I admit that he is remarkable and a little mysterious, but that is all. And tonight we are here to have supper and some entertainment provided by your servant as on many another evening.'

'You liar!' she retorted with a giggle and, again, that excessive note of excitement. Her hand pressed mine more firmly. 'But surely something is afoot? The house is guarded so closely that a mouse could not get in, and the servants are armed.' I had in fact noticed that the door-keeper had a cutlass strapped to his belt.

'No doubt it is for your safety.'

'Pshaw! Why should a murder in the street, committed by brigands, cause us to lock up the house like a prison? It is most . . . inconvenient!'

I could not see the inconvenience. Visitors could come and go in the normal way, and, in any case, Angelica was always closely chaperoned by her women and, when outdoors, escorted by a lackey. Signor Morosini was not a strict parent but he observed the proprieties. I could not understand what freedom she might have lost. There being nothing else to be said, I gave Angelica the slightly flirtatious bow that I reserved for her and continued up the staircase past the footman and entered the great salon.

The salon of the Ca' di Spagna was not familiar to me. It was used only for balls and receptions of importance. A line of ogee-arched windows gave on the Grand Canal and along the wall, between each pair of windows was a console table with a marble top worked in *pietra dura* and supported by a pair of gilded griffins or chimaeras. Large vases or bowls of blue and white porcelain stood on the tables, and on the wall behind each was a pier-glass in a glided frame carved with fanciful subjects in the Chinese style. Opposite the windows a heavy fireplace occupied a great part of the other, long wall. This was painted with the arms of the Morosini and held a fire which did little either to warm the room or to disperse the smell of the canal. This would, in any case, be impossible. In winter the canals give off a miasma that fills these ancient palazzi with odours of disease and disuse that herbs and rose-water cannot hide. Thus it is with Venice. The theatre of all our ceremonies, our splendour and fastidious courtesies stinks at times like a cemetery.

The room, as I have suggested, was enormous and a gallery ran around the upper walls. No care had been taken to light it all. The fire created a patch of brightness, and other points of light flickered from candles held aloft in the ebony hands of carved and turbaned blackamoors standing each side of the tables. The centre remained a pool of blackness around a huge table in the heavy, ancient style suggesting a tomb or altar. I shivered, not entirely on account of the cold.

I was able to take in the appearance of the room because I was a person of no consequence and no-one addressed me. On the walls other than the exterior one, paintings had been hung in great number. I was aware that Signor Morosini was a *cognoscento* of painting, but he had never cared to show me his collection. Nor should I have been greatly interested, since I am ignorant of these matters. Now, with due allowance for the gloom, I could see them and I suppose that they were very fine. I observed a number of Madonnas and a host of saints undergoing divers tortures, and still other paintings on classical themes. The backgrounds, the facial expressions and the contortions of the figures reminded me of the opera, and it was therefore difficult for me to attribute any genuine passion to these scenes: no more than I credit the passions of the whores and reprobates who strut the stage with me and whom I call my friends. Enough! I have confessed my ignorance.

'Will you not join us, Signor Ludovico?' Monsieur Arouet called to me in a pleasant tone from a place by the fire where he was warming his backside and talking to the others. I made my bow and joined them.

Not including myself, there were five in our company: my patron, the Avogadore, Signor Feltrinelli, Monsieur Arouet and Signor Balsamo. I am conscious that I have said little about the manners and appearance of my patron, except that he was a man of some taste and sophistication. I suspect that this is because of the triviality of my own nature. I am used to acting and actors, and therefore look to the surface of things, seeing people in the theatres of their imagination. And this night I saw Signor Morosini in the theatre he had created; for undoubtedly that was what the great salon was. The pride of his family's achievements was painted on the fireplace; and the gallery of pictures, the porcelain, the fine furniture, all were testament to his wealth and discernment. Tonight he was of a piece with his surroundings, wearing a coat and silk breeches in the palest of peach, embroidered with sprigs of flowers and pricked with silver; his hair curled, powdered and pomaded; his skin dusted so that it appeared ivory in the firelight. He was a handsome man of some fifty years, his face lean without being gaunt, his nose large, aquiline and assertive, his mouth full about the lower lip, his eyes a little protruding so that they seemed large and caught the light. As to his manners, I have indicated that, except where his vanity was concerned, he was indulgent. But this should not be understood as a lack of firmness or intelligence in his character: more in the nature of aloofness from ordinary concerns. He was, and knew himself to be, a very superior person.

The presence of Signor Balsamo was a matter of some surprise. He had not been party to the discovery of Signor Molin's body or the subsequent investigations in the kitchen of the Ca' di Spagna. He was, as I had noted before, completely at his ease, dressed handsomely but not extravagantly in a suit of deep crimson velvet without ornamentation except a small, curious medallion worn round his neck like a chivalric order. Smooth-skinned and delicately constructed, he maintained his faintly clerical air, somewhat that of a Jesuit confessor to a noble family: modest yet faintly foppish, worldly but as one who knows the world above. Considered as a performance (and I have marked my propensity so to judge things), his was nicely judged and inspired a confidence in him that was remarkable for his age.

'Our present affairs have been made known to Signor Balsamo,' explained Monsieur Arouet with a note of amusement. 'He has knowledge and skills – I know not their exact nature – which it is felt may be useful to us.'

'I am overwhelmed by the condescension of so distinguished a person as yourself,' replied Signor Balsamo.

'We are all distinguished in our own way,' said Monsieur Arouet, dismissing the compliment briskly. I was conscious that my friend's 'distinction' was a mystery still kept secret from me.

'Let us eat,' proposed Signor Morosini. However, this invitation was not addressed to me. I was directed to a pianoforte that I had not previously noticed in a dark corner of the vast chamber. Signor Feltrinelli began to serve a collation of cold dishes, the servants having been sent away.

I am not fond of the pianoforte. To my ear its notes have a hardness and clarity that do not go well with singing. I prefer the soft vibrato of the harpsichord as a foil to the limpid tones of my soprano voice. But these are matters of taste, and I was provided with a fine instrument. I set to and, from the darkness, sang some arias made popular by Farinelli, but the effect was to make me melancholy. My companions sat at the other end of the room at a small table lit only by two small candles and I sang, as it were, from darkness into darkness, like a lover outside his mistress's window not knowing if she were there. I sang of love while they murmured of murder. I sang of sadness, exile and longing.

When they had finished, I was invited to join them and sup upon the broken meats. To cheer me, Signor Morosini with his own hand and a charming smile offered me a glass of *refosco*. Monsieur Arouet looked kindly at me. Perhaps, at times, I take my condition too sorely to heart.

They were finishing a conversation I could only dimly follow.

'San Cipriano can be agreeable at this time of year,' said Signor Morosini languidly.

'It would mean re-opening the house,' remarked the Avogadore doubtfully. 'Would you hire servants or send some from here?'

'Angelica would have her women, but the others I could take from the estate. The Contessa has volunteered to accompany Angelica, but I confess I should miss her society.'

San Cipriano was the family estate in the Terraferma. I had known Angelica go there only in the hot months when

Venice was unhealthy. In winter it would be a dull place. Evidently Angelica did not know of her father's plans, or they would have formed a part of her complaints to me. I was curious but could not enquire about this proposed departure from custom. In particular, was there any connection with the murder? I recalled the arming of the door-keeper. Was it that the crime in some fashion affected Signor Morosini's own security?

It was apparent that there had been some discussion from which I had been excluded. I was there only as an inconvenient bystander whose loyalty must be ensured. Not that I believe my exclusion was a matter of deliberate policy. Rather it came from my half-visible existence in the world of great men such as Signor Morosini and the Avogadore. I mused on this while cards were proposed.

As usual a table had been prepared. The game was basset, which requires four players and a banker. Again I was overlooked. My companions fell to playing in a careless fashion, as if waiting on some event. Such conversation as there was consisted of remarks by Signor Balsamo concerning Egypt and the Hermetic Sciences, which were listened to respectfully. Signor Morosini said to me, 'Please be so kind as to go to the door and ensure that any callers for Signor Dolfin are brought directly up' – he smiled knowingly at the Avogadore – 'no matter how unlikely they may be.'

I went to the door. There had been no callers. I passed a few minutes with the door-keeper. 'Oh, yes,' he remarked in connection with his cutlass, 'all of us armed to the teeth, we are. Blessed if I know why!' I returned to the salon and my station at the pianoforte and played in the gloom while servants came to remove dishes, stir the fire and replace the candles.

Having no watch, I could only guess the time. At three or four by the angelus, a knock came at the door and the steward entered. He went to Signor Morosini and whispered in his ear, before departing with some instruction. I saw the cards being put away and the coins taken from the table. My patron and his guests stretched themselves after sitting.

As I ceased playing, Signor Morosini clapped his hands almost inaudibly and muttered in my direction, 'Charming, Signor Ludovico. Truly you have a voice . . . a voice.'

'You are too gracious.'

'Salimbeni must look to his laurels.'

'I am overwhelmed.'

The door opened again and, to my astonishment, half a dozen men, generally dirty and greasy in aspect, entered, dragging with them another who was their prisoner by virtue of his chains. The leader (having that character by the size of his belly and newness of his hat) made a flourish and announced, 'My excellent Lords and Mightinesses! I bring, as commanded, *the miscreant*!'

He pushed the fellow forward, who fell under the weight of his shackles. Signor Morosini studied the prisoner and then, glancing at the *sbirro*, gave him a coin and said, 'Speak to my steward and take some refreshment until you are sent for.'

The *sbirro* made another deep reverence and answered, 'We are at Your Holiness's service. Command and we shall act. Whatever Your Magnificence desires—'

'Yes, yes – My Magnificence desires you to go and eat.'

'And drink in moderation,' interjected the Avogadore.

'And perhaps this fellow, too, requires a drink to ease his burden,' said Signor Morosini. Signor Feltrinelli poured a glass of *refosco* and, kneeling, helped the poor creature to drink it, while the four great men stood in the glow of the fire and looked down on him with detached interest.

I left my place in the shadows and insinuated myself next to Monsieur Arouet. He spared me the briefest of glances and signed that I should be silent. He asked Signor Dolfin, 'This is the man of whom you spoke?'

The Avogadore nodded in assent. He nudged the prisoner with his foot until the fellow looked up. I saw the face of a man of thirty or so, hard-used and very pale. His head was shaved and scarred by ring-worm. His face spoke of suffering, bitterness, hatred, resignation. For clothes he wore the ragged slops of a labouring-man.

'Confirm your name,' commanded the Avogadore.

'Fosca,' croaked the other, 'Beppo Fosca, called Codardo.'

'Occupation?'

'Sail-maker.'

'At the Arsenal?'

'Yes.'

Signor Dolfin turned to Monsieur Arouet and announced, 'This is the man.' And to everyone: 'Well, shall we have his story out of him?'

This seemed desirable and the Avogadore, taking a seat while the prisoner lay at his feet like a cushion, proceeded to interrogate him. I shall pass over the small details of how this was done, since the sail-maker spoke in a Venetian dialect so gross that it bore only an approximate resemblance to human speech, and at every point Monsieur Arouet had to ask Signor Feltrinelli for a translation. This the factor gave, while making no effort to hide his contempt for the poor soul who lay before us.

The substance of Fosca's story was simple. On his own admission he was a double-dyed villain, a footpad and cut-purse who should have been hanged long ago. On the previous night, after several hours' carousing with his intimates, he had found himself fuddled and in search of a bed in the vicinity of the Duodo bridge. At this unlikely moment Signor Molin, alone, chanced to come by and Fosca, with – so he swore – no evil intent in his mind, approached the stranger in the guise of a beggar seeking the price of a night's lodging. Signor Molin stopped and seemed disposed to give Fosca a few coins. (At this point my patron interrupted and sighed, 'How like Alessandro. He was a good Christian, a member of the Confraternity of the Blessed Sacrament.') As Signor Molin reached for his purse, the villain took in the richness of the other man's clothing and, in a spirit of drunken resentment, resolved on the spur to rob him. His victim was taken by surprise and Fosca was able to stab him cleanly in the chest with the knife he carried for use in his trade. As for the mutilations, they had no sense or meaning. The murderer was possessed by fury at his own poverty and the wealth of the dead man, and had taken his horrible vengeance upon the corpse. The rope used to hang the body was something Fosca also carried, since he worked as a porter if opportunity arose. He hung the body from the bridge partly to hide it from any passers-by and partly to consummate his act of revenge.

At the end of this account the prisoner prostrated himself in the form of the cross and begged the Avogadore for mercy.

We had drunk a little and Signor Morosini called for the piss-pot, which we passed among us while Fosca lay sobbing and begging for his life. Then we washed our hands in a bowl of rose-water.

While the others were distracted by their ablutions, I whispered to Monsieur Arouet, 'Surely this is nonsense? This poor fellow has not explained the second knife which, if our reasoning is correct, must have been used.' Again, I was signalled to keep silent.

At length the Avogadore asked, 'Are there any more questions to put to this animal?'

Monsieur Arouet said, 'Set him on his feet. I wish to look at him.'

Signore Feltrinelli helped Fosca to stand. Now that I could study him more closely, though short of stature he was a well-made man, unusually large in the chest, as if he too were a singer.

Monsieur Arouet walked around him and then demanded, 'Show me your hands.'

Fosca presented them. They were, so far as I could tell, a labourer's hands: calloused and strong-fingered. Each of us examined them as if they were cheap trinkets.

'What does this mean?' asked Signor Morosini.

'Pray, have patience.' Monsieur Arouet pulled open the prisoner's shirt, and I saw on his chest a number of white scars. They were not the relics of cuts but more in the nature of shapeless splashes. I could not puzzle out their origin.

'I am satisfied,' said my friend. We, on the other hand, were far from satisfied. It seemed again that the Frenchman could see things that we could not see – and, yet, had we not all seen the same things?

He turned to Signor Dolfin and said sadly, 'Alas, Excellency, you have been misled. This man is not what he seems.'

'How so?' enquired the Avogadore, cautiously.

'He is not a sail-maker. His hands bear no needle-pricks nor the cuts that come from handling canvas. He is, rather, a glass-blower. Note the size of his chest and the scars where, in the course of his work, he has been splashed with burning metal. He is not a sail-maker, and, if he has lied about that, we may fairly take it that he has lied about the rest. Villian he may be – but not a murderer.'

Yes! It was so! Exactly as my friend had said. And no attempt was made by the Avogadore to contradict him. For Signor Dolfin *knew* that Fosca was a fraud: it was written plainly on his face! But, of course, nothing could be said of this.

'Do you wish to interrogate the creature on this point?'
enquired Monsieur Arouet. The question was malicious.
How could the Avogadore answer without revealing his
complicity? As for Fosca, he had not been prepared for his
exposure, and his eyes darted wildly between the Avogadore
and Signor Morosini to see who would come to his aid.
However, Monsieur Arouet had too much tact or caution to
press his advantage, being satisfied with the demonstration
of his superiority above the wiles of others. He looked again
at the prisoner, and when he spoke it was with a strange
tenderness for the other man's condition.

'What are you, then?' he asked. 'A galley-slave?'

Fosca nodded.

'And you were suborned with threats and promises to
make this confession?'

The fellow nodded again. When he would open his mouth
to speak, Monsieur Arouet put a finger to his lips. 'Hush
now,' he murmured. 'You have confessed enough for one
day.' To the rest of us he said, 'Well, Signori?'

'Truly I know nothing of this subterfuge,' said Signor
Dolfin.

'No, no – I see at once that this is an affair concocted by
your minions.'

'You are too kind,' the Avogadore acknowledged archly.

'How so? Can I question the word of a gentleman? Put
it out of your mind and bid the sbirri take the fellow away.
However, if I have done some small service, you could return
the favour by sparing the creature's life. Call the request a
whim on my part.'

Signor Dolfin smiled graciously and gave a bow mingled
with I know not what emotion. The *sbirri* were summoned
and, by now full of wine and food, came tumbling into the
room like a troupe of mountebanks, under the captaincy of
their chief, he of the new hat.

Grinning and wiping his mouth, he made a grovelling bow and asked, 'I trust that this miscreant has conducted himself proper and given every satisfaction to Your Highnesses?'

'Return him whence he came and go gently with him,' answered the Avogadore and passed out a few zecchini for their trouble.

'A thousand thanks to Your Resplendency,' said the captain, and, grabbing his prisoner by the scruff, he dragged him from the room to the accompaniment of giggling and scraping from his colleagues. We were left with that hollowness of emotion which can affect an audience at the end of a performance.

For the moment my companions were at a loss for words. They helped themselves to more wine and took a seat according to their fancy. I observed Signor Balsamo wink in my direction. He had stayed silent during the proceedings and now disguised his merriment by taking snuff and hiding his face in a cambric handkerchief. Evidently he had known of the deception but not been party to it.

'Shall we now address a more serious solution to this mystery?' said Monsieur Arouet at last. He reached into his pocket and produced the note I had transcribed that afternoon. 'I have here a scrap of paper which I found in Signor Molin's hand. In the excitement of yesterday evening I forgot it was in my possession.'

A further candle was brought by Signor Feltrinelli to the card-table and the note was placed on it while we stood about and, in turn, read it. In their surprise, and chastened, perhaps, by the discovery of their own lies, no-one was disposed to challenge the Frenchman's own falsehood – not, I think, that he cared. He had mastered us. Signor Dolfin might carry himself with all the majesty of the law and Signor Morosini affect an aristocratic disdain, but we were all conscious that Monsieur Arouet was capable of penetrating the slightest nuance of word or gesture. Or was it only I who felt naked before him?

'What do you intend we should make of this?' asked Signor Morosini, once we had all read the document. 'Surely it is nonsense?'

'It is a code,' said Monsieur Arouet.

'Are you able to decipher it?' enquired Signor Balsamo carelessly.

Monsieur Arouet turned his eyes slowly on that young man, who did not flinch from his gaze. I believe I am sensitive to these things, and I saw in that exchange of glances a mutual recognition though I could not define the quality they shared. It was the merest flicker but it troubled me. With jealousy, perhaps?

'Alas, it is at present obscure,' admitted my friend.

'Even to you, Signore?'

'Even so.'

'I find it hard to believe that of one so wise.'

'Perhaps my wisdom extends to a knowledge of my own ignorance. But let us not barter compliments. I have laid the problem frankly before our company and invite you all to cast light upon it.'

I had already exhausted my store of ideas on this subject. I was a little sleepy from wine but also anxious. The subtleties of courtesy and deceit crackled among us like the thunder of a summer storm, still distant but causing foreboding according to the direction of the wind. I sensed that it must break but did not know when or upon whom. The gale that presaged the storm had already snapped the dead branch which was that poor creature Fosca, and he was a sign that this storm was no respecter of persons and that the innocent must look to their safety along with the guilty.

Thrifty as always, Signor Feltrinelli was moving silently about the room dousing the candles.

As he approached, I asked him, 'Have you no thoughts to solve this riddle?'

'I am not so bold as to test my powers where greater men have failed,' he answered. 'I shall wait until I am asked.'

'Who is Signor Balsamo?' I enquired, glancing at that gentleman.

'Who indeed? He intimates that he is Greek or perhaps Egyptian. He claims to have studied ancient mysteries with the Jews of Abyssinia and to know the secrets of the Templars. He speaks Coptic and Persian and the tongue of the Hindoo, and who can gainsay him? Signor Morosini and Cardinal Aldobrandini are his patrons, as — if he is to be believed — are the King of the Two Sicilies, the Prince of Wallachia and the Grand Turk. In short, everyone grants him honour upon the authority of someone else. I also understand that he is one hundred years old — if not older.'

'How much of this is true?'

'Every word,' said Feltrinelli evenly.

I could hear Signor Balsamo speaking in his limpid and rather beautiful voice. 'Clearly, Monsieur, what we have here is not a simple substitution of one letter for another. I see only two repetitions in the terms, where there should be more.'

'So I have noted,' agreed Monsieur Arouet.

'And it cannot have passed your powers of understanding that the whole text is founded upon a sequence of ten items arranged in some series.'

'Your perspicacity does you credit.'

'But you do not know the series?'

'There you have the pith of the matter.'

'Do you know the answer?' interjected Signor Morosini to his protégé.

With a lack of modesty which only his lightness of manner

could soften, Signor Balsamo replied, 'Oh, I don't doubt I shall discover it, even though it be put together with the wisdom of Solomon.'

Signor Morosini fell silent at this reply, which seemed to trouble him.

Our gathering dissolved with no firm plans to meet again. Monsieur Arouet volunteered to accompany me as before. It was late, and the servants were mostly abed and the house in darkness. From somewhere – I did not know where – I heard a petulant cry: 'I will *not* go to San Cipriano!' And from elsewhere came a squeak as a cat killed a mouse.

A fine rain was falling and our link-boy had waited for us huddled in the doorway, denied shelter by the door-keeper.

'I trust, Signori, you will reward me for my faithfulness?' he said hopefully. Monsieur Arouet instead dismissed him with a coin and asked the door-keeper if the man had waited all night. Finding that the link-boy had been gone for at least part of the time, he sent the door-keeper to search out another.

'Look to your sword tonight,' he said to me. 'Fidelity without cause is ground for suspicion. That fellow is the stalking-horse for some ruffians, but now that they know that there will be three in our party, and that we are not to be taken by surprise, they may leave us alone. Come, Ludovico, it is not a matter for concern.' He took my arm and we set off into the night with a new guide.

'Well, my friend,' my companion said as we walked. 'What do you make of our entertainment?'

'Are you playing with me, Monsieur?' I asked, guardedly. 'It is not kind of you if I am to be a mere block upon which you beat your ideas.'

'Do not be so tender. Truly I value your native wit and

honesty. But there, you are tired, while I am in a turmoil of thought. A code put together with the wisdom of Solomon! Is that not a revealing suggestion?'

'Not to me, Monsieur. However, you are right, I am tired.' I was missing the warmth of Tosello, who was a comfortable if not exciting bedfellow. Nevertheless, I felt slightly ashamed that I had not complimented my friend on the cleverness with which he had exposed the fraud of Fosca. In his games of the mind there was, I believe, something innocent in Monsieur Arouet's character. When he had carried off a coup, he wished to be praised for it, like a cat presenting a dead bird.

'I am tired,' I said, 'but that does not excuse my ungraciousness. I am sensible of your triumph this evening. Why did the Avogadore try to perpetrate such an outrageous falsehood? Is he – or, God forbid, Signor Morosini – implicated in the murder of Signor Molin?'

'I do not know the answer to the second question, but the first is easy. Priests and rulers are instinctively shy of the truth, whether they know the truth or not. From experience they know that it is damaging to their reputations, since they govern by ignorance. No doubt the Council of Ten has need to consider the present matter and seen immediately that Signor Molin may have been murdered because of some personal depravity or the machinations of his political enemies. These are explanations which they are not prepared to risk since they would reflect upon the condition of the State. It is altogether preferable that he should be killed by a ruffian such as Fosca, and therefore – in public at least – that must be the explanation.'

'The Council of Ten has sanctioned this fraud?'

'Undoubtedly. But, as I have just indicated, the fact may be of no significance in itself.'

'That I understand, Monsieur. But it may assume significance when one notes that the coded message left by the
murderer is based upon the number ten.'

'Indeed. The code is based on the number ten, Venice is
ruled by the Council of Ten, there are Ten Commandments,
and' – he smiled and flexed both hands before my face –
'I have ten digits. Numerology is a game without rules,
and the results can be whatever one wishes. I predict
with confidence that young Signor Balsamo will arrive at
a solution to our riddle.'

'And will it be the truth?'

'It will certainly be revealing.' He saw my lack of understanding and explained, 'It will tell us a great deal about
Signor Balsamo.'

For me this was a curious notion. It opened the possibility
that the coded message might be meaningless in itself and
yet not without meaning. For it would reveal something
of the character of the person who wrote it and, more
interestingly, of him who interpreted it.

We fell silent under the influence of tiredness, the darkness and the rain. Burdened by riddles, I was conscious of
a sense of guilt. If Fosca were not who he had proclaimed
himself to be, no more was I, the fake man, the fake Angelica.
If the Signor Molin's murder was indeed a crime without
form, a shapeless thing to be moulded into a solution by
whoever cared, then – though the notion was absurd – I
could myself be the murderer. Had that not been the case
with Fosca?

We passed a priest in a greasy soutane, a drunken soldier
lying in his vomit, a servant furtively emptying night-soil
into the canal. In their moored vessels, the gondoliers slept.
The torches in their brackets flickered and died.

To cheer my spirits and win my companion's good
opinion, I asked, 'Where, Monsieur, did you acquire your

knowledge of sail-making and glass-blowing with which you confounded the Avogadore? Lord, but I have never seen a man so put out of countenance!'

Monsieur Arouet smiled. 'I know nothing of either. I was certain only of the Avogadore's own ignorance of the subject, the fact that he was lying, and that Fosca was so cowed that he would not contradict me if I were wrong. On the other hand, my speculations did not seem improbable and, I fancy, were correct. Reason does not exclude the possibility of error. One advances hypotheses and tests them by events. Tonight I was right. On another occasion I may be wrong.'

'Your reason seems like a species of cheating,' I said.

'No. The cheat is to hold to a certainty that does not exist. Nothing exists so clear in itself that it excuses us from interpreting it.'

'Not even God?'

'Least of all God.'

'That is atheism!'

'So be it.'

I shook my head and attended to watching my feet in case I slipped on the path. We halted at some waterside steps where a body wrapped in a winding-sheet was being carried from a doorway and loaded on to a gondola. A young woman looked down on the scene from a lighted window. The heads of the doctor and his attendants were shrouded in hoods of fine muslin and I supposed that the dead man had been carried away by some infection of the air. I crossed myself and turned with my companion to walk another way.

CHAPTER TEN

An Extract from A History of My Life
by Jacques de Seingalt

I woke in my own bed with the grinning homunculus stooped over me, breathing into my face.

'You are alive, Signore?' he rasped.

This proposition seemed incontrovertible, though it was a mystery, since someone had tried to blow my head off. I enquired of the dwarf how I came to be here. He explained that my would-be assassin had fired high. The ball had struck my skull a glancing blow from which I had been saved by the cushioning effect of my wig. Both wig and hat were ruined.

'And your mistress?' I asked. 'What of her?'

'There was much, much noise and many peoples,' he said. 'She have to hide.'

She had fled, leaving me in the care of the homunculus. Apparently, I was dazed but not senseless and had been able to advise the fellow of my lodgings. The faithful servitor had brought me here. My lady would visit me, she had promised.

'But very secret!' he cautioned.

Satisfied that I was well, the dwarf left me, but only after refusing any particulars of his mistress's identity, though I offered him a bribe. A little later the physician arrived. He cupped me of some blood as a precaution against swelling and brain fever from my injury, and gave me a further nostrum against the other wound I had suffered in Love's service. As he quit the room, I asked him to pass me my brace of pistols. I was determined that if Ludovico and Tosello should call, I would extend to them the same courtesy with which they had served me. I was annoyed and deeply perplexed.

And in due course they did call upon me.

Tosello, who is a fat fool, was whimpering and shame-faced. Ludovico, who is made of bolder stuff though as winsome as a girl, stepped forward and asked after my health.

'What, Signori!' I exclaimed. 'You ask me that, who tried to despatch me unshriven to my Maker!' With which I threw back the bed covers and displayed my pistols.

'But Giacomo, my dear fellow,' expostulated Ludovico, 'we do not know what you are talking about! We did not follow you last night.'

'You did not?'

'No. We tried to' – he laughed – 'but we were so foxed with wine that after a few turnings we lost you. The homunculus is a cunning rogue and he doused the lantern. In the dark we mistook another gondola for yours, and it was half an hour before we realised our error.'

I was dumb-founded. I believed them. There was no reason why these light-minded pederasts should desire my death. But, if it was not they, who had tried to kill me? A moment's reflection told me that it must have been my lady's guardian or some other who claimed title to her person. This cast my amorous campaign in a different light. I had engaged my affections but not my life. I have as much courage as the next man, but it must be expended wisely. I decided that when my lady called upon me I would withdraw from the field and tell her, with regret, that I had been recalled to my regiment and must leave for Slavonia.

Some two hours later she arrived. She wore a hat, a mask and a black hood and mantle over a modest dress of deep plum-colour. No sooner did she see me than she fell upon her knees at my bedside as if she were worshipping me, and her tears prevented all words. Alas, I am too sentimental! The sight of a beautiful creature in such distress swept away all doubts. I was beloved, and it would be ignominious to abandon my efforts when they must be crowned with success. I raised her face by putting a finger under her chin, and gazed frankly and kindly into her eyes.

'Oh, Giacomo,' she cried, 'my dearest darling – my heart – my love!'

'Hush now!' I whispered. 'You must not say so. I have risked the final sacrifice to protect your honour and repu-tation. You must not throw away what has been so dearly won.'

'Ah!' she swooned. 'You are too noble, too gallant! You risk everything for a poor, sad creature and receive nothing as reward.'

I saw then that a portion of the reward had been brought with her. I had cause therefore to regret that I had filled Cupid's treasure-chest in Corfu and must clear it of base coin before I could receive any other – in short that I must cure myself of the pox. In any case, I was in no haste. Pleasures gained at leisure would be all the sweeter. Moreover, I was not certain that I knew their full price. After all, I had only one good hat and wig.

'Dearest one,' I said, 'I am sensible only of doing my duty. For that I ask no reward. If, on the other hand, not out of gratitude but from a sincere and affectionate regard for my person you wish to bless me with Love's tokens, then and only then I shall receive them. But,' I added, 'it is too soon. Your mind is swayed by the events of last night. They were no more than the trivial acts of valour that any honourable man would perform for a lady. They merit nothing. I disdain to be rewarded for such dross when I am after a greater treasure.'

'What is that?'

'The love of a pure heart.'

I confess I believed this to be so. I could not but credit the purity of this beautiful and melancholy lady. If I had beguiled her, so had she beguiled me. My natural virtue – which, I admit, has often been belied by my conduct – made me wish to protect her. At the same time, there was a delectable novelty in being wooed by a woman, and that was my situation. The more my honour forbade me to press my suit, the more her longings became apparent. Words were unnecessary. She held a cup of cordial to my lips with her own fair hand. She applied her own perfume to my temples. She cooled my brow with a cloth moistened by her own tears. I was in an ecstasy of restraint!

However, I could not put entirely aside the attempt upon my life. I said, 'Tell me, dearest: Who is this enemy who threatens us?'

She shuddered. 'That I cannot say without revealing all. Do not ask. You have been so good, so kind, so generous and true! I can say only that he is driven by a devilish lust and jealousy.'

'Has he some right upon you – of law or morality?' I was thinking of a husband.

'Of a kind,' she answered reluctantly. 'But he presses those rights which Society grants him into areas which are beyond all propriety. It is too horrible!' she cried, and burst into tears again.

Cautiously, not wishing to suggest any fear on my part, I asked, 'Does he know my identity?'

'No!' she said firmly. 'He followed us from the Ridotto, but he has seen you only cloaked and masked. After his attempt he fled and my servant was able to bring you here unremarked. Nor does he know that I am here today. As he spies on me, so I spy upon him, and I can assure you I have not been followed. It is in part his ignorance of your name that fires his anger and jealousy. Surely,' she exclaimed, 'you do not intend to challenge him to a duel!'

I hesitated over my reply and allowed my face to twist in bitter relish at the thought. I had no intention of fighting an unknown opponent who had shown some skill and determination, but it did no harm to convey the impression that I burned to avenge the wrongs done to my fair lady. For her part, her lower lip trembled with the exquisite counterpoise of desire that I should fight as her perfect knight and fear that I should be killed and she denied those more tender joys to which she aspired. Women are like that: perfectly unreasonable.

When this had gone on long enough, I shook my head regretfully and said, 'It cannot be. I must swallow my pride, though it choke me. The result of a duel must inevitably be a scandal and, though for me the opinion of the world is a trifle compared with my duty and the true honour known only within my breast, for you the result must be disastrous. Your reputation would be destroyed. No, alas! the cure is worse than the disease.'

Did I detect a little disappointment? To soften this I added, 'But it is not I who count. I am a slave to my adoration. Command me and I shall do it. From my own desire I urge you to command me!'

'No! No!' she cried with a frisson of fear. 'It is enough. You have shown me the unalloyed gold within your heart and I will not have you expend it on one so unworthy as I. I die almost at the thought of the danger to you!'

With that we fell into each other's arms, though at some inconvenience because of my lady's mask, which no outpouring of emotion would induce her to remove.

I said, 'My own one, I have given full testament of the love I bear for your soul. May I not now be granted sight of your face? I swear I shall love you even if your skin be pocked and dark. For it is the woman whom I love and not the fleshly integuments that hold her.' I felt it safe to make this offer.

She withdrew in silence. At length she shook her head. She said, 'That I cannot do. The danger to us both is too great. Do not ask it of me. Yet,' she added, 'I would not have us part without some token. You say that you will receive nothing out of gratitude. Take this, then, from the love I bear you.' With that she swept back the folds of her mantle, exposing the swell of her bosom beneath her dress. She passed her hands behind her back and untied her lacings. A moment, and first the dress and then the bodice slipped from her shoulders, and my eyes were given full liberty to revel in the sight of her pale breasts – so white against the blackness of her mantle!

Her perfect knight was welcomed with open arms to feast himself on these mounds of joy!

I made no further visits to the Ridotto. If I were seen in the company of my lady, my rival might gain the means to discover me, while I remained ignorant of him. Fortunately, I was able to explain my actions (which must not appear to want courage) by the occasional fever derived from my wound, which had the further benefit of eliciting the sympathy of my mistress. My funds meanwhile grew low, but she supplemented them by loans. I scorned any outright gifts of money, and only circumstances have prevented me from repaying her.

It mattered not that I was confined. My lady visited me whenever she could, which was with a frequency calculated to excite rather than to satisfy desire. We were in a frenzy of longing, which only her inexperience and my disability could restrain. Now, when she called upon me, she disrobed from her mantle, retaining only her mask and her dress below the waist. I was granted sight of the beauty of her chestnut hair and the fullest freedom to explore those lovely portions of her body that formed the glacis* to the fortress of her maidenhood. To add to the exquisite pleasures of the hands, it was her custom to perfume her voluptuousness with variations of scent, so that each visit was to a new and enchanting wilderness, discovered, as it were, for the first time.

The continuation of this preliminary dalliance was dictated not by the progress of our feelings (which were aflame) but my own indisposition, of which I could not speak. She teased me that I was bashful. At times she would say crossly that my sense of honour went beyond all reason. I could tell her only that a delight postponed was a delight more than doubled. The very thought of this would cause her to fall into a swoon in which she would lie in her half-naked *déshabille* like an houri contemplating Paradise. I was not certain how long I could maintain her in this state of unconsummated bliss – nor how I could stop myself from going stark mad.

Though my lady was now committed to *guerre à outrance*, it was still necessary to advance our amorous experiments slowly. For though she understood the goal of our operations

* For a guide to de Seingalt's use of military terms, refer to *The Compleat Military Art, with Reflections on the Famous Siege of Namur* by Tobias Shandy Esq. – London, 1759.

(rather dimly, let it be said, as a new-baptized Christian understands Heaven), she had not surveyed the route and was not certain of every turning of the road. For example, though my manly breast was the object of her worship and anointed with tears and unguents, she was not aware that something quite different might lurk beneath the bedclothes, and she made no essays in that direction. How to school her in these interesting details was the object of my study at those times when we were not together. This, you will understand, was not from any calculation on my part but because Love owes a duty to Virginity, and, though the act may sometimes be brought to the crux by modest force, I am not a common ravisher. I desired to lead her tenderly and, as if she were a thoroughbred filly, encourage her only lightly with the whip as we came to take the jumps.

Having spent some time in reconnoitre of those positions made known to me, I decided to move my campaign to new territories. I began with her foot, playing with first the toes, then the instep and then the ankle. By happy chance she was one of those women whose feet are an organ of pleasure and she would faint with delight at my ministrations, in the touching belief that a place so far removed from the point of decision was endowed with an aura of innocence. So, in this innocent way, she grew used to the disturbance of her skirts and failed to notice that the boundary of my activity was as ill-defined as a Cossack frontier.

In due course we came to the point where it was natural for her, after her partial disrobing, to seat herself on my bed with her skirts arranged to reveal a goodly part of her leg: but as if this were an accidental thing sprung from ordinary comfort. And, of course, I was careful to continue my attentions to those familiar mounds of delight, so that she should not think that my expeditions into the netherworld had any particular significance. She had forgotten now that, once,

I should not have dared venture beyond her toes, and she crooned to the stroking of her calf outside the sheer silk of her peach-coloured stockings. It was clear that, though my condition did not permit me to attempt the summit of my endeavours, I might send forth a party to scout the way.

And so it proved. My fingers – the light cavalry of my forces – finally sat upon an unstockinged thigh, creamy to the touch.

'Is this not the goal to which our desires aspire?' I asked. (Of course, it was not – but she could wait to be enlightened as to that matter). 'Would you deny me that for which I have sacrificed?' To make my point I applied a light touch of the whip: which is to say that, with my free hand and some gentle force, I removed her own hand. She gasped, a little shocked and outraged, but my cavalry had brushed aside her pickets and had a free run of the field, an event which soon elicited a moan near to delirium. Such was my success that I might have proceeded incontinently and breached the final defence but for a timely reminder, a burning sensation in a certain place that was necessary for my assault.

And so it was left that we should part and meet again. And, in the meantime, I berated my physician for the slowness of his cures.

The homunculus brought me a message. My lady was not able to visit me but she urged me to go with her servant, for she must see me 'lest she die'. This seemed to me to have a sinister import, and I feared that she had been imprisoned by her husband or lord and that I was discovered. Though this was an unwelcome thought, courage and honour forbade me to refuse the challenge. So I armed me with a brace of pistols of the large calibre (and not the effeminate instruments of duelling) and a hefty sword of the cavalry pattern rather than my small-sword, and, comforted by these, followed the dwarf.

He led me to the gondola and I was in haste to be bound about the eyes. My blood was up. Let the Devil himself face me! I should give a good account of myself. It was a night full of revellers – I forget which saint's day or festival – and my ears were afflicted with merriment and music and there were lanterns and fireworks. I would have none of them. Death stalked me and, as if to announce his presence, the canals were smoky with a stinking miasma. I was chilled to the marrow.

By twists and turns we arrived at the palazzo and my guide admitted me by the water-gate. He was impatient, and urged me by darkened stairs and corridors until at last we arrived before a door below which glimmered a faint strip of candle-light. And then he was gone.

I faced the door. I took out my pistols and checked that they were primed and cocked and that the flints were sharp. Mentally I prayed for Absolution, though at the time I was conscious of my virtues not my sins. After all, had I not dealt honourably with the lady? And, if I were to die, would it not be for Love? I opened the door.

The sight that met me amazed me. I saw a figure clothed, as it were, in gossamer which radiated like a pale flame in the flames of the candles. It was my lady, masked as always but now a thing of wonder. She seemed without form, her chestnut hair tumbling over her shoulders and her body a shadow under the contours of the gossamer gown. She smiled at me in innocence and joy, and I gave a small mewling cry like a new-born babe and fell to my knees in awe. She removed her mask.

'At last, my beloved,' she said in a caressing voice. 'Is this not the night to which all our hopes have tended? Come, do not look sad or amazed. This is joy incarnate and it behoves us to take it. For are we not one in soul and spirit?'

She *was* beautiful. She had the face of an angel. I was a blunderer, a stammering fool, and had I not been conscious of my own righteous conduct I should have felt abased. She came to me and by degrees raised me, pressing my face in turn against her *mons veneris* and soft breasts outwith the gossamer gown, and then allowing me to gaze adoringly at that lovely countenance before our two faces blended with each other, each taking its full measure of ambrosia.

A fire had been lit and wine and meats set upon the table. This must have been my lady's own chamber since it was furnished with a bed draped in damask. When we had eaten to satiety with our lips and pleasured each other with our hands, she led me to the table and bade me eat. This I did, but scarcely a morsel, for what was food but gross matter? I was a thing of pure spirit!

I confess I did wonder where my rival was. I would have asked, but it seemed inappropriate. I could only assume he was out about his business – murdering other strangers, no doubt. If this was a risk that my mistress could take, it would have been ungallant for me to do otherwise. In any case, I was full of fire and courage and so full of the manly humours that, after I had done my duty by my beloved, I believe I would have served him in the same manner, so little did I care for him.

Having disposed of all preliminaries, we turned at last to the bed, where I was resolved this night to complete my mistress's education. She, I believe, had undertaken some private study of her parts, for she placed my hand upon the tender place and with all the enthusiasm of a wanton conveyed that she was largely, if not entirely, aware of its purpose. I say 'not entirely', since I had about me an item which caused her eyes to open and whose improbable function required an explanation. This I gave, which caused surprise and laughter; but seeing that it was attached to my body she conceded that it must be good and she thereupon dealt it those loving kindnesses that she had bestowed upon other portions of my person. Delightful though these were, perforce I had to stop her before the premature occurrence of the happy moment put an end to our pleasures.

'What?' she asked. 'Do you mean that all our bliss can come to an end?'

Alas, it did! But not before I had acquitted myself with Love and Honour and entered the Temple.

*Fu il vincer sempre mai laudabil cose, Vincasi o per fortuna o per ingegno!**

---

* Victory has ever been worthy of praise, even when due to fortune or trickery – *Ariosto*.

CHAPTER ELEVEN

Signor Ludovico's Narrative

Much though I loved my friend and bedmate, Tosello, it had to be admitted that he was a talentless fat-guts. I acknowledge that his voice was finer than my own, but he was overweight and could not act though his life depend on it. I, at least, could play the soubrette and get cheers of approval for a turn of the ankle or a glimpse of *décolletage*. Tossello's tragic heroes, on the other hand, trundled about the stage with as much grace as the scenery and looked as if they would expire from gluttony. Very well – I confess! I was envious when he had work and I did not.

When I arrived home in the small hours of the morning, I found him in bed crying and the whores complaining of the noise. His face was covered in chocolate from the *nonpareils* that he eats when upset.

Between the tears the story came out. His King of Persia was a disaster. His rivals had hired a claque and, in the banquet scene as he was singing his great aria *'Cosa prendo per primo?'*, the rabble on its feet in the pit let out a yell and pelted him with fruit, offal and dead cats. The opera closed and the management was talking of re-staging *Il Pandolfo*, which had been done a few years ago and would require little rehearsal. Since he was now out of work, I felt more kindly towards him; I slipped between the bedsheets.

A few hours later we set out to get some breakfast and repair our finances. We walked to the *magazzeno* of Santa Croce. The *magazzeni* combine the offices of tavern and pawn shops, so I was able to raise a few soldi on the security of my second-best suit and drink some of the bad wine which was given in part-payment according to custom. I sent out to a cook-shop for breakfast. With wine and food inside us, Tosello and I felt more comfortable with the world and went our separate ways to look for work: Tosello to the seven opera houses that grace the city and I to make a round of the orphanages in the hope of employment teaching singing to the brats. I called at the Pietà and the Incurabili with no luck.

I had made no appointment to see Monsieur Arouet. Indeed, I was of two minds whether I wished to see him again. The murder and the confession forced out of Fosca had convinced me that we were blundering into dark and dangerous mysteries, and that innocence was not in itself a defence. Yet, it seemed to me that for reasons of his own Monsieur Arouet was not willing to let matters lie. There was something within his character that accepted the challenge flung down by the murderer. This was, perhaps, the true significance of the coded verse. Had it not been written, my friend might have left the crime to be solved by others. But the verse defied the world to solve it: it asserted the cleverness of the murderer and challenged Monsieur Arouet on that very ground where he was vain enough to suppose himself the master.

My motives were simpler. I required food and money, and hoped that Monsieur Arouet might supply me with both. And, in truth, I was a little infatuated with him, seduced by his mind despite his ugliness and rudeness.

At his lodging I found him in bed, eating gruel from a small porringer. His head was wrapped in a turban against the cold and his face was unshaven and horribly grey. He composed his features into a painful leer and said, 'I am indisposed today, Signor Ludovico, as you see.'

'I trust that it is but a slight malady.'

'It is the cross I bear. My constitution is a delicate one and my regimen is ordinarily limited to gruel and sops. Alas, to be sociable I am obliged at times to eat richer meats and they take their toll.'

'Have you tried eau des carmes?' I asked.

He gestured at several vials and powders by his bedside. 'That and every other specific prescribed by my doctors. They tell me I have the constitution of an ox and that my ailments are in my fancy only. But you can see me, my friend. Am I not sick?'

He looked so pathetic that I wanted to laugh. However, I was more politic and made some sympathetic cluckings.

'Ah well,' he sighed. 'And how is the day?'

'As fine as may be expected at this season.'

'Be a good fellow and open the shutters,' he said. I obliged him and let in the daylight. He, meanwhile, had got out of bed and was attending to his toilet behind a screen. To my mind his bedclothes gave off the meaty stink of a man in good health, not the sour odours of sickness. I inclined to the doctors' opinion that my friend's ailments were in the mind, a consequence of the same airy humours that drove his restless spirit of enquiry.

'Your arrival is timely,' he said when he had finished dressing. 'I have made an appointment at twenty o'clock*

---

* Time was counted from the evening angelus. In winter twenty o'clock would be sometime in the afternoon.

to see the relict of Signor Molin. I hope to learn from her the character and circumstances of her husband.'

'It is your intention, then, to continue your investigation?'

'It pleases me to do so. If that troubles you, tell me.'

'My concern is for you, Monsieur.'

'Indeed?' Monsieur Arouet saw the disingenuousness of my answer and his lip curled in a half-smile. 'You are too solicitous of my welfare. But there – I cannot let this problem go.'

No, he could not. And neither, it seems, could I. My curiosity had been engaged, and my affections, and they both dragged me in the train of this strange old man.

'Well?' he said. 'Out with it. I see there is something you wish to say. What is it?'

'An observation, no more,' I murmured.

'Yes?'

'Signor Molin's cloak.'

'What about it?'

'It was the wrong colour.'

Expecting surprise, I saw only a raised eyebrow. 'How so?'

'Signor Molin comes of a patrician family. It is the custom of the city – and, for all I know, the law – that the cloaks of our nobility are red and not the common black of the cittadini. Yet Signor Molin was wearing a black cloak when he was killed. His mask signifies nothing, since it is normal to go about masked in the theatre season. But the cloak is a different matter. It tells us beyond doubt that Signor Molin was in disguise at the time of his death.'

'Oh,' replied Monsieur Arouet blankly. Perhaps he had already drawn this conclusion. Perhaps, in his graceless way, he declined to acknowledge anyone's contribution but his own.

*   *   *

The Palazzo Molin is situated in the Campo San Maurizio. This is a large square but depressing to the spirits, being flanked by decrepit buildings constructed in the Gothic style. I have no prejudice against the ancient fashion but here it has contrived to become flat and dreary, and the Palazzo Molin is of such mournful and unrelieved dullness that one is pressed to discern where it ends and its neighbour begins.

The palazzo was in mourning, the shutters closed and the servants in black. The major-domo introduced us to a small, darkened chamber where the widow was waiting for us in the company of a gentleman in the garb of a notary. He was not, however, there in his capacity as a lawyer but made it clear to us that he was, in fact, Signor Girolamo Molin, the second son of the family; the elder being at present in Corfu in the service of the Provveditore. In appearance he was a solemn, heavy-set man of thirty or so: not fat but large in every dimension, with sleepy eyes and slow movements. Whether moving or speaking, there was a palpable lapse of time before any action was initiated. This contributed to an air of stupidity, though he did and said nothing that was stupid.

Signora Molin was seated in an antique chair that was too great for her slight form and added a note of vulnerability to her pathetic situation. She wore a widow's dress of plain black stuff and her head and breast were draped in a *zendale* of the same colour. Her hands held a rosary and her wrists and neck were hung with religious medallions. It was my impression that these were part of her daily attire and not assumed for the present occasion. I say this because her face expressed a pious resignation to the will of God and not the grief and tears we had reason to expect. When I had opportunity to examine the room, my impression was confirmed. This was a religious household.

The room was in darkness but for a few candles. It was hung as a picture gallery, the only major items of furniture being a large writing-table and a single book-case, its contents bound in vellum. The pictures, as far as I could judge them, were of an ecstatic religious taste and held as little appeal for me as similar works owned by my patron, Signor Morosini. In addition, there was a prie-dieu and, on it, a small whip with knotted thongs for self-flagellation. Directly above it, lit by candles, hung a devotional painting: Saint Dominic, I believe, with a silly expression on his face.

What I have not said about Signora Molin is that she was a woman of rare beauty. I confess this though female beauty holds no particular charms for me. Hers was of the ethereal sort; her skin pale and flawless; her eyes large and clear; hair smooth and glossy; teeth white and regular. A little pulse beat in her throat.

Monsieur Arouet made several remarks of profound condolence to the widow and her son. They sounded unusually sincere and elicited a mournful smile from Signora Molin. He took her hand gently and sank to one knee as he spoke. Was this for show? I cannot say. I felt at times that my friend's scornful, even arrogant, demeanour hid an exquisite sensibility to the situation of others. Despite the tone of his speech, was he not always kind to me?

'Your husband's room?' he asked.

The widow nodded. 'He found his inspiration in paintings. Will you look at them with me?'

'I should be honoured.'

Signora Molin rose and together they made a slow circuit of the room while she murmured explanations of the various works.

Signor Girolamo said to me in a low voice, 'I had understood that Monsieur Arouet was an atheist?'

'You are acquainted with him?'

'His reputation.'

I would have enquired further but my piping voice had

alerted Signor Girolamo to my condition and he moved slightly away and turned his attention to Monsieur Arouet.

'Are you able to help us in discovering the terrible facts of this case? You bring a letter of recommendation from Avogadore Dolfin.'

'I claim nothing' was my friend's answer. 'I am your family's servant for what little service I may be able to give.'

'I have heard something of a coded message left with my father's body.'

'I have it here.' Monsieur Arouet produced a copy which he must have written in his own hand. 'Does it suggest anything to you?'

'Not in the least.'

'May I see it?' asked the widow. Signor Girolamo gave it to her and I thought that, within his natural slowness, I detected a reluctance. A mental computation suggested to me that the Signora was too young to be his natural mother; indeed, one might wonder which was the older. In turn, this led me to wonder if there would be some difficulties over the deceased's estate. I assumed that, in accordance with the custom of these Venetian nobles, one of the sons would be obliged to maintain his bachelor condition to avoid dissipation of the family's fortune. Was that son Signor Girolamo? And, if so, what did that signify for relations with his pretty stepmother? There was something dark and uncomfortable about the Palazzo Molin which was not explained by the obsequies of its late lord. Or perhaps it simply oppressed my frivolous spirits. I was, after all, only twenty-one and ignorant of most things except singing and sodomy.

My companion had lingered by the paintings on the far wall of the room, apparently lost in thought. He was fiddling with something, which in the gloom I took to be his snuff-box. The candles lit his grey face to the colour of tallow and the shadows exaggerated the gauntness of his limbs.

'This means nothing to me,' said the widow with disappointment and passed the paper back to her stepson, who took it with a nod of acceptance like a servant. In that gesture I was certain of the distance between them and that Signor Girolamo did indeed fulfil the role of disinherited bachelor son like the other penniless *barnabotti* who occupy the pit at the opera and hoot the players. However, he carried himself gravely, like a gentleman.

'Can you tell me, Signora,' asked Monsieur Arouet, 'what caused your husband to be abroad two nights ago?'

'He was attending the Confraternity concerning some charitable matter.'

'Was that a regular appointment?'

'No. There was something in the affair that was vexing him. I do not know the details. He was summoned to attend.'

'How so? And at what time would this be?'

'It was about half an hour after the angelus. A man came bearing the message.'

'What did he look like?'

'I did not see him. Jacopo came to inform my husband that a visitor had called.'

'And?'

'My husband saw him alone in this room and then sent to tell me he was called away urgently. I did not speak to him.'

'Did you note what he was wearing?'

'I have told you: he did not come to speak to me after receiving his visitor.'

'Signor Girolamo?'

'I caught sight of him as he left. He was wearing a hat, mask and cloak – what else should he wear?'

'What colour was the cloak?'

'Red, of course.'

'Of course,' repeated Monsieur Arouet with a sigh.

From his pocket he took a box containing some violet pastilles. He nibbled at one in a close movement as if biting his nails. He glanced at Signor Girolamo and by way of statement rather than question said, 'May I suggest that he was carrying something? An object wrapped in a black cloth?'

'Dio!' answered the notary in a breathless murmur. 'You speak as if you had been present! It was exactly as you say. I could not tell what was in the bundle, but it was black and of a size my father could carry under his arm. How did you know?'

'You must allow me my secrets,' came the reply and, with it, the cruel smile by which my friend expressed the superiority of his intelligence. 'Let us pass on,' he said briskly. 'May I take it that Signor Molin went out alone?'

'I believe so. None of the servants has reported being with him.'

'Do you not find that strange? To be abroad at night with no-one for his security or to carry a lantern? — I may take it that he did not go by gondola?'

'He did not go by gondola. As to the rest, I admit the appearance of strangeness and cannot entirely explain it.' Signor Girolamo paused to marshal his slow words. 'You must understand my father's character. Despite the history of our forebears and the wealth of our family, he was a man of deep inner simplicity and pious intention. He maintained only that outward show which his station required. His natural tastes were frugal. These paintings' – he indicated those hung about the room – 'reflect piety, not ostentation. Therefore that he should go abroad at night like a common citizen is, while unusual, not wholly incomprehensible.'

'My husband had no enemies,' said Signora Molin with quiet sincerity. 'He was loved and respected by all the world who knew him.'

113

Even by my patron, Signor Morosini, I thought, who was a worldly man far removed from religion except in the common decencies.

As we left the Palazzo Molin, my friend did something that I had seen before only in the case of excited children. He clenched his teeth, gave a little shudder and rubbed his hands together.

'So!' he exclaimed. 'Was that not well done, Signor Ludovico?'

'I confess I have no idea how you know that Signor Molin was carrying a bundle as you described it.'

'No – no?' he answered with pleasure and took me by the arm. 'We must find a tavern, for I am in need of wine to settle my stomach. I am a creature of mercurial disposition, without the heavier humours. My digestion is affected by my mental efforts. Wine to settle my stomach and lift my spirits!'

'I am afraid that I am inconvenienced in the matter of money.'

'Ha! Never mind. You shall be my guest.'

'I feel like your pupil.'

'Saul at the feet of Gamaliel? Well, so it may be, my boy. So it may be.' The conceit entertained him and he beamed and winked at me for the distance until we found a *malvasia*, where we ordered some Sangiovese wine. Where now was my invalid of only a few hours before? Gone – all frailty transformed into the litheness of a dog after a hare. And my philosopher? Playing with ideas like toys.

Settled over our refreshment, I raised again the subject of the bundle. How had my companion divined its existence?

'You told me,' he said.

'I?'

'Certainly. How else could the cloak be explained? Do you not see? Signor Molin left his house wearing the red cloak

114

of a patrician. He was found wearing the black cloak of a common person. Whence did it come? From the murderer? It seems improbable, since no other attempt was made to disguise the victim's identity — indeed the coded message cries aloud that we are to pay attention to the crime and the victim. Therefore the black cloak must have been carried by Signor Molin himself, and for what purpose would he do this except as a wrapping for something he was carrying? Then, somewhere on his journey, Signor Molin recalled the secrecy of his mission and decided that he would exchange the red cloak for the black. Quod erat demonstrandum!'

He took a mouthful of wine and nibbled at another of his pastilles. A note of violet covered the foulness of his breath, a cheesy smell from the milk-sops he ate.

'I see a doubt in your eyes,' he said.

'Not doubt as to the correctness of your conclusions. As to those, I understand them and am amazed. But from such trifles of information I cannot see how you were able to be so certain of the truth before Signor Girolamo confirmed it. Many things occurred that night which we do not know and cannot at present imagine. One of those unknowns might have been the true explanation of the facts.'

Monsieur Arouet put down his glass and now he spoke solemnly, even painfully. 'I was *not* certain,' he answered. 'No more than I was certain that Fosca was a galley-slave and not a murderer. I speculated and risked being in error. I judged on probabilities, not certainties. Even now I may be wrong.'

'How so? Signor Girolamo confirmed that there was in truth a bundle.'

'He may have lied.'

'Surely you are not serious?'

'It remains a possibility. Conflict between fathers and sons is a commonplace. Perhaps he wished to misdirect me.

Perhaps, too, I am wrong about Fosca. If you recall, I proved only that he lied about his trade as a sail-maker rather than a glass-blower. That he was therefore lying about other matters was merely an inference. My young friend, you display the contradictions of mankind. It demands certainty and is too eager to believe it has found it. I, on the other hand, am satisfied with probabilities and open to contradiction.'

Thus Monsieur Arouet stated his position to me. But, on reflection, I believe that he did look for certainty and was no more amenable to contradiction than the rest of us. Still, it was a fine speech and gave me cause for thought.

CHAPTER TWELVE

A Letter from an Unrequited Lover to his Sister

Venice
17th December 17—

Dear Sister,

Your letter arrived by the carrier, together with the hams
and a barrel of salt beef. The hams are mouldy and the
salt beef stinks. You are to insist on return of the money.
Thank you for your account of the Mass said for the Soul
of our Mother. According to the number of candles, you
have overpaid the priest and he should return two soldi.
However, to show that I am not the Avaricious person
whom you insultingly describe, I am content that the money
be given to the Poor. I am glad that the choir accepted the
cheese. Thank you for sending my cloak.

So we come to the meat of your letter. You do not wish
to marry Rachitico because of his Infirmities and rustic
manner. You say I am a Monster for pressing the fellow
upon you for the base reason that he is rich.

Yes, he is rich. And, as the World goes, this is a just
consideration for a Brother who loves His sister. Consider

my situation in this House of Fools. Who can tell if or when. I shall be dismissed? And what then will become of our family? Does it not occur to you that I am our Sole Support? Our Father is aged and Tognolo is a wastrel who consumes rather than provides money. Is my life to be dedicated wholly to feeding the Maws of my Dependants? Venice is an expensive city, and to keep myself in my Proper Condition and to maintain you all in Decency I am forced at every turn to find Money. I am at my wits' end.

Now, having done my duty, I am to be Insulted. You say I have a stiff manner, without warmth or affection. My Soul is arid except in the pursuit of Gold. I am a mere Lackey, lifeless except at the Command of Others and incapable of understanding Love.

Would it were so, dear Sister! Do I not pray it were so! True it is that I am stiff and lacking the address of those whose background is polite. True, I lack many of the civilised Accomplishments — though many of those who possess them are Worthless Creatures. True that my Condition, though respected by many, is Servile. Yet these are all matters of the surface and disguise a Heart that is as Ardent as your own.

My curse is to creep like an unregarded mouse in the society of the Great. I may look upon their tables but not eat. I may look upon their womenfolk but not admire. Am I a deaf, blind thing of Stone? Would it were so!

I am Afflicted, Struck to the Heart, for I have seen and admired. I have been given a sight of Heaven and told that I may not enter. I am living in Hell and every day I cast up its accounts, manage its estates, and praise my Demon Masters as worthy and wise and just.

Only one is excepted — and she is an Angel. But she stares not into the nether pits of Hell — or only to extend a drop of water on her finger to soothe the Torments of this

Damned Soul. I wail and chatter and gibber, but she hears me not, since my Agonies are Imprisoned within the stiffness of manner you so despise. How shall she love me? How can I charm her when my only Accomplishment is to be a Lackey? Why, then, I shall be a Lackey such as was never seen! No Service shall be too great or small for her, but she shall command my attention. No! though that Service shall cost my Soul, she shall have it. She may not Love me, but my Abasement before her Altar will demand her Regard. I shall so lead her to depend upon me that she shall not walk or breathe or eat or sleep, having no knowledge how to do any of these things without my aid. No! No! She shall not enter Paradise except borne by her Slave.

Thus it is with your Brother. Pray for me.

With your next letter send a suit made in black of English wool but in the French style. The tailor has my measurements. The tailors here are more expensive than those at home. If he does not know the French fashion, let him speak to Signor Bellimbusto who has a suit of the same kind though more extravagant than I require. Finally, you may order wood in the necessary quantity for the winter, but you must not pay for it to be cut. Tognolo must do it. Send me an account of the cost, together with the account of the rest of your housekeeping, which is late.

I kiss you and send respects to my father, while remaining

> *Your loving brother,*
>
> *Giangiacomo*

CHAPTER THIRTEEN

Signor Ludovico's Narrative

I was much affected by the melancholy state of Signora Molin. Or, at least, so I believe. In my present decrepit years I am touched by the slightest of things, and, above all, the memories of youth bring tears readily to my eyes. At twenty-one I was frivolous and hard-hearted. Yet I had a streak, if not of morality, of sentiment. This is a quality of youth and also of my unnatural state; for, if my powers of observation do not deceive me, we pederasts are a sentimental crew. However, as to my thoughts upon that day I cannot be certain. I am separated from the truth by layers of illusion beyond the passage of years. I am a creature of artifice and I lived at a false time and in a false city. It can be said with confidence only that I was *probably* affected by the sad state of the widow, but beyond that I cannot go. This much I learned from Monsieur Arouet.

It was not a feeling that possessed me in the lady's presence. Then it was the gloomy air of the house that oppressed me. The pathos of a pretty woman was merely one element in the composition of a picture of something malign and mysterious. In itself it was no more significant than the image of her stepson, Signor Girolamo, whose slow, saturnine manner also added to my disquiet. And in my youth I was embarrassed at the sight of bereavement. As I emerged from the tavern to which we had repaired after our visit to the widow, I felt a fine rain falling on my face from out of a dull sky and sad at the thought of that melancholy lady.

'What do you intend?' I asked Monsieur Arouet.

He seemed distracted. His grey face was speckled with liver spots and beads of moisture.

'We shall see – I am thinking. What say you of the widow Molin?'

'A sad and pretty lady.'

'Pretty?' He shook his head and declared warmly, 'You show the limitations of your age and condition. She is a most beautiful lady – most beautiful! Still, let that be as it may. Sad and beautiful, and perhaps not above causing her husband to be murdered. Who can tell?' He slipped his arm round my shoulders, and continued murmuring as if to himself. 'What are we to make of the Palazzo Molin? Is the widow the object of our sympathy or our suspicion? What do we think of the son? Is he a dolt or are there depths beneath that still surface?'

'He seems a grave and religious gentleman.'

'Indeed – and may he be forgiven for both those sins, in which he follows the footsteps of his father. Perhaps we, too, should trace them – but in our character as rational men and philosophers. We are told that, two nights ago, Signor Molin was summoned to a meeting of the Confraternity of the Blessed Sacrament, which accounts for his being abroad at the time of his death. Shall we test the truth of that statement?'

Huddled in our cloaks against the rain, we proceeded on foot to the church of Santa Maria Zubenigo. It was there that Signor Molin had made his devotions. My companion was no respecter of churches. He muttered profanities as he removed his cloak and shook the water from it. We entered a building made dismal by the failing light but filled with a dim splendour of half-seen paintings and stinking of candles and incense. I shuddered, being both cold and also struck by recollections of my youth in Rome, where the priests had assured me of my damnation while at the same time requiring that I sing like an angel or provide other favours. I fervently wished myself elsewhere.

The priest proved to be the usual creeping fellow. He was not especially ill-favoured, but pale and poorly fed. We found him making a round of the candles and poor-boxes, removing the former for his own use and rattling the latter for a few copper coins. His soutane was stained with polenta and smelled of fish. Seeing that we were gentlemen, he smiled and approached us with a gliding walk.

'Lustrissimi,' he began in deference to our rank, 'you do me great honour in visiting my humble church.'

'You do us honour in receiving us, learned Father,' returned Monsieur Arouet, to the priest's delight.

'What service may I do the noble Signori? Do you wish to see the church? It is much admired for the beauty of its decoration.'

With that the old fellow proceeded to point out to us *The Coronation of the Virgin* by Zanchi, *The Last Supper* by Giulio del Moro, a *Madonna* by Tintoretto and much else in the same vein which I have forgotten if I ever knew it. My interest was sparked only by a bust of one Girolamo Molin in the style of two centuries ago which was in the vestibule to a small chapel. It bespoke a long and pious association between the Molin family and this church.

I have remarked that I am not much affected by paintings of a religious character. My companion, however, gave every sign of being pleased with the priest's tour and at the end gave him a zecchino 'for the poor'.

'I am told,' said Monsieur Arouet, 'that your parish is much regarded for the zealousness of the laity: that there is, in short, a chapter here of the Confraternity of the Blessed Sacrament which is highly respected for its works of charity and devotion.'

'God be praised,' said the priest, 'it is true. Forgive me, Lustrissimo, but have you friends in the city who tell you these things?'

'I had a friend – now dead, alas.'

'Ah! All flesh is grass. Give me his name and I shall say a Mass for his soul.'

'His name is known to you – Signor Alessandro Molin.'

The priest looked away.

'Tell me, Father, was there a meeting of the Confraternity two nights ago?' my friend continued affably.

The priest blessed his face with a smile as if crossing himself. In that brief interruption I had followed his glance and observed another cleric who, to all appearances, was occupying himself in the shadows with the study of his breviary. However, this was no ordinary parish clerk but, from the style of his *soprabito*, a Jesuit.

'Two nights ago? I am not aware of such a meeting.'

'It was of an exceptional nature. Signor Molin was called suddenly from his house.'

'Truly?'

'Indeed it was so,' said Monsieur Arouet and he tendered him another zecchino.

'There are,' said the priest slowly, 'other associations of the laity, not only the Confraternity – associations of a special character of which I know nothing. It is possible that Signor Molin was a member of such a brotherhood.'

'Who would know?'

With a brief nod the priest indicated the Jesuit.

'I am grateful,' acknowledged Monsieur Arouet.

'I have said nothing,' answered the priest, and it was as if we became invisible to him. He returned to his candles and his poor-boxes and passes out of our story.

Here I pause with the image of the priest before me. He is an undistinguished fellow. Indeed, have I captured him or is he merely a compound of the many priests I have met? What does he think? I have little notion. Just as I was crafted into a eunuch, he was crafted into a priest by dint of catechism and seminary. And just as I (I do not flatter myself) appear to all the world a frivolous little sodomite such as many another, so the priest appears to me one priest among thousands. As with him, so with others. Addicted to trivia, to manners and the surface of things, how could I expect to see our murderer *in himself?** Priest, sodomite or philosopher, surely he would to all outward seeming be but an exemplar of his kind? So (to return to my tale), if I conjure a picture of a Jesuit, will he not be, in those parts visible to the eye, merely the type of all Jesuits?

'May I disturb you, Father?' asked Monsieur Arouet.

The Jesuit closed his breviary and held it on his lap. He was sitting on a stool. I saw a young man, five or six years older than myself, handsome and cleanly dressed. His eyes were large and clear, his nose straight and properly proportioned, his lips well-formed but without sensuality, his ears small. He was, in brief, a beautiful person, yet manly in his dimensions and speech, not skulking and soft-voiced.

---

* The term is derived from the works of Immanuel Kant. The author's contribution to German idealist philosophy was the subject of bitter controversy in his lifetime. Refer to his polemics: *Kant hat meine Ideen gestohlen*, Berlin, 1795; and *Hegel, der Meisterphilosoph der Onanie*, Prague, 1810.

125

When he did speak, it was with his gaze directed at his interlocutor and in a voice of depth and mellowness.

'You are a visitor to our city?' he asked pleasantly. Monsieur Arouet answered that he was, and thereupon they exchanged the usual courtesies. The Jesuit was called Fra Angelo Sebastiani.

'I have come,' said Monsieur Arouet, 'to see the church where my friend Signor Alessandro Molin conducted his public devotions.'

'A most Christian gentleman,' came the answer, and with it a look of curiosity perfectly natural in the circumstances. 'I do not recall your name among those of his intimates.'

'In younger days, I believe Signor Molin performed some service of a diplomatic character for the Republic?'

'Exactly so.'

Here I stumble over my unnatural attraction to one so handsome. Fra Angelo conveyed an innocent receptivity to the conversation of others while saying little himself. It is a quality appealing to women and I fancied him the repository of many an interesting confession. So now he seemed to wait.

'My friend,' said Monsieur Arouet, 'intimated, though without details dangerous to confide in a letter, that he was a member of a society or brotherhood of an especially pious nature. You were mentioned – that is to say, a priest of your Order was mentioned – as the spiritual director of that brotherhood.'

'That is possible,' admitted the Jesuit. 'There are many societies among the devout. Their purposes are charitable and devotional.'

'May I suggest that, in this case, the objects were more extensive?'

'Such cases also exist,' conceded Fra Angelo. 'To what purpose do you enquire?'

'To contribute of my means or services. To ascertain if there is, perhaps, a similar brotherhood in my own country.'

The Jesuit did not reply for the moment but studied Monsieur Arouet with his peculiarly clear and innocent gaze. Then he smiled and shook his head. He said, 'I am appreciative of your interest, Monsieur, but I cannot help you. The society of which you speak is a confraternity of friends, all intimately known to one another and admitting none except by special invitation. Still, you may hope. In your character of friend to Signor Molin, you are doubtless known to others in the society, whether or not they have revealed themselves to you. If it is thought that your purposes are of a kind pursued by the society, you may expect that someone will speak to you. Until then, I must bid you good day.'

With that the Jesuit stood up and would have left, had my companion not arrested him firmly with one hand. Putting aside all smiles he asked, 'Tell me one thing, Father. Did this society or brotherhood meet two nights ago?'

The Jesuit removed the restraining hand.

'It did not,' he answered. 'On my soul I assure you of that.'

With the priest and the Jesuit gone, we were left alone in the dark confines of the church.

My companion drew his cloak about him and muttered, 'Tantum religio potuit suadere malorum.* A religion which worships torture and idolatry is contemptible. What say you to our friend? Is this supposed pious society mere Jesuitical flummery hiding a cause as innocent as the redemption of fallen women, or does it betoken something more sinister?'

* So great are the evils Religion has encouraged.

He was in an ill temper and of no mind to listen to my opinions. 'Their conspiracies will be their downfall!' he expostulated. 'We live at a time when the Jesuit Order is already in conflict with the Crowns of Spain and Portugal over the South American territories. Still, there is nothing to be done. Until mankind realises that nonsense wrapped in a mystery is not the same as wisdom, we must bear with all this priestcraft and find the truth as best we may. But it is annoying – yes, annoying! This murder is at heart a simple business: a certain person killed the victim at a certain time and place. Yet it seems that we must solve all the world's riddles to get there. And why? Because we cannot confront either the world or ourselves in their stark nakedness!'

'You preach a severe doctrine,' I suggested tentatively. 'Admitting that they cloud our perception of the truth, could we face the truth shorn of our illusions and vanities?'

My friend regarded me sternly for a moment. Then his face broke into one of his strangely sweet smiles and he said, almost with affection, 'You are charitable towards the rantings of an old man.' He laughed. 'And let me confess that such pig-headed rantings are also an obstacle to wisdom. Come, let us take some refreshment!'

The rain, which was frequent that winter, had ceased. The sun had come out and raised a mist over the lagoon. We walked in search of a tavern and my friend talked the while. Here I reach my limitations. How to capture Monsieur Arouet's speech? His erudition was far greater than mine. He had made a study of philosophy and acquired the forms of logic and the terms of rhetorical discourse. I can reduce what he said to principles which are comprehensible to me, but I cannot convey the subtleties of his argument nor his playfulness. For he was playful. Ideas, for him, were like coins risked in a wager. They had a value in themselves; they could be won or lost, and to lose was bitter. Yet he possessed that balance between commitment and detachment which is the mark of a true gambler, who never forgets that he is wagering the sum of all his substance and yet that it is at bottom but a game.

In brief, the drift of his philosophy was this. Truth is in essence simple, reasonable and comprehensible, though it may also be stark and terrible. Mankind has the gift of reason and should use it to ascertain the truth by logical argument. What cannot be known *a priori* or by logic should be discovered by enquiry and experimentation. The whole field of knowledge should be tested by this process, whether it concerns the Divine Being or human institutions. Ignorance, obfuscation and traditions are enemies of truth. All mysteries are false because the truth is simple. Until everything is known, nothing is certain. And false certainties cannot replace reasoned probabilities.

Thus he explained it to me, though I have reduced his speech to the bounds of my understanding. When *he* spoke, it was with animation: eyes flashing, hands gesturing. There was in *his* voice something of magic. I was at the same time dazzled by the lambent clarity of his main theme and entranced by the argument and wit with which he developed it. Though he was, in his object, the most serious of men, in the means to that end he could be frivolous: playing with ideas as if they were baubles. If the mind of God could be explained with sly winks and guffaws, Monsieur Arouet was the man to do it.

So it was in a state of some merriment that we arrived at a tavern, the second since departing the Palazzo Molin. I commanded wine and my companion a glass of hydromel for the sake of his digestion. We sent to a cook-shop for some food.

Satisfied on these counts, Monsieur Arouet asked me, 'Well, my dear Ludovico, have you produced the list that

I requested? The names of those persons who attend the suppers given by Signor Morosini?'

I had done so. I produced a sheet of paper upon which I had written the names as best I could recall them. They were:

> Sig Tomasso Morosini
> The Contessa della Torre da S——
> Sig Alvise Grimani
> Sig Silvestro Loredan
> Sig Giovanni Corner
> Sig Marcantonio Dolfin
> Cardinal Aldobrandini
> Sig Alvise Foscarini
> Sig Nicolò Venier
> Sig Agostino Ruzzini
> Sig Feltrinelli
> Sig Ludovico il Tedesco
> Sig Lorenzo Barbarigo
> Sig Pietro Dona
> Sig Balsamo
> Conte de la Ferté
> Monsieur Arouet

'This list includes everyone who has at any time attended Signor Morosini's suppers?' asked Monsieur Arouet.

'To the best of my knowledge. If you except Signor Feltrinelli and myself, who were there as dependants of our patron, and Signor Balsamo and the Conte de la Ferté about whom I know almost nothing, you will see that they are persons of the highest consequence, patricians of Venice, Senators and others holding important offices in the State.'

'Am I right that the Cardinal, Signor Balsamo and the Count attended the supper for the first time on the evening of the murder – you did not know them before?'

'That is correct.'

'Ha!' murmured Monsieur Arouet, and he shook his head. He glanced at me. 'You do not see?'

I was puzzled. 'What is to be seen?'

'There are seventeen names in your list. However, if we omit yourself and Signor Feltrinelli — being, as you say, servants — and those of us — namely Signor Balsamo, the Cardinal, the Count and myself — who were guests only for that evening and, furthermore, the Contessa, who as a woman is doubtless of no importance, we are left with ten names. Reduced to essentials, your patron's suppers were meetings of a club of ten persons.'

'To play cards,' I interjected.

'Nonsense!' said my companion impatiently. 'I have played cards with these men and they play for a few soldi only. If they were bent on playing deep they would go to the public Ridotto, or to one of the many private ridotti in this city. The card-playing is a mere distraction. These ten men meet for some serious purpose — a purpose with which Signor Molin was known to disagree. That is why he was not invited, even though in other respects he was their friend.'

'The number ten is the base upon which the coded message is constructed!' I exclaimed as the coincidence struck me belatedly.

'Precisely!'

'Does that mean that you can now decipher it?' I asked.

In a tone of frustration, Monsieur Arouet answered, 'I regret not. The figure ten, as used in the code, is not simply a number but a series, having a definite order. If we assume that it refers to ten names, they must be in some form of hierarchy: a first, a second, a third and so on. The order of the names in your list is merely that in which you recall them; in itself it means nothing. And' — he sighed — 'we must always bear in mind that we may be mistaken. The number ten, as we see it in the code, *may* allude to Signor Morosini and his friends, but the code may not specifically employ their names. If their club has no definite hierarchy, our cryptographer would have had to use some other series which does have a hierarchy. Moreover, it may be sufficient for his purposes merely to serve Signor Morosini and the others notice that he is aware of their activities. Indeed, perhaps he wishes to draw an analogy between the ten members of the club and some other body, for example the Council of Ten. Do you follow me? A code is not one message but several. Firstly, there is the text transcribed into code. That, at its most superficial, contains a message. Secondly, there is the fact that a code is employed at all. It is not self-evident why a code, rather than clear words, should be used. Therefore the very fact of the code contains a message. Thirdly, there are the details of the code. For example, we do not know that it employs Italian – why not Latin? If the latter, would that not also have a message for us? Fourthly . . .' My friend laughed. 'Aye, and why not fifthly and sixthly? This code is a piece of glass with messages like bubbles frozen within it. Some of the messages are true and some are lies. Some are intended and others are not. What do you say?'

I answered nothing. I was oppressed by my ignorance.

CHAPTER FOURTEEN

Signor Ludovico's Narrative

I behaved badly towards Tosello. I treated him as a thing for my convenience, like an ill-regarded wife. Using him as a foot-warmer on cold winter nights, it was easy to forget the bond of affection that had put us in this situation. He provided love and companionship, a shoulder on which to weep and a purse that was always open to my demands. In return he asked only that I bear with his mindless cheerfulness, his occasional fits of temperament and his thoroughly uninteresting conversation. Thus it was during that cold winter and Carnival season of 17—, and I should be a brute if I did not acknowledge his qualities. I mention this because, if I have learned anything from that strange Frenchman Monsieur Arouet, it is that there are messages within messages, indeed messages encoded in the simplest gestures. I warmed my feet on poor Tosello and he allowed it. Does that not say something about us?

It seemed to me that Monsieur Arouet was pursuing a mental duel with the murderer of Signor Molin, and I could not understand what place I had in my new friend's world. Was I there merely so that my ignorance should reflect his brilliance with greater effulgence? Or, as Persius put it: *Usque adeo ne scire tuum nihil est, nisi te scire hoc sciat alter?** This was a humbling thought. Indeed, such was my ignorance that I could not know whether in truth he were brilliant. Such an intellect possesses a quality that is not self-evident. A certain education and show of cleverness, when combined with verbal fluency, are the stock-in-trade of every charlatan. Bedazzled by these, perhaps I failed to see an essential shallowness in my friend. The point remains for me, even now, unresolved.

Burdened with these thoughts, I was in low spirits when I returned to my lodgings. Tosello was squatting on the bed, draped in a turban and loose robes, rocking and crying to himself, moping over his failure to find work. In his gay silks, which wound about his fat body, he looked like a gorgeous melting pastry.

'What now?' I said.

'Don't speak to me!'

'Come, you are depressed?'

'Hah!' he exclaimed, chins wobbling.

I kissed his cheek. 'Alas,' I said, 'I'm in no state to cheer you unaided. We must go out – eat – drink – gamble!'

'No money,' he replied gloomily.

'Then we shall not eat, nor indeed gamble. But drink – there is always money for wine!'

'I want to kill myself,' he answered. As I say, his conversation is uninteresting.

His gloominess seemed to relieve my own sorrows. I stirred him from his torpor and we decided to parade our finery, cover our sad faces with powder and patches and venture into the night. Though we had no money, the price of wine can

* Does knowing mean nothing to you unless somebody else knows that you know?

always be raised as if by some manner of alchemy. If this were not so, the poor would never get drunk – which is a horrible idea and against Nature. So we went out with a few coins in our pockets and filled our bellies with brandy and water.

The night was foul, like so many that winter. We were early in the Carnival season, but the wind and rain had driven even the pickpockets indoors. Only a few street acrobats, looking sorrowful in their damp motley, took tumbles to the spitting light of flares, and the occasional bedraggled Jew, in broad hat and black gaberdine, hurried about his business, doing Jewish things. No gondolas were to be had, the waters of the lagoon being choppy. In the *bascino* was every kind of craft: galleys and galleasses, *burchielli* and *bragozzi*, *sandali* and *sandolini*; *peote*, tartans, *bastarde*, caïques and feluccas; sails furled and oars shipped, all of them rocking at their moorings in a stately dance, and the waters spangled with the light of their lanterns.

'We must take shelter indoors,' I said above the wind, and proposed the public Ridotto. We might be poor, but we were dressed fit to be princes and filled with enough drink and arrogance to overawe the doorman with a mere gesture at our small-swords; and so we gained entrance. As often on these occasions, I carried a purse filled with pebbles, which gave the appearance of wealth.

The various salons within the gaming-house were more than usually crowded, no doubt because of the weather, which had put paid to the usual distractions of the Carnival season. Except for the servants, most of those present were masked in accordance with the custom. I except also those who held bank at the tables, patricians in red robes and long, old-fashioned wigs.

We passed from room to room to watch the various games: faro, *panfil*, *tarocco*, *zecchinetta*. I took a glass of wine and a piece of sausage to still my hunger but, if truth be told.

Tosello and I were throughly fuddled and my head was swimming. In consequence, the gamblers appeared not as people but as dolls mantled in black and cruelly masked in white, puppets pirouetting against a backdrop of crystal, paintings and candle-light.

In this dizzy state I found myself in a room where faro was being played. To my surprise, my patron, Signor Morosini, was the banker. He glanced in my direction and gave a polite smile, but of course he did not recognise me, for which I was grateful. The effect, however, was to instill in me at least the appearance of sobriety, and I retired to seek the support and anonymity of the nearest wall, from where I paid some attention to examining my fellows, having nothing better to do.

Signor Morosini conducted himself with his usual suavity, attending quietly to the game, but sparing a smile and an affable remark for those who addressed him, and taking both gains and losses as if they were of no interest to him. His smile was, truly, a thing to admire. It seemed to express at once humour and detachment as if he would say, 'Why are we here? Surely this is the most absurd of occupations? Still, since we are here, I suppose we must play.' It seemed to me that the run of cards was against the bank and, in fact, I heard another bystander comment, 'Does he not have the most confounded luck? I hear his losses are enormous.' If this were so, my patron seemed indifferent to the fact.

The custom of masking is tantalising in its attractions, for we hide not merely our faces but our persons, and put on such airs as we see fit. Yet an accent of voice, the colour of an eye, the shape of a lip or turn of hand or ankle may reveal much, though not all of it true. Thus, as Monsieur Arouet would have said, there are messages behind the mask as well as in the very fact of masking. How many times has an unwitting husband sought to make a fair mistress from an unrecognised wife? Or a wife discovered a husband in the guise of a would-be lover? Certainly I have found many a family man who, hidden behind his mask, has been willing to make sport in the manner of the ancient Greeks. Here lie the excitement and danger of masking! Without it, are we known in our true character? Or, indeed, with it?

I remarked two ladies. The first was to the fore, playing the game with some determination. She wore a white half-mask, revealing the lower part of her face and a certain extent of neck, all prettily powdered, and about her neck several collars of fine stones. At the corner of her mouth was a patch – an *assassina*, as we call it – and there was another, a *galante*, on her throat. Her hands, which always betray the fair sex, showed her to be beyond the first flush of youth, but they were still fine and delicate, and I would hazard that she had seen thirty years but not yet forty. She drank wine and her manner seemed very free, though not improper. I assumed her to be a courtesan – or a lady who was exercising the freedom of the mask to appear so.

The second lady seemed smaller, frailer, younger – though this was all impression, since little was visible behind her costume. Whereas the mature beauty had set aside her mantle to display the charms of her neck, this other still wore a *bautta* which covered her head and body to the waist; and, as for her face her features were entirely hidden by a black *moretta*. It was held in place by a button gripped between her teeth, so that she was necessarily mute. Moreover, she wore gloves of a fine grey silk. A more complete disguise cannot be imagined.

That the two women were together was clear to me. The younger (as I assumed) held herself modestly behind or to the side of the elder, and did not play except when the latter passed her a small sum in the way of a stake in the game. This she would place, but I cannot say if winning or losing gave her any pleasure, since the restriction of the *moretta* meant that she maintained her silence. Her companion, though, greeted each turn of the cards with a smile, a frown, a soft cry, or the spreading before her lips of her fan, behind which she would murmur something to her young friend.

I had moved from the wall, feeling a little clearer in the head and no longer in need of support, and behind me I heard two persons speaking in low voice.

A woman said, 'I do assure you that she is both lovely and accomplished.'

The man replied, 'Fie! This is another example of your sweet cruelty. Admit that you are tired of me. I have been too chivalrous in my addresses to you, and now you wish to discard me because you have found another lover.'

With some emotion the woman said, 'My dearest one! How can you accuse me of lack of faith? Have I not given *everything* to you? Can you not imagine the sacrifice I am making in directing your attentions to another? But I am aware of your ardent nature and the imperious demands of virile passions and it is from my love for you that I wish another to provide you with that which is at present beyond my power.'

It is another consequence of the mask that, trusting to anonymity, voices are raised and things said that would not be said if the speaker were known.

'Also, my darling one,' continued the lady (who had a voice of sweet familiarity, though I could not name it), 'you must have a care for your situation. Though you hide it from me, I know that your purse is not the fullest. And I' – there was a catch in her voice – 'I do not wish to speak of my own affairs, but I am beset by debts and enemies. It is from my love and duty to you that I direct you to another. I cannot bear to see you both embarrassed in your worldly affairs and denied the consolation of tender caresses. I know that she will not take away the firmness of your true heart, and that this sacrifice on my part will only bind us more closely.'

At this point I ventured a glance over my shoulder. I noticed a gentleman of my own height and slight build, who beneath a *maschera nobile* was wearing the white uniform of one of the Empress's officers. As to the lady, there were several in the vicinity and I could not tell to whom he had spoken.

Tosello now came into the room with a grin on his lips and a certain stagger to his walk. He was brandishing a silver coin between two fingers. He exclaimed, 'A ducat, my bravo! A whole ducat! Let's get another drink.'

'Where did you get it?'

'Poof! From the floor – ha ha! – from the floor!'

Frankly, neither of us was above pocketing any unattended coins, whether from the floor or otherwise. A beggar's purse is that of his neighbours. I followed Tosello in search of further refreshment. He drank brandy. To my own surprise, I ordered chocolate. I was becoming wise – or, at any rate, sober. While we were there among the topers and the losers at cards who were fortifying themselves for another battle with Fortune, the soldier whose conversation I had overheard, approached me.

'My compliments, Signor Ludovico,' he said with an elegant hand to his breast.

'You know me?' I answered.

'I fancy I am acquainted with every stitch of clothes that Signori Ludovico and Tosello possess. So, unless a stranger has found his way into that suit, I believe you must be the former, also called il Tedesco.'

'You have the advantage of me, Signore.'

The stranger laughed heartily. 'Nay! "At tibi nil faciam, sed lota mentula lana."* When I have the advantage, it is

---

* I'll do nothing to you till you've washed your cock with wool – *Martial*.

with the fairer sex and not with some Giton who treads the boards of the theatre.'

'Now you insult me!' I bridled. 'Shall I call you Scaramuccia in return?'

'If you please, Ludovico, as between friends.'

With that remark the stranger's voice changed to one that I recognised and my temper cooled, which in truth pleased me, since I doubted my skill in crossing swords.

'Giacomo?' I said.

'Hush now!' he whispered with a finger to his lips.

I eyed his uniform. 'I was not aware that you had entered the Austrian service.'

With a smile, 'Nor have I. This is something I had made by my tailor. It lends me a certain distinction, don't you think?'

'Indeed I do.'

It was some time since I had seen my friend Giacomo. He had been afflicted by that poverty which occasionally keeps us in bed. Then there was an affair of a mistress whom he was pursuing. Tosello and I had done him a small favour. His character as an Imperial officer was probably serving him well, since he had an equivocal reputation and enough cause to employ more than one identity. I had known him variously as a priest in minor orders, a notary's clerk, a magician, and the adopted son of a patrician family. His amorous inclinations and reckless judgment prevented him from sustaining any reputation for long. In this respect he was an ideal representative of the time and the place.

'We have a silver ducat,' said Tosello like a child with a toy. At times he embarrassed me.

'And how are your funds?' I asked of Giacomo.

'I am adequately served by loans from my lady,' he answered.

'Loans?'

'On my honour, I have every intention of repaying them!'

'I do not doubt you. Are we speaking of the same melancholy mistress whom you were courting with our assistance? The one whose guardian served you with a box on the ears?'

'The very same,' said Giacomo. Confidingly (he, too, had been drinking), he put an arm round my shoulders. 'All appearances to the contrary, dearest Ludovico, I am a fellow with a simple and affectionate heart. Faithful when circumstances allow.'

'You are, perhaps, the author of those circumstances that do *not* allow.'

'I confess it. "Il cazzo non vuol pensieri."'*

'But now the affair goes well?'

My friend was thoughtful. 'Well enough,' he replied. 'But strangely.' And he gave me an account of events.

An Extract from A History of my Life *by Jacques de Seingalt*

By virtue and restraint I had at last gained entry into the twin temples of my mistress's body and home. As regards the former, I was in Paradise. The fact that I did not know my sad lady's name only added to her mysterious charms and made our transports more exciting and piquant, since I could not tell if I should ever see her again. I was in a fever of anticipation at each assignation and did my duty to her with all the fervour of a man who eats his last meal knowing that on the morrow he will be hanged. Indeed – and I admit this because I am an honest man so far as concerns these memoirs – the force of my passions sometimes caused them to be prematurely spent, to the disappointment of my

* The prick does not want to think – proverb.

fair charmer. She was, however, both generous and ignorant, and did not reproach me if my infantry were exhausted before they had thrust the bayonet home. But on the latter count, that is to say, my penetration into the secrets of her home, I was more cautious of my success. Although the homunculus kept watch to see that we were not distracted during our amorous exercises, I was not convinced that the little fellow could protect us if we were interrupted by the jealous brute who had already done me injury. In such a case I should be found with only a blunt sword in my hand.

'It is possible,' I explained to my lovely, 'that it is this fear of interruption which is causing me to worship your body with such intemperate haste. Would it not be to our advantage if we found a private chamber elsewhere, a place where we could attend at leisure to our tender devotions?'

Clinging to me, my lady answered, almost in tears, 'Surely you would not leave me if we could not continue as we are? I could not bear it, dear one! I should kill myself!'

'I have no intention of leaving you,' I assured her, and demonstrated the sincerity of my feelings by serving her in the usual fashion. 'But,' I continued when we had finished, 'we act in continued fear of discovery. It is against my honour as a soldier to be so craven. If we cannot show our love for each other except under this shadow of fear, give me the name of this monster who oppresses you and I shall call him out and kill him.' Such was my passion for my mistress that I believe I might have done so, too – though my enemy was a huge animal who might easily have tipped me into the lagoon with a blade in my gizzard and left me to float with the turds and the dead dogs. However, I was spared. The thought of my death terrified my lady and I was obliged to set to again in order to calm her.

She said, 'Dearest heart, you have no knowledge of the difficulties under which I labour. I am watched at every turn.

142

My visits to the Ridotto are the only indulgence granted me. I have admitted you here into my own chamber only because my enemy cannot conceive that I should have a lover so bold as to venture into the lion's den. Nevertheless, if it would calm your spirits and assuage your offended honour, I am willing that you should find some quiet place elsewhere.'

Thus it was decided.

There are in Venice many *casini*, suites of private rooms prudently provided so that affairs such as ours may be pursued away from the public eye. They are a wise institution, reconciling the frailty of human nature with the outward appearance of virtue. I am firmly a believer in the latter. Only courage, virtue and honour allow a small number of men of breeding to overawe the rude temper of the mob. I knew of such a set of rooms in a quiet house located in a bywater of the city. It was frequented by persons of discretion.

Some days after our discussion, I hired a chamber in this private house and saw to its appointments. From his stock of furnishings the keeper provided a divan, carpets and cushions in the Turkish fashion, and the walls were hung with paintings showing in suitable detail how the gods of old disported themselves in love. I laid in a store of sweet Cyprus wine, which my lady was fond of and which added to the affection of her disposition. And I called for a supply of ambergris, styrax and other essential oils to perfume the air and also, because it pleased my lady, a pipe and some crab's-eye tobacco so that, at the close of our endeavours, I could recline like a Sultan while she bestowed some final caresses. It was, in short, an arrangement of the most perfect and delicate taste.

Alas, it was not to be enjoyed to the full.

My lady came to the house by subterfuge. She found a wench to dress in her clothes and attend the Ridotto, masked and accompanied as usual by the homunculus. I provided her with an escort to my prepared chamber; a fellow was prepared to do the service in discharge of a gambling debt. When she arrived she was in a state of distress which I attributed to her nervousness. It was only reluctantly that she disrobed to that state of partial undress that lends interest to the amorous event.

'You must take some wine,' I urged her. 'It will calm you. You have no need to be concerned about the discretion of this place.'

She took the wine hastily. Finished, she said, 'I thank you for the wine and also for the care you have taken with this apartment. But it is not that which concerns me.'

Gently I slipped some fastenings of her undergarments. I thought some kisses bestowed upon her fair white mounds would cause a melting passion that would remove all tension from her. To my surprise she restrained my hand with her own.

'You do not desire it?' I enquired, aggrieved.

In a choking voice she replied, 'Desire it? Ah, dear Giacomo, if only you knew how my soul floods with the heat of love at the thought of your touch! I stop you because, once begun, all thought of prudence vanishes and I am a very wanton and slave to your desires.'

She added much more to the same effect. Her words were not calculated to halt the virile movements of my body, which were beyond the control of my will. She had not repaired my attentions to her clothing and my eyes were feasting upon the tender swell of her bosom, like pearls in candlelight. It was in some mutual discomfort that we continued our conversation.

'I pray you, then,' I said haltingly, 'tell me what it is that causes you to turn prude.'

At this my prude flushed to the very peaks of her breasts.

'Do not be cruel!' she answered.

'How can I not be so?'

'Because it is for you that I play the nun. Only I know not how to explain to you what has happened.'

I waited.

At last she said, 'Have we committed a sin?'

What question was that?

'Only in the eyes of the vulgar,' I answered.

'Does God place a curse on the innocent and the blessed?'

'It has been known.'

'Is that truly so?' she asked eagerly. 'A woman may be cursed and yet innocent?'

'On occasion,' I answered circumspectly. 'Do you have a particular curse in mind? Is it . . . ?'

'No – not the usual one.'

'Ah!'

'You cannot guess?'

'I am at a loss. God has so many curses at his disposal. He seems to be very free with them.'

'Monster!' she exclaimed angrily yet pathetically. 'You cannot help me! I am the unhappiest woman. In love but unable to grant the tokens of love.'

'So you say, Madame.'

I relented. I extended my hands and raised her from my feet where she had fallen in tears.

'You speak in riddles,' I said gently. 'What is this curse?'

'I do not know its name.'

'Ah! We have a conundrum. Can you describe its particulars?'

My lady calmed herself. She remembered her bosom and covered it with a fichu. She said slowly, 'Yesterday, at dressing, I had to attend to . . . the necessary offices.'

'Yes?'

'I called my maid for a pot and performed . . .'

'The usual things?'

'Yes.'

'Good. And?'

She buried her hands in her face. 'I was afflicted with the most terrible burning sensation. It was as if the fires of Hell were contained within my waters!'

'Ah!' I said for the third time.

Well, at least there was no mystery as to the nature of *that* curse! In His wisdom God had visited me with it on several occasions. Indeed, I had been suffering on this count when I first met my lady. But, as behoves a gentleman, I had moderated myself until my spagyrist had assured me of my cure. It was not from me, then, that my mistress had acquired these effects of love. Imagine, therefore, my distress. I have told the reader how lovely my lady was and nothing – nay, even though my love for her should crumble in an instant – could detract from her unsurpassed beauty. I was in an agony of conflict between my adoration of her and the knowledge that she had played the strumpet. I shuddered. I trembled. Inwardly, I desired to kill myself on the spot, as all my belief that I had found the paragon of womanhood was dashed. Yet such was my situation! As some wise Roman or other put it: *Pinguit amor nimiumque potens, in taedia nobis vertitur, et stomacho dulcis ut esca nocet.** What sublime and unaffected language; and how true! I could only conclude that the woman was a jade and that others had sacrificed on the same altar.

Whilst I was lost in mental turmoil, she asked, 'Do you know anything of the cause of this affliction?'

'What? Oh, it was God, no doubt, as you say. The fellow gets everywhere.' I suppressed the knowledge that I had been wickedly deceived.

---

* Too strong and rich a love-affair soon turns loathsome, just as sweet food sickens the stomach—

I was at a loss what to do. In a trice my love for my mistress had disappeared. But this was not an end of the matter. I could not simply dispose of her. In her service I had incurred many debts, and I would be embarrassed until she provided me with the specie to discharge them. Moreover, unlike the villain who had bestowed these painful tokens upon her, I am a creature of sentiment. Who but a brute could not be? She was truly beautiful and she bore such an appearance of pathos and distress that one could almost believe her innocent, though, I am sure, she was experiencing no more than a salutary guilt at her own infamous conduct towards me. Yet I have a forgiving nature and the code of a gentleman required that I aid her. Indeed, I could not even tell her of the change in my feelings, but must maintain the pretence of my true affection.

'Do not despair,' I told her. 'I have friends who know of doctors who have philtres and specifics that can cure this condition. It is a matter of a few weeks only, and our continence during this period will only double the bliss when we resume our union.'

With that we set about the food and wine, which relieved our spirits. In fact we came to a point where we could engage in some amorous dalliance short of the main attack. So my time and expense were not entirely wasted.

This was the time of the famous murder. And I think it was only a day or so after that crime that my lady, heavily disguised in black, came unannounced to my lodgings, in company with the faithful homunculus.

'I come at some danger to myself,' she said. 'And I cannot stay long.'

'You are in mourning?' I asked.

'A close friend of my family has died.'

'Signor Alessandro Molin?'

My lady nodded and her face – which even now was dear to me – was bathed in tears.

'Pray tell me what I can do,' I said.

Her bosom, which I knew so intimately, heaved with emotion. 'We must end this thing between us,' she said. 'I have been visited with a warning. Sin is sweet – but it remains sin.'

'You would desert me?' I asked. I was hurt that she would discard me so lightly.

'Nay, not desert! Not that! I shall ever love you!'

'Then what?'

More calmly, she continued, 'I know only too well the demands imposed upon you by your virile nature. I cannot abandon you to satisfy them by means that may be even more sinful. Also, though I know you to be a hero in the service of Mars, I am well aware that a soldier's profession does not bring the rewards of this world.'

'What would you, then?'

'If you will let me guide you, I will provide you with the love of another. She is a sweet creature, possessed of a great fortune, and I have some influence over her. It would comfort my soul to know that you have gained the affection of one whom I esteem.'

'But will she have me?' I asked.

'There you have it. Though you are a gentleman, your condition is not such that you may approach her openly. Her family is ancient and has great pride. I shall show her to you and we must consider how you may pay her some secret addresses to gain her favour. Then, if Fortune favours you, it is possible that you may be able to advance your cause publicly.'

Since my lady was evidently still attracted to me (though her proposal was infamous), I assumed that she wished to place me safely in the custody of a rich, old harridan from whom she could have my occasional use. This was not my ambition, but since our relations – which on my part had always been characterised by the purest feelings – had been reduced to mere commerce, I decided that I was owed the wages for my service. I therefore resolved to see how events would unfold, thinking that they would, at least, be interesting.

CHAPTER FIFTEEN

A Letter from a Very Old Lady to a Long-dead Lover

Venice
29th February 18—*

My Dear One,

In a long life I have been loved by three men. Of these
I chose to love the most Worthless, the most Faithless. I
loved you. The other two I killed.

So you have written a memoir of your Life! Boastful
to the last, how typical of you to do so and to flee
the consequences by another daring Escape — this time
into Death.

Does the tittle-tattle of this World circulate in Hell?
The Serenissima is no more, and we are all Austrians
now. No longer 'Donna' or 'Signora', I have become
'Gnädige Frau' to a legion of viceroys and emissaries

* This letter dated circa 1820 is the most serious example of
the chronological impossibility of the events described in *Scherzo*.
For a scholarly discussion see Lügner's *Ludwig Bauer and Seine
Lebensbeschreibung — Quatsch oder was?* Berlin 1939.

151

*from our Masters in Vienna, and our young folk have
abandoned the* furlana *for the waltz and wear their
own hair, discard the mask and smoke cigars. I know of
what I speak since I have such a one, my great-grandson
Alberto (or Albrecht, as his tastes will have it). He
is a member of the Reichsunsinnrat in the Imperial
Civil Service, and has acquired the necessary Freedom of
Thought, Speech and Manner.*

*In the service of His Majesty, my dear Alberto found
himself a little time ago in Leipzig. There he met a man
named Carlo Angioloni. Do you recall the name? You
should. His father and Namesake married your niece
and was present at your Death — surely an occasion
to remember? This Carlo Angioloni was on his way to
visit a man called Brockhaus and bearing with him a
Manuscript.*

*He and Alberto fell to talking. What was the
Manuscript? asked Alberto. A Memoir, answered Signor
Angioloni. Of someone famous? my great-grandson pressed
him. Perhaps. The Author had had some little fame years
ago before the Revolution and the World changed. However,
he was now Dead some twenty years, a sad old man who
had outlived his Time and was buried in the churchyard at
Dux in Bohemia. His name was Baron Neuhaus, though a
Venetian by birth.*

*Learning that Alberto was also Venetian, Signor
Angioloni offered to give him sight of the Memoir. It
was very lengthy (you were always a prolific Writer, my
dear, and led an eventful Life), and he was quite unable
to study it all, but he read with Interest — not to say
Fascination. And when he came to certain passages,* he
stole them. *It is these that have come into my possession.
Thus, you have written to me from beyond the Grave, and
now I write to you.*

SCHERZO

*Let me begin by allowing, with some Admiration,
that you have been Constant in your Inconstancy. Your
Memoir is a faithful Mirror of your Soul: dishonest,
self-glorifying, witty, debonair, cruel, blind, sentimental,
false in its modesty and its claims to Honour. In short,
the very image of you: a monument to a Baseness so rash
and glorious as to be almost a Virtue. How could I not
weep on reading it? And how could I understand the
Nature of my own Tears?*

*But enough! This is a Dialogue. I have spoken a little
about you (quite prettily, I think). What do you have
to say about me? Do I even figure in your discourse?
Certainly I see there a Lady whose Lineaments in general
follow my own and who from certain circumstances
and description may be called by my Name. Yet is she
truly me?*

*She is a Lady. Well, so are many, and this Lady
wears the Clothes and Courtesies of any other Lady. She is
'melancholy'. What? Nothing more? Is this the sum of her
Character, like the heroine of a French novel? No Wit or
Charm or Vivacity — not even the occasional spark to enliven
her Sadness? Apparently not. Unlike other Human Beings,
she lives without contrariness in the pure, dull light of
her Gloom.*

*Ah, no! you say. She is also a Virgin. Virginity
seems to me like Melancholia by another name. And how
improbable, since by your own account she was a married
woman and hastened to bed with you after showing no
more Restraint than common Decency would require. No,
I cannot admit her to be a Virgin, though you will have
her so. Yet, as men always dominate women, I shall
concede (in form at least).*

*So let us have her — have me — a Melancholy Virgin.
Let us look now at her appearance.*

*She is 'beautiful'. I am not certain that we need go
beyond that. Her Beauty comprises a woman's parts of
the usual order and number, and white as Alabaster.
I recognise in them none of those Flaws that trouble
me before my Mirror. I see none of those details that
inconvenience a woman's Body. I smell the perfumes of
Araby but none of the live scents of a vibrant Female who
loves. In brief, I know this creature for the marble Statue
that she is.*

*Do you understand me, my Dearest? Where you purport
to describe me, what I see is you. The Mask with which
you say I hid my face was in truth the Blindfold that
you placed before your own eyes so that you should not see
me as I was. Thus it is that, when I removed my Mask,
you too removed your Blindfold and saw no longer your
melancholy Virgin but a woman of Passion and carnal
Appetites – and you recoiled.*

*Oh, my dear, I do not blame you that you abandoned
me. I was never yours to abandon. I do not blame you
for forswearing your Love, since you never loved me. You
pursued your melancholy Virgin and, finding her not in
me, you sought her elsewhere. And found her nowhere.
How could it be otherwise? Having no knowledge of real
Women, but only the sad Images of bad Poetry, it was
scarcely possible that you should ever fall in love. What
you conceived of as love was only shallow Sentiment. You
liked being 'in love' but did not like women.*

*I shall say little as to your account of our Relations.
From what I have written above, it is entirely natural
that if I were not your sad Lady I should be no better
than a Whore and Procuress. Shall I resent your Cruelty?
No, I am too tired.*

*I am old, Dearest, old. I have killed one husband
and two lovers and spent a lifetime in Repentance. It is*

enough, and I shall not complete my Crimes by killing you in my Memory.

Rest peacefully until we meet in that Place where all Masks are torn away. There we shall see each other as we are, and, if two Souls can love apart from bodily Joys, perhaps we shall.

Rest peacefully in my Love

CHAPTER SIXTEEN

Signor Ludovico's Narrative

That night a wind, the *bora*, got up from the north-east, bringing the threat of snow and ice. Not a lantern could stay lit under this gale; the city was in pitch blackness and every shutter creaked and clattered like so much applause. Tosello and I retired to bed and slept fitfully until, in the small hours, we were disturbed by two of our favourite trollops, Giuseppina and Angelina, seeking lodgings for the night. The weather had put an end to any hope of business, even during Carnival season. They, however, attributed their problems to competition from the lascivious habits of the nuns.

Our room was of necessity a sparse one. The girls made a nest on the floor from such rags of sacking and old clothes as were available. But the floor was cold and fierce draughts blew through every crack in wall and shutter so that even the waters in the piss-pot were stirred like a tempest.

Eventually Giuseppina raised her head and said, 'Can we come into bed with you?'

'You smell and your neck is dirty,' I said.

'La!' she retorted. 'You should see my feet!'

I fancy I am more soft-hearted towards women than many an entire male. I could not resist the sight of their shivers and so, in the end, invited the girls into our bed; for this purpose rousing Tosello. In any case, there was no sleep to be had from the sound of crashing tiles and chimneys. And so the four of us in bed together entertained each other merrily, according to our various tastes.

The following morning the funeral of Signor Molin was held. It had been delayed by the enquiries following his death, but the corpse was beginning to stink and there seemed no reason to delay the obsequies further. So the family and mourners were packed into a flotilla of *peote* and we set off under our damp banners across the grey and choppy lagoon to the sad cypresses and the tombs of San Michele. Not surprisingly, many of us were sick.

My patron travelled with other notables in one of the leading vessels. I travelled at the rear in one of the smaller craft that bore persons of lesser importance. Above the wind we heard drums and snatches of lugubrious music, and the curses of fishermen baling out their waterlogged boats. I saw the Jesuit, Fra Angelo, intoning prayers in a craft full of priests. They seemed like so many ghosts.

I was in company with Monsieur Arouet and Signor Balsamo. The former, huddled in his cloak against the weather, appeared sickly, his face drawn and his expression at its most unpleasant. Signor Balsamo, on the other hand, retained the suavity and blitheness that went with his youth and elegant manners. He might claim – as Signor Feltrinelli, another of our companions, had suggested – to be a hundred or more years old, an ancient creature possessing arcane knowledge of the Hermetic Sciences, but there was still a hint of naivety in his brightness. He looked about him eagerly, taking in the views of our city. For Venice was wondrous even on such a day as this. If she did not sparkle like a jewel set in sunlit waters, she was, in the veils of spray and mist, and the bars of pale sunlight between the scudding clouds, a thing of glamour and illusion: neither land nor sea but existing in only partial solidity in a vaporous world between sea and sky.

'How did you spend your day after our parting?' I asked Monsieur Arouet.

He grunted like an old man woken from slumbers, and said shortly, 'I've been attending to my literary labours. Minding my own business as I ought to do. The affairs of others have properly nothing to do with me.'

He was dispirited. It seemed that his great mind had wrestled in vain with the mysteries of the code. I imagined him struggling to draw meaning from the ten names I had given him: twisting their order and letters into innumerable combinations. I looked away. I saw ahead of me the barque holding the catafalque of the deceased accompanied by his beautiful widow, Signora Beatrice, and her lumbering step-son, Signor Girolamo. With them was a host of holy relics and banners as befitted the pious life of Signor Molin. And with them, too, was Cardinal Aldobrandini, representing the Church's acknowledgement of its true son, though from his expansive gestures and animated conversation it seemed that His Eminence had refreshed himself liberally with wine.

Just behind was a vessel holding a company of the deceased's friends, including the Avogadore Dolfin and my patron. Signor Morosini was every inch a patrician, bearing himself today with gravity and the perfect demeanour of his breeding. The Contessa sat with him, chattering merrily, and there, too, was my Angelica, demurely pretty and as sad as a little girl who has lost her dog. In the way of this world, we all carried our characters and troubles to the funeral. And who was to say that the murderer was not also among us?

'I went upon a tour of the literary academies,' continued

Monsieur Arouet. 'I hoped to find some true writers and philosophers there.'

'Which academies?' asked Signor Feltrinelli.

'The Granalleschi and the Messanici.'

I stifled a laugh* and was rewarded with a sharp look.

'This is a frivolous city,' said Monsieur Arouet.

'Indeed it is,' I replied. I have always drawn comfort from this fact.

Signor Feltrinelli asked, 'Have you had success in deciphering the coded message left by the murderer?'

'I have thoughts upon the subject,' replied the Frenchman.

'Are they leading you to a solution?'

Monsieur Arouet shook his head. 'The code is founded upon a series, and I need a clue to identify the nature of that series.'

The factor gave a thin-lipped smile, meaning whatever such smiles mean. He said, 'In the matter of codes you have the advantage of me. I know nothing of them.'

As I have explained, my relations with Signor Feltrinelli were respectful but distant, even though we were both, in a sense, servants of the family. For me, in my then youth, he was too old, too serious and too bland of manner to attract me. It may be that, within his factor's soul, there welled deep springs of passion, but nothing of them was known to me. I found him inscrutable but not in the least mysterious. That is to say, he was like the closed cover of a book that I did not wish to read.

'However,' he continued, 'although I know naught of codes I do, from the course of my occupation, understand something of figures. Behind all the figures in the cryptic

* The Granalleschi would have particular meaning for the narrator. Its nickname was the 'Balls Academy' and its emblem an owl holding a pair of testicles. The Messanici favoured writers of pornography.

message is there not a single figure and that the number "one"? I quote from memory: "I speak of the First and the Second of the First and the Ten that are First." Is not that "First" the key to the entire cypher?'

A glimmer of alertness flickered in Monsieur Arouet's narrow eyes. 'I pray you, go on,' he said.

With more energy Signor Feltrinelli explained, 'The "First" is the thing to be identified. The word describes not its number but its significance as, for example, when we speak of God, He is not the first of many but is the One and Only, above and beyond all other things. So *this* "First" is of the same character, signifying that it is the first in importance not in number.'

'And the "Second of the First"?'

'The "First" has two components and it is the second that forms the basis of the code.'

'So I have concluded also. And the "Ten that are First"?'

'Of this "First" – this thing of supreme importance – there have been many, a series of at least ten.'

'That is most interesting,' said Monsieur Arouet.

Signor Feltrinelli was uncertain whether his notions had been approved. 'That, at all events, is my opinion,' he murmured. 'Though I have confessed my ignorance.'

'No, no!' answered Monsieur Arouet, and he granted the factor one of his wintry smiles. 'You are too modest. Your explanation is clear and full of insight. I believe you are right and that we must renew our enquiries to find this thing of unique importance that justifies its title of "First". I have misdirected my researches in seeking the meaning of the "Ten".'

With that both men fell into silence.

On reaching the cemetery island we went through the mournful pomp of consigning Signor Molin to his ancestors. The wind and rain contributed their lamentations. It seemed to me that, with all our finery and the circumstances of the deceased's reputation, we made a poor collection of humanity. Many were wretched with sea-sickness, and the Cardinal could not escape the muddying of his scarlet robes even though he was sheltered by a baldequin. Also, as I had suspected, he was damnably drunk.

We returned to our boats and were rowed back to the Sacca della Misericordia. Only Signora Beatrice and my patron maintained an entire dignity, the first from an unearthly beauty and the second from pride of race. For my part, I was sick and threw up a porridge of chocolate and brandy which I had consumed the previous night. Monsieur Arouet, who had brightened since his conversation with Signor Feltrinelli, vouchsafed me one of his displays of affection. He patted me on the back and said warmly, 'There's my good fellow!'

While our unhappy party were tossed on the waters of the lagoon, only young Signor Balsamo and Monsieur Arouet seemed lively.

The latter asked, 'Tell me, Signore, have your own researches into the coded message borne any fruit?'

Signor Balsamo and my friend exchanged knowing looks. This was one of the mysteries that I could not fathom. As I have remarked, it seemed that there was some quality of mutual recognition, but I did not know what it might be. Granted both men were savants of a kind. But whereas the Frenchman was a philosopher and *littérateur*, Signor Balsamo pretended to a darker knowledge of Egyptian writing, ancient rites and other esoteric matters. And in appearance what could be more different? Monsieur Arouet was crabbed, abrupt and sly in manner and dressed in an untidy fashion. Signor Balsamo, in contrast, was suave and elegant, and his dress, if not exactly foppish, was *à la mode*. Nor could I say that the two men were open in their recognition of each other. Rather it was as if they were exchanging mutual deceits, neither caring much if the other knew of this fact.

In a most blithe way, Signor Balsamo said, 'I am reluctant to expose my theories to the scrutiny of a greater mind, Monsieur. However, since you are so kind as to value my opinion, I will tell you that I make progress and perhaps within another day shall have reached some conclusions. If you will do me the honour to call at my lodgings tomorrow, may I present them to you?'

Monsieur Arouet chuckled at the other's polite impudence.

'Ha, Signore, you are altogether too generous in your condescension to the vanities of an old man. But, if it pleases you to let me examine the result of your labours, by all means let us meet tomorrow.'

Meantime, at Monsieur Arouet's insistence he and I were landed on the Fondamenta dell'Abazia and exchanged compliments with the others by way of farewell. It was inconvenient for me to be so far from my own parish, since I was minded to return to my lodgings to find Tosello. He had been about the city in the hope of obtaining work or credit, and I aspired at least to fill my belly, since I was hungry after the dissipations of the previous night. I had nothing in my pocket except a small loan from my friend Signor Giacomo — or from his mistress, since I knew him to be as poor as I. However—

'You will, pray, come with me?' proposed Monsieur Arouet cheerfully.

'I regret, Monsieur,' I answered, 'but you find me embarrassed again. I am faint with hunger.'

'Fie, but you must come with me! I need your clear young head to clear my own. If it costs me the price of some food, so be it.'

We found a cook-shop and satisfied ourselves on that

count at modest cost. I note this last point, because, as I had remarked in viewing my companion's rooms, it was my impression that his own funds were not extensive. I saw, too, that his linen was a little soiled, though that may have been a result of his lax habits. Our stomachs now more comfortable, we set off I knew not where into the artisan quarters of Cannaregio.

Monsieur Arouet spoke as we walked. 'Did you observe, Signor Ludovico, that, at the Palazzo Molin, I gave some attention to the paintings?'

'I saw some such thing. You admired them?'

'No, not at all!' he answered sharply. Then, in a more friendly way: 'Not at all. There is something hideous, not to say ridiculous, in the spectacle of so many martyrs offering their mutilated bodies to the Creator in the highest state of ecstasy. No, it is repulsive, the faith of Signor Molin – but it is not for me to criticise the religion of another so long as he does not try to impose it on me. My interest lies in what the paintings can tell me about the deceased, as a guide to the solution of his murder.'

'And did you find something?'

'I do not know. At least, I do not know if it is relevant.'

To my astonishment he produced a pin from out of his pocket. Still more astonishingly, he asked, 'What do you know of the habits of the woodworm?'

I laughed. 'You jest with me, Monsieur?'

He looked at me narrowly. He said, 'I perceive that everything is a jest with you, my light-hearted young friend. Still, it is forgivable in the young and in one whose condition does not permit any family attachments. No, I do not jest, Ludovico.'

I was duly chastised and asked more humbly that he should tell me something about the lowly woodworm. His vanity was, however, affronted and only when we had walked a little further did he continue, as if speaking to the air.

'The woodworm is a creature of decided tastes, revelling in its own woodwormish delights, no doubt finding this piece of wood a juicy tit-bit and that one not. And, even having found a dish to its liking, selecting the choicest cuts: preferring the tender fibres to the tough, and avoiding gesso and varnish if it can feast on three solid dishes of ash or beech.'

'No doubt,' I agreed.

'There is *no* doubt,' he confirmed. 'I have proven the fact by experimentation. Now, what of it? This! In the course of its diet, the woodworm does not travel as straight as an arrow, but follows the whims of its appetites here and there in a meandering fashion through its chosen food. And, being of deplorable habits, it fills up its hole with worm casts and turds, and in the fullness of time throws off its mortal shackles and leaves its body behind. Requiescat in pace!'

'I understand.'

'Yes! Yes! Thus it is with the common woodworm. But *not* with the uncommon woodworms that inhabit the frames of several of Signor Molin's pictures. *They* are firm of purpose and, like true geometers, travel in a straight line between two points. Nor do they leave behind them the detritus of their lives; but, like good housewives, sweep out their abodes so that not a turd or corpse lies therein. In short, these holes are not made by woodworms at all. I know this because I have tested them with a pin. In fact, I believe that the holes are made with a heated needle, since I have detected slight signs of charring around the entrances. Is this not strange?'

It was indeed! But, as my companion had observed, what did it mean?

'A great deal – but perhaps nothing to our purpose.

It is too early to say, though we may conclude that the frames surrounding some of Signor Molin's paintings belie their antique appearance and are in fact of recent manufacture, got up by artifice to seem ancient. And, if the frames are recent, perhaps the same applies to the paintings themselves? However, what I cannot yet tell is whether Signor Molin was the unwitting victim of a cheat or whether his taste or vanity required him to dress his collection in the appearance of age.'

'I do not think that likely,' I said.

'No?'

'No. By all accounts, Signor Molin was an honest man, not a hypocrite, and nothing in his house showed him to be a play-thing of vanity. If his paintings are indeed not what they seem, he has been grossly imposed upon.'

Monsieur Arouet halted and stared at me. He said, 'My dear boy, truly there is something clear-sighted in your nature.'

I was flattered (I was speaking of Signor Molin's lack of vanity – not my own).

We now found ourselves in the neighbourhood of the ghetto, as was evident from the number of Jews in gaberdine reaching to their ankles and a chatter of Hebrew cant in what seemed to be a bastard Spanish. It was a filthy hole of chicken-runs and piles of ordure.

'We are nearly there,' said Monsieur Arouet.

'Where?'

'I have been making enquiries among various artisans and craftsmen to ascertain where we might get such work done as was provided to Signor Molin. If his paintings were produced here in Venice, this is the place.'

We were in a narrow lane of workshops, part of a tumbled-down warren stinking of wood-shavings, tar, rotten vegetables and fish. The canal was covered in a scum of trash and night-soil. The footway was unpaved and blocked here and there with smouldering middens. My companion made enquiry of a baggy-trousered Albanian. Having taken directions from this cut-throat, he said, 'We are at our goal, Ludovico!'

It was an undistinguished building of crumbling brick and stucco, facing the lane at the front and on one side standing straight out of the canal and stained with weed and dampness. I discerned the remains of a yard or garden behind it. The shutters were in ill-repair and the roof lacked tiles in places. We knocked.

A little fellow came to the door. He was covered in paint, dust and wood-shavings and wore a leather apron. As is often the case with a labouring-man, his trunk and arms seemed built of oak and properly belonging to someone much taller. His face was pink, well-fed and bristly like a pig's backside. He spoke the Venetian dialect with which my friend had difficulty.

'Signor Pasticcio?'

The man scanned our faces and clothes with unabashed frankness and suspicion. Then, seeing that we were persons of quality, his own face broke into an ingratiating leer. 'Lustrissimi!' he said, touching his breast, and bade us enter.

We went into the first of a series of rooms lit only by tallow dips. My nose was assailed by a reek of hot oils, soap and lye. One of our host's apprentices was priming various boards and canvases, confirming that we were in some fashion of studio, though perhaps 'manufactory' would be a better term; for, on the next floor, half a dozen young men were at work. Some were painting draperies, others figures, and yet others trees and sky. We passed on to still another floor, which comprised Signor Pasticcio's private apartments, though, again, words fail me to describe a den occupied by slatternly women of various ages, a brood of brats, and a scrawny, wall-eyed bitch that was suckling a litter of pups. Using a piece of carved framing-timber, Signor Pasticcio cudgelled his children and women folk into clearing a space for us among the filth and disorder, and commanded wine to be brought.

Monsieur Arouet introduced us, giving our history with some embellishments. He was, he said, the man of business to the Duc de Richelieu; commissioned by His Grace to tour Italy and buy works of art. I was a confidant of the noble Signor Tomasso Morosini, and guide to my friend in his visit to Venice.

'Your name, Signore, was given to me as that of a craftsman of distinction and – discretion,' said Monsieur Arouet with delicate emphasis upon the last word.

'By whom?' asked Signor Pasticcio.

'Signor Girolamo Molin.'

Our host showed no reaction to that name. His face was of a kind that changes expression rapidly. At rest (which was their usual condition), his features were those of a perfect ruffian: coarse, lined and fleshy. At will, however, he could switch them to those of a jolly fellow, smiling broadly, eyes twinkling, in short the most genial body one could wish to meet. Now, having listened to us thoughtfully, he wiped his lips and revealed a cheerfully evil grin. He slapped his leg.

'Come, Lustrissimi!' he exclaimed. 'Leave your wine! Leave it! It's Jew's piss!' He proceeded to cuff his wife and berate her for insulting his honour by poisoning his guests. I fancy that Signor Pasticcio believed this mixture of brutality and rough courtesy constituted the manners of a gentleman. 'Follow me,' he invited with a theatrical bow.

We descended again to the painting-studio on the floor below. The good craftsman introduced us to his chief jour-neyman, one Bastianini, who was supervising the apprentices about their work. At the request of his employer, the fellow gave some explanation of grounds of glazes, tempera and oils, and painting in the Byzantine manner and that of the Spaniards and the Dutch. This was all beyond my comprehension. To my surprise, however, I noticed that, though the incomplete works appeared in all their freshness, the finished paintings seemed in the last stages of decrepitude: the images obscured by smoke and dirt; the frames damaged so that the gilding was worn and tarnished; and chips revealed the underlying gesso.

From here we went down and into the yard. This was filled with wood and stone and various sculpted articles upon which still more apprentices were working under the guidance of another journeyman, a modest young fellow named Dossena. He was supervising the turning over of a pile of earth and manure, in which, so far as I could tell, was buried the bust of some ancient philosopher.

Monsieur Arouet guarded his nose with a copious pinch of snuff and offered the same to me. We were, in truth, in one of the smelliest places it has been my misfortune to visit. Our host now attended to us.

'Well?' he said, with a foul wink. 'What do you think of my trade? Aren't we the lads who can do the business for you?'

'I see that you can deliver pieces done in the antique manner,' said Monsieur Arouet circumspectly.

'Anything you like! Greek, Roman, Siennese, Spanish, German – this is the shop!'

'Isn't this all a kind of cheat?' I said unwisely.

Signor Pasticcio regarded me with contempt. To my companion he said, 'Understand, now. It's not for me to know what my patrons do with my work. They know what we do. We sell stuff that's all got up in the antique fashion, but fair and above-board and no gammon. What they do with it – well, that's their business. Let me tell you a story,' he said to me.

This is his story, which he related with some relish. Lorenzo de' Medici, tyrant of Florence, was a patron of the young Michelangelo. He commissioned the artist to ornament his park and palazzo with sculptures in stone. One of these products was a *Sleeping Cupid* done in the classical manner. Recognizing its quality, the Prince decided to sell it for a high price, and saw that its value would be enhanced if it could be sold as an original work of the Roman period. He put this proposition to the artist, and Michelangelo, not averse to making money, agreed to bury the piece in some sour earth, from which it was dug up once it had the appearance of age. The prince then sold it to Cardinal Riario of San Giorgio for two hundred gold ducats, using a dealer, Baldassare de Milanese, as his agent, to secure his anonymity. In brief, it was a complete imposture.

Signor Pasticcio continued his lesson. At one time, in the Medici palace, there was a portrait of Pope Leo X by Raphael. Now it happened that Federigo Gonzaga, Duke of Mantua, saw and was enraptured by the painting and so embarrassed his host, Prince Ottaviano de' Medici, with praise of the work that the latter felt obliged to make a present of the same to his guest. This he was most reluctant to do, because of the beauty and value of the painting. There was his dilemma. What should be his remedy? The Prince was at a loss. Then he remembered that a certain fresco, the *Baptism of Christ*, in the Chiostro dello Scalzo, painted by Andrea del Sarto, was considered worthy of Raphael. He therefore summoned the painter and paid him to make a copy of the Pope's portrait indistinguishable from the original. This he did and the Duke, unaware of the deception, was delighted.

'I recall the story,' said Monsieur Arouet. He addressed me. 'The fraud was uncovered finally by the painter Giulio

Romano, who informed the Duke. The latter said: "I value this picture no less than if it had come from Raphael's own hand; on the contrary, I value it more highly, for it is past nature that one distinguished man should so fully succeed in imitating and catching the style of another." I believe that the forgery – if such it may be called – was given a place of honour in the Duke's collection.'

Signor Pasticcio hooted with pleasure that my friend had so appreciated his story. By way of compliment he placed an arm about him and called him 'a devil – a villain – a very Greek'. Monsieur Arouet was also pleased at his own sagacity and in no way annoyed with his host for the latter's nice manners.

Instead, smiling, he said to me, 'There are several lessons to be drawn from these stories, my dear Ludovico. The first is that one can place no faith in the honesty of either princes or artists. The second is that a work of art cannot be judged by the purity of the artist's intentions, but only in and of itself. And the third is that such work indeed has no value except such as we, in our wisdom or folly, bring to it.'

At this Signor Pasticcio was so delighted that I wondered that he did not bless my friend with the title of 'Satan'. For my part, though I make no claims to morality, I confess I was offended that art should be such a cozening business and its practitioners nothing but rogues.

'But enough of this jollity,' said Monsieur Arouet to our host. 'Let us speak confidentially.'

Signor Pasticcio coughed and murmured, 'Not here, Lustrissimo. Not if you follow my meaning.' He led us again to his private apartments and obliged us by driving out his family with sundry blows and curses, excepting only the brown bitch, which growled and seemed disposed to defend herself and her litter.

'Right then,' he said. 'Let's come down to cases. What

does your patron, the Duca de' Ricchezze, want? Depending on the period and the quality, I can sell you by the square yard for bulk, or by weight in the case of sculptures. If you take from my stock I can give a discount – though, since I'm an honest man, I'll tell you that the stuff in stock has been returned as not being of the best, and it won't pass muster under a discerning eye. I can't say fairer. How much do you have to spend? I don't doubt we can strike a price that will leave something with Your Honour for his trouble.'

'You are a good fellow and a plain-dealer, I can see,' answered Monsieur Arouet good-naturedly. 'And I shall be frank also with you. I shall be still a little time in the city, and feel obliged to fulfil my master's commission by enquiring of others in the same trade – though I do not doubt that in the end I shall find that your good self will meet the requirements of the situation. Nevertheless,' he added, 'it would assist me if you could name me some persons who are the proud possessors of your work while remaining in ignorance of the fact. There could assuredly be no better test of quality.'

At this Signor Pasticcio's face abruptly lost all trace of geniality. I saw his cruel and mercenary nature undisguised.

'So that's your game, is it?' he snarled. 'Coming here to spy on my business!' He rose to his feet and grasped one of the handy batons. He shook this at us. 'All right, out with you! That's it, right this second if you know what's good for you. D——d spies! I'll swing for you, see if I won't!'

With this encouragement, Monsieur Arouet and I were bundled out of the premises and Pasticcio would have called his apprentices to toss us into the canal had we not beat a hasty retreat. Monsieur Arouet, however, insisted on returning briefly. He said it was to get his hat.

CHAPTER SEVENTEEN

Signor Ludovico's Narrative

Upon my return to my lodgings, I found Tosello in bed, though it was barely dusk. His face was covered in chocolate from the *nonpareils* he had been eating and he was grinning like a dog.

'My dearest fellow!' he cried. 'I have some things to tell you!'

His first piece of news was pleasant but mundane. Giacomo had called to deliver me a suit of clothes of which he was no longer in need, being in funds from his mistress. Whatever his failings, he was a generous fellow, and the suit was of pale-blue velvet that would pass as fine by candle-light.

The second story was more curious. Tosello is of a religious and mystical turn, superstitious to fault (he cannot see a statue of the Virgin or hear a choir without crying). So he is a frequenter of churches, even though he may not take Holy Communion. That was where he had been that afternoon – to the church of Santa Maria Zobenigo.

Now it happened that the priest was hearing confessions. Tosello was on his knees before the Virgin when he heard the door of the confessional open. He thought nothing of it until, to his surprise, he heard a sympathetic voice from close behind him say, 'You are in tears.'

Tosello turned. Behind him was a stranger, masked, mantled, and gowned in patrician red.

'Do not let me disturb you,' said the stranger gently, and he himself appeared to pray.

'I am making my devotions to the Mother of God,' Tosello explained somewhat needlessly. 'When all the World denies me forgiveness, She at least will forgive.'

'Why does the World deny you forgiveness?'

'Because I am an actor.'

'Ah, how sad!' sighed the stranger with great sincerity. 'To commit great crimes and other sins, and to find no forgiveness! Yet Our Lady will surely forgive a contrite heart and make intercession with the Saviour.'

'So I trust,' answered Tosello fervently.

As I say, my dear Tosello is an actor – albeit an inadequate one. And like many actors he carries his part for the time-being with an interior conviction. So, now, he was not a fat fool but a humble penitent, and his smooth round face, which is naturally sweet, must have seemed most touching, bedewed as it was with tears. Certainly it seems to have stirred the stranger, who, in the conversation that followed, admitted that he had come to confess his own sins and yet was left unsatisfied. Was it, he asked, that he was not in fact contrite? There was hidden in his manner an anger that belied his outward gentleness. It seemed (according to Tosello's imaginings, for what they are worth) that the man was crushed by a burden of guilt of which he could not rid himself because he was still committed to dangerous courses. He was, said Tosello, truly frightening.

However that may be, the part must be played out. And Tosello, dimly influenced by the roles of priest or confidant he had sometimes acted, was the sympathetic listener to this troubled creature. No doubt Tosello had a few peccadillos to get off his chest, but for the benefit of his new-found friend he confessed that he, too, laboured under the oppression of unnameable offences that bound his soul in torment.

The pair therefore got on famously.

I do not wish to mock. My fat friend felt pain behind his foolishness, and doubtless the mysterious patrician experienced his own agonies, but I cannot but perceive the absurdity of these two, each finding in the other a fellow-pilgrim on the soul's journey. But, then, what is to be made of myself and Monsieur Arouet?

Engaged in deep conversation of the heart, Tosello and his patron went to seek refreshment but found only a convenient *malvasia* where they imbibed cheap wine and little else. This further depressed their melancholy spirits and increased their feeling that they were men of sentiment, a species of Promethean hero despised by the World. Signor Prometheus, as I shall call him, claimed, rather surprisingly, to be ignorant of the Theatre. He knew nothing of comedians and their lives, and to meet such a one as Tosello was akin to religious conversion: he must needs know every particular of his friend's existence.

Diffidently, Tosello volunteered to show Signor Prometheus his chambers. He prayed that the whores were not in occupation with their customers. In this he was fortunate. Ah! exclaimed Prometheus. The squalor! The degradation. Well, yes, allowed Tosello, perhaps a little cleaning and some patching to the roof would improve the place. (My poor benighted friend, who could see the condition to which sin and debauchery had reduced you! And yet you had a good and sincere heart.)

Signor Prometheus was genuinely moved by Tosello's state. The latter, it seemed, was not, as some might think, an effeminate reprobate, but rather an innocent who had been cruelly mutilated and then ensnared in the toils of sin.

It took very little of this to reduce both Tosello and Prometheus to tears of mutual pity and affection. And this, of course, led to its natural conclusion. Signor Prometheus swore that he felt for my friend a profound Christian love, and proceeded to prove his point by serving him *à la turque*.

'The fellow was a virgin!' exclaimed Tosello, his face all joy and chocolate. 'At least insofar as concerns our merry customs. He gave me to understand that he has been left bereft by some heartless mistress who resists his advances. Not, I may say, that I am wholly surprised. He is an enormous beast and his character is saturnine, not to say gloomy. But, if his mistress is pious and miserable, I daresay he would do her very well.'

'You seem much taken by him.'

'He is rich! I admit that he caught me in a sentimental vein and therefore I was unable to derive financial profit from our enterprise; but I am more sober now. I doubt that he is a man committed to the merry life or he would not be pursuing his reluctant charmer; but, for as long as she resists him, it is natural that he will seek other distractions. Why should we not provide them? Fortune has put him our way, and she is a dame I never refuse.'

'You shall see him again?'

'Not *I* but *we*! I have made an appointment for this very evening, and not for myself alone. I have mentioned your own name and explained that you, too, are a Spiritual Person who has been trapped in Vice by an unforgiving World.'

I confess that I was amused at this notion of my spirituality. And, in a corner of my mind, did I not believe it to be true? Thus it is with us trivial fellows: always imagining that we are other than we are. I confess, too, that I was curious at my part in the proposed encounter. Three in a bed was calculated to disturb any recent virgin.

'No, not for that,' said Tosello when I explained my concern. 'You are right, I have no desire to frighten him. But he may regard our amorous episode as an aberration, and the presence of a third may persuade him that he need fear no more than polite conversation. And for my part it may remain so, for, as I say, he is a brute so far as concerns his physical parts.' With that Tosello extended a hand to me. I saw the nervousness in his eyes and asked what ailed him. Only then did the sparkle of wit and pleasure vanish from his face, and he said, 'Truthfully, Ludovico, he terrifies me.'

Signor Prometheus had retained some sense of caution and decorum. He would not return to a house where sodomites and whoremongers plied their trade. The arrangement was made that we should meet at a certain discreet casino, identifying ourselves by wearing tokens, since we should be masked. This we did and found Prometheus sitting in a gondola – a mark of a doubting person who might wish at the last moment to escape. But he alighted and bade us good evening. I had advised Tosello that, if he could not sustain his character as a man of religion, he should try at least not to appear a simpering pederast.

'So this is your friend Monsieur Louis?' said Prometheus. For some reason, Tosello in his fancies had decided I was French. We exchanged circumspect looks. Tosello had spoken the truth. He was indeed of an uncommon size, a veritable bear.

I touched breast and hat. 'I am honoured to make your acquaintance, Monsieur.'

The acknowledgement was curt. And yet he had not repented of the earlier encounter. This shortness of manner must represent what Tosello had detected: the trembling cork stopping a bottle containing who knew what emotions.

'Come, let us go in,' said our companion.

The casino in question held not only a number of chambers dedicated to intimate encounters, but also a private gaming-room. Although he showed no interest in the punt as such, Signor Prometheus was disposed to linger over the faro-table. I wondered if, like many another recent virgin, he was of two minds whether to repent of his loss or dedicate himself fully to his new-found pleasures. At all events, though he did nothing but haunt the room in various postures of gloom and moroseness, he was generous enough to advance a few ducats so that we might play. And this I did, since there was evidently no conversation to be had.

I gambled and Fortune was with me – perhaps because, from a sense of tension, I did not care. So I proceeded from *paroli* to *sept et le va* and finally carried off *soixante et le va* on a turn of the knave. This was one of those *ridotti* where the gamesters conducted themselves solemnly and silently, making their calls by bending and mutilating the cards so that scarce a word was heard except a murmured command to a servant or the whispered encouragement of a courtesan to her lover. I felt troubled.

And not only I. Tosello drank. He became jocular and addressed the servants as 'dear heart'. Signor Prometheus, meanwhile, seemed to press himself deeper into the shadows. I tried to engage him, making, as I thought, a pretty and witty little speech on the perils of gambling.

'I do not gamble,' he replied. 'It is contrary to the laws of God.'

'La! Signore, then why are you here?'

'I indulge my friends,' he said, as if any indulgence were a torment to him.

'Most assuredly you are right,' I said, pretending to

some morals. It seemed to me that his dark mood could become only more sinister if we remained at the tables. I began to wonder what crimes they were to which he had made confession. 'Let us leave this place for more convivial surroundings,' I proposed.

A servant, a mincing popinjay with roughed lips and a patch on his cheek, showed us to our chamber with nudges and winks of lubricious intent. He lit the candles and revealed a small apartment laid with a cold supper of ortolans, larks' tongues, and hung with paintings depicting appropriate pastimes for a reclining position. I felt disgust rising like bile in my throat, made worse by Tosello's Oohs! and Ahs. Was I indeed becoming more spiritual? More moral? Or was this merely the effect of fear?

Signor Prometheus entered the chamber with a firmness of step like that of a husband surprising a lover, dismissed the servant and poured himself a brandy which he drank in one mouthful.

'Well, my dear fellows!' cooed Tosello. 'Shall we take our ease?'

'Indeed,' I agreed, wondering what ease was to be had in the company of a monster. Tosello removed his hat, mask and cloak. In powder, patches and periwig he looked the very image of a woman. I glanced at Signor Prometheus. 'Shall we do likewise?' I invited him.

Until then my inner garments had been largely hidden by my cloak. As I removed this outer layer, I revealed the pale-blue suit that Giacomo had given me.

At this, Prometheus uttered one word: 'You!'

I was abashed, lost for words. What had I done to deserve this? For though but a single word, it was delivered with a ferocity and hatred that were palpable.

'I?'

'Yes, *you*!' repeated Prometheus, his voice rising.

I collected such nerve as I possessed. 'Pray, Signore, we are strangers. What can I possibly have done to deserve this coldness of manner?'

'We are not strangers,' said Prometheus slowly. 'And as for what insult you have given me, I know you for what you are: a fornicator, a ravisher of women!'

'What?' spluttered a wide-eyed Tosello. 'Ludovico? Women?'

'You mistake yourself, Signore,' I said, coolly. 'There is here some confusion of persons. I am no ravisher – of either sex. I know of no occasion of offence. Pray consider and give me such particulars of the insult as will allow me to defend myself. On my honour, I am innocent.'

All restraint now gone, Prometheus shouted, 'Honour? You have no honour! You are a libertine and the most forsworn man in Venice!' He took a step towards me, and the candles threw his massive shadow against the wall so that it seemed to fill the room. Then he collected himself. He said, more calmly, 'Nay, though you are without honour, I shall not slay you in cold blood. But I demand satisfaction upon the instant.'

In horror, I understood that he intended a duel!

Now, as Signor Prometheus correctly said, I am a creature without honour. I took to my heels. Nor was honour the only consideration. Beneath my enemy's cloak I perceived that he came armed with a rapier and poniard, whereas I carried only a small-sword, and that more for ornament than use. In addition, he was a very Behemoth. At the first pass of our blades he was like to pin me to the wall, upon which he could fillet me at leisure. I had no fear for Tosello. Indeed, I had no thought for him.

I bounded down the stairs. Prometheus came roaring after me. I bowled over the scullions and chambermaids who stood in my way, and at every turn in the passages tipped over such chairs or tables as I could find, in the hope of slowing the monster. But I was lost. The house was a labyrinth.

I had thought to gain the gambling-room, where Prometheus would be restrained or restrain himself, but this was not to be. Though I had covered but a little distance, I halted in trembling exhaustion. My enemy halted, too, for I could not hear him. In some twist of my flight he had lost me.

Where were all the lackeys of the house? I supposed that we had made the most indecent noise, but perhaps this was not so. Or perhaps it was discretion. This was a place where intimate violence was tolerated with every other vice.

I considered a cry for help. Immediately I repented it — at least for as long as any other course offered salvation. If Prometheus chose to disclose himself, the house would obey his commands. On his whim I could be arrested, and I fancied being strangled as little as I did being run through the belly. I must be cunning.

I found myself among the private offices. Here there was a coming and going of servants taking wine and sweetmeats to the guests and otherwise going about the concerns of this gambling-hell and bawdy-house. My presence was not questioned. I stopped one of the kitchen drudges and enquired for an exit. She showed me to a water-gate. It seemed that I was saved.

Several gondolas were moored in the canal. I remembered that I had money. I waved a gold piece and summoned a boat.

'To the Riva degli Schiavoni!' I said, thinking I should be safe in such a public place.

We cast off into darkness along a stinking side-canal. I encouraged the gondolier to row faster, but the fellow had been drinking and seemed befuddled. He thought I had asked him to sing, or perhaps the mood was on him.

I in terror of my life and my guide singing a melancholy love-song.

At length we came to a crossing, but, alas, it was only another bywater overhung by crumbling houses. The buffoon who rowed me seemed as ignorant of his bearings as I was. I urged him on with an offer of more money but the fool only grinned and sang louder. Answering calls in song came out of the darkness.

The other gondola came upon us by stealth. Our lantern dazzled me and illuminated the approaching craft only at the last second. I heard a roar, and knew, although the words meant nothing, it could be no-one except my enemy. Prometheus, of course, had his own craft and more powers of encouragement over his man than I possessed over mine. They came up strongly, gliding alongside us so that the vessels touched.

'Ha!' yelled Prometheus. He made a pass at me with his rapier and snagged my cloak. I could make no riposte as I struggled to free my own blade from the toils of my clothing.

'Ha!' He came at me again and this time stuck his poniard into my cloak and tore it from me. He proceeded to worry at it like a terrier at a rag until he was free of it, than threw the remains into the canal.

'Row, you fool!' I cried to my gondolier. The fellow seemed to think that this was no more than drunken sport and was laughing like an idiot. I returned my enemy's thrust, but both my reach and the length of my blade were less than his and I struck only air.

The energy of our strokes had caused the two craft to separate. I turned to my man and belaboured him with the flat of my sword, urging him to row, damn his eyes, row! A glimmer of understanding of our danger now seemed to flicker in his brain and he made an effort. As did Prometheus's fellow. Our craft slid a while in silence through the darkness.

'Douse the lantern!' I shouted.

'What?'

'The lantern, fool!' I seized it and threw it into the water. Now let Prometheus see me! He replied by dropping his poniard and taking up the light from his own vessel. Holding that in his left hand and his rapier in his right, he jabbed at me as best he could while we maintained our crazy course, bumping and nudging each other and the walls of the canal.

Now, I claim no skill as a soldier, but I had learned the rudiments of fencing as part of the comedian's art. If my reach did not enable me to strike my enemy, I could at least parry his blows. My concern was that he would wear me down. He was a powerful beast, and at each blocking stroke I shuddered to my boots. Moreover, his energy was demoniacal. There was no tiring of him.

'The devil take this!' cried my gondolier. He abandoned his oar and dived into the water. Without direction my boat glided to the canal-side, where there was no path, only the wall of a house. The other vessel slipped past me. Prometheus yelled furiously at his man to come round again and pull alongside. I could do nothing to avoid this: I was stuck fairly against the bank, caught on some obstacle in the water.

The way was too narrow to turn in the darkness. In coming at me again, my opponent back-paddled and it was the oarsman who was nearer me. I saw then that I had a second's advantage. Stretching as far as I could, I made a thrust at the fellow and raked him down the forearm. He screamed and, truly, I was sorry for the poor devil, but what choice had I? He let loose the oar and again his vessel slipped past me. And this time we passed closely, like lovers kissing, and as we did so Prometheus rained a series of blows on me which drew sparks from our blades. Then he was gone — drifting into the darkness with a chorus of threats and curses. I picked up the oar of my vessel and with a little struggle pushed myself free.

CHAPTER EIGHTEEN

Ten Sefirot from nothingness. Ten and not nine; ten and not eleven. Understand with wisdom; be wise with understanding. Probe with them and explore from them. Establish a thing in its essence. And return the Creator to His rightful place.

Sefer Yetzirah 1:4

Signor Ludovico's Narrative

My encounter with Prometheus left me terrified and exhausted. I was set to go home, having nothing in mind but to cry myself to sleep, miserable creature that I was. Then I realised the impossibility of that course. Prometheus knew the whereabouts of my lodgings! He had been taken there by that fat fool, Tosello! I could not with safety return there.

At a loss for anything better, I presented myself at Monsieur Arouet's chambers and knocked up the house until a servant answered. Lord knows I was a pitiful sight, shaking with cold and fear and weeping like a baby. Monsieur Arouet, in nightcap and shirt, came downstairs to see who was visiting at this hour, and, recognising me by candle-light, reassured his landlady's people that there was nothing about which to be concerned. Putting his arm about me, he led me to his room, where he promptly gave me a cup of wine and a rug to wrap about my shoulders. And then we settled to talk.

I had had some time to reflect on the explanation of my predicament and I began by telling my friend as much as I understood of Giacomo's paying court to his melancholy mistress.

'I see,' said Monsieur Arouet. 'And you think that this murderous fellow, whom you call Signor Prometheus, is in some fashion the lover or protector of this sad lady?'

'I have no doubt of it,' I answered. 'He is a monster of jealousy and has already attempted to put a bullet into Signor Giacomo. Tonight I was wearing a suit of clothes which belonged to Giacomo, and it seems clear that Prometheus has confounded our identities.'

'So it seems,' agreed Monsieur Arouet. He grinned. 'This custom of masking is the devil, is it not? Still, Ludovico, I do not believe that you will have cause to fear much longer. Once Signor Prometheus's temper has cooled, he will act more circumspectly and no doubt make some enquiries at your lodgings in order to understand the character of his enemy. A moment's reflection will tell you that he will quickly learn of your unfortunate condition and will realise you are a most unlikely rival for his mistress's affections.'

My friend's reasoning was sound. A brief enquiry would soon reveal to Prometheus that I was nothing but a poor eunuch. I was reassured.

'Your story is, however, curious on another count,' said Monsieur Arouet thoughtfully. 'You have not remarked it?'

'You have the advantage of me,' I answered hesitantly.

'No matter. Perhaps it is only a coincidence.'

'Yes?'

'The church,' said Monsieur Arouet. 'Your friend Tosello encountered Prometheus at the same church where Signor

Molin used to make his devotions. Still, a man must pray somewhere and the fact may mean nothing. Let us put this night's business out of mind and look to the morrow. You will recall that Signor Balsamo has undertaken to reveal to us the mysteries of the code.'

My bed was made on the floor and I slept well. Not so my friend. He was afflicted with night terrors and moaned and groaned the night long. I mention this fact in order to show that, for all the clarity of his great mind, Monsieur Arouet was also troubled by obscure fears that no philosophy could remove. In the morning we breakfasted on the milk-sops that were his preferred diet.

Signor Balsamo had taken apartments in Cannaregio in a decayed palazzo, the property of a decayed family. Such families arise not uncommonly by reason of the customs of the city, whereby younger sons are kept unmarried to preserve the patrimony, and war or disease can carry away the hope of future generations. In was my belief that such was the situation of Signor Girolamo Molin: a younger son whose hope of marriage was blighted unless his brother should die in Corfu.

The servants at Signor Balsamo's palazzo – what we saw of them, skulking in doorways and under staircases – were of a character with the house: shabby villains hired by the tenant for a season. The major-domo who received us was such a one, perhaps of some ancient family now broken down. His hair and face were liberally powdered, his sunken cheeks rouged, his lips puckered and pouting. He made a bow of great civility, declaring that we were expected and that he was honoured, and so forth, as if he were master of the house. And, with mincing steps and the aid of a long-handled cane, he escorted us by cobwebbed stairways and abandoned chambers palely lit by daylight, through dust, ruin and detritus, commenting gaily all the while that this or that wreck of furniture or painting was some splendid monument of glory.

I was well rid of the fellow but his successor was even more disturbing. He seemed to spring at us from behind an arras door that disguised the entrance to some other apartments – a great blackamoor with cicatrised cheeks and drooping moustachios. He was dressed as a Musulman in baggy pantaloons, his feet bare, as indeed was his torso except for a short embroidered jacket. On his head he wore a scarlet tarboosh, and held across his breast, as if warding off evil spirits, was a great curved sword.

'Ahmed, my dear friend,' said the exquisite who had first greeted us. 'Pray advise the master that his honoured guests have arrived.'

'Your slave obeys, Effendi,' replied the blackamoor, though in accents that reminded me of a Venetian seaman.

'My master may still be about his prayers,' the exquisite informed us, airily. 'The rising of the sun, the setting of the same, the changing seasons in their due time, these are all occasions for his devotions.' I nodded sagely, though, by the clock, the sun was well risen. He continued, 'May I oblige you with some further history of this melancholy mansion?'

We consented and our guide took us on a further tour of those sad rooms full of dust, dampness and the ruins of ancient splendour.

'This,' he said, pointing to a fireplace, 'was constructed for the Emperor Charles the Fifth. Alas, he never visited. And this' – indicating a portrait, much spotted and torn – 'is the same Rodrigo Borgia that was Pope Alexander the Sixth. A good likeness, I am told. This marriage-chest of the quattrocentro was made for the wedding of – no! I forget the name of the poor lady; she was poisoned. Do you know her?' The fellow's absurdities were not of a kind to cause mirth. He laboured under some madness which depressed my spirits even as it made him merry. 'Hark!' he concluded. 'I hear something! Is the master now ready, Ahmed dear?'

'As ready as he'll ever be,' returned the slave, bad-temperedly. He beckoned us with a finger and we followed. My last view of the major-domo was of his white face smiling pleasantly, and I was reminded of the moon on a winter's evening.

The desolation of the other parts of the gloomy palazzo had not been carried to Signor Balsamo's apartments. From here daylight had been excluded by heavy drapes and, as my eyes became used to the flames of some brass lanterns, I saw that the whole chamber was hung in exotic stuffs, giving the appearance of a tent or pavilion of an Ottoman Pasha. In the space so created, divers carpets, cushions and divans were scattered, and Ahmed the slave invited us to take a seat at our pleasure.

I was conscious that, since our arrival, Monsieur Arouet had not spoken, except for a few words of politeness. A glance at him now, as he squatted on one of the cushions, confirmed his subdued manner and I wondered at its cause. Was it Signor Balsamo? I could not tell whether that young man were a magus or a charlatan. I knew only that he was an extraordinary person. No-one else could so easily have engaged the interest of my patron. But what did this signify for my companion? It was only on reflection that I understood the nature of his fear. His honesty would not allow him to disguise the fact that he was defeated by the intricacies of the code. But his monstrous vanity could not allow that Signor Balsamo should succeed where he had failed. This was his danger and it was, I suppose, courageous on his part that he was willing to face this humiliation.

To the sound of a gong, Signor Balsamo entered through a corner of the drapes. His man made an unconvincing show

of fawning and cringing in front of him until dismissed by
a clap of his master's hands. To us Signor Balsamo smiled
and raised an eyebrow as if to comment on such silliness.
I mention this because it was a measure of our host that he
was above these theatricalities as well as part of them. Such
were his lightness of manner and his perfect self-assurance
that one was equally impressed by the display and by his
effrontery in imposing it upon us.

In accordance with his assumed character, Signor Balsamo
had set aside his wig for a striped turban of ivory and
green, fixed in place with an aigret feather. He wore a
shirt of the same ivory silk, and a short jacket similar to
his servant's covered this ensemble, the whole set off with
pointed slippers. The entire costume was worked in gold
thread and semi-precious stones.

He took his seat and turned his eyes upon us with a frank
and engaging smile. 'Greetings, Signori,' he said. 'You do me
honour in attending on me, and I am yours to command.'

Monsieur Arouet murmured a civil reply but his tone
seemed to me ungracious. While waiting for our host he
had ferreted among that young man's books and a selection of
them lay at his feet. He fingered one. 'You have an interesting
and curious library,' he commented.

Signor Balsamo shrugged insouciantly. 'You are familiar
with the Sefer Yetzirah?'

'As the need arises,' replied my companion obscurely.

'Our task will be made easier if you have studied the
Jewish philosophers.'

Monsieur Arouet grinned for the first time, as if he
expected some pleasure from the meeting. 'Ah, the Jewish
philosophers! You excite me, Signore. Indeed you do! The
Sefer Yetzirah, Luria, the Zohar – the whole Abracadabra.
"Wisdom is found from nothing," wrote Dov Baer, the
Maggid of Mazritch. You, on the other hand, have books.

Yet, I understood that you were a Hermeticist rather than a Kabbalist?'

Signor Balsamo indicated some other books, by Pico della Mirandola and Giordano Bruno.

'Truly,' said Monsieur Arouet, 'you are a most extraordinary young man – I speak frankly.'

In face of this compliment, I noticed that our host made no reference to his great age or immortality such as Signor Feltrinelli had hinted at.

'Very well!' said my friend. 'I come to learn. Instruct me!'

Signor Balsamo clapped his hands and his slave entered to light the contents of a brazier. It gave off a heady scent of incense.

'Come now,' said Monsieur Arouet, 'we are not to be made dizzy with magical hocus-pocus, are we?'

Signor Balsamo laughed. 'I see that I deal with an enlightened philosopher! No, there will be no more hocus-pocus than goes naturally with the subject – though, in truth, there is more than enough of that. I shall lay my theories before you and you may consider them as a rational man.'

'I am deeply obliged,' acknowledged my companion and again there was between these two men that smile, that look in the eyes of shared knowingness. Was it shared wisdom or shared deceit? Are the two separable? I was at a loss to answer this and, indeed, at a loss to follow the sense of their subsequent discussion. For they spoke of ancient mysteries, arcane sciences and the attempts of mystical speculation to name the Ineffable. I was left dizzy with words and can set out for my reader only this poor fool's understanding of what was said.

'We begin, do we not,' said Signor Balsamo, 'with the "First" and the "Ten that are First"? We begin, then, not with words but with numbers! Does this not tell us something of the writer of our cryptic verse? His concern is not with words in themselves but with their reduction to a numerical value. To what end? To the end that the number generated by one word has correspondences with the same number generated by another word, or to a symbolic correspondence between the number contained in the word and some greater mystery. Thus he may take a clear text and produce from it a mystical sense.'

'You are speaking of Gemateria,' said Monsieur Arouet with interest.

'Precisely!' answered Signor Balsamo.

'Gemateria' was a word unfamiliar to me and I was forced to ask its meaning. It was explained to me that Gemateria is a Hebrew science, having as its object the divination of the mystical sense underlying the open text of the Torah. According to this theory, the Word of God has two senses: that which is plain in the literal meaning of the words and that which is hidden within the words. To uncover this hidden meaning, numbers are assigned to each letter in the Hebrew alphabet, and each word within the sacred text may therefore be assigned a number. Where two words have the same number, it may be supposed that there is a connection between the two. Likewise, if the number of a word suggests a correspondence with some other thing – as, for us Christians, three is the number of the Holy Trinity – the word may refer symbolically to that other thing. This was explained to me by Signor Balsamo by way of example. So, according to the thirty-ninth chapter of Exodus, the furnishings of the Ark of the Covenant comprise thirty-two items. These correspond to the thirty-two mystical paths of wisdom set out in the *Sefer Yetzirah*. Moreover, thirty-two is the *gematria* of *lev*, the centre of the body, the temple within each man corresponding to the Temple of the Jews.

As I say, thus it was explained to me and much else completely beyond my understanding. Was it true or false? Who can say?

'Now,' continued Signor Balsamo, 'it is plain, is it not, that the "First" refers to the Lord God, who is above all things first. What then of the "Ten"?'

'What indeed?' asked Monsieur Arouet soberly.

'Ten is the minyan – that is to say, the number of observant Jews who must gather together for prayers. Ten is also the number of the sefirot or mystical attributes of God.'

He presented a sheet of paper upon which he had drawn a schema of the *sefirot*, somewhat in the form of a tree. I still have it.

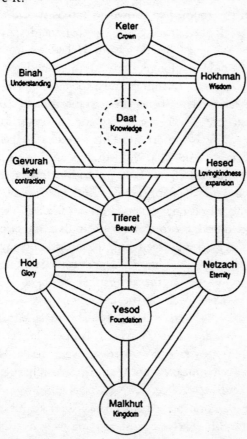

'What am I to make of this?' asked Monsieur Arouet when he had finished his scrutiny of the paper.

Did I discern malice or amusement in the eye of Signor Balsamo? He said, carelessly, 'I have indicated only the major connections between the sefirot. Each sefirah is in some degree connected with the others and, together, they are God. Ahmed!' he called. 'Wine for my guests!'

He reclined on his cushions with a smile that was unfathomable in its guile and innocence. I, too, felt a desire to lie down. The incense, which at first had merely perfumed the room, had grown in intensity and its smoke now lay thick above everything, so that the drapes forming the room and the objects within it had assumed a hazy quality. I could no longer look at them and see them as they were. Instead, strange patterns began to form, whether from the materials or from the juxtaposition of the several objects, so that, as they came to me in succession, I said to myself, 'This is important! This I understand!' But what was important? And what did I understand? Nothing – and yet everything! As Signor Balsamo had intimated, there was beneath the surface of appearance a hidden Essence, ineffable and beyond all rational comprehension. Indeed this Essence fled before all efforts to name or formulate its nature, for it existed not in things seen but in things unseen, and not in thoughts but in silences. Logic could not capture it, because it existed in the interstices of logic. Ambiguity and contradiction were in the nature of its very being.

Ahmed brought the wine. I sipped mine and gagged and felt sick. I glanced at Monsieur Arouet. He was sitting bolt upright, his face drawn to a severe mask. He asked, 'What does this mean, Signore, for the decipherment of our cryptic verse?'

Signor Balsamo passed his empty glass to his slave. He answered indifferently, almost as if we were not there. 'The verse is not in code – not in the sense in which the word is usually understood. It is a prayer, an invocation, a mystical meditation upon the sefirot and who knows what else. It is useless to look for a meaning outside the mind of the Kabbalist who composed the verse.'

'You believe, then, that the writer was a Kabbalist?'

'I am convinced of it.'

'And the mutilations to the body of Signor Molin? Let us not forget them. What say you?'

'They are of a piece with the rest. Each sefirah corresponds to a part of the human body. Therefore the mutilations. The Kabbalist has taken the result of his sefirotic meditations and, as it were, written them upon the corpse.' The young man shuddered. 'It is horrible but it must be so. The very excess of the violence done to Signor Molin betrays its symbolic intent. The problem before us is only to discover which system of symbols underlies the crime. And this question I believe I have answered.'

'Quite so,' said Monsieur Arouet. 'You have gone to the heart of the matter. The murderer has confronted us with a pattern of symbols and it remains for us to understand the scheme from which they are drawn. Kabbalism, you say. Very well, so it may be. So' – he sighed – 'if I understand you aright, the origin of this matter is some conspiracy of the Jews and it is there we must look?'

'Signor Molin was a very religious man, a member of some holy confraternity, I am told. Perhaps he and his brethren have pressed the Hebrews too hard? Perhaps there is money at the root of it? Usury or trade? That would perfectly explain the matter.'

'Yes, yes,' said Monsieur Arouet impatiently. He rose from his cushions. He continued brusquely, 'We must go. Indeed we must. I am infinitely obliged to you for your wisdom. Yes, infinitely.' He glanced at the embers smouldering in the brazier. 'If I were you, I should put that out and air the room,' he said. 'The fumes confuse the brain.'

We emerged on to the Fondamenta degli Ormesini, and the cloying vapours of Signor Balsamo's apartments were replaced by the common stink of the city. My head began to clear. As it did so, there vanished all the confused fancies, the sense I had had for a moment that I had been granted – absurd to say – a glimpse into the mind of God. Until that morning I had not known how intense my longing was for such a moment. Foolish! Foolish! Yet, though its liveliness and intensity had passed, I was left with the recollection. I have it still.

Monsieur Arouet was in an ill temper. 'They play games with us!' he snapped, without saying whether Signor Balsamo or the murderer were meant. 'But I am not a toy! They may lie to me, but even their lies will set me on the road to the truth.'

'You do not accept what Signor Balsamo says?' I asked.

My friend did not reply directly but muttered: '"Unicuique ista pro ingenio finguntur, non ex scientiae vi."'*

He walked a little further, then halted and gripped my upper arms. He said with great fervour – indeed as if pained, 'I do not *know*, Ludovico! That is what plagues me. And Signor Balsamo defies me to contradict him, because he advances a hypothesis that cannot be tested by evidence. At bottom what does he tell us? That the murderer's message is a mystery – as if that were something a reasonable man could not see for himself. No! I cannot accept that! A mystery is not a solution: it is the avoidance of a solution. It makes sense if the numbers are understood in a Jewish fashion, he says. Yes!

* Such theories are fictions, produced not from solid knowledge but from their individual wits – *Seneca*.

And probably the same is true if understood in the fashion of the Persians or the Hindoos. For what are we doing but playing with the symbolism of numbers which may mean all things to all men? "Somnia, magicos, terrores, miracula, sagas, Nocturnos, lemures portentaque Thessala."* No, I tell you, it will not do!'

'Gently, Monsieur,' I urged, freeing his hands from my arms and turning my eyes from his fixed gaze. 'You will do yourself some violence of the spirit if nothing more.' He continued to stare at me with that wildness in his eyes, and my heart went out to him. He was a man ridden by an incubus of intellectual pride: his vanity in his own powers challenged by any contradiction. He was a man esteemed for those powers, a philosopher known as such (though I had not yet discovered why he was so esteemed). Yet he acted as if he were a man despised, uncertain of himself, fearful that he would be exposed and all his mental prowess shown to be pretence. I could not account for this.

My friend grew calm. He patted my shoulder. 'Yes,' he murmured. 'You are right, I take the matter too nearly.' He smiled affectionately – if his smile could ever be so called. 'Now I see why I need you,' he said. 'You are a man of uncommon sense.'

Well, perhaps I am uncommon. But not, I think, in that particular. Still, we were now both at ease and disposed to walk on. However, we had not gone many paces before, from round a corner, came a party of *sbirri* slouching and shuffling behind a tall fellow who bore the clothes and manner of a gentleman. He seemed to know me, though I could not return the compliment. He approached me

* Dreams, magic, terrors, miracles, witches, nocturnal visits from the dead or spells from Thessaly – *Horace.*

and asked directly: 'Are you Signor Ludovico, called il Tedesco?'

I made a bow. 'I have that honour,' I answered.

'Very well,' came the stern response. 'In that case I must inform you that you are under arrest.'

CHAPTER NINETEEN

Signor Ludovico's Narrative

The gentleman who had arrested me was Signor Sregolato, the Messer Grande or chief of the city's police force. Monsieur Arouet endeavoured to protest, but he was ignored and was not allowed to accompany us. I was removed by a gondola, but, instead of being led to one of the prisons, I was first taken to Signor Sregolato's own residence in the Campo San Stefano.

No reason was given for my arrest and I was not minded to ask for one. To do so might be dangerous, and, in any case, pointless since the Council of Ten proceed in secrecy, and, if they had decided that I should be imprisoned during their good pleasure, so it would be. In such cases the prisoner must look to the influence of his friends and patron. I was comforted that someone, at least, knew that I had been taken and could therefore advise Signor Morosini. Whether he would extend a finger to aid someone as insignificant as myself was a questionable point.

There is many a good reason to arrest an actor or foreigner, whether it be an unpaid fishmonger's bill or something more weighty. By definition our lives are indecent and offensive.

However, falling as it did so shortly after my encounter with the brutal guardian of Giacomo's sad lady, I supposed that my arrest was the result of his denunciation. It is a feature of Venice that the State encourages such acts. There are about the city boxes, the *bocce di leoni*, in which accusations can be deposited. It seemed I was the victim of such a one.

I maintained an outward calm. Inwardly I was trembling. My accuser was a patrician and I a nobody despised by all respectable people. I might be tortured and garrotted and my body flung into a canal and no-one would know or care about my fate. I therefore made the cowardly and reasonable resolution that, on being shown the instruments of torment, I would promptly betray both Giacomo and Tosello. They were lively enough to take care of themselves. In this frame of mind I arrived at Signor Sregolato's house.

On entering I had a sense of familiarity, though I had certainly never been there before. Then I recognised the source. The house had the same oppressive air of gloom and religion that had hung over the Palazzo Molin. The furniture was ancient and decrepit. The walls were plain and lime-washed. For decoration there were crucifixes and some pious paintings. The smell of dampness and decay pervaded all.

'There is someone who wishes to speak with you,' said Signor Sregolato. He was a serious gentleman, somewhat damp and musty like his house. Within the restraint of his good breeding, he bore himself as if I were a rank stink under his nose. Lord knows we were different enough: he in his suit of drab wool and I in my blue velvet and braid. My voice is naturally high and, let it be said, my pronunciation affected. Now, all I could do was ask, 'Am I to be interrogated?'

'You would be advised to answer honestly any questions that are put to you.'

'Most certainly, Lustrissimo,' I babbled, thinking to fawn

my way into his favour. 'I am at your service. Command me. Anything!'

He responded by opening a door and pushing me into a dimly lit chamber. The door was barred behind me.

'Damnation!' I piped, believing the room to be empty. 'May your wife be a whore and all your children sodomites!' I took a few paces up and down behind the door, as if it would miraculously open. I uncorked a small flask of cologne which I carry about me and dabbed my wrists and neck, muttering to myself like a child afraid of the dark, 'There, Ludovico, now we feel ready to face the world. Bear up like a good fellow and we may get out of this alive.' Meantime I scanned the room briefly and saw nothing to raise my spirits: a chest, a table and some chairs in a heavy Spanish style, the rags of an old tapestry depicting a classical scene, a shuttered window admitting only a little daylight, a tallow candle smoking on the table. I sobbed, 'Lord save me!'

'Perhaps He will,' said a voice.

I gave a start. A slight figure, black as the Devil, rose from the obscurity of a high-backed chair and casually lifted the candle from its place. I saw a face only partly lit. A hand beckoned and the same soft voice invited me, 'Come, Signor Ludovico, take a seat beside me and let us talk.' Hesitantly I crossed the room to where a stool was indicated. Only then did the face resolve itself from the haze of light and shadow and did I identify the speaker. It was the Jesuit, Fra Angelo.

I was not comforted. As I have said, he was a young man of considerable beauty and suave address. But so, we are told, was Lucifer. In my state of terror I found his sinister physical perfections horrible, his calmness to be evidence of an absence of feeling, his carefully modulated voice soulless. In shock, however, I fell to my knees, seized the proffered hand and kissed it, crying, 'Father, help me!' He had fine, pale fingers.

The hand was withdrawn. Was I mistaken that it had lingered a while in mine? He resumed his seat and I withdrew to mine, where I sat like a penitent in front of a confessor. He eyed me studiously. I could determine neither liking nor revulsion in his manner, but to call him indifferent would be an error. Rather, he examined me without malice but with the purest calculation.

'Well,' he said, pleasantly, 'why do you think you are here?'

I bore in mind what Signor Sregolato had said and answered as frankly and humbly as I could. 'I do not know why we are having this interview, Father.'

'You misunderstand me. I mean: why do you think you have been arrested?'

That was more comprehensible.

'I fear that a gentleman believes I have offended him by making impertinent advances towards a lady who is in some manner under his care and protection.'

'Do you know the accuser's name?'

'Truly I do not – nor that of the lady, whom I have never met. I should recognise neither if they were to walk into this room, since I have seen them only when masked.'

'Are you lying to me?'

'On my soul, Father, I am not lying,' I protested. 'I make no claim to be believed upon my honour, since I have none in the World's eyes. But consider my condition and the evidence of your own senses. I am a comedian and singer by trade, and a poor effeminate pederast in appearance. Is it for a second conceivable that I should direct my advances at a respectable lady or that she would receive them? It is a thing so against nature and experience that surely no-one can credit it. There is some confusion of identity behind the affair.'

Fra Angelo nodded, though I could attribute no meaning

to the gesture: whether it denoted understanding, agreement or sympathy. He asked, 'Do you love God?'

I was surprised at the question or would not have replied so boldly. 'Ask rather whether God loves me. Am I not excommunicate?'

'Answer me plainly. Are you a good Catholic?'

'I acknowledge no other faith, Father. I do not know how else I may answer you.'

He stood up and extended his hand again. I grasped it and we shook hands firmly, while his eyes remained fixed on mine. It was not friendship that made him do this. Rather, he seemed in some manner to be testing my grip. I did not undertand. He indicated that we should resume our seats.

'You are acquainted with Monsieur Arouet, the Frenchman – you will recall that I have seen you in his company. Is he your friend?'

'I trust you mean that in no special sense? Yes, I do regard him as a friend and hope that he so looks upon me.'

'Do you know that he is an atheist?'

I answered cautiously, 'I cannot judge of another's beliefs. I admit he has an enquiring mind and a free tongue, but when he speaks of the Almighty it is with reverence.'

'He is an atheist,' repeated the Jesuit. 'I put that to you not as a question but as a statement of the opinion of the Holy Church. Tell me, how stand you with your patron, Signor Morosini?'

Perplexed at this change of subject, I said, 'He does not speak his mind to me about many matters. Since he continues to employ me, I must suppose that I am in his favour.' Perhaps, I thought, he was considering whether Signor Morosini would take steps to intercede for me.

'What are your sentiments towards your patron? Are they warm? Affectionate? Grateful? Would you die for him?'

I laughed – I fancy because terror had made me a little

mad, unless we are to think I had become courageous. That was a sufficient answer for the Jesuit.

I am a glib, prattling fellow. I enjoy gossip and hate silences, especially the deep sort that are pregnant with significance. When Fra Angelo fell silent, my bowels churned.

At last, he said, 'There are within this World and within this State a party for good and a party for evil. They struggle for the control of affairs and the soul of Man, and their struggle is often unwitnessed, since it is conducted away from the eyes of the vulgar multitude in high counsels and dark conspiracies. Such a struggle is presently under way in this city of Venice. On the one side are ranged the forces of Truth, the Church and Religion; on the other, the forces of Reason, Pride and devilish speculation into ancient mysteries and idolatrous practices best forgotten. Which side are you on?'

Hearing the two cases so unequally put, I voted for Truth, the Church and Religion. 'But,' I added, 'how does this concern me? I am by my own confession a foolish fellow and part of the vulgar herd. No-one takes me into his counsel.'

'The stone which the builder rejected can be the headstone of the corner. It is not your affair to understand your part but merely to play it. You are moving in the circles of the Ungodly, Ludovico, even if you do not know it. Arouet, Balsamo and Morosini – yes, even your patron! – are bent on courses which will let in the reign of Satan, even though they believe they do no more than pursue enlightened thought and hidden science.'

In a moment of inspiration I exclaimed, 'Signor Molin! Are you saying that they were implicated in his murder?'

'He was a member of a pious confraternity engaged upon our good work. And, as I imagine you have guessed, so is our host, Signor Sregolato. You, too, in your small way may become a part of it. That is my offer to you, Ludovico.' The

Jesuit leaned forward in his chair and, though it was perhaps only an effect of the candle-light, his eyes seemed to glitter with an insane fervour. 'Help us!' he pleaded. 'My Order is pressed on all sides by its enemies. The Crowns of Spain and Portugal are against us, and other Princes will follow. Even the Holy See itself is being suborned by agents bent on our destruction. I hold nothing back from you. Satan is everywhere, and he will capture this State unless the righteous rise to fight him. You *must* help us!'

'But how?'

'You are close to Signor Morosini and the others. You have entry to the Ca' di Spagna. Papers are written, and things are said. You must spy them out for me and report what you learn.'

'How can I?' I answered, and came down to practical matters, since my imprisonment seemed even less attractive if I were to be in the power of this madman. 'I am under arrest.'

The Jesuit sighed and reverted to his tone of sinister pleasantness. 'That matter can be arranged,' he said. 'Your accuser is a good man whose judgment is affected by jealousy. And, as you say, the case is one of mistaken identity. Your stay in prison will be a short one, I assure you. But,' he added in the most friendly manner, 'your fate will be a hard one if you betray us.'

Thus we concluded our interview. And, as a coda, fell to our knees and offered prayers to the Saviour and His Mother. The Reader may believe that my prayers were as ardent as those of Fra Angelo. I doubt, though, that they were the same.

I was taken by Signor Sregolato to my prison in the Leads, under the roof of the Doge's Palace. It seemed I was to be no common criminal but a prisoner of the State. My mind was in turmoil. The conspiracy described by the Jesuit could not be dismissed as mere priestly fantasy. Had not Monsieur Arouet intimated that the supper-parties given by my patron concealed some other purpose? And was it not above all things clear that the death of Signor Molin was not a simple slaying by a robber, but rather an action arising from some incomprehensible ritual fraught with esoteric symbolism? So much I could accept. But that Monsieur Arouet was himself involved? How could that be? Unless in my simplicity I had misunderstood him, he seemed wholly ignorant of the truth of the matter and bent on discovering it.

'At least,' I consoled myself, 'you are on the side of righteousness. Though who would have thought it?'

From Messer Grande's house, I was brought by gondola and landed at the quay on the Rio delle Prigioni. Escorted by four *sbirri*, I was led up some stairs and across an enclosed bridge and through a number of rooms until at length I found myself in a large chamber where, I was to understand, the State Inquisitors held their meetings. Those gentlemen, however, were not present but only their secretary, the Circospetto. He regarded me bleakly before proceeding to interrogate me as to my identity and antecedents. He made no enquiries concerning my crime; indeed, I was not even told what was alleged against me. Satisfied that he had the right man, the Circospetto directed that I be taken away.

I went now up two small flights of stairs and into a gallery which ended in a locked door. We passed through this into a second gallery which led likewise to a locked door. At length, I was shown into an attic immediately below the roof. It was about twelve paces in length and two in breadth, and was dimly lit by a dormer window at one end, set high and inaccessible. The attic was filled with ancient chests and other débris, mostly legal papers, records of trials, long-forgotten documents left to moulder, and what went with them: ink-pots, pens, sand-trays, seals.

The door of my cell, which opened off the attic, was as thick as my hand from finger-tip to wrist, nailed, bolted and provided with a judas-hole. The floor, walls and ceiling were planked. It was not the worst of cells (and I have seen a few) being of a good size and unaffected by the dampness of an underground dungeon; and, unlike the cells on the west side, which were windowless and low-ceilinged, this one had a window, albeit barred. But like all of its kind it was a dreary place. I had the comfort that, with the aid of Signor Morosini or – God forbid – Fra Angelo, the error leading to my arrest would be discovered in a day or two and I should be released.

I was not alone. Another poor wretch was huddled on a cot, sleeping. His back was towards me but I could see that he was a powerfully built fellow, crop-haired and dressed in rags. He was either exhausted or an habitué of prisons, for his slumbers were untroubled despite the cold and his thin clothing. I was not inclined to disturb him. He was a murderer.

My gaoler was the common sort: a venal, sociable drunk-ard, civil enough to a gentleman who might have money. We had chatted amiably as we walked the length of the attic and he informed me about those who shared my accommodation. Mentioning no names (or perhaps I did not hear them, being still in low spirits), he told me that such a one was a forger, another a lecher imprisoned at the request of his family, and a third a father who had killed and eaten his children and was possibly mad. It was this big-bellied, wall-eyed turnkey who cheerfully said that my fellow-prisoner was a murderer, 'but quiet, Signore, very quiet' – this last quality being a recommendation. I gave Signor Biradonna (his name) one of my few copper coins and asked him to deliver news of my whereabouts to Monsieur Arouet, who would reward him. He agreed to this and also obliged me with the tariff for bringing wine and tobacco to me. As to food, 'since I am sure, Lustrissimo, that you won't want the State's grub', he would for a charge obtain whatever I wished from a cook-shop or, with his own fair hand, cook whatever raw comestibles were brought by my friends. If I were troubled with the pox, he would summon my doctor. And upon this friendly understanding he left.

I began an examination of my surroundings, which took but little time. There was a single cot, at present occupied by the murderer (Signor Biradonna was to bring a second cot), a plain deal table, a stool, a crock with a jug, a wooden spoon, and, in one corner, an upholstered chair, rather the worse for wear. I also discovered that, for moral education, the cell was provided with a copy of *The Mystical City of God*, though this had failed in its purpose, since the leaves were still uncut. With that the survey of my empire was complete and I had to consider how to pass my time.

Some five hours later I had browsed *The Mystical City of God* and was heartily praying that Sister Maria of Agreda was roasting in Hell. Allegedly inspired by the Holy Spirit, she had written the biography of the Blessed Virgin. I asked myself: if the spirit of fanaticism was capable of moving a person to produce such a work, what credence could be placed in the Gospels themselves? Who was to say that the Evangelists were not as deluded as the nun? I suppressed this impious thought.

Night had fallen. My gaoler returned with a bottle of wine and a letter from Monsieur Arouet. I took it and read: 'The worthy Cerberus has told me how matters stand with you. I have advised Signor M——and we shall work for your release.'

'Have you read this?' I asked.

'I have,' came the reply, 'but your friend is either deaf or don't know what he's talking about. It wasn't Cerberus as called on him but me personally myself.'

'How did he seem?'

'A queer old cove.'

'He's a philosopher.'

'I spotted he was a foreigner.'

At that Signor Biradonna sat himself upon the stool, leaving the luxury of the chair to me as his host. It was clear that we were to share the bottle, which proved on examination to be arrack. We broached it and were soon on most convivial terms and indeed touched upon the deeper mysteries of life. So I learned that my gaoler was a great believer in the power of education to reform a man's character. He said that he regularly educated his wife by breaking her nose, and his children were properly catechized with a good whipping. And as for criminals – 'saving your honour's presence' – he believed that they should all graduate to a state of innocence with the aid of a rope. Naturally I concurred.

'Now, what about a song?' he suggested, when we had done with moral philosophy. I said I thought that would be a splendid idea. 'Then I'll begin,' he volunteered and launched into a bawdy song. His voice was a lively bass, the kind whose timbre is improved by bad living, a rumbling of gravel and phlegm. 'And now you,' he said.

I stood up, a little unsteady and flushed with drink. I sang 'Vedrò con mio diletto', perhaps, as I thought of my sad condition, with more tears than it merited. My good Biradonna eyed me cautiously and then raised his heavy frame from the stool.

'I'd best be going,' he said, and lurched towards the door. He turned for a last look at me. 'I'd watch those high notes, if I were you.' He added, pointing at his groin, 'you don't want to strain yourself.'

He was gone. And at the brute's departure I was left with the mood of sadness. On reflection, it was not caused by my imprisonment, which promised to be short and jolly. It was, I suppose more that condition of melancholy which can affect the young who expect of life more purpose and achievement than it can give. I shall not bore the Reader with the details of my thoughts, which were trite since I am a trivial person, but I ask you to share briefly in that moment of self-pity and forgive me. I was twenty-one years old, a penniless outcast living by his wits in a world which was confusing him. In addition, I was frightened and wanted to vomit from the arrack I had taken. I should have done so, too, had a voice not come from the bed.

It said, 'Has that drunken swine left?'

I looked at the speaker.

It was Fosca.

He looked even worse than he had only those few nights ago when he had been dragged into the presence of the great and had confessed to the murder of Signor Molin. His wrists were raw from chains, though he wore none now, and his face showed signs of a beating: indeed in the lower part it seemed collapsed and boneless. He was shivering, and looked starved.

'Good God, man!' I exclaimed, startled.

'Hush! We don't want that bastard to come back!'

'Why not? Does it matter? He seems a merry fellow.'

'To you he may be, but not to me. He knows that I'm heading for a good strangling.'

As it happens, Biradonna had shown me the instrument of execution. While we were passing through the attic I had observed a metal half-ring attached to the wall. My gaoler explained (with relish, I thought) that the half-ring was a collar. The condemned man was seated on a stool with his neck held in the collar, and a silken thread was wound about his neck and tightened with a winch. The notion was horrible and I tried to console Fosca.

'Surely not? You've been found innocent of the murder. At worst they'll return you to the galleys.'

'You poor fool,' he sneered. 'No wonder you're in here as well.'

He stood up and went to the window.

'What are you doing?' I asked.

'Trying to judge the time by the moon. Why are you here?'

I told him something of the sad lady and my duel with the monster.

'So it has nothing to do with the murder, eh? Then it may be you will get out of here. I wasn't expecting to share this place.'

'Why not?'

'Because of what I know. But I suppose they think I'm safe with you.'

He finished his study of the moon and left the window so that a faint grey light was admitted and we could see one another. He returned to the bed.

'What do you know?' I asked. 'Surely you did not in fact kill Signor Molin? But, of course, you wouldn't tell me if you had.'

'No? And why not? It makes no odds since me and Satan are going to be shaking hands in a few days, whatever happens. As a matter of fact, I didn't kill him. Like your friend, the clever bugger, said, I was in the galleys and in no position to murder no-one.'

'Then do you know who committed the crime?'

Fosca shrugged. 'Dolfin and Morosini, I suppose – or more likely, someone they paid.'

'No,' I protested, 'not Signor Morosini. He was a friend of Signor Molin.'

'Don't be a simpleton!' Fosca snapped. 'It was the Avogadore who dragged me from my boat and told me I'd better confess if I knew what was good for me. He and Morosini are thick as thieves, and what one knows both know. As for being friends with Molin, who knows if it's true and what does it matter anyway? That kind are always bowing and scraping and smiling at each other. It don't mean nothing. All the time they're after money and places. And even if they was friends, friends fall out with each other and it's them that we knows best as is most likely to kill us.'

'Even so,' I answered, 'you have no certain evidence of their guilt. What, then, is it that you *do* know?'

He looked at me intently. 'I know that Molin was murdered and didn't die in his bed like what they said.'

'Is that all?'

'It's enough.'

'Enough to take a man's life?'

'Yes, when the Great Ones are scared and it's meant to be a secret.'

'It's a very small secret.'

'It is. And mine's a very small life – almost nothing at all. How big a life is yours?'

I did not reply.

Fosca rose from the bed, went to the window and checked again the moon and the course of the stars.

I decided to ask him a question that had been vexing me. 'Why did you say you were a sail-maker rather than a glass-blower? It was that lie which caught you out.'

He chuckled grimly. 'Yes, you have to hand that one to the Frenchie – he is a Frenchie, isn't he? Work it out for yourself.'

'I cannot.'

'It's simple. As a glass-blower I'd have lived in Murano.

I'd have no ordinary reason to be on the Rialto at night. See? I had to give some sort of story. I could have said I was visiting my dying mother, but, instead, I said I was a sail-maker at the Arsenal. It was six of one and half a dozen of the other. Who'd have thought it would make a difference?'

'It did it to Monsieur Arouet.'

'The Frenchie?' Fosca shrugged again. 'He's too clever to live is that one. Can you hear a noise?'

'No.'

'Who is he?'

I told him something of my friend's circumstances, conscious that I knew very little. Because of the drink I was a little warm in my praise of him.

Fosca laughed. 'I know your sort. Always falling in and out of love. There's a lot of it goes on in the galleys – singing, I mean.' I believe he winked, but it was too dark to tell. 'Are you sure you can't hear a noise?' he asked.

'Perhaps something.' Indeed I thought I could hear something, a crepitation like rats scurrying in the roof-space above us.

'The moon's in the third quarter,' said Fosca. It was a remark that sounded oddly mystical, as if from a horoscope. He stared at the ceiling and sang softly the first few lines of a barcarole.

'I know that one,' I said.

'Shut up!'

He repeated the lines of his song, and said again that the moon was in the third quarter. He seemed more vastly agitated with every second. He paced the room several times and then went to the upholstered chair, where he ferreted in the horse-hair. Fine particles of lime-wash began to fall from the ceiling like snow.

Then, suddenly, Fosca was on me. He bore a metal spike,

sharpened to a point. He grabbed me before I could resist and held the point to my throat. He hissed, 'One whisper from you – a whisper, a peep, a chirrup – just one, and I'll kill you!'

CHAPTER TWENTY

Signor Ludovico's Narrative

As I shivered in terror at the spike pressed against my throat, and in danger of being pinioned to the wall, I realised that Fosca had a plan of escape. How, in the few days of his imprisonment, he had contrived this I could not imagine. But there he was, quaking with bitterness and anger while wood-shavings and powdery lime-wash fell from the ceiling to dust his hair and shoulders until he looked like a spectre in the moonlight. As abjectly as I could – which was, in truth, abject enough – I promised, 'As God is my witness, I won't betray you!'

Fosca snarled, 'God and I have nothing to do with each other. There's no need to piss yourself as long as you behave, my little sweetheart. But as to trusting you, you must think I'm as big an idiot as you are.'

'Then what do you mean to do?'

'You're coming with us.'

'But I don't want to escape!' I cried. 'I've been promised my release.'

'It's your choice,' said Fosca icily. 'You can escape with us or die on the spot now. Which is it to be?'

Suddenly I was in favour of escaping.

Fosca relaxed his hold. I believe he realised that I was not about to cry for help. Also he was in a high state of excitement and anxiety. He stood on the stool and began to chip at the ceiling with his metal bar to assist his confederate above. However, despite his powerful physique, he was weakened by hunger and beatings and soon gave up. He became subdued and, instead, sat on the stool, and was disposed to talk. There was time, since the work of enlarging the hole went forward slowly. This was his story of the escape so far.

As I suspected, it was not Fosca who had initiated the attempt. That had begun with his neighbour, a coiner named Count Ducato who was even now above us in the roof-space. This Ducato was also a glass-blower by trade, and he and Fosca had known each other for many years before Fosca was condemned to the galleys as a robber and Ducato sent to the Leads for assaulting an official of the Mint.

The tools for the escape had been obtained by Ducato from the rubbish that littered that area of the attic where the prisoners took their exercise. He obtained a metal bar similar to Fosca's and his first plan was to make a hole downwards into what he believed to be the Inquisitors' chamber immediately below us. He had worked on this for a considerable time, chipping away at the wood and using vinegar to soften the marble *terrazzo* he encountered. To avoid being discovered, he had to prevent his cell from being cleaned, and so he feigned a sickness of the lungs which he said would be made worse if the dust were disturbed. This first venture was aborted by several circumstances. Firstly, he encountered a large wooden beam that resisted his efforts and he was forced to deviate round it. Then he became concerned that, once he reached the plaster ceiling of the Inquisitors' chamber, if he failed to breach it in a single attempt, he would be discovered by reason of the débris fallen on to the floor. Finally, he was entirely thwarted when he was moved to another cell – an event not without its risks since he was obliged to smuggle out his metal spike under cover of a dish of gnocchi.

Installed in his new lodgings, Ducato revised his plan. He would not go downwards into the Inquisitors' chamber where the disturbance to the plaster might be discovered by the cleaning-women. He would break out on to the roof and make his way from there. He was engaged on this, hiding his work with a piece of canvas, when Fosca arrived.

Fosca was held in stricter confinement than the Count. He exercised alone and was not allowed to speak to the other prisoners. However, the garrulous Biradonna had revealed the identity of his neighbour and they had commenced communication by tapping on the dividing wall. Ducato was more than willing to have an associate in the escape, since he feared venturing on to the roof alone in darkness. It was this last point which explained Fosca's preoccupation with the phases of the moon. He was torn between a desire for its beneficial light, so that he would not slip and break his neck, and fear that the light would lead to their being seen by the Arsenalotti who patrolled the courtyard.

Thus Fosca's story. And by the time it was finished, Count Ducato had enlarged the hole in the ceiling so that it was big enough to admit the body of a man. He pushed his face through; it was chubby and rascally and scarred from his trade as a glass-blower. He scowled at me.

'Who's he?' he demanded.

'Nobody,' said Fosca. 'Just a harmless queer.'

The Count ran his finger across his throat.

'There's no need for that,' Fosca responded. 'Him and one of his friends did me a good turn when the bastards were trying to stick a murder on me. It wouldn't be gentlemanly to pack him off to Jesus.'

'Suit yourself,' said the Count. He extended down from the ceiling a hand, which Fosca clasped warmly. 'It's good to see you, mate. I won't hide it from you. I didn't fancy tackling that roof on my own. Here now – look sharp – the rope.' Hand and face withdrew, and a length of rope snaked down from the opening in the ceiling.

Fosca turned to me. 'You first.'

'I'm not good at climbing.'

'You are now. Don't mess with me, Fragoletta, or you'll regret it. Come on with you.'

I swallowed my objections. It was clear that I was living on sufferance. I seized the rope, and Fosca cupped his hands and made of them a step so that I could climb more easily. Ducato grapsed my wrist and by one means and another I scrambled through the hole into the roof-space. Fosca followed.

'Right, what now?'

'The roof is covered with lead sheeting,' said the Count. 'We should be able to knock a hole through at the joints.'

'But what then?' I asked. 'We must be a hundred feet in the air!'

'We have the rope – not a hundred feet, I admit, but enough to get us to one of the lower floors.'

'It's a long way to fall.'

'I know some shorter falls with a rope that are every bit as fatal. Come on, now, we can't wait here: the night is wearing on and we've only the one candle.' He was referring to a mere stub, which flickered uncertainly.

The roof-space was indescribably dark and littered with nests, dead birds and builders' debris. There was no purpose in moving far from our position, and we each of us began to grope for the edge of one of the lead roofing-sheets, after first breaking through some rotten timbers that clad the interior.

It was Fosca who found it, and he and the Count proceeded to attack it with their metal spikes. I feared that the noise would betray us, but the thick layers of dust exercised a deadening effect. The work took only a few minutes and then these two strong working-men were able to roll the sheet back as if it were thick paper. After our time in darkness the moonlight seemed as bright as day.

We clambered on to the roof. I tried to take my bearings and saw that on one side we overlooked the Piazza San Marco, but saw also, to my horror, my own shadow seeming to stalk across the square. I tapped Fosca on the shoulder and pointed this out to him. 'Back!' he whispered urgently. 'Back!' He grabbed Ducato by the collar and the three of us scuttled like crabs back into the roof-space.

'Damnation!' said Fosca. 'It's as I thought. We must wait until the moon sets.'

'We can't wait!' protested Ducato. 'If Biradonna or one of his pals looks into the cells, he'll see we're missing.'

'Then we must go back to our cells,' answered Fosca. He shook his friend gently. 'Don't worry. By my calculation, the moon will set in three hours at most, and then it will be at least six hours until sunrise. We have time.' His reasoning seemed irresistible and we returned to our prison.

Our wait proved to be two hours, and they were among the longest, dreariest and most fearful I have spent. I was still drunk and weary. Fosca, on the other hand, was feverish. Each of us was suppressing his terrors. Fosca would be strangled if our escape failed; and I expected to be murdered by him if I did anything to lose his faint confidence. Yet, in his brutish way, he was not a bad fellow. Unable to rest, he told me his life's story. To my shame I cannot remember all of it, but it was a tale of hardship such as would drive any man to crime or despair. He had a wife, he said, and two children of the seven born to her. Sickness – some failing of the lungs I believe – and injury had cost him his employment and he had turned to robbery; but he was inept and had been caught and condemned to the galleys. In turn, I told him something of my own life: how I had been taken as a boy and neutered in order to preserve my voice.

'You poor bugger,' he said, and tousled my hair.

At the end of our waiting, Count Ducato's grinning face appeared once more above us.

'I've cocked an eye outside,' he said. 'The moon has set and there's a fog got up. Come on, lads, it's time to be going.'

We clambered up on to the roof once more. The Count was right. We found ourselves in darkness with fog billowing around us.

'Wait here,' said Fosca.

'What are you going to do?'

'We haven't got enough rope to reach the ground. I'll look around and see if there's a lower point we can reach. Then we can descend in stages.'

Fosca slipped away, using his spike to drive hand-holds into the lead sheets, and I was left shivering in the company of Count Ducato.

'Well, dearie,' said he with horrible cheerfulness. 'This is a pretty pickle, isn't it?'

'As long as the night lasts, we can hope,' I answered.

'Me and Fosca can hope,' said Ducato. 'You don't have to, do you, dearie? Your posh friends are going to spring you. In fact, it would suit you fine to be back in your nice warm cell.'

'Hush, we may be heard.' This was not fanciful: the thud of Fosca's spike driving into the roof was still reaching my ears.

Ducato ignored me. 'Speak up! Speak up! Don't you want your friends to hear?'

'Why do you say that? Am I not here with you?'

'Only because Fosca threatened to slit your gizzard.'

'Let that be as it may. I have done nothing to betray you.'

'Only because you haven't had your chance.'

'Stop acting like a fool!' I snapped – which, on reflection was as foolish a remark as I have ever made.

'Three of us is one too many for this business,' said Ducato and he lashed at me with his spike. I raised a hand to defend myself and so lost my grip on the ridge of the roof. I went sliding down the leads.

'Where are you, damn you?' came Ducato's voice from above me. I had been brought to a halt by a parapet. I looked up, but in the dark and fog I could not see my enemy. I could hear him, though, moving about furtively, using his spike as Fosca had done. He cooed softly, 'Sweetheart, where are you? Fragoletta, my darling, come to me.' I stayed mute and terrified, clutching the parapet for comfort but with no other idea of where I might be. At that moment a thunderous clamour broke the silence.

I was stunned. Then I recognised the chimes of San Marco striking the hour. It was a familiar sound, but here on the heights of the palace roof with my nerves drawn to a pitch of acuity, the noise was ear-shattering and full of every portent of doom. This, I suppose, was also Ducato's reaction. He, too, had been caught unawares, but, unlike me who was clinging to the security of the parapet, he was endeavouring to move freely about the roof. As I say, this is what I suppose. The only certainty is that there was a cry, which I knew to be his, and, a moment later, a splash as a large object fell into the canal. And then silence.

I released my grip on the parapet and, gaining such purchase as I could by spreading my body flat, climbed back to the ridge of the roof. There I was joined by Fosca.

'You!' he said with as much surprise as he could afford

under the circumstances. I had straddled the ridge and made ready with my fists to defend my life as best I could. He stared at me and his face broke into a grimace. 'Ah, well,' he continued, 'so be it. I heard the racket Ducato made. He was an idiot and has come to an idiot's end.' With that the subject was ended. Fosca was concerned only with his own life. 'I've had no luck,' he said. 'The only chance for us is to break through a window into one of the rooms below.'

'And then?'

'As God wills, my friend. I've found a barrel of mortar and a ladder left by the builders. They should be of use.'

'Have you chosen a window?'

'Over the Rio di Palazzo. If we secure the ladder with the rope, it should extend far enough.' He moved to set about this work, but I reached a hand to stay him.

'Listen!'

There was a noise below us: voices coming from the canal into which Ducato had fallen. I crawled to the edge and looked down. I could not see the gondola, but the lantern was clear enough and the voices suggested two men searching for whatever or whoever had fallen. I informed Fosca.

'Enough,' he said. 'We must wait.'

So wait we did, for an hour, while below us the two busybodies plied a gaff and chatted and laughed. But they did not find Ducato and at the end of that time grew bad-tempered and left. By then Fosca, poor soul, who had been sick to start with and was dressed only in rags, was drenched in fog and frozen to the marrow. His feverish energy had gone and he was sunk into a kind of torpor, unable to move except to shiver.

'I'm all done in,' he said. 'You'd better find your way back to the cell. You can call Biradonna and tell him that I've just now escaped. He won't know any different.'

'And leave you?' I answered.

'If that's how it must be.'

I fell silent. Of course what he said made sense. I had no reason to be hazarding my neck on this roof. If I had not been a sentimental person, I believe that I should have abandoned him there and then: but, at bottom, I am just such a sentimental fellow and I was moved by Fosca's sufferings and the fate that awaited him if he should not escape.

'Come now, take courage,' I said. 'We have a plan and we should at least try it. If you are too tired to go on, leave the affair with me and I shall try my best.'

Fosca was too exhausted for gratitude; and, to be frank, I do not think that gratitude was in his nature, any more than regret at Ducato's death. His life had spared him little in the way of feeling. However, I had no time to meditate on this.

The barrel of mortar and the ladder, as reported by Fosca, were on a flat section of the roof like a terrace, by a cupola. I tied our rope to the barrel and, with considerable difficulty, manoeuvred it so that it would fall on the other side of the ridge from our descent and so act as counterweight. The other end of the rope I tied round a rung of the ladder, and I then dragged the ladder and placed it so that we could gain access to the window. The window was barred.

I tackled the bars with the spike borrowed from Fosca. It cost me considerable effort, but, since they were not mortared into stonework, they eventually came loose. My problem then was to enter the room.

The matter was not a simple one. The window was let into the roof itself and it followed that there was an unknown drop to the floor. I had already used up the rope. Having no other resource, I had to retrace my steps, retrieve the barrel of mortar, untie the rope and hope that the ladder would not slide down the damp slope of the roof. It did not. I tied the rope to a rung of the ladder and let it fall into the room. Whether it reached the floor I could not tell. I went to get Fosca. He was where I had left him.

'How are you, my dear?' I asked. He smiled faintly and shrugged. 'Well, we must make an effort,' I said, and at this he stirred. I offered him my support but this was a mistake since neither could be nimble when encumbered with the other, yet nimbleness was needed on the glassy surface of the leads. We straightway lost our footing and went skating downwards into the blackness.

I was brought up suddenly and painfully by the parapet and went pitching over it. I scrabbled with my hands to grab anything within reach, grasped something (I know not exactly what) and found myself in the pretty situation of dangling over the edge of the roof with my legs waving in the air.

'Here! Hold on to me!'

I felt rather than saw Fosca's hand. He held mine and dragged me back; and for five minutes or more we sat sobbing: I in thankfulness at being rescued and he from whatever moved his spirit. At length, I said, 'The window,' and we made our way there.

Here we had a little good fortune. I descended the rope first and found (which I had not known) that it reached nearly enough to the floor. I called to Fosca and he made the same descent. The room in which we found ourselves was about ten by thirty paces and in darkness except for a little starlight through the windows, which served to give us our bearings. It was, at all events, unfrequented at this hour and when Fosca insisted that he must sleep a while, I consented. And that is what we did, the pair of us cuddled together like orphan boys.

I doubt we slept above an hour, but it was enough to restore Fosca's strength and will to go on. We made our way to the door, which proved to have only a flimsy lock;

I broke it with my spike. In a second room I found the
door-key on a table. From there it is difficult to be exact
about our course, since it was night and we were in an
unfamiliar building and at times retraced our steps. I recall
a succession of deserted halls which I must imagine decorated
with hangings and paintings of the greatest splendour; but I
saw none of them. We passed through these rooms and along
galleries and through various chambers which I believe were
part of the ducal Chancellery, since some were lined with
archives of papers. Always our steps were directed downward.
In daytime this would have been the work of minutes, but we
were moving in virtual blackness, easily disorientated, and
having to test each wall of every room to determine where
lay the doors. Some were barred and had to be forced with
the spike. One could not be forced in this easy fashion and
we had to make a hole through it, a noisy business which
I feared might lead to our discovery. At last, we reached a
passage on the courtyard side of the palace, near the Giant's
Staircase by the office of the Savi della Scrittura. Here we
were halted by a door of such strength that it could not be
broken or forced by any means at our disposal. We collapsed
behind it in despair. Outside the sky was glimmering with
the false dawn.

'Well, my friend,' said Fosca with a broken-toothed smile,
'it seems we have reached the end of our attempt. I'd advise
you to go back to the cell, but I fancy that choice is no longer
open to you.'

'At least we shall be garrotted with a good conscience:
that we did not die for want of striving to avoid the event,'
I answered. I got to my feet, intending to take stock of our
situation in case any further avenue of escape were open to
us. I examined my clothes. I was still wearing the handsome
suit Giacomo had given me, but it was in a sorry state, torn
and besmirched. I had also, by some miracle, retained my

hat, though its white feathers were bedraggled. As for Fosca, he was in his ragged slops and these were scarcely fit to avoid indecency. He was moreover covered in filth and smeared in blood from many cuts; and I could only imagine that I was the same. Wanting some air, I opened a window. A man was passing through the courtyard. Ruefully I gave him a wave of my hat and he halted, astonished, and then walked on.

So we waited. However, not many minutes passed before I heard a clank of keys on the other side of the door and a voice spoke. 'Excuse me, Lustrissimo. I swear by Our Lady that I had no notion you were locked in here last night. Why didn't you call out? I've been doing my rounds and I would have heard you.'

I stared at Fosca and then I realized. The passer-by whom I had seen through the window must have supposed that I had been inadvertently locked in the Palace overnight and so have alerted the door-keeper. The latter was turning the key in the lock. Surely he was not going to free us? It was enough to make one believe in the grace of God!

The door opened and a small, wheezing fellow stood before us. In the exchange of astonishment it would be difficult to say who won. But there is no doubt as to who was the quicker. Grabbing Fosca by the hand, I brushed the door-keeper aside and rushed down the Giant's Staircase and into freedom. To make doubly sure, I ran to the gondola jetty, leaped with Fosca into the first boat, and yelled so that all the world might hear, 'Take me straightway to Fusina!'

CHAPTER TWENTY-ONE

Signor Ludovico's Narrative

I had no intention of going to Fusina, which was miles away at the mouth of the Brenta canal. It was merely a ruse to fool anyone who might overhear me. We had no sooner rounded the Customs House point than I directed the gondolier to take me to a place hard by the Ca' di Spagna. I had, of course, the problem of Fosca to deal with, who was still with me, shivering in his rags. However, he proved surprisingly amenable and I was able to drop him by Santa Maria della Salute. He had, he said, colleagues in the underworld who would hide him and set him on his feet again in the robbery trade. So we parted in a friendly fashion and he went off to cut throats and get himself hanged as a respectable thief, free of the Byzantine mysteries of the present affair. I felt, to my own astonishment, a flush of tenderness towards him. Not that we were in any sense friends since he had threatened to kill me and had dragged me even deeper into the mire of misfortune because of our escape. But he was at bottom a pitiful wretch and perhaps my tendency to pity my own situation inclines me to pity others. At all events, I never saw him again.

My own position was more difficult. Unless I intended to take to my heels, I required shelter and assistance. Leaving the city was scarcely a choice open to me. I had neither money nor patrons outside Venice; and my trade (or, at least, my primary trade) could not be plied on street-corners. Also, I should have to abandon Tosello, who was a dear fellow of whom I was genuinely fond. There were therefore three possibilities: to return to my lodgings; to seek out Monsieur Arouet; or to beg the help of Signor Morosini. Neither Tosello nor Monsieur Arouet could protect me from the agents of the Council of Ten, who must know of both. That left Signor Morosini, who had the means either to hide me or to procure my lawful freedom. Whether he would do so had become questionable. I remembered Fra Angelo's suggestion that my patron and his circle were deeply implicated in the murder of Signor Molin. Yet what could I do?

The Ca' di Spagna was in a bustle. A *burchiello* was moored in the canal and there was a great to-ing and fro-ing of servants under the direction of Signor Feltrinelli. I saw trunks, bales, boxes, parcels of all descriptions; dogs, parrots and pet monkeys; wine, hams, cheeses and other requisites for a journey; fans and folding chairs, smelling-salts and pots of unguents; a travelling-desk, a lute, a harpsichord; and, as if they too were furniture, a hairdresser and other lackeys of the useless sort, all being loaded into the vessel. Only the factor was calm amid the chaos.

He saw me and observed, 'Signor Ludovico? Indeed it is you, though I barely recognise you. Your clothes and linen are soiled.'

'What is happening?' I asked.

'Signorina Angelica and the Contessa are moving to the house at San Cipriano. And you?'

'I do not know where to begin. You have heard of my misfortune?'

The factor nodded.

'Then you are looking at one whose misfortunes have been doubled. Against my will I was forced last night to make my escape from the Leads, and you see before you a fugitive.'

'Come,' said Signor Feltrinelli without more ado, 'let us get you out of the public gaze.' He took my arm and, forcing his way through the army of fools, led me into the house. 'Your arrival catches me at a busy moment, but you may rest for a while in my chamber while we consider what to do.'

He led me to a small room near the kitchen and the servants' quarters. I had not visited it before. It was a place which served at the same time for the factor's office and as his private apartment, so that, in addition to a desk with the usual accoutrements and shelves holding books of accounts and other papers, there were a trunk for Signor Feltrinelli's private effects, a truckle-bed, and some modest touches of ornament. Everything was in great order and neatness and the room smelled of beeswax.

'Rest yourself,' said the factor. 'I shall inform Signor Morosini that you are here and return as soon as I have finished the present business.'

I was left alone. As I contemplated the last few days, and in particular my encounter with the guardian of the sad lady and my escape, both of which had destroyed my sleep, a wave of tiredness came over me. I was not so ungracious as to use my host's bed but curled up on the floor and, feeling sorry for myself, I dozed for an hour. At the end of this period I woke.

Signor Feltrinelli had not returned and I was still alone in possession of his room. That being so, I could not resist prying into corners to see what I could learn of his character. As I have already indicated, our relations were distant but correct. I believed he held me in contempt, but so does the World and I did not resent it: he had, at least, the decency to be polite. For the rest I knew almost nothing.

My eye fell first upon a framed silhouette. It was of a young woman and the head was prettily surrounded with a garland of hair. Who was she? A mistress or a sister? I decided upon a sister, since the picture was on open view and altogether respectable. I imagined a girl living somewhere in the countryside: fresh-faced until the day she caught smallpox, and speaking atrocious Italian. What else? Some books among the ledgers. A collection of homilies and sermons, carefully read and noted in the factor's hand. A book on mathematics by Gassendi. A little something by Algarotti. My man, it seemed, had some claims to education and culture.

I turned to his desk, but here had no luck, it being locked. His wardrobe? Alas, dull. A spare suit of black and another in bottle-green; waistcoats in black or snuff-colour; linen shirts with plain clean bands and neck-cloths of bleached cotton.

In sum, I had looked for Signor Feltrinelli and found no-one there. I confess I was sad. I am by nature a friendly fellow and was open to friendship with the factor.

Signor Feltrinelli returned. As much from habit, I fancy, as suspicion, he cast a scrutinising eye around his chamber and then became at ease.

I asked, 'You are finished with your work? Signorina Angelica and the Contessa are gone?'

'The luggage is loaded; I can say no more. Our young mistress is pleading with her father that she should not have to leave Venice. He, of course, will listen to her with every sign of indulgence but in the end he will insist.'

'Why?'

'Who can say? Signor Morosini is given to disguising his true sentiments behind the urbanity of his manners, but he has been preoccupied with something ever since the murder.'

I was left to pluck significance from this last comment.

'Perhaps he has reason,' continued Signor Feltrinelli. 'Last night the Watch-man disturbed someone trying to break into the house. One assumes it was a thief . . .'

'But?'

'But nothing. Our superiors are engaged in mysteries and we are merely spectators, Signor Ludovico. It was a thief or a rogue enterprising some other villainy. I have no opinion.' He took a seat. 'But enough. You must tell me what has happened to you.'

I was at a loss how to do this, both because of the complexity of the tale and because it contained little to my credit. However, with suitable evasions, I told him of how the guardian of the mysterious sad lady had mistaken me for her lover, how we had duelled, and how he had caused me to be arrested.

'And you truly have no notion of her identity?'

'On my honour, I am innocent in the matter.'

'Go on.'

I omitted my interview with Fra Angelo but gave an account of how I had found Fosca a fellow-prisoner in the Leads, and how he had prevailed on me by force to aid his escape.

'And he is free?'

'He was two hours ago.'

Signor Feltrinelli sighed. 'I am glad. I have not met the fellow except upon the occasion of his interrogation, but it is plain that he is innocent. So he feared that he would be garrotted? He was right to be afraid. Believe me, Ludovico, there is *nothing* that the Great Ones of this World would not stoop to in order to preserve their reputation and privileges. I speak frankly to you.'

Indeed he was speaking with unusual frankness. And his observation, though it might be just, was a strange one for the factor to such a great man as Signor Morosini to make. I used the new freedom in relations between us to tell him so.

He looked at me cautiously, as if troubled by a burden he desired to share, then said earnestly, 'What is your opinion of our situation, Ludovico? Granted that we are creatures of our patron, that he may call upon our loyalty and service – does this mean that we have no souls or passions?'

Somewhat discomfited I answered lightly, 'La! I cannot swear that I have either a soul or passions. The World holds me in such low esteem as a frivolous fellow that I must suppose that it is true.'

'Do not denigrate yourself,' returned Feltrinelli impatiently. 'It is one of the instruments of this power that we hold such a low opinion of ourselves. For all that I am engaged in the position of a menial, and that my manners are unsociable, and my appearance (do not contradict me, for I know it to be so) stiff and unbending, I hold myself to be a proper man with honour, courage, intelligence and feelings equal to any other's.'

'You frighten me.'

'I frighten myself. Always before my eyes is this difference between my outward and inward life: between servitude and freedom. Do you not also feel it? Could you not explode from the conflict between the two?'

'I? . . . Well . . .' I did not know what to reply. I was moved by the sense of oppression under which the factor laboured and, in a way, I supposed that he was right. But did I share his feelings? It was true that I felt a slight prickle under the World's contempt, but at bottom my attitude was 'So much the worse for the World'. It could think what it liked so long as I was permitted to eat, drink, kiss the boys, and play my trivial games. Was life not a joke?

Signor Feltrinelli must have detected my lack of comprehension, for he looked disappointed. He said, 'I have spoken to you in confidence, Ludovico, trusting to your honour.'

'I am very sensible of your friendship,' I answered in what I hoped was a pleasant manner under our new condition of intimacy.

'Friends? Yes, I suppose we may be considered friends,' said the factor, returning to his usual stiffness. 'Now you must forgive me if I leave you. If you are to remain in the house *incognito*, I must put about the story that you have left, and find you some articles of disguise.'

Upon that he stood up sharply and quitted the room, and I was left to ponder the mystery of what had caused this sudden change in his manner towards me.

Signor Feltrinelli returned about half an hour later, bringing a bundle of clothes with him.

'These are women's clothes,' I pointed out.

'They belong to Signorina Angelica's maid. There is a bonnet to cover your hair, though you have the advantage that you wear your own. On another these things might look ridiculous, but in your case you may wear them with perfect safety and they will form the most complete disguise that could be wished.'

I acknowledged that this was true. Thereupon the factor left me to change. I found that he had provided not merely a dress and bonnet but stockings and a shift. The maid being taller than most women and I being of a slight build, everything fitted quite acceptably, even the shoes. I decided upon an entire change, even to the shift, thinking to increase my security. I have played prettier girls upon the stage, but still the effect was quite pleasing: I became a lady's maid, rather more pert and becoming than the original.

As I was examining myself before the mirror, there came

a tap on the door, which opened and a voice said, 'Ah, it's you, Maria. Have you seen Signor Feltrinelli?'

I turned, startled, and whom should I see but my dear Angelica! She was equally startled and peered at me short-sightedly. Then her hand went to her mouth and she exclaimed, 'Why, it's not Maria . . . it's . . . Ludovico!' She gave the most light and delicious of laughs, rushed towards me, spun me round and planted a kiss on my cheek. 'My, my!' she prattled on. 'It's my own sweet Ludovico become a maid – and what a beauty you are. I am positively jealous! You are . . . you are Angelica! Do you remember how you were when I first saw you at the opera? I wanted you then as my own dearest friend, and now I've got you!'

She stepped back and an expression of puzzlement crossed her lovely face. 'But why, Ludovico? Though I infinitely prefer you in your new sex, what has caused this change? Surely you are not coming to San Cipriano with me as my maid? That would be excessively naughty and altogether delightful!'

I was not certain how much I should reveal to her. I answered, 'Please, Signorina Angelica, you must be quiet and discreet and not betray me.'

'Betray you?'

I was at a loss. 'I am in disguise.' I said.

'Disguise?'

'Oh, Lord, what can I say? Signor Feltrinelli knows all, as does your father. I am here with their consent and beyond that I cannot tell you. You must trust me.'

This, as it turned out, was enough to satisfy her curiosity. Her concern was with her own childish pleasures. She said, 'And San Cipriano? Shall you be coming with me there?' She looked at me pleadingly.

'I think not,' I answered.

'I shall ask my father.'

'He will refuse you. It would not be decent.'

'Oh, fie for the proprieties!' Angelica retorted. Then she became glum. She went on, 'Do you know San Cipriano? It is bearable in the summer when I have the society of other girls from the neighbouring estates and their lovers; and there are routs and balls. But in winter! It will be so dull! Only the Contessa and I shall be going, and we shall be alone, in a small apartment within the house, and everywhere else will be under dust-sheets, and it will be cold, and we shall have nothing to do but needlework and write letters. I shall die of ennui!'

'I am sorry,' I said sympathetically. 'But it seems that it is necessary.'

'Fiddlesticks!'

'Your father thinks otherwise. I am told that a robber tried to break into the house last night.'

'Who told you that? Signor Feltrinelli? It's what they all think, but it isn't true.' She stared at me with her disarmingly innocent eyes. 'The explanation is something else.'

I intended to ask her what she meant, but at that moment the door, which had been imperfectly closed, swung open and, in the passage outside, I saw Signor Feltrinelli engaged in earnest conversation with, of all people, Signora Beatrice Molin. Glancing in my direction, the factor closed the door.

'Was that Signora Molin?' I asked Angelica.

'It was,' she answered without interest.

'Do you know her?'

'She is a close friend of the Contessa.'

'I did not know that.'

'You do not know everything, Ludovico,' Angelica said petulantly.

'She seems to have business with Signor Feltrinelli?'

'I do not know, nor do I care. She came to say farewell to

the Contessa before we go into our horrid exile. Perhaps she wishes to satisfy herself that all the arrangements are made for our comfort.'

'Yes,' I said, 'no doubt that is the explanation. Tell me, Angelica, what is she like? I have met her only once, and that briefly. Monsieur Arouet and I paid our respects at the Palazzo Molin. She seemed a sad and lovely lady.'

'She is that and more besides. Unlike you, you unfeeling brute, she is a true woman and was once a girl.' Angelica pushed me away. 'She, at least, understands what I feel and tries to help me. I know what you think. You consider me a creature without sense. But I am not. I am a . . . woman! I have inherited my portion of womanly feelings and she understands this!'

'Angelica?'

'No! Enough! I no longer like you, Ludovico. You are only a pretend-girl. They say you are only a pretend-man, too! A real girl would be a friend to me, and a real man would be my cavalier. You are neither.' With that Angelica withdrew to the door. As a Parthian shot she stuck her tongue out at me and said, 'And, by the by, you look ridiculous in that dress.'

She was gone, leaving me alone. It was, I reflected, a morning when people – first Feltrinelli and now Angelica – revealed that the surface of their behaviour hid obscure passions. Only I was exempt: a shallow fool. On the whole I was content that this was so, and I hummed a merry tune while I considered what these revelations might mean and concluded – nothing.

Signor Feltrinelli returned, looking starched and preoccupied. Noticing my costume, he gave a cold smile and said, 'You make a very passable maid, a true Corallina. Yes, you will do very well. However, one must not take risks and I therefore suggest that you remain here until nightfall when we shall hide you away elsewhere. Signor Morosini has agreed to make representations on your behalf and we have hopes that by tomorrow the matter will be resolved.'

'I am grateful to Signor Morosini.'

The factor looked at me sharply. 'He does it in his own interest. Always bear that in mind.'

I did so and remembered that Fra Angelo had cautioned me that my patron and his supper-guests (who made up the magical number ten) had some part or interest in the murder. Yet, if their involvement had been direct and bloody, Signor Morosini must have been abroad at some time on that fateful night. I was myself a witness to the fact that he had been at the Ca' di Spagna for some hours during the supper-party; but, since the exact time of Signor Molin's death was not known, the possibility existed that he had been murdered *before* my arrival and the commencement of supper. Monsieur Arouet had made no enquiries as to my patron's whereabouts in the earlier part of the evening because there had been no reason to suggest a connection, and even now I doubted that it existed outside the Jesuit's imagination. How to satisfy myself? It was a question I should not have dared raise before this day. But, now that Signor Feltrinelli had disclosed his resentment against that whole class of society to which Signor Morosini belonged, it seemed possible that I could at least hint at my concern.

'Signor Feltrinelli,' I began, 'as you rightly say, our master acts in his own interest where our affairs are concerned. Have you considered whether he has been entirely frank in the matter of Signor Molin's murder?'

The factor paused in the collection of some papers. He shot a glance at me. 'I have not considered the point,' he answered.

I continued, 'I was thinking of that poor devil Fosca. We are both convinced of his innocence and yet the Avogadore made efforts to implicate him in the crime. We have supposed that he did so because of interests of State; but might there not have been another interest?'

'Is this question to some purpose? Signor Morosini and the Avogadore were both at supper on that night. You and I both saw them.'

'But before supper? It had been dark for about two hours when I arrived. I cannot swear to that period.'

'I was in this chamber casting up the estate accounts.'

'And Signor Morosini?'

'I assume he did as he usually does on these occasions.'

'Which is?'

Signor Feltrinelli resumed the sorting of his papers and began to tie a bundle with ribbon. His fingers fumbled over a knot. He stopped and examined me again. He said, 'What can I tell you, Ludovico? I have no more idea than you what Signor Morosini does. On the evenings of the supper-parties he leaves the Ca' di Spagna some two or three hours before supper and goes I know not where.'

I was astonished. 'Do you mean on every such occasion?'

'Without fail. And if for some reason the supper is cancelled or postponed to another day, so also Signor Morosini cancels or postpones his sortie.'

'But you must know where he goes. His lackey will know.'

'I assure you he goes out entirely alone.'

'Does he return alone?'

'No. Normally he is accompanied by one or two of the gentlemen – most often the Avogadore, Signor Dolfin.'

'And on the night of the murder?'

'I cannot say. As I have told you, I was myself occupied and did not see Signor Morosini until the beginning of supper. However, since his practice has been invariable I would assume that Signor Morosini did go out. If the point is important, one could interrogate the servants. His valet, Alfonso, would have dressed his hair and would certainly know if his master were abroad that evening. You look astounded, Ludovico.'

In fact my mouth had turned dry at what I heard. I had posed my question as an idle enquiry, not expecting that it would lead to anything. But now? Was it possible that Fra Angelo was right and that my patron was a member of some evil brotherhood? The supper-parties at which I had so innocently sung now began to take on a wholly different character. It seemed to me that they, too, were in the nature of a code: having one meaning upon the surface and another, more sinister, one beneath.

CHAPTER TWENTY-TWO

An extract from A History of My Life
by Jacques de Seingalt

My sad lady (as I still fondly thought of her, though she had
shown herself to be a harlot and procuress) having directed
my attentions at another – saying that she was conferring
this blessing out of love for me – I had to consider how
I should embark upon this new amorous campaign. It was
not a simple matter. This new charmer was as unknown to
me as my lady had been; she was attended by an older female
relative; and for all I knew she might have a legion of *bravi*
and bully-boys in her train. After my experience of being
shot at by my lady's own protector, I was not disposed to
volunteer for more of the same.

'May I know the name and connections of this young
person – for I assume her to be young?' I asked.

'Nay,' said my lady almost merrily. 'It is part of your
charm that you are a man of honour and discretion. Have
you not allowed me to preserve my own anonymity? I have
told her of this quality in you and it is one which appeals
to her. You must understand that she is a maiden. She
looks for one who has the delicacy to relieve her of that

condition without pain, and the sagacity to preserve her reputation.'

'So you have spoken of me to her?' I said in a tone of offence. 'Discussing my points as if I were a prize bull?'

'Or stallion. Come now, my love, of course I have spoken of you to her. How is a young girl to be prepared for the ways of the world if an older woman will not take her under her wing?'

'You were not so experienced yourself, as I recall – or was I mistaken?' I asked pointedly.

'My upbringing was very sheltered and a cause for regret. My married life was a sham, as you well know from the rosy tokens left upon the sheets at our first essay in love. My happiness was that, at the hands of my teacher' – here she gave me a kiss – 'I was introduced gradually and with delicacy of feeling to the paths of Cupid, so that my ignorance proved a blessing and only heightened my bliss at each step along the way. However,' she added, 'most women must be content with brutes and it is therefore desirable that they should be schooled.'

At this point I should mention to the Reader that I was in due course to learn the true name of the young person in question. However, she is still alive and, as I write, resides in Venice, a matron of advancing years married to a patrician of excellent morals and family. Honour forbids that I call her by any name but that which my lady gave her: Dulcinea.

'I confess,' I said, 'that you are introducing me to new aspects of the society of women. Was she not appalled that you should have a lover?'

'La! Every Venetian woman of rank has her cicisbeo to keep her amused, unless – as has been my unhappy case – she falls under the dominion of a jealous oaf. And whether this confidant is also her lover is a question which no wise husband asks and no prudent wife answers honestly.

In short, my Dulcinea was entranced, not appalled. She trusts me implicitly and therefore is willing to trust you. My dearest, you shall love her as you have loved me, though the experience will be different. My life and character have been melancholy and you came to me like a gaoler releasing a captive from a long imprisonment. She, on the other hand, is gay, her nature soft and joyful. Having received no ill at the hands of men, she burns with desire to know one intimately. Lest you think badly of me, I will tell you that, unless I help her in this matter, I fear she will do something imprudent and cause a scandal. It is only my tender regard for her, my knowledge of your fine nature, and the unhappy condition of my own health, which at present disables me from love, which together make me beg this service of you.'

Now, dear Reader, I set this exchange at length before you so that you may consider my situation, for I would hide nothing. I am not a common despoiler of virgins, and a respectable man may leave his daughter with me as safely as his money in a strong-box. However, every moral principle has its exceptions; or, perhaps, I should more properly say is liable to be modified by a principle of a higher order. So the sanctity of unmarried maidenhood, which I acknowledge along with the Church and Philosophy, may be violated in the interest of a higher good. In particular, if a maiden is bent upon changing her state by one means or another, then a gentleman may, without losing his character, guide her choices in a direction which will enhance her joy in the event and leave her reputation intact. These were the considerations which went through my mind. I will not play the hypocrite and deny that I looked forward to some pleasure from my encounter with Dulcinea; but I aver that such pleasure as I took was subordinated to the demands of Duty.

'Very well,' I told my lady. 'I am persuaded by you and I trust that you will not call me faithless.'

'My dearest, you are in everything faithful to me.'

'Then I must rely upon your aid. For if you will tell me nothing of Dulcinea, I shall not accomplish my task.'

My lady acknowledged that this was just, and promised to arrange everything.

I confess that I had hoped our lovers' tryst would take place in some pleasant bower or private chamber hired for the occasion. I was being unrealistic. Dulcinea was a girl from an ancient and revered family. And, though her father was of enlightened opinions and displayed some liberality of manners with her, he had a keen eye for the limits of propriety and she was kept under the narrow eye of an aunt. This aunt was herself a handsome woman of a lively disposition and an intimate of my own sad lady (indeed, she knew of the connection with myself); but, said my lady, she dared not reveal her plans to her friend. Firstly, the friend might not wish to risk her brother's wrath, which would inevitably follow discovery; and, secondly, having herself an amorous disposition, she might be jealous to find her niece plucking fruit from an orchard of which she considered herself the mistress. These considerations meant that the field of battle would have to be Dulcinea's own bedchamber. Had I the courage for this?

'Surely, my dear one,' I said, 'you above all women know the fixity of my purpose.'

Since my intended *inamorata* was already aware of me and more than willing to co-operate, no purpose would be served by delay, and we resolved to undertake the enterprise forthwith. Dulcinea would retire for the night and unlatch the shutter of her window. The homunculus would be my servant and keep guard.

The night proved to be typical of that gloomy winter:

dark and full of stinking vapours. Our approach was to be from the canal-side and we therefore proceeded by gondola. I, of course, was to be blindfolded in the usual manner.

My sad lady gave me a fond kiss as if I were setting forth to slay a dragon. I promised the faithful performance of my duty and suffered the blindfold to be applied. However, we had not gone very far – only as far was necessary to be out of sight of my mistress – when I removed the blindfold, produced a pistol from under my cloak and, pointing it at the homunculus, informed him that I was tired of mysteries and would blow his brains out if he betrayed me. The dwarf duly promised his discretion, and, satisfied upon that point, I was able to see where we were going.

By twists and turns through bywaters so as to avoid the attention of late revellers (who nevertheless could be heard as an unseen chorus), we arrived in the shadow of a large palazzo, which on this side reared directly out of the water. The lanterns had not been lit, and we had doused our own; the only light available to us was the febrile light of the moon, which scarcely reached down to the canal. It was under these conditions that, rather in the manner of a besieging force, the homunculus and I were to scale the walls of the fortress.

The manipulating of a ladder, in the dark, against a vertical wall, and from the uncertain platform of a rocking gondola, was a skill which I had inadvertently failed to study in sufficient detail. The homunculus was of limited assistance to me, since there was no convenient mooring pole and he was obliged to apply his strength to the oar in order to keep our vessel on station. I cursed him as a misshapen dwarf of as much use as the private member of my friend Signor Ludovico; for his part, the homunculus informed me that I was a pox-ridden popinjay who was not fit to kiss his mistress's arse. In this spirit of co-operation, I laboured to erect the ladder against what I determined to be the window of my *inamorata*. And, after much swearing and many appeals to the Deity, I satisfied myself that I could make my ascent in tolerable safety.

I hide nothing from my readers. I wish to be judged as I am. If, in the impetuosity of youth, I acted the very fool, I own to it. So on this night, fired with an amorous ardour, I was determined not to be thwarted by any difficulties. Figure to yourself, therefore, your author, masked, cloaked and booted, climbing a wall in pitch darkness. It is a miracle that I did not fall at the first step! As it was, my situation became increasingly precarious. With each rung I scaled, the gondola was pushed away from the wall by some principle of leverage, and the homunculus had to redouble his efforts until at last he was splashing like a mill-race. Nevertheless, I reached the level of the window, where I paused for breath.

I am not a professor of Natural Philosophy and therefore cannot explain in the fashion of Newton what exactly happened next. However, in the manner of planetary motions, which go now forwards and now backwards against the background of the firmament, so the gondola moved in one direction, the ladder moved in another, and I moved in a third in accordance with the laws of Nature and with predictable effect. I was pitched into the foul waters of the canal.

Neither the dwarf nor I was silent upon this event. I shouted an appeal (to the Virgin, I believe), and the dwarf cried out to whatever Chthonic spirits he worshipped; and between the pair of us and the falling of the ladder and the splashing of the water, we set up a fine racket that woke the whole house. Shutters were thrown open, urgent cries were issued to bring candles and lanterns, and a general shout of 'Thieves! Robbers!' went up. The homunculus promptly turned tail and rowed himself away as vigorously as he could, leaving me swimming in a black soup of turds, dead fish and vegetable-peelings.

I swam to a quay where I could leave the canal in safety, and, soaked and bedraggled, I returned to my lodging. I was not daunted by the failure of this adventure. Rather, I was even more determined to succeed, and, for the sake of my courage and self-respect, to do so at the earliest opportunity. However, this time I was resolved not to rely upon the homunculus, who had proved himself a coward as well as impugning my reputation. I did not turn to my lady. Instead I recruited a pair of likely villains from the Arsenal and, to overcome the problems of the ladder, provided myself with a grapple and some lengths of rope. So equipped, we set out the next night upon my second attempt.

By the expedient of money and a pistol in his face, I persuaded a ruffian to serve us with his gondola. Our assault party was therefore four in number. The night was as before, black and filled with mists. Having previously discarded my blindfold, I had no difficulty in finding the palazzo without the aid of the dwarf. The fact that I had only succeeded in rousing the house on the last occasion did not trouble me. I calculated that no-one would expect robbers to be so bold as to try the same crime twice. And, if I were disturbed whilst effecting my entry, I had three brutes in the gondola to support my cause. Once I was in the maiden's chamber, I relied upon her discretion to protect me.

Using the additional lengths of rope, we were this time able to secure our craft against two mooring-posts, which gave us greater stability. In any case, this problem was not so acute, since I had abandoned the ladder which had been so great a part of its cause. Not that there were no problems. The swinging of a grapple at the end of a length of rope is not so easy a matter; but, at my third attempt, I was able to lodge it somewhere among the roof-tiles directly above the window. I clambered up.

The shutter was not fastened. However, a gentleman does not burst in upon a lady, even when he is expected – in particular, if she is a maiden who must be tickled out of her modesty like a trout out of a stream. I tapped upon the shutter and waited somewhat uncomfortably suspended on my length of rope until the glimmer of a candle told me I had attracted attention. The shutter opened.

'Signore?' enquired a sweet and nervous voice. A candle was held before a female figure, who peered at me.

'Signorina,' I responded, as gallantly as I could under the strain of hanging on the rope, 'I am the cavalier whom, I trust, you were led to expect.'

'I was not certain you would come,' she answered. 'I left the shutter unfastened more in hope than expectation. After last night, I thought that courage would fail you.'

'Courage never fails me. However, may I beg your indulgence to relieve myself of the discomfort of my present situation by entering your chamber? Then we may talk freely.'

Flustered, the girl answered, 'Forgive me! I am ungracious and inexperienced. Please come in.' She then retired to her bed, where, from modesty, she covered her charms.

The interview that followed was conducted by the light of a single candle, but it was enough for me to form an estimation of my fair companion. She was a maiden of some eighteen years and had that pert beauty that is so lovely in the flower, though often overripe in the fruit. Her hair was dark and of a deep lustre. Her eyes were almond-shaped and bright with mischief. Her lips quivered with a mixture of uncertainty and promise that was touching and inspiring. I have loved women who were more beautiful and experienced, but I have never encountered one who seemed in her inner being to be more created for delight.

However, first she must be won. What? say you. Surely she was already won? There speak brute lust and inexperience. A world of difference exists between the inclination and the deed, and the crop may be trampled in the harvesting. Rather than pouncing upon her like one who already possessed her, I was initially at pains to maintain the distance of a respectful suitor. She took refuge in the presumed fortress of the bedclothes, I took position upon a small stool, and we continued to converse.

'You seem much exercised by your climb,' she said.

'It is not the physical effort but the motions of my heart that disturb me,' I answered. I looked down at the floor and raised my eyes only gradually to her, as if ashamed and penitent. 'Does the ardour of my language frighten you?'

'Certainly it is not language to which I am used. But no, I am not frightened for as long as your boldness of speech is not matched by boldness of behaviour.'

'Alas, I cannot promise that,' I said. 'You may be assured of my gentleness but beyond that I cannot go. Your loveliness – I speak frankly – calls forth the normal manly passions and to deny them is to go against Nature.'

'Truly, then, you do frighten me.'

'I should add that honour and duty stand always above passion. And in this you may trust me: that, though I will make no secret of the longing which even the merest glimpse of your charms inspires in my breast, yet I shall take no action which is against your desires or inconsistent with the conduct of a gentleman.'

To that she made no answer, but I do believe a blush stained her cheeks and travelled her neck and the bosom that was at present hid from me. I settled upon my stool and resolved to be patient. In my experience, curiosity will always overcome modesty, especially when accompanied by desire.

At length my Dulcinea grew bored, and my inaction

convinced her of the purity of my intentions. Her boredom, you understand, was not with me but with her own pose of maidenly prudence. On her exquisite lips I could see the inward struggle. At length, she asked, 'Am I, then, beautiful?'

This is a question which virgins put to themselves; and the more guarded their upbringing, the more urgent and doubtful they are.

I answered, 'I see you poorly in this dim light, but what I have seen leads me to believe you may be so.'

'Only "may be"?' she said, disappointed.

'Fie, Signorina! Am I to lie? I wish to be your true cavalier and play my part with all honesty.'

'But you said I was lovely – I distinctly recall it.'

'And so I believe you to be. However, your question was directed at my knowledge, not at my fancies. Yes, I believe you to be beautiful, but I do not know you to be so. Only you can impart that knowledge. I shall not simply seize it.'

I fell silent again, which disturbed her. She prattled a little about her education, her books, her dolls, her desire to see the world, the restrictions of her life and all the petty stuff I knew so well. And all the while the same question nagged at her: *Am I beautiful?*

I met her little offerings with my own: telling her that I was the unregarded scion of a patrician family forced into the theatre; that I had become an *abate*; had been despatched to Constantinople; and was now a soldier. These were *louche* occupations but they held the hint of dangers which I had made safe by my admirable restraint. My Dulcinea could enjoy the *frisson* of a flirtation with such dangers, protected by the fond belief that she was the mistress of her situation.

As we exhausted these subjects (which – so that you may trust my honour and restraint – I tell you lasted above an hour, during which she had lit a second candle to replace the first) she reached over for the candle and held it to me to examine me more closely. And as she did so, in the most easy of manners (so that I was not to think it was of her volition) she permitted the bedclothes to slip from under her chin and there was afforded me – admittedly still masked by a fine fichu – a glimpse of the most tender and promising breasts I had ever seen.

Affecting only now to notice her disclosure, and doing nothing to replace the bedclothes, she blushed again and asked, 'Well, dear cavalier, what do you think now? Am I beautiful?'

'You astonish me!' I said, sincerely. And I fell upon my knees.

I then proposed a game of cards.

Why cards? you ask. The game I suggested was a childish one which brought to her fond memories and a sense of security, while at the same time provoking laughter. Laughter is the greatest solvent of inhibitions. Moreover, cards cannot be played from a stool placed in darkness across a room. Perforce she must admit me to the circle of candle-light, and I placed my seat alongside the bed and we played upon the counterpane. Childish card-games are vigorous. Who could play them without allowing the bedclothes to fall about her waist?

Only a few minutes of cards and laughter sufficed to make Dulcinea used to my viewing her *en déshabille*. And, such is the nature of these games, her play caused her fingers to graze against mine, and then she tapped my hand and kissed my cheek with all innocent affection, as if I were a playmate of her toddling years. Yes, she knew what she had done; but since I took no advantage of this accidental prize, she bestowed upon my cheek a kiss of greater meaning. Yet I said nothing.

So we ran through the gamut of infant card-play. I even sat patiently while she giggled and instructed me in new games. Her confidence both in her own powers and in me grew boundless. So she suffered her hair to fall from beneath her cap most becomingly and, in the rough and tumble of our play, my forearm brushed her breast and, in a moment of such dizzy excitement that I thought I would either faint or fall upon her in carnal desire, I was given the briefest sight of that most tender object: a nipple so fresh and rosy, so unkissed and unsucked, that I have never seen another like it. And this, I believe, was done in genuine innocence, so trusting was she.

Now she said, 'Dear cavalier, do fetch another candle, for this one fails.'

It was giving off smoke and guttering its last. I saw then the means of bringing to an end the preliminaries and completing the education of my pupil.

'Where are the candles kept, my dear one?' I asked.

'In the chest – yes, there, in the corner.'

I took the stub of the old candle and held it before me to shed light upon my investigation of the chest. What can I say? The candle went out and the room went black.

'What a silly you are!' she said, merrily.

'So I am,' I confessed in the same spirit. 'But now I shall never find the candles.'

'Then I see I shall have to do it myself,' she answered. I heard a creak as she rose from the bed, and a patter of soft feet across the floor. 'Where are you?' she asked. I extended a hand and her own outstretched hand found mine and our fingers touched.

Thus, hand in hand like children, we stumbled towards the chest and, as she opened it and stooped to explore, I supported her with my hands held around her slender waist.

'What are you doing?' she asked with surprise but not alarm.

'Helping you, my dearest. Are you still frightened?'

'Of you? What nonsense you do talk!'

'Then thank your uncle – for such I consider myself to be – with a kiss.'

Her lips pouted and she searched where she thought to find a cheek, though what she found were my own lips. She pressed against them in ignorance, withdrew, and then applied her own again in uncertain excitement.

'You taste of' – I felt a sliver of tongue slide across my mouth – 'salt,' she said. 'Why salt?'

'I do not know.'

She kissed me again, and again in her innocence her tongue explored the full circumference of my lips. 'Yes, salt! How odd!'

'May I taste yours?' I let my tongue engage with hers.

'Good Lord!' she exclaimed, meaning, I think, that this was a plesant novelty of whose meaning she was uncertain.

I allowed this to continue for a little; I increased my advantage only gradually by pressing my body gently closer to hers so that she would slowly sense those interesting particulars in which it differed from her own. Becoming aware of some movement in response, I applied my hands to caress my Dulcinea's lovely form; but even now I kept them outside her undergarments and, at the same time, I made as if I were merely aiding her to find the bed again, bearing the object of our search, namely the candle. And I accompanied my actions with reassuring words about finding the tinder-box so that we might have light again.

'I feel strange,' she said, and halted to turn my face to hers and cover it with kisses.

'This is love,' I said.

'It is? Then how can people bear the exquisite excitement?'

I placed my hand inside her shift and touched a place that conveys the most delicious of sensations.

'It will be still more wonderful,' I told her, 'if you will but let me instruct you.'

'Can I trust you?'

'Tell me to desist. Have I done anything except at your invitation?'

Her reply was a moan which I took to be consent. I decided that further introductions were unnecessary and forthwith took her to the bed. I laid her in a demi-swoon and accomplished the tender victory.

At that moment the door opened.

At this abrupt entry, I tumbled from the bed and scrabbled after the pistol in my coat pocket. However, I then saw by the light of the candle carried by the intruder that I was dealing not with one of the family bully-boys but with a woman. From her carriage and the fine quality of her gown it was evident that she was not a servant, and I could only suppose that this was the aunt mentioned by my sad lady, and whom I had seen only once before, masked and mantled at the Ridotto. As my lady had indicated, the aunt was herself a handsome woman who must at one time have been a considerable beauty. This creature now stared quizzically at me.

My Dulcinea had taken the wisest course. She pretended to be asleep. I, however, had to decide whether I was in my fair one's chamber in the character of lover, ravisher or robber.

'Do you intend to murder me, Signore?' enquired the aunt with utmost coolness. I hastily put my pistol aside, tidied my disordered clothing and gave her as pretty a bow as I could contrive.

'I apologise a thousand times, Signora,' I said, 'but you came upon me unawares.'

'Really? Is it not rather that you have come upon *me* unawares. I, at least, have some title to be here.'

'I must allow the justice of your claim,' said I.

Well, here was a strange situation! I was at a loss for words, while the aunt seemed not in the least discomposed by the appearance of a villain with a pistol in her niece's bedroom. Indeed she continued to regard me wholly without fear but with the same *froideur*.

She came further into the room, closed the door behind her and walked in a circle of inspection around me.

'To be sure, what an elegant animal it is,' she commented.

'I am pleased that my person finds favour with you.'

'Please be silent until invited to speak.'

I bowed.

'So, what are we to make of this? Evidently you are not a common robber; your clothes are not suited to the occupation: indeed, they seem to be of a military cut. Have the Empress's operations against the Prussian King reached Venice? If so, I had not noticed.'

Annoyed at this barbed way of speech, and suspecting that I was not in immediate danger, I said, 'You seem inclined to deal ironically with me.'

'Fie! I may deal with you as I choose. But let us not banter. Are you the valiant fellow spoken of by' (she named my sad lady) 'or some other?'

'I am indeed he.'

'And did she commission you to ravish my niece?'

'Honour forbids that I answer that question.'

'It needs no answer. It seems that my friend has designs upon my niece's education which she has not discussed with me. Well, then, have you completed your task? No, do not answer that. Doubtless the girl is complicit, and perhaps it is no bad thing that she is introduced to the ways of Eros by someone who has the appearance, at least, of a gentleman.'

'Then have I your approval?' I asked hopefully.

'I cannot say that,' she answered. 'I cannot approve a teacher whom I have not myself examined.'

With that, she advanced more closely upon me, still subjecting me to her cool regard; and, with an imperious gesture of the hand, commanded that I sit upon the bed. She sat next to me.

Her first reaction was to restore my dress to the same disordered condition in which she had earlier found it. Supposing that this was intended as a prelude to the usual pleasures, I responded by extending a hand to touch her breast.

She slapped my hand gently. 'You misunderstand me, Signore. It is I who am examining *you*.'

Thus admonished, I was forced to assume the role of spectator while the aunt completed my undressing to her satisfaction; whereupon she studied me with some admiration and then applied to a sensitive organ certain attentions which are too indelicate to describe.

At the conclusion of these operations, bearing in mind my earlier exertions of very recent memory, I was doubly spent.

'Are you content, Signora?' I enquired, breathlessly.

She smiled slyly at me, and by the candle-light I could see that she was indeed a lovely creature. She answered, 'Have patience. So far we have proved merely that you are a man composed of the usual parts. Your capacity to give instruction and pleasure to a woman still remains an issue between us. We must attend to that immediately.'

Appalled, I cried, 'Have mercy on me, Signora!'

'Hush now!' she whispered with a finger to my lips and a

kiss to the lobe of my ear. 'Have courage. Surely it is a part of your pedagogical talent that you can sustain your teaching in the face of an unruly pupil?' So saying, she reclined upon the bed with her garments in a state of interesting disarray and the entrance to Elysium clearly on display. I sighed, realising that I should not escape from the clutches of this wanton until I had fulfilled her desires. Accordingly, I attended to the amorous act and disposed of her as quickly as I could.

Throughout this, Dulcinea had continued her pretence of sleep, and the discussion between the aunt and myself was conducted to the soft trill of Dulcinea's girlish snores; except when she was listening so intently that she forgot. Now, my forces exhausted, I collapsed in the space on the bed between aunt and niece.

It would be unreasonable, I suppose, to expect that Dulcinea should listen to her relative's efforts without their having an effect upon her own energies and imagination. So, as I lay in a state of mortal exhaustion, the younger of my two beauties turned towards me, embraced me with one arm and, with her free hand, grabbed (too vigorously in the circumstances) a portion of my anatomy made tender by its earlier exercises. This action could not go unobserved by the aunt. She seemed to view it as a challenge, to which she responded by turning also towards me and indicating her desires by abundant caresses. Caught between these two harpies, I was obliged to rally my troops for the fourth time to the flagpole and pleasure the pair of them. In due course I despatched them to Paradise; but for my part I was beginning to feel that I had stumbled into some species of erotic Hell.

At last! I thought, when I had reduced my charmers to moaning contentment. I gave some consideration to effecting my escape. In my state of physical shock (having fired my artillery four times in rapid succession), I feared I was going to be taken captive in this place and confined for the enjoyment of aunt and niece like a Musulman slave. It was a prospect so horrible (given my suspicion as to the frequency of their appetites) that I determined to flee the field of battle although I could barely walk.

Yet it seemed that this amorous pair were not finished. True, my Dulcinea had been reduced to the gentle condition of a well-fed cat, but the beautiful aunt had not yet exhausted her inventiveness. She turned upon her niece, ran her fingers over the latter's bosom (which even now had charms to arouse me) and proposed, 'My dearest, shall I instruct you in certain religious exercises practised by the nuns?'

'Will they also take me to Paradise?' asked Dulcinea languidly.

'Assuredly,' said the aunt, using her hand to give her niece some preliminaries of this new experience. She glanced at me and enquired amiably, 'Shall you stay to watch, Signore? You are welcome to enlarge upon your present learning.'

I was hurriedly gathering my clothes. I answered her glance with a bow and replied, 'Alas, I must fly. My ladies have shown themselves the mistresses of my more modest powers and I must leave lest they send me shortly to Heaven without the benefit of a priest.'

This gallant reply provoked a tinkle of laughter from both my houris, and it was with this sound in my ears that I opened the shutters and began my descent by the rope. Behind me the candle was extinguished.

It was the wreck of a man who at last slipped into the gondola and ordered that it be cast off incontinently. My fellows obliged, and, as I thanked them, it seemed to me that they were less brutish than the two bawds I had just left upstairs.

CHAPTER TWENTY-THREE

Signor Ludovico's Narrative

Before my darling Angelica left with the Contessa for the estate at San Cipriano, she came to visit me again in the factor's chamber. She was dressed in her travelling-clothes, contrite and dabbing the tears from her eyes.

'Dear Ludovico, forgive me!' she sobbed.

'Why, Signorina Angelica?'

'You know why. I have been a cruel and capricious mistress to you, forgetting that we are used to dealing as friends. I withdraw my calumnies. You are indeed a proper man in spirit and intelligence. And as a girl – why! Have you not always been the prettiest?'

'Then I forgive you,' I said tenderly.

She kissed my cheek and I kissed her forehead.

I tried further to comfort her by telling her that a short stay in the country would not be so bad. She would have the companionship of the Contessa, who was a very gay person and undoubtedly would receive visitors, for example her dear friend Signora Molin.

'That is so,' she sniffed. 'But oh, Ludovico, I had such hopes if I had remained here at the palazzo even a little longer.'

'What hopes?'

'I cannot speak of them,' Angelica replied evasively. And shortly after that she was gone.

I was left for the rest of the day to occupy myself in Signor Feltrinelli's chamber while he attended to his business. I was not without subjects to entertain my thoughts: the unexplained absences of Signor Morosini prior to his supper-parties (including that on the fateful night); the attempted robbery which had provoked my patron to exile his daughter; the mysterious hints by Angelica that she was shortly expecting a momentous change in her condition; and the sudden appearance of emotion in the dry manner of Signor Feltrinelli and his new confidence in me. However, materials to answer only the last-named question lay to hand in the factor's papers, and (I say this shame-facedly) I straightway violated his confidence and began to ferret out what I could find. Alas, it was very little.

In addition to the works I have already mentioned, I found a commonplace book in which the factor jotted his thoughts, and, with it, several volumes containing fair copies of his correspondence.

As to the commonplace book, Signor Feltrinelli had the habit of inferior minds of writing bad verse and philosophical notions in portentous language. The train of his thoughts was as he had briefly indicated to me. That is to say he was (as we would say in present troubled times) a very Jacobin.* His hatred of the nobility, and of all privilege was palpable. I was astonished by the violence of his language, and I wondered if this loathing of the patrician class were

---

* Unless the dedication to the 20th edition (circa 1765) is a forgery, this passage (post 1789) must have been added later. This problem was discussed in a symposium. See the rare *Études sur la Pornographie Musicale*, Nanking 1938 (reprinted by Satyricon Press, Las Vegas, 1975).

sufficient motive for him to have murdered Signor Molin as its representative. However, even a moment's consideration revealed the unlikelihood of this explanation. For, surely, the proper object of the factor's vengeance against his oppressors would have been Signor Morosini? It was most unlikely that he could harbour strong feelings against Signor Molin, whom he could have known only distantly.

The other volumes contained the whole of Signor Feltrinelli's correspondence. He was, as I expected, a most meticulous fellow. And there, among his letters to horse-dealers and corn-chandlers, were for my perusal his personal communications. Disreputable character that I am, I read them.

He was a narrow correspondent. Of friends he seemed to have none to water his arid soul. His letters were confined to exchanges with his sister, and even these consisted of instructions as to what she should and should not do, as if she were managing an estate under his supervision. Yet, within their crabbed style there were indications of the passionate creature who had written the polemics contained in the commonplace book. He was clearly fond of his sister, even as he criticised her. And, it seemed, the poor devil was going through the tortures of an unrequited love for some lady far above his station (though this last point may have been an affectation: a milkmaid may be a goddess to a lovelorn churl). I sympathised with his agonies, but they were not to my purpose.

Study of these documents occupied me until evening had fallen and Signor Feltrinelli returned. He greeted me with a little of his earlier warmth and enquired how I had passed my day and whether anyone had discovered me.

'I saw only Signorina Angelica, who bade me farewell before she left. She was distressed to be leaving.'

'She is a foolish girl. If she took instruction from Signora Molin, she might improve in wisdom and manners. The

Contessa, although a lady, is too worldly to provide a good example.'

'As to that,' I answered, 'I have only recently become aware that Angelica and Signora Molin are acquainted.'

'Signora Molin has a sympathy for the young and can see that Signorina Angelica's education has been neglected by the indulgence of a fond parent. She has tried to take our young mistress in hand and, to speak the truth, has had some success. Angelica has become better-mannered, if no less imprudent.'

There was no more to be said, and Signor Feltrinelli sat himself down and began working on his business papers. It is a measure of his single-mindedness that the presence of another person – even a eunuch dressed as a maid – had no effect upon his concentration. As I watched him work by candle-light with a dedication beyond that generally shown by a factor, several thoughts came to mind, though I reached no conclusion as to their truth. The first was that, engaged in his pettifogging daily concerns, and from what I had seen of his doggerel, Signor Feltrinelli must possess only a mediocre understanding. And the second was that he was withal a most singular man, capable of great or monstrous things from the concentration and dedication of his forces. I admired him vastly for that quality. I, on the other hand, would ever be condemned to inconsequential things because, whatever the power of my intelligence, my character was so slight and trivial that in future men would doubt even that I existed. These thoughts, which I offer for what they are worth, made me wonder further if there were not a species of genius, especially of the terrible sort, that was merely an alliance between mediocrity and force of character in revenge upon the world; or if, even when genius seemed benign, it was often no more than a conjunction of energy and vain self-promotion. I do not know. I know so little.

As evening drew on, and because of my exertions of the previous two nights, I grew tired.

Signor Feltrinelli noticed and asked with amiable concern, 'Are you fatigued, Ludovico? I have been inconsiderate. Do you wish to retire?'

'I should like that,' I admitted.

'I have spoken to Signor Morosini and he has agreed that it is impossible that you should sleep with the servants. Therefore, it is proposed that for tonight you shall sleep in the Signorina Angelica's chamber. It is hoped that tomorrow the matter of your arrest will be resolved and you will be able to return to your lodgings.'

I thanked him, and he led me by candle-light, up stairs and along corridors of the great palazzo, to my young mistress's chamber.

It was furnished in as pretty a fashion as could be wished, and filled with the dolls, trinkets and bibelots of a girl who, in her habits of thought, was scarcely out of childhood. It was delightfully perfumed with lavender-water and, in all, so soothing that I looked forward with relish to the best sleep for several days. Accordingly, I undressed to my maidenly shift, made a comfortable place for myself in the bed (which added to the animal pleasure of my slumbers the slightest whiff of virginal farts), and within minutes had drifted into dreams.

I cannot say how long I slept or when I became aware of an exterior noise, since the latter became incorporated within my dream. It was an insistent tapping which, in my slumbers, became the dripping of water on to a drum. Only gradually, by its interminable quality, did I realise that the noise came from outside myself; and I then awoke.

A night-light was burning by my bedside. By it I identified the noise with a trembling of the window-shutter. I would have considered it an effect of the wind, but it was not the wind that was whispering bad-temperedly, 'God's blood and damnation!' If I excluded the possibility of a foul-mouthed spirit floating in the air outside my window, it seemed that someone was trying to gain entry – though how he came to be fifty feet or more above the canal was a mystery to me. Evidently it was not a robber, unless he were expecting an extraordinary degree of co-operation from his intended victim.

In curiosity as much as trepidation, I picked up the candle and advanced to the window, where I unfastened the latch of the shutter. Immediately the wind blew the candle out and a dark figure tumbled into the room with a breathless flow of 'Damnations' and further colourful profanities.

The man lay upon the floor for some seconds, then stood, tidied his dress, gave me an elegant bow (so far as I could discern these things in the gloom) and said, 'I apologise . . . Where are you? . . . Damn this darkness! . . . Ah, I think I see you . . . Yes. I apologise, Signorina, for the abrupt manner of my entry. I am greatly obliged to you, since I do not believe I could have hung on the rope much longer.'

In the face of this civility, I answered, 'You have me at a disadvantage, Signore. You are . . . ?'

'May I present myself?' Another bow. 'I am the Chevalier Jacques de Maison-Neuve. And your name, Signorina?'

'What? You do not know my name?' I answered coyly.

'Alas not. I have admired you humbly from a distance since first seeing you at the Ridotto, where your identity was hidden from me.'

'You are bold then, Signore, to pay your addresses to a maiden whom you do not know.'

'I confess it. If I possessed any prudence in matters of the heart, I should not be here, but' – he started me by falling to one knee – 'such is the fascination you have wrought in me that all caution has been overturned and I have come, as you see me, a perfect fool for love.' This pretty speech was somewhat spoiled by another cry of 'Damnation!' caused, I think, by something he had knelt on in the darkness. At all events he leaped to his feet again and peered at the floor.

Well, here was an odd turn of events! I was not in the least frightened by this fool, since his intentions appeared to be peaceable, if not exactly decent. On the other hand, how he had come to this state was a mystery. However, I could not criticise the fellow too much, since an idea of equivalent foolishness now came to me which was this: if he were prepared to take his mistress upon such blind trust, why should I not be that mistress?

To understand the delirium which now gripped me, the Reader must know me thoroughly, which is scarcely possible. But the notion that I, who had so often played the false, should be taken for the real Angelica filled me with such exquisite joy that I could not resist it. For I had before me that which had never been before; a lover who desired me in my womanly nature!

'You are weeping, Signorina?' interrupted my cavalier with concern.

I touched a hand to his cheek. 'It is nothing, Jacques – a maiden's tears – nothing . . .' I burst out sobbing and ran to the bed to bury my face in the pillow, leaving behind me my perplexed lover. I believe I heard him muttering something unflattering about virgins, accompanied by more 'Damnations', but I was unconcerned. I was in a state of ecstasy.

He laughed and emitted some 'Hahs!' and 'Hums!' as he collected his thoughts. Then he said, cautiously, 'May I take it, Signorina, that my attentions are not unwelcome?'

I nodded, but, of course, he could not see me. In a stifled and tearful voice I whispered, 'Yes, Jacques . . . oh, yes!'

My lover proved a brisk and saucy fellow and without

any further pretty words he removed some of his garments and loosened others so that we might be at amorous ease. But he was no brute and was content gradually to overcome my girlish bashfulness with caresses and rustic humour. He had apparently learned (I know not where) that coarse speech may be used to effect in making merry a high-born virgin. At all events he knew some interesting jokes and entertaining games. We laughed – each of us whispering 'Hush!' to the other so that we should not be overheard – and my heart swelled with gratitude and my eyes grew moist in anticipation.

'You laugh, you jade!' he said at last, and added, 'Come now, it is unjust that you should poke fun at things of which you have no knowledge.'

'Will you instruct me, Signore?' I asked – and, truly, I felt for a moment as if I were wholly ignorant: as, indeed, I was in my character of a true woman.

'Aye, that I will! he said and clapped his hand to my bosom.

This was an occasion when I had reason to bless my caponized condition. For though (as I have remarked) I do not labour with the heavy dugs that can afflict those who are cut out for my profession, I do possess breasts as neat and comely as those of any maiden and it was to these and then to my lips and then to these again that my lover applied his kisses, so that I was in a swoon of delight – still more so when from somewhere about his clothes he produced an unguent with which he anointed my belly and my thighs and which he then worked into my too-receptive flesh with strokes of his fingers and licks of his tongue.

There were, of course, certain obstacles of anatomy to the consummation of our desires in the usual fashion between man and woman but I gave no thought to inevitable discovery. Firstly, I had tucked the useless remnants of my virile member between my legs so that I presented an unencumbered face to him. And, secondly, it was possible that, in our mutual transports, I might persuade him to embrace me from the rear and enter me by one gate, while thinking he was entering me by another. Who could tell? And, in God's name, was I not entitled to hope? Poor sinner that I am and caught between two sexes, surely there was some purity in being loved wholly as one?

Be that as it may, it seemed that we must soon try conclusions. Tired of simply pleasuring me, my cavalier issued a low groan, took my hand and wrapped it round his member (as to which I needed no encouragement) and at the same time placed his own hand where he thought the entrance to Venus' temple must lie.

He quipped, '"Discite grammatici cur mascula nomina cunnus. Et cur femineum mentula habet."'*

I replied, '"Disce quod a domino nomina servus habet."'†

'Why, dearest Angelica, I did not know you had so much Latin in you!'

'If you are a true heir of Rome, I shall shortly have still more Latin in me.'

He laughed. 'Why, it is a witty thing that the girl is!' he said and with that he kissed me on the lips and at the same time slipped his hand between my thighs, thereby causing my own *membrum virile* (which had been under some strain) to pop out like a jack-in-a-box – and change the direction of our conversation.

A silence fell upon us. At length, in a voice that was a little above a squeak, my cavalier enquired, 'Bellino?' When I did not reply (I was holding my breath in an agony of

---

* Teach us, grammarians, why 'cunt' is a masculine noun and 'cock' is feminine.
† It is because the slave takes its name from its master.

disappointment), he began to feel more searchingly about my parts and gave me some pinches that were harder than the caresses to which I had looked forward. 'Damn me!' he muttered. 'If that's a fake, it's the best I have ever come across.' It came to me then that he was still uncertain if I were not in fact a woman – a circumstance which may seem odd since the answer was, if not poking him in the eye, at least poking him in the belly. However, this will not appear so strange if the Reader is made aware that there are within my profession certain mock-castrati, women who assume the guise of castrati in order to be permitted to sing within the territories of the Holy Father where women are forbidden to tread the stage. To perfect such an imposture, an imitation of the male member is made of gutta percha or the like which is intended to fool the gropings of a priest. Evidently my lover had encountered such a person in the past. That on the other hand, he should expect one to turn up in the bedroom of Signorina Angelica Morosini is testament that his brains were addled by his lust.

'Alas, Signore, I must disabuse you. The object you are handling is as tender as any other part of my person. You are hurting it.'

'Ah!'

'May I have it back?'

'What? Oh! Yes, of course.' He released me, but at once applied a hand to cup the fullness of my breast and stroke the nipple. 'And these?' he asked. 'Fakes?'

'Mine, too,' I said, feeling still an amorous faintness quickened by his caress.

'Good Lord . . . Hmm! . . . May we have some light?'

I fumbled a while to find tinder and then strike a spark with which to light the candle. When I had done so and we turned to face each other we exclaimed as one:

'Ludovico!'

'Giacomo!'

Indeed my lover was none other than my friend Signor Giacomo. He stared. I stared. He grinned. I grinned. 'Damnation!' he said, shaking his head. And then we both began to laugh.

'Well,' he said at last, as we sat together amiably upon the bed, 'we find ourselves in a merry fix. May I enquire what has happened to my Dulcinea?'

'Angelica has been despatched to the country by her father. The house was assailed by robbers last night.'

Giacomo smiled wryly. 'That was I – not as a robber, you understand. Alas, I failed in my attempt. Ah, well! There is no purpose in regret. I have never seen the maiden except at the Ridotto, where she was masked. Is she pretty?'

'Yes, delightful.'

'Pity. Still, I may perhaps reserve her for a future occasion. Meantime, you must tell me how you come to find yourself in this situation.'

This I did, and we spent an entertaining hour. I described how, having been mistaken for my friend by reason of the clothes he had given me, I had engaged in a passage of arms with the sad lady's protector.

Giacomo was profuse in his apologies for this accident. 'The fellow is a dunderhead, but persistent and very dangerous. It seems that anyone with designs upon his mistress runs the risk of losing his life, though my lady loathes the man heartily. But pray go on – what then?'

I told him of my arrest and my reluctant escape from the Leads in the company of poor Fosca. Giacomo paid close attention to this. He explained, 'Prison is a hazard of our way of life, and who can say when we shall next be there?'

'That may be,' I answered. 'And now you – what turn of events has brought you to this house?'

'I came to collect a present and to give instruction – or so it was put to me. My sad lady told me of a virgin who dwells here and said I might oblige both of them by relieving the girl of her embarrassment. As a rule I have no truck with virgins, who in my experience are unpredictable and unsatisfactory, but it was explained to me that I should be performing a service that I could not in honour refuse.'

'So Angelica was expecting you?'

'I must suppose so. My mistress told me the girl was eager to make my acquaintance. Do not look so offended, Ludovico. I have spoken the truth. I would not have undertaken the enterprise unless the maiden consented.'

'I believe you,' I answered sadly. I remembered Angelica's reluctance to depart for San Cipriano and the air of mystery and excitement about her. On the other hand, it was possible that the light-headed creature had been deceived as to the nature of the intended assignation and that she had expected no more than a flirtation. In which case, she would have been most rudely surprised.

I asked, 'Have you yet discovered the identity of your sad lady?'

'I have,' answered Giacomo. 'With familiarity she has grown lax in her precautions, and from papers and other items inadvertently left about her apartments I have ascertained that she is none other than Signora Beatrice Molin.'

'Signora Molin!'

'The very same. And I may add that it pleases me that she has decided to direct my attentions at another. Though she is a most beautiful lady, it has occurred to me that the murder of her husband may be the start of a curious vice.'

'Nonsense!' I exclaimed. 'She cannot have murdered her husband!'

'Not in person, I admit,' said Giacomo. 'But – as you are well aware – she owns the affections of a monster who seems to regard murderous assault as a form of courtesy. I daresay that by a look or glance she could set the brute upon anyone she chose – even her husband.'

I could not deny this – I knew the brute in question. Yet I found it difficult to reconcile my recollections of that grave and lovely lady with the person whom Giacomo sought to present as procuress and possible murderess. I could accept that she might turn from an old and gloomy husband, such as I imagined Signor Alessandro Molin to have been, and seek instead the comfort of a lover. But even in this vicious age, I could not believe that she was so sunk in vice as to procure the virtue of my dear Angelica or be intentionally an accomplice to her husband's death. I leave the matter to the Reader to decide. You have my impressions and the story told by Giacomo. You know the truth as well as anyone. I will add only that, in matters of the heart, Giacomo is as great a liar as I am.

Our tales finished, we sat regarding each other in silence. I cannot explain how it came about, but I had taken on my character of maiden so completely that I now felt strangely abashed and covered my breasts, which still tingled under Giacomo's gaze.

'So lovely!' he muttered to himself.

'Fie!' I answered in gentle modesty.

'I speak only the truth,' he said, looking me in the eye, and sighed. 'It seems, dear Ludovico – so far have you aroused me – that we must complete the work we have started.' He took my hand, kissed it and pulled me towards him. He covered my neck and bosom with the most tender embraces. Thus *vota puer solvit, quae foemina voverat Iphis.**

Ah, well, I thought as I gave myself to him, the World is a queerer place than I had imagined.

*   *   *

* Iphis fulfilled as a boy vows made as a girl – *Ovid*.

I shall pass over the rest of that night spent with Giacomo, and finish with a footnote in the matter of my escape from the Leads, which I had narrated to him as I have to you, dear Reader. It is an account the truth of which affects my credit in your eyes.

I have been sparing in those to whom I have confided my tale (until now when my world is dead and buried) since it was bound up with such intrigues and considerations of high policy that a man might die for the telling of it. In consequence, there has grown up a story, unchallenged and put about by Signor Giacomo, of his own daring escape from the Leads, which in all material particulars (except the identity of the hero) is the same as my own. The Reader may compare the two. True, there are differences: Giacomo's account is more elaborate, more exciting and amusing than my own. But these are the very qualities, in comparison with my own more sober story, which should put the prudent Reader upon his guard. For they are part of the art of a story-teller, mere scribbler's tricks to beguile his readership. I rest my case upon unadorned fact. Giacomo did not escape from the Leads. He was released after his patron, Senator Bragadin, bribed the gaoler. All the World knew it at the time but has since forgotten.

I grow angry and should not; but it annoys me that another should claim the credit of my achievement. We cannot both be telling the truth. For it is certain that, as between Giacomo and myself, one of us is a shameless plagiarist.

CHAPTER TWENTY-FOUR

Signor Ludovico's Narrative

Giacomo departed with the dawn and with a kiss; and I, telling myself that I was the luckiest of creatures, fell into a pleasant sleep of delightful dreams. I was awakened some hours later by Signor Feltrinelli, who in his stiffness and with his eyes averted from my person, seemed to have a regard for my maidenly modesty. Indeed it was a character with which I was so imbued that I was ashamed to be seen by any man in my state of undress.

'You wish something?' I asked, pulling the bedclothes about me.

'Have you slept well, Ludovico? Did you hear anything during the night? The servants have suggested that robbers were again about the area.'

'I heard nothing. I have been robbed of nothing.'

'I am glad of that. I do not suppose that you have broken your fast. May I ask you to defer that until later, when we have found more suitable attire? The servants would be curious if you were served in Signorina Angelica's room; and your appearance as a woman would, if the disguise were penetrated, cause even more consternation. Your own garments are rent and soiled following your escape, but I am taking steps to procure some others. I shall return shortly.'

The factor was true to his word and brought me a set of clothes about half an hour later. He had caused a man to visit my lodgings and bring my own suit and linen. I washed face and hands, sprinkled myself with some of Angelica's rose-water and went down to the kitchen, where I was given some bread and cheese and a glass of wine. Signor Feltrinelli had busied himself about other matters, but he now came to tell me, 'Signor Morosini wishes to see you.'

'I am honoured.'

The factor looked at me sharply, then said, 'Honoured you may be, but I trust that you will have the discretion to stay silent on certain subjects we discussed yesterday. Yes? Very well, come with me.'

We went by stairs to Signor Morosini's private cabinet in a part of the house to which I was not ordinarily admitted. It contained those items of furnishings of which my master was particularly fond: some paintings of exquisite though erotic taste, some volumes on the subject of Natural Philosophy, and various instruments of a scientific kind such as an orrery and an astrolabe. My patron was sitting at his ease in a quilted robe, having his hair dressed by his valet, Alfonso. Noticing me after a moment, he motioned me also to be seated and then, so that nothing should disturb the perfection of his toilet, he sat quite still, with an expression of serenity upon his face, until Alfonso had finished the last application of powder and a final spray of perfume. Then he dismissed the valet and gave his attention to me and, to a lesser degree, to Signor Feltrinelli, who was attending upon any orders.

'Well, Signor Ludovico,' began my patron affably, 'I hope that you have recovered from your considerable physical exertions.'

'You find me as you see me, grateful that you have noticed your servant and extended your aid and protection when they were needed.'

'Did I? Oh, well I suppose I must have done something of the sort since you are here and in apparent good health. Why do you say you were arrested?'

'I incurred the displeasure of a gentleman – a stranger, I assure you – who held the mistaken belief that I was a rival for the affections of his mistress.'

'I see.' My lord did not ordinarily acknowledge that he was as short-sighted as his daughter, but now he picked up his quizzing-glass and eyed me through it. 'Was there, do you suppose, any connection between that incident and the murder of Signor Alessandro?'

I saw at once that there might indeed be a connection, though it made little enough sense. If, as Giacomo had told me, his sad lady was Signora Molin, it seemed entirely possible that the monster whose violent presence haunted her was her stepson, Signor Girolamo, and that he was my assailant and accuser. Though his manner had seemed slow and ponderous on the occasion I had seen him, that did not preclude a propensity to violence. And in his general configuration, he was of a size to fit the beast whom I had fought. I did not doubt that he had attacked me because of a confusion of identity and not for any reason directly connected with the murder. But the former might be related to the latter in an indirect way: they might both be manifestations of a temper given to insane jealousy.

'I know of no connection,' I replied. 'I am not aware of the identity of my enemy and, as I have explained, the incident arose from a mistake.' I waited for my patron to enlighten me, since he had surely obtained the name of my accuser from the Avogadore; but he was not disposed to do so.

Instead he turned his eyes from me with fading interest and said, 'Whatever the truth, it seems, Signor Ludovico, that you are innocent in the matter. You have been dragged firstly into the death of Signor Molin, which is none of your affair; and now into some intrigue concerning women – whether the two subjects be connected or no. It is' – he searched for a word – 'an inconvenience to have one's dependants dragged into problems that are none of their business; and one has an obligation . . . an obligation . . . Well, I have spoken to Signor Dolfin and he has put your case to your accuser and the latter has handsomely acknowledged that there was some confusion and that you were not the . . . In short, you are free. The business of your escape will therefore be forgotten, yes?'

I rose from my seat and bowed. In his great condescension Signor Morosini smiled on me most amiably, but my own smile was clouded by a thought. Had he deliberately directed my suspicions at Signor Girolamo Molin?

As we descended the stairs, Signor Feltrinelli commented, 'You were very polite not to mention the subject of Fosca.'

'I was afraid that, whatever my general innocence, I should be held complicit in his escape.'

'Evidently that is not to be the case. And, frankly, it suits the Council of Ten that Fosca should have escaped.'

'How so?'

'He was an embarrassment to them: a testament to their incompetence as well as their injustice. They would have killed him but for the promise which your Monsieur Arouet wrung from the Avogadore. Free he cannot harm them – but to free him would have meant an admission of their fallibility. Now, if it so happens that they catch him, they may suppress the fact and string him up quietly. Therefore, Ludovico, you have done a service to the State.'

'You are a Machiavellian,' I said admiringly.

Signor Feltrinelli returned a dour smile. 'Ah,' he said. 'There is something I had forgotten. Signor Morosini intends to hold a supper-party tonight for his usual guests as well as Signor Balsamo. You are to provide music.'

'I see,' I answered, and posed the question he had known I would ask. 'Do you think Signor Morosini will make one of his private expeditions from the house before supper?'

The factor raised an eyebrow. 'Who can say?'

I did not return directly to my lodgings. Instead I called upon Monsieur Arouet, hoping to find him at home and wishing to tell him of my various discoveries for such light as they shed upon the murder. I found him abed, complaining of an attack of some flux or griping wind, unable to bear the light and saying he doubted he would be able to walk again unless the clyster he had applied was successful in removing a stool, the size of an elephant, which was presently stopping up his back passage. I tried to get him to listen to my story, which in its main points was as follows.

Firstly: my patron, Signor Morosini, was a party to some sinister conspiracy against religion, if Fra Angelo were to be believed.

Secondly: it was certain that Signor Morosini's supper-parties were other than they appeared. It was his habit to leave the house two or three hours before supper, for unknown purposes, and to return in the company of one or more of his guests.

Thirdly: Signor Alessandro Molin had been a member of a pious but secret confraternity organised by Fra Angelo which was in opposition to Signor Morosini and his friends.

Fourthly: Signora Molin had not been content with her elderly husband and had taken at least one lover (unless Giacomo were lying — which was entirely possible).

Fifthly: Signor Girolamo Molin nourished a forbidden passion for his stepmother and was of a violent and jealous temper.

Monsieur Arouet opened an eye slowly and painfully and gave me a lop-sided smile of hideous cunning. 'And sixthly?' he enquired.

'I do not know that there is a sixthly,' I answered.

'And sixthly,' he persisted, 'Signor Pasticcio, the jolly painter whom we visited, has been murdered – no doubt a matter which you consider as unrelated to our problem, except that—'

'*What?*'

'Seventhly, I have divined what the object was that Signor Molin carried from his house, wrapped in his cloak, when he went forth on that fateful night. It was a painting. I had suspected it was so, and the murder of Pasticcio seems to confirm it. Signor Molin was carrying a small painting, and it has disappeared: stolen by his killer. What say you to that, Ludovico?' Monsieur Arouet finished triumphantly.

I had nothing to say. I had no theory that fitted this latest discovery.

After delivery of his last news, my friend became brighter, which tended only to confirm my suspicion that his ill-health was a product of his fancy rather than his constitution. He beamed at the effect he had made, and said, 'I believe I have partly recovered my spirits and will rise. Indeed, considering your recent adventures, you look well yourself, very well – you have a certain glow about your skin and cheeks that I would call feminine if I did not know you better.'

I blushed at his perspicacity.

'Come on – come on,' he continued with cheerful impatience. 'While I am dressing, and then while we walk, you shall give me a more circumstantial account of the points you have raised. Omit nothing. The stories of your friend

Signor Giacomo; your interview with Fra Angelo (God curse him!); your imprisonment and escape; your return to the Ca' di Spagna. I want everything!'

In this I tried to oblige him. However, I omitted one matter which seemed to me inconsequential because it did not fit into the scheme I had half devised. Since it was a point that could be established only by knowledge and not theory, and since it was a point unknown to Monsieur Arouet, it fell entirely outside his calculations and proved to be a *lacuna* in a solution which was otherwise complete. However, I am in advance of my tale.

As requested, I told Monsieur Arouet as much as I could of my friend Giacomo's dealings with his sad lady.

'But I must caution you,' I concluded. 'If I understand your philosophy aright, all purported truths must be judged according to the source from which they come. In this case I will tell you that – though I doubt not that he has some acquaintance with the lady – Giacomo cannot be believed upon any matter which touches his standing in the World's eyes. He is full of bluster and rodomontades and, as rogues go, I have never met one so concerned about his honour; so that he will persuade himself that his depredations are a benefit to his victims and bring him no satisfaction except the fulfilment of his duty – I say this, who love him. Not that there is no truth in him. The sad lady's protector (whom I believe to be Signor Girolamo Molin) certainly exists and Giacomo has had an unfortunate encounter with him, or else the attack upon my own person cannot be explained. But it does not follow that Signor Girolamo's jealous suspicions have any foundation in fact. It may be that, being suspected and, indeed, assaulted for the sake of the lady, Giacomo feels he has paid the price and may therefore fairly claim the goods – if only in reputation. For my part, while I would not go so far as to say that Signora Beatrice is wholly innocent, I should want firmer evidence before I would admit that she had entirely lost her virtue.'

Monsieur Arouet scrutinized me closely. I did not know if it were wryly or from a growing wonderment. He said, 'What shall I make of you, Ludovico? First, like a rational man, you expound the rule by which truth must be tested empirically. Then, in the same vein, you apply the rule consistently to the case in hand, sifting the evidence to test its weight and purity. But next – what? – you introduce a new test, namely that the evidence must overcome your sentimental regard for a woman.'

'You yourself expressed admiration for the beauty of her person and demeanour,' I protested.

'So I did. And I also admire a fine piece of beef. But I eat it with the same teeth that grind coarser meats. Enough! Let us see the widow and her pet monster.'

We were at the Palazzo Molin, whither Monsieur Arouet had sent a boy to make sure that Signora Beatrice and her stepson were at home. We were admitted to the same chamber as before, which I had found so oppressive from the religiosity of the dead man but which on this occasion seemed more expressive of his dullness. For some minutes we were left to admire the furnishings and paintings (though I found little admirable in either); then there was a tap at the door and two people entered.

I tried to remember my first sight of Signora Beatrice. Was my recollection pure or was it inextricably confounded by Giacomo's stories of his ethereal mistress? Certainly I had thought her beautiful (as beautiful as my neutered state would allow). But had I been overawed? Had I any sense that I was in the presence of an unearthly being, but one bound painfully to the earth like an angel trapped by its wing? That was how she now appeared: reflecting those two qualities, beauty and pain, each to a terrible degree so that it was an irresistible agony to look at her. And I did not resist. I looked and was dismayed. It felt as if I were emptying myself: pouring compassion into a receptacle of such despair that it was like water on sand. How was it possible to look at – let alone speak to – someone so inconsolable?

Thus my impressions. I was incomprehensible to myself. Why should I, who had such slight regard for women beyond the moderate affection that comes from a naturally kindly disposition, feel such a profound compassion for this woman? I cannot explain it, except that there was a change in both our states. As to hers, it must remain for ever to some degree unknown, but there are some bubbling chemistries that work slowly towards the climax of their effects and are held trapped within alembic and retort with little outward seeming. So with her. While all surface appearance was as before, yet I could feel the heat of the ferment within.

But I? What of me? It seemed that, having discovered the real Angelica within me, I could not dismiss her and I was still exploring her qualities. One of these, I now learned, was that whereas the false Angelica was *effeminate*, the real Angelica was *womanly* and a world of difference lay between the two. For in my effeminate state I was vain and self-regarding but in my new womanly glory I quivered with receptivity towards others. What other discoveries lay to be made within the stew of emotion and sensation that was my new condition I could not imagine.

Two people had come into the room. The second was Signor Girolamo Molin, who looked large and sombre in the black suit and white linen which is called the 'Spanish' style. If my suspicions – which were near certainties – were correct, he must know me as the man he had assaulted and wronged, but he gave no sign. As Signor Feltrinelli would have put it in his Jacobinical way, I was beneath the notice of such a fine, patrician gentleman. He acknowledged Monsieur

Arouet and displayed the same lumbering slowness I had remarked at our first visit to the Palazzo Molin.

Signora Beatrice spoke first. Her voice held the limpidity and gayness of one under uncertain control. 'Well, Monsieur, it was you who asked for this interview. What have you for us? Is it news or questions?'

'It is both.'

'Have you decoded the message left by the murderer?' enquired Signor Girolamo.

'Oh, that?' replied my friend indifferently: 'Yes. I have cracked the shell of the thing and it remains only to extract the kernel.' (I shot a sharp glance at him but he waved me away with a flick of his hand.) 'However, my news is of other matters. Have you heard that Pasticcio is dead?'

Signora Beatrice gave no sign of recognition.

Signor Girolamo said, 'Pasticcio?'

'The painter. Do you know him?'

Signor Girolamo looked questioningly at his stepmother (I say 'stepmother' though language renders truth absurd: she could have been his wife). He answered, 'I do not know the name – but I know little of painters. Is the information relevant to the present purpose? I suppose it must be, but I fail to see how.'

'No? It had occurred to me,' said Monsieur Arouet, 'that the object your father carried concealed in his cloak when he sallied abroad on the night of his death might have been a small painting.'

Signor Girolamo scanned the walls where his father's collection hung. 'I knew he had carried something but could not imagine what it might be. To go out at night with a painting? I thought he had been summoned to a meeting of the Confraternity.'

'His priest denies it.'

'He does?'

'You doubt him?'

'No. But it had not occurred to me to doubt my father.'

'Signora?' asked Monsieur Arouet, turning to the widow. She returned his gaze but, as it were, with borrowed eyes that had been fixed on a melancholy infinity and were only momentarily withdrawn from that object.

'Please,' she said. 'Examine the paintings. Like Girolamo I have given little attention to them; but, if it appears that something is missing, I may be able to assist.'

'You are most gracious,' answered my friend and bestowed upon her a leer that passed for sympathy.

Monsieur Arouet now attended to the walls, seeming not to examine the paintings nor even to look for obvious spaces (there were none).

'You seek what?' I asked him.

'Paintings are hung and they leave their marks, but that has often been the case here and one can learn nothing. But there is something else. Paintings are not hung randomly. Even without intention, they follow principles of composition upon any given wall. The artistic eye cannot live with a distribution that contains no harmony and will strive for it without plan or thought. Yet, here it does not exist. There was once a small canvas – *here*!' He pointed at the spot. 'It was removed and the other paintings were slightly rearranged. Signor Girolamo!'

'Signore?'

Monsieur Arouet spun on his heel, pointed imperiously at the spot on the wall and demanded, 'What picture hung here? Come, now! No! Don't think! See it in your mind's eye and the name will come.'

The big man looked disbelievingly, then puzzled, then open-eyed. He stammered, 'It was . . . it was . . .'

'Well? Well?'

'Christ and the Woman Taken in Adultery!' murmured

Signor Girolamo and stared at his beautiful relative. And here was the difference between us: for Monsieur Arouet smiled with radiant satisfaction that he was right, but I burned with shame as if I, too, had been accused of infidelity.

'Well, Madame?' asked my friend.

Signora Beatrice spared him a glance. She answered evenly, 'There was such a painting. Was it there, Girolamo? Perhaps. I do not know.'

'Was it, to your knowledge, removed?'

'No.'

'Signor Girolamo?'

'No.'

'Yet it is gone. Who painted it?'

Signor Girolamo answered, 'Raphael, according to some. According to others it is a copy by Andrea del Sarto. It is not recorded among the works of either. There is some doubt in the matter. But I am told that it is a very fine painting of its period, and on that account valuable.'

'And it is gone,' Monsieur Arouet reminded him.

'Yes, so it seems.'

The Frenchman continued to examine the other works. Without bothering to look at us, he went on, 'When was the painting acquired by Signor Alessandro?'

'Five or six years ago,' answered Signor Girolamo.

'Before my marriage,' said the widow.

Monsieur Arouet paused in his researches and glanced over his shoulder. 'You were married only a short time?'

'Twelve months.'

'I see.' He returned to a small canvas which for some reason attracted him. He asked, 'Have any of these works been removed recently for cleaning or restoration? I notice that several appear to have been treated.'

'Yes,' answered Signora Beatrice.

'Since your marriage?'

'Yes.'

'Including the painting in question?'

'I cannot say.'

'I believe so,' said Signor Girolamo.

The widow smiled sadly. She added, 'If Girolamo says so, then it must be so.'

'Very fine!' exclaimed Monsieur Arouet with satisfaction. He returned his attention to Signora Beatrice and her stepson. 'The collection is very fine.'

'I cannot say. I have no knowledge of these things,' answered that sad lady.

'My father collected these works to assist in his religious devotions,' said Signor Girolamo. 'If they are fine or valuable, let that be as it may. It is not a consideration that would have moved him.'

'No? Well, you may be right. However, it is my experience that the value of a thing is often established by its loss rather than its gain. A painting which Signor Alessandro acquired without consideration of cost might become a familiar and well-loved object and its loss occasion sharp pangs of regret.'

'I do not understand you,' said Signor Girolamo. 'The painting was not lost – that is to say, it was in my father's possession until the moment he was killed and robbed of it.'

'Very true,' agreed Monsieur Arouet with a sigh and a smile.

Signora Beatrice appeared much relieved. She asked, 'May I offer you refreshment?'

Monsieur Arouet bowed. 'Sadly I must decline. Ludovico and I have business to attend to. May I ask you: were the paintings – those that have been cleaned – put into the hands of Pasticcio?'

'I have told you: I do not know the name.'

'So you did tell me,' my friend acknowledged graciously. 'My apologies. I am impertinent with questions, but so many things trouble my mind. Ah, yes – one point. Signor Morosini is a *cognoscento* of paintings. Did he admire Signor Alessandro's collection?'

Signora Beatrice answered, 'I am not aware that Signor Morosini ever visited the house during my marriage. I do not know his opinion or that he has ever seen the collection.'

Signor Girolamo placed a hand gently upon her shoulder and said, 'You disturb my mother with your questions.'

'I have confessed my impertinence and begged forgiveness,' answered Monsieur Arouet, 'but I hope only to elucidate the truth of this affair to the benefit of all. I had understood that your father and Signor Morosini were close friends. It would therefore seem natural that—'

'They *were* friends,' answered the son abruptly. 'However, in recent years they have dropped their former intimacy. There was – as you must have observed – a growing difference of outlook between them. After the death of my natural mother, my father's interests became increasingly directed to matters of the spirit: he became, in short, a serious and religious gentleman. Signor Morosini, however, continued in the ways of his youth. Whether the accusations against him of debauchery and atheism are true, I cannot say. Nor can I confirm that he occupies himself with forbidden philosophies and strange sciences. The World exaggerates these things in rumour. What I can say is that Signor Morosini is lax in manners and outlook, and considers his own notions to be superior to the truths of Revealed Religion. In those circumstances, though my father and Signor Morosini remained friends out of former affections, their differences did not allow close intercourse between them to continue. And now, I pray you, let all questions cease. My mother is distressed.'

Indeed Signora Beatrice did appear distressed, though deriving no comfort from the sympathy of her stepson. I noticed that she shuddered when he placed his hand upon her shoulder and, when he gazed at her with an expression in which I discerned adoration, I detected a fleeting glimpse of horror behind her melancholy composure.

Poor lady, I thought, so young, so beautiful, and so trapped.

It was to be rid of us that she consented that Monsieur Arouet should borrow a small painting he had selected.

CHAPTER TWENTY-FIVE

Signor Ludovico's Narrative

We took a gondola, Monsieur Arouet and I. I remarked that my friend was in a free-spending mood.

He gave a jolly laugh. 'There is no hiding from you, Ludovico, though you consider yourself a fool! Yes; I have been attending to my own affairs – the publishing of my book – as well as this business of the murder. It seems that I have some reputation among a section of the patrician class, and they have proved eager to subscribe to the work and I find myself in funds.'

I wanted to enquire about his 'reputation' but felt too embarrassed to do so. It seemed this information must ever be denied me. I asked, 'Where are we going?'

'To Pasticcio's. Where else?'

'You think this matter of the paintings (which I confess I do not understand except as a simple robbery) is relevant to the murder?'

'Yes, though I cannot be certain. Undoubtedly there is some mystery attached to Signor Molin's paintings, but whether it is directly connected to his death remains an open question. It is in the nature of these affairs that, in uncovering a thing that is hidden, we uncover other things that are hidden. Not everything we discover will lead us to our goal.'

I put to him the matter which had astonished me when he mentioned it to the widow and stepson. 'You say that you have deciphered the code.'

'What? Oh, that. Yes. It was Signor Feltrinelli who gave me the clue – for which I am grateful: he is a helpful fellow, witness those things he has told you and the aid he gave you. He reminded me that I should not concentrate my attention on the "Ten" but rather should identify the "First", which, like God, is above all things and of which the "Ten" are merely exemplars.'

'And?'

'What is this "And"?' my friend snapped. 'Do you interrogate me, Signore?'

I stammered my apologies. 'I ask only, Monsieur, that you tell me the message we have been at such pains to discover.'

Monsieur Arouet did not immediately answer. I saw that he was wrestling with an inward frustration. Then he spoke frankly, reverting to his usual warmth. 'As I feared, the message is nonsense – a distraction, a piece of misdirection, an illusion, in short. Or, at least, so I believe, unless I misunderstand the affair entirely. I shall explain it to you more fully, but this is not the time. To do so requires that I lay it out with my ciphers and calculations.'

'Then it is valueless,' I said, somewhat surprised.

'No,' answered Monsieur Arouet. 'I did not say that. The message in itself is designed to confuse. But, as I have told you before, any message reflects the character and purpose of him who composed it. Our murderer has laid himself bare in that message, even though he does not know it. Our task is to read it aright. Alas, that is beyond me for the moment.'

'You refer to the murderer as a man. Are you sure of that?'
I was thinking (I may as well admit it) of Signora Beatrice,
whose tragic beauty had beguiled me as it beguiled any
proper man.

Monsieur Arouet threw me a sidelong glance, full of his
own vanity and superiority. He said, 'I know to whom you
refer. Be at peace, dear Ludovico. She is no murderess.'

'It would be wholly beyond her character,' I affirmed
enthusiastically.

'On the contrary! She is a passionate woman and had
profound reason to wish her husband dead – he was a very
dullard, and I could have wished him dead myself. However,
murder is a practical, not a theoretical, matter. And it was
beyond the widow's forces to carry out the crime in the way
in which it was committed. Nor, I think, did she suborn her
stepson into doing the deed; for that would be to put herself
wholly in the power of that oaf, whom she rightly fears and
despises. No, if Signor Girolamo is a parricide, he murdered
for his own reasons; perhaps so that he might take possession
of the widow. As to Signora Beatrice . . .' He paused. 'No, I
shall not say what I believe.'

So by degrees we arrived at the workshop of the late
Pasticcio. On the way, Monsieur Arouet told me something
of the circumstances of the rogue's death, which were plain
enough, the very obverse of the complexity and ritual which
had attended the death of Signor Molin. It seems that at
three or four o'clock by the angelus, the painter had gone
out to take a cup of wine with his cronies. When he had not
returned by morning, his apprentices were sent to search for
him and found his body floating in the Rio del Battello near
the ghetto. He had been bludgeoned and knifed, and the
little money he had had about him was stolen. The crime
would have seemed one of robbery but for two details. The
first was that none of Pasticcio's fellow topers had seen him

or arranged to see him on that evening. The second was that, in the afternoon, some villain (a Friulian by all accounts – though that means nothing, since they form the common class of link-boys and other loafers) had brought a note for the painter and taken away a reply. The note could not be found, and it was surmised that Pasticcio had sortied that evening for some purpose other than the one he had admitted.

'How did you learn these things?' I asked Monsieur Arouet.

His answer showed me something of his far-sightedness. 'When we last visited Pasticcio, I gave the address of my lodgings to his journeyman, Dossena, together with a gratuity, and advised him to send word to me should anything untoward happen.'

'What!' I exclaimed. 'Do you mean that you expected this murder?'

'No, not that. But it seemed to me there was some deep business between Pasticcio and the Palazzo Molin. Anything was possible. However, that is enough. We are here. Please God we shall not be called upon to make our condolences to the widow. She is no Signora Beatrice.'

In evidence of the truth of that last remark, as we approached the doors of the late Pasticcio, we could hear the wailing of females from one of the upper rooms to a chorus of brats screaming, barking dogs, clucking chickens and an accompaniment of curses and fisticuffs as if the mourners were trying to prove their grief by assaulting one another. An apprentice answered the door, and upon our introductions summoned Signor Dossena. He arrived covered in marble-dust.

'Lustrissimi, forgive me,' he said. 'Come in, come in. I was not certain you would respond to my message. Alas, our poor house is too disordered to offer you refreshment.'

This was certainly true if the noise of breaking furniture were an indication. The building seemed to rock from the tumult. Signor Dossena cast his eyes upward (whether to Heaven or the upper floor, which was shaking and causing a general descent of dust, I know not). 'Money,' he whispered confidingly. 'The master was a close man, and no-one knows where he kept his money. He owes wages to everyone.'

'You are an obliging fellow,' said Monsieur Arouet, taking up the hint, 'and I shall see that you do not go unrewarded.'

'Signore, you shame me!' protested Dossena insincerely.

'As you please, but no doubt we all live with shame as we live with bad teeth and falling hair. May we speak somewhere?'

We were taken to the painting-studio, which was the lightest part of the house. As before, the room was crowded with canvases, batons, pots of glue and varnishes and a pervasive smell of oils and soaps. Dossena despatched the apprentices to play ball, torture cats, or what-you-will in the yard. We seated ourselves upon stools.

'What is that lovely painting?' I asked. My eyes had let upon a canvas which, so far as I could tell, was almost finished. It was of a supper scene. The painter had captured such an extraordinary subtlety of light, and the serenity of the central figure was so perfect, that even I, who claim no knowledge of these things, was moved by the beauty of the work.

Dossena glanced at the piece and answered indifferently, 'It is Christ and the Disciples at Emmaus, done in the Dutch manner. Now, Signori, how may I help you?'

Monsieur Arouet fixed his eyes firmly on the other. 'I will be direct with you,' he said. 'I wish to know what work you have done for the Palazzo Molin. No more evasions.'

'I am embarrassed,' came the answer. 'Truly I do not know,

nor how to discover it. Signor Pasticcio was – Lord save him – but a bad painter, fit only for copyist work, and poor enough at that. For that reason, among others, he kept us at a distance from his patrons so that he could claim credit for our work and we should never have the chance to build a reputation free of his.'

'I suspected as much,' said Monsieur Arouet, and he now unwrapped the painting he had brought with him, which was of St Sebastian. 'I will try to help. Tell me: this canvas, was it painted here?'

Dossena looked at it, but only briefly. 'My own trade is that of sculptor and wood-carver,' he said. 'A moment, please.'

He went to the window and through the broken shutter yelled, 'Enrico!' into the yard. He continued, 'We have a painter who is a Dutchman. While we wait, may I examine the frame?' Monsieur Arouet gave it to him and Dossena inspected it closely. 'It's modern,' he said, 'but well done. Not my workmanship. One of the apprentices could have made it. How did you discover its secret?'

'The woodworm holes,' said Monsieur Arouet.

'Ah, yes. So difficult to imitate. Here is Enrico.' He handed the picture back and introduced a small, neatly made Dutchman of unassuming appearance. Dossena indicated the painting to him with the question, 'Did you paint this?'

Signor Enrico wiped his hands on his apron and took the painting. He went to the window and examined it by daylight. Quite at ease and with a note of pride in his voice, he returned it to Monsieur Arouet. 'Yes,' he said. 'That's mine. Quattrocento, Sienese school. Not my favourite kind of work, but I think I didn't make a bad fist of it.'

'Is it a pastiche or a copy of an original?' asked Monsieur Arouet.

'A copy. The original was brought in supposedly for cleaning, but Signor Pasticcio asked me to paint a copy.'

'Do you know to whom the original belonged, or where it is now?'

'Not a clue. I never saw the client.'

'I see.' Monsieur Arouet wrapped the painting thoughtfully. 'It obviously goes without saying that you have done other work of a similar nature. Do you recall a painting' – he gestured – 'a little thing about so big? It was of Christ and the Woman taken in Adultery?'

'Style of Raphael?'

'Yes.'

The painter looked to Signor Dossena for guidance. The latter nodded.

'Very well,' said Signor Enrico. 'I confess to that one, too. It was a nice piece, but not Raphael – an imitator. Very nice for all that. And don't mistake me: it was old, not a modern copy. I don't know if you'd call it a forgery or just something done in the same style. It was very passable.'

'At all events,' interrupted Monsieur Arouet, 'whatever the status of the original work, you copied that one, too?'

'That's right. And, before you ask, no, I don't know who the client was. It wasn't of any interest to me.'

It was evident we should get no further, neither with Signor Dossena nor with Enrico the Dutchman – not that I believe they were hiding anything from us. Signor Pasticcio had been secretive about his business, and his secrets had gone to the grave with him. Nevertheless, we had learned certain facts that seemed incontrovertible. Someone at the Palazzo Molin had committed a fraud against the late Signor Alessandro: had stolen certain of his paintings and replaced them by forgeries executed at the studio of Pasticcio.

'However,' said Monsieur Arouet as we set off towards our lodgings, 'there is an insuperable obstacle to the theory that whoever killed Signor Alessandro was an inhabitant of his house. What? You do not see it?'

Humbly I confessed that I did not. (And I confess also to the Reader that I was not much appreciative of my friend's repeating his question: 'What? You don't see?' and other remarks to the same effect. But I was learning to live with his vanity.)

'No, I do not see,' I told him firmly.

His malicious old eyes glittered with pleasure. 'The point is simple, though perplexing,' he said. 'If the murderer had had access to the Palazzo Molin, he would have returned the picture to its rightful place on the wall. Any connection between the forgeries and the killing (if we assume such a connection to exist) would then have been disguised. Therefore, dear Ludovico, though both matters would seem to be inextricably bound together, it follows that the thief of the paintings and the murderer of Signor Alessandro cannot be the same person: for the thief, by definition, had entry to the Palazzo Molin, whereas the murderer (as I have just demonstrated) did not.' And now, seeing my discomfiture, he smiled sadly and, I believe, compassionately at one whom he had defeated and said, 'Those are the facts, I'm afraid. "Qui nisi sunt veri, ratio quoque falsa sit omnis." '*

I had *not* seen. I had *not* understood. The facts were plain and the inferences irrefutable. Yet the obvious is not obvious except to a mind that sees clearly. Recalling my childhood in Bavaria, I thought, "Kinder und Narren sagen die Wahrheit."† Was Monsieur Arouet a child or a fool? In retrospect it is possible to understand the logic of his thought, and treat it as a simple case of reasoning. What is impossible to convey is the shock, the sense of

---

* If they are not true, then Reason itself is totally false – *Lucretius*.
† Children and fools speak the truth – *proverb*.

outrage, experienced when his light suddenly illuminated my blindness. For I thought myself fit for all the common experiences of the world and as able to link two thoughts together as well as the next man. To be confronted by one who, in his curious simplicity, collected ideas like a child picking stones from the road and who could see the perfectly commonplace relationships between them was humbling. Was I a fool, or was he?

However, I am neither quick of intellect nor eloquent and, faced with my own consternation, I changed the subject and asked, 'Shall I see you tonight? Signor Feltrinelli tells me that my patron has invited his friends to supper. I am to sing.'

'Indeed?' said Monsieur Arouet, and raised an eyebrow. 'No, I am not invited. Signor Morosini has become cold towards me and no longer offers his society or confidence. What do you think, Ludovico? Am I pressing too hard upon his heels?'

CHAPTER TWENTY-SIX

A Letter from one Nobleman to Another

Venice
15th February 17—

My noble Lord,

Some time ago I was pleased to receive a letter in Your Grace's hand recommending to my attention a certain Personage who was then travelling Italy under a nom de guerre, *but whose true name was one which ornamented the pinnacle of Art, Philosophy and Letters. Moreover, though Your Grace used language which was not intended to be understood by the vulgar or uninitiated, I recognised in it the call which any Widow's Son may make upon another, and this added an onus of Duty to what I would have done in any case to oblige Your Grace. Indeed, I did not regard Your Grace's request in any other light than that Your Grace was conferring a Favour upon me. For to receive into one's society a person of such Renown and at the same time have the opportunity to be of some small service to a Brother is in the nature of a Blessing not a burden. Therefore*

*you may imagine that it was with Joy and Anticipation
that I opened my house to the gentleman and that I looked
forward to the stimulation of his Wit, the wisdom of his
Philosophy, and the lustre which he would confer on my
own Reputation. Nor can I say that in these respects I
have been entirely disappointed. Why, then, do I write to
Your Grace?*

*Supposing Your Grace to be a connoisseur of Art and not
a mere collector of furnishings, you will, I doubt not, have
experienced on occasion a sense that a piece, notwithstanding
all outward appearance, is wrong. To put a name and
reasons to this sensation is impossible: indeed, it often seems
to belie what one sees before one's eyes, so that if one had
to give Reasons one should feel foolish. Truly, there have
been cases in which a piece has filled me with Uncertainty
because of its very Perfections, its exact correspondence to
the Platonic type of such pieces. Do I make myself clear?
I fear not.*

*Your Grace informed me that the person in question had
incurred the displeasure of His Most Christian Majesty
because of a certain Freedom of Thought and a suspicion
of Irreligion, so that he might no longer publish his Works
in France. Under those circumstances he purposed to visit
Venice to have a book printed and published here and then
disseminated into his own country. This I understood and
accepted; and, as a corollary, that the Author would seek
subscribers to defray the Cost of the exercise – in fact, I
have myself subscribed and feel honoured that in so small
a way I can increase the Treasury of Letters. Thus far I
make no complaint. Genius must earn its bread. And, if
the operations of our Friend were confined to those strictly
necessary to this end, I should applaud them. But – or so
it seems to your Correspondent – it goes beyond the demands
of our Friend's situation when he produces proposals for*

the undertaking of a new State Lottery and importunes my connections to endorse this object. Likewise when he offers, upon commission, to invest any funds placed at his disposal in the security of the Rentes sur l'Hotel de Ville at a certain favourable Discount. At this I ask myself if he is a Philosopher or a common stock-jobber: Aristotle or Law?

Of his Wit and Brilliance I have no doubt, though they are often expressed with an acerbity of tongue and asperity of manner that offend Polite Discourse. He has a mind of great Acuity and, to the embarrassment of lesser mortals, incisive powers of Reasoning that lay every Proposition bare to its essentials. Undoubtedly he is clever. But is he wise? It seems that I see in him not Olympian detachment but waspishness and Vanity. Moreover his Erudition — upon pressing him — appears to be all on the surface. His knowledge of music and painting is no more than that of a Gentleman of moderate Education. His Latin consists of well-chosen Maxims from the Classical Authors but has no depth; and when have Knowledge and Virtue ever been accounted the same? Odi homines ignava opera, philosopha sententia.* He has no Greek. In short, Your Grace, though our Friend is a man of uncommon parts, his title as Philosopher does not seem to justify the high opinion of the World. Indeed (and here I come to the Heart of that which troubles me), I begin to wonder if he has not earned another title: that of Rogue and Charlatan.

I apologise for disturbing Your Grace with my misgivings and for the Severity of my language with regard to one (if it truly is he) who enjoys the World's good opinion and Your Grace's Favour and Protection. And indeed the matter would be of no importance if our Friend

---

* I hate men whose words are philosophical but whose deeds are base
— *Aulus Gellius.*

should prove to be merely some Mountebank in borrowed clothes, amusing himself for a little space at our expense. However — and I come to the crux and beg Your Grace's discretion — the fellow begins to meddle unbidden in Deep Affairs which touch upon the interest of the State and affect my own Position closely. He delves and speculates and uncovers those things which were best left hidden, and will not be diverted from his Quest. He might be despatched and told to involve himself no more in the business of the Republic. However, for so long as he is reputed a Philosopher and Sage, I am reluctant to incur the Censure that would attend such an action or to displease Your Grace by such apparent Ingratitude. Hence this letter and my request.

I beg Your Grace that you should by the next post after receipt of this letter either confirm the Credentials of our Friend or expose the Imposture of one who trades upon our Good Will and the Reputation of a greater man to whom all proper Honour is due. I beg all indulgence and Forgiveness if I should have misprised myself as to a person of genuine Merit. I appeal to Your Grace in the interest of that Work upon which Hiram first embarked, and as to which we are mere stones in the building.

I remain as ever Your Grace's true Friend and Brother in the Great Work.

et cetera

CHAPTER TWENTY-SEVEN

Signor Ludovico's Narrative

It was the middle of the afternoon when I returned to my garret. My mind was in turmoil as I struggled to comprehend a problem in which nothing was as it seemed. We were moving – so I thought – not towards a solution but towards the uncovering of ever deeper mysteries. It was as if the Almighty were drawing veils of illusion and misdirection over the affair, in mockery of our mortal powers of reasoning. This conflict between Reason and Mystery was, I believe, the motive force behind Monsieur Arouet's passion to search out the truth. He could not allow that Reason should fail; for, if it did, he would have to admit that his Philosophy lacked all foundation and that he could not do. Consider his character. If he were wrong about the intelligibility of the world and his own intellectual powers, what was left of him? He would become no more than a ridiculous old man full of arrogance and vanity.

I mounted the rickety stairs that led to my room, thinking nothing of the stillness that had settled on the house. I opened the door and entered. Immediately I was seized from behind, my left arm pinioned to my back, and a dagger-point was pressed to my throat.

'Good day to you, Ludovico,' said Fra Angelo.

The Jesuit was sitting on the bed that Tosello and I shared. He had been reading his breviary, waiting patiently for my return.

'You may release him, brother,' he said to the unseen stranger who held me in his grasp. 'You will do nothing foolish, will you, Ludovico?'

I composed myself and, with such shreds of dignity as I possess, swore by the Virgin that I should do his bidding, and asked how I had occasioned his anger that I should be so treated. Fra Angelo made a gesture and I was released. I glanced over my shoulder and saw a huge masked figure armed with poniard, rapier and pistol. Was it Signor Girolamo Molin? I do not know, because in the interview that followed he spoke not a word. The shock of release caused me to fall to my knees where – I admit my weakness – I shed some tears.

The Jesuit raised himself to his feet, approached me, extended his hands to mine and lifted me up. In a kindly voice he said, 'Have no fear, Ludovico. Are you not our brother in the work of God?'

'Most assuredly, Father,' I answered.

'And you will keep the vow you made when last we spoke?'

'As God and His angels are my witness.'

'Then sit and let us talk.'

The fellow in the mask offered me a stool and I took it gratefully. The mild tones of my Jesuit interrogator, belied by his calculating eyes, were peculiarly horrible. He continued, 'Well? I am pleased to see that you are free. Did I not promise you that you should be freed?'

Foolishly I replied, 'I had understood it was my patron who procured my pardon.'

The priest's companion grunted angrily. Fra Angelo,

however, said in an even tone, 'No, Ludovico, you are mistaken – though you may be forgiven for your mistake. Only your accuser could withdraw the charge against you, and he is a bitter enemy of Signor Morosini. So, you see, your patron could do nothing to help you – *can* do nothing to help you. He is concerned now only with his own name and reputation and would cheerfully sacrifice you to that end. Place no faith in him. He is deeply embroiled in this affair and his destruction, by the will of God, is assured.'

I thanked the Jesuit for that information and for his efforts to obtain my release. He disclaimed any praise. He was merely an instrument of the Almighty – apparently.

'But now,' he went on, 'I must call upon you to return the favour that has been conferred on you by Divine Grace.'

'Command me,' I said. What else could I have answered that would not have left me dead upon the spot? It was my impression that the masked man would have been more than happy to assist Providence by despatching me.

'Tonight,' said the Jesuit, 'you are to sing at a supper given by Signor Morosini for his brethren. Wait! I do not require an answer yet. At about one hour after the angelus, your patron will leave the Ca' di Spagna to meet in secret conclave with his fellow conspirators.'

Astonished, I blurted out, 'How do you know this?'

'I know it because I have Signor Morosini watched narrowly' was the patient reply. He leaned forward. 'Now I come to your part. Knowing what I have told you, I require you to follow Signor Morosini and spy upon this gathering; and then report to me. I require a witness to the activities of these vile atheists.'

'But . . . I . . . I mean . . . Surely you already have a spy who can undertake this task? Why do you require my service?'

There was no answer. The Jesuit's face showed only his

insane calmness and calculation. And, as to his companion, he was masked and I could see only the implacable whiteness of the mask and a pair of eyes glittering with (so I fancied) anger. However, a moment's thought told me that no answer was needed. I said, 'If I am discovered, Signor Morosini and his fellows will kill me, will they not?'

With pleasant indifference to my terror, the Jesuit answered, 'In such a case you will be a martyr to the cause of the Church. There is no greater glory.'

Following this invitation to commit suicide from my two friends (as I suppose I must call them, since they expressed such concern for the well-being of my soul), I sat for while in a state of terror accompanied (I confess) by swearing and the occasional tear. Then, having told myself for the tenth time that I was out of my depth in these matters, I decided I must go to Monsieur Arouet and lay everything before him. I put on my hat and cloak and ventured forth.

The day had turned foul with wind and rain. On such a day, when everything is obscured by cloud and spray, Venice looks like a great fleet fleeing a storm: the churches rearing from the sea like galleons battling the weather, but everything else like dismasted wrecks streaming with water and pounded by the waves. I forswore a gondola and, huddled in my soaking garments, scuttled through the maze of narrow lanes, empty of all life, until I had reached the Frenchman's lodgings. There I was received with kindness and good-tempered amusement at my bedraggled state. I was given a glass of brandy, and the landlady was commanded to take my cloak and dry it as best she might.

'Well?' enquired Monsieur Arouet. 'And what brings you here?'

While he was being so solicitous about my comfort, I had taken the opportunity to look about my friend's room.

I noticed, upon his writing-desk, a quantity of gold coins, and various notes drawn upon banks, appearing at a glance to be a large sum. This contradicted my earlier impression that Monsieur Arouet was in straitened circumstances, if not actually destitute. It seemed to me also that he had commenced packing his possessions – more than he had brought with him, since there was a new trunk – and these included some new clothes rather finer than I had ever seen him wear.

'Are you intending to leave Venice?' I asked, sounding perhaps more distressed than was appropriate. But you must remember that I was still reeling from the shock given me by Fra Angelo. And, also, I must allow (as should be obvious to the Reader) that I admired my friend intensely for the qualities of his mind and he had been unfeignedly kind towards me and did not despise my condition.

Monsieur Arouet studied me for a moment and gave a crooked smile. He extended a hand to cover mine and said, 'You reveal yourself, Ludovico. I am touched at your concern. Yes, I do intend to leave Venice shortly, since my private business is almost completed. But do not be afraid. I shall not leave you naked before your enemies. I shall throw light on all the mysteries that have troubled us, because it amuses me to do so. After that – well, after that, I shall quit this city, and then everything that has passed between us will be a fond recollection. Now – we have digressed – tell me your story.'

This I proceeded to do, relating to him everything that had passed between myself, Fra Angelo and his masked companion. Monsieur Arouet listened and his face became sombre and thoughtful.

At the end he asked, 'Are you certain that the masked man was Signor Girolamo Molin?'

'How can I be certain?' I answered. 'He did not speak a

word. I could form only a general impression. He was . . .
I mean . . .'

'Calm yourself. I understand. You are not certain, but it
seems likely that it was Signor Girolamo. Very well. Let
us continue. Those two fanatics desire you to follow Signor
Morosini this evening and to spy on the proceedings between
himself and his friends – do I understand you aright?'

'You do, and, Monsieur . . . I am . . . Oh, my God!' I
broke off and sobbed. 'God help me . . .'

'You are terrified,' said Monsieur Arouet. 'That is under-
standable.' He stood up and paced the room quietly for a
moment, stretching his angular limbs so that they cracked.
Then he returned to me. He said, 'I, too, wish you to spy
upon Signor Morosini but – stay, Ludovico, I have not
finished – I shall not leave you unsupported as those two
villains would do. No! We shall meet, shortly after the
angelus has chimed and we shall do this thing together.
There! Does that please you?'

'Monsieur,' I mumbled, 'as always I am grateful to you.
I was . . . I am a coward – there, I've said it!'

'No. You are a man of ordinary courage, Ludovico, neither
more nor less, and that is not a bad thing. Consider Signor
Girolamo. He is a man of unusual courage, willing to fight
strangers at every turn. But would you wish to be like him?
Jealous and an idiot? Let us recognise ourselves for what we
are and then, if we prepare ourselves rightly, we may yet do
extraordinary things. So rest assured, I shall be with you
tonight, and you shall protect me as much as I protect you.
However . . .'

'Monsieur?'

He looked at me seriously. 'I have one further request.
There is a point that I must resolve, and only you – by
cunning and courage – can get me the knowledge I need
to resolve it.'

Thereupon he told me his request. And, though it was not without its risks, such was my confidence in my friend and my desire for his regard that I undertook to fulfil it. Thus he was proven right. I became courageous above the limit of my natural courage.

'Now,' said Monsieur Arouet when he had finished giving me his instructions, 'we come to the matter of the coded message which has so vexed my intelligence and which I promised to explain to you.'

'You have indeed deciphered it?'

'Certainly. Did I not promise you that I should?'

He had laid out upon the table a sheaf of papers which, so I supposed, represented his calculations. He pondered over these awhile so that I began to wonder.

I asked him, 'Do you have doubts?'

He shook himself like one rudely awakened, pierced me with his gaze and answered, 'No. That is, not insofar as it concerns the words. They are plain and my calculations are irrefutable. But the meaning to be drawn from the words — ah, Ludovico, who can ever comprehend the significance of language when used by another? Still, let us see what we can make of it.'

With that he laid before me his copy of the cryptic message and I mentally recited its haunting rythms:

> I speak of the First and the Second of the First
> and the Ten that are First.
> My First is the Third of the First.
> My Second is the First of the Seventh.
> My Third is the First of the Fourth.
> My Fourth is the Third of the Second.
> My Fifth is the Sixth of the Fifth.
> My Sixth is the Seventh of the Sixth.
> My Seventh is the Third of the Eighth.

My Eighth is the Fourth of the Fourth.
My Ninth is the First of the Fourth.
My Tenth is the First of the Seventh.
My Eleventh is the Second of the Seventh.
My Twelfth is the First of the First.
My Thirteenth is the First of the Third.
My Fourteenth is the Third of the Fifth.
My Fifteenth is the Twelfth of the Ninth.
My Sixteenth is the Seventh of the Fourth.
My Seventeenth is the Fifth of the Eighth.
My Eighteenth is the Ninth of the Tenth.
My Nineteenth is the First of the Fourth.
Thus are nineteen contained in ten that are in the First
who is the Greatest.

It was difficult to regard the lines as other than verse and they possessed (or so I felt) a mysterious beauty. Yet, I suspected that these qualities were mere accidents and lay in the receptivity of the reader and not in the inventions of the author. The latter had created something that he had not thought to do: achieving by chance an effect that others could not do by artifice. I thought: how unfathomable is our nature! – and then rejected the thought for its banality.

Monsieur Arouet now set down another sheet upon which the following was written, which I have tried to represent as accurately as I can just as he wrote it.

Orso IpAto
Teodato IpAto
Galla Gaulo
Domenico MonEgaRio
Maurizio GaLbaIo

SCHERZO

Giovanni GalbaiO
Obelario DEgli Antenori
Angelo PaRtIcipazio
Giustiniano ParticipaziO
Giovanni ParticipAzio

Ten names (for I recognised them as such) but names I did not know. They were not the names of Signor Morosini's supper-guests; they had never been mentioned in our enquiries. I was at a loss, and Monsieur Arouet could see that I was, for he treated me to a smile of good-humoured malice.

'I see I have you foxed!' he said. 'Well, so be it, and you are not to be blamed since I have wrestled with this conundrum until I thought my brain would burst with the effort. And yet,' he added as if regretting something, 'it is, at bottom, a simple substitution code requiring no great understanding once one has grasped the key. It was Signor Feltrinelli who gave me the latter when he said I should direct my attention to the "First" rather than the "Ten".'

'But these *are* the "Ten",' I interjected.

'Indeed they are. But the "Ten" of what? There is the heart of the puzzle. Can you enlighten me?'

'I cannot,' I admitted humbly.

'No. But think, Ludovico! Where are we? In Venice! And who, in this State, is the First above all others, the god within this little teeming world?'

'The Doge!' I exclaimed, as the realisation broke upon me.

'Precisely! The "Ten who are First" are none other than the first ten Doges from the foundation of the Republic. And "the Second of the First" as appears in the introduction to our cryptic verse refers to the second word in the Doge's name. Now, consider this!'

He placed a second sheet before me, which I reproduce for the Reader. It was a column of nineteen figures – a number which I saw corresponded to the number of lines in the core of the verse. Thus:

3/1
1/7
1/4
3/2
6/5
7/6
3/8
4/4
1/4
1/7
2/7
1/1
1/3
3/5
12/9
7/4
5/8
9/10
1/4

'I have merely reduced the verse to numbers in the order of the lines. So "My First is the Third of the First" means that the first letter of the message is the third letter in the surname of the first Doge and I have represented it numerically as 3/1, being the number of the letter and the number of the Doge – it is in fact the letter A. The other numbers follow correspondingly. And' – he picked up the first sheet – 'I have marked all those letters so identified, though not in the order they are used. The order is represented in this column of numbers. Now let us marry the two: letters and numbers in the order given in the verse.'

For my benefit (since he was well familiar with the message) he showed me how each letter issued from the list of Doges, taking each in its correct turn, and I transcribed the result which appeared thus: ADMAIOREMDEIGLORIAM

I did not immediately recognise the language nor the intervals between the words, since the latter were not represented. I repeated the sounds as best I could until, by some process of natural understanding they seemed to fall into their proper components. And when this was done, as if the clouds had parted and light shone upon me which burned my eyes, I gave a shout. And what a shout! in which relief, joy and — yes — fear were intermingled.

'Ad maiorem Dei gloriam! That is it! Ad maiorem Dei gloriam! Yes! Yes! So simple! My God, it is so simple!' If I did not dance in my exuberance it was only because I was under the dark, thoughtful eyes of my friend.

He allowed me my moment of enthusiasm and then said curtly, 'Well, Ludovico, there you have it: "Ad maiorem Dei gloriam — To the greater glory of God." It is the motto of the Jesuit Order and as fair an emblem as was ever made to disguise a foul conspiracy of hypocrisy and ignorance. You have met its representatives, Fra Angelo and his deluded minion, Signor Girolamo Molin. What do you make of them? Are they not fine specimens, these men who would terrorise you into doing their bidding?'

'Perhaps they are themselves afraid,' I answered. I was thinking of what the Jesuit had told me: that the Crowns of Spain and Portugal had turned against the Order and that this might presage the end of all they held dear. I held no particular fondness for the Jesuits or any other class of priest, but I was not as fiercely anti-clerical as Monsieur Arouet. He saw the Church as the enemy of Reason. 'Like all of us, they have their fears,' I said by way of repetition, and for reasons inexplicable to myself I felt sorry for those two madmen and all those like them – not excluding Monsieur Arouet who (I now realised) understood himself but dimly and did not see the fanatic in his own soul.

'We shall see,' he answered less ferociously. 'Yes, we shall see. What this message does not tell us is whether it was written *by* the Jesuits or *against* them. Does it claim credit for the murder or seek to divert blame from the true murderer?'

Monsieur Arouet put down the clue, which was no clue because it could be understood in two ways. Yet it was not without meaning. It told us something of the mind of the person who had devised it.

CHAPTER TWENTY-EIGHT

Signor Ludovico's Narrative

To execute the commission imposed upon me by Monsieur Arouet, which was no less than to discover the evidence which would prove the guilt or innocence of a certain person, I returned to the Ca' di Spagna in some trepidation. It was now twenty o'clock or thereabouts.* I was admitted without difficulty and asked the doorman the whereabouts of Signor Alfonso, my patron's *valet de chambre*. I was told that I should find him in the kitchen.

Signor Alfonso was a small, ill-favoured fellow; but, like others in the tribe of valets, he fancied himself a Macaroni, and Signor Morosini, in his liberal way, indulged his servant's habits of dress and mien. These were to wear his master's old clothes, suitably tailored to his figure, together with a wig and a lavish application of powder, patches and rouge. I found this dandy paying court to one of the maids, promising to advise her upon her wardrobe and to dress her hair in the Parisian fashion. Signor Alfonso was also a *friseur*.

---

* Counted after the evening angelus and therefore some time in the afternoon of the next day.

'Signor Alfonso,' I said, 'may I have a moment of your attention?'

The valet broke from his conversation and made me a bow (it being his habit to address any well-dressed fellow-servant as a gentleman, so sustaining his own character, and to lard his conversation with references to antique authors of whom he understood not a word).

'La! Signor Ludovico, you disturb me in friendly intercourse with this fair Scylla (as the Romans would call her) or Charybdis (in the language of the Greeks). Excuse me, my dear,' he added, directing a killing smile at the maid. 'Your servant, Signore.'

'I am infinitely obliged.'

We went to a corner of the kitchen near the close-stool or privy.

'You afright me!' said Signor Alfonso. 'Is the matter so secret that we must discuss it in this fragrant place?'

'Truly it is a matter of some confidence and I therefore rely upon you, knowing you to be a gentleman of discretion.'

The valet pouted and put an arm around me to prove the justice of my confidence in him. 'I am all ears.'

'My thanks to you. By the by, where is Signor Morosini at this moment? I imagine you must dress him for this evening. I know he intends to make an excursion of a couple of hours once the angelus has sounded.'

'That is a little time away and I flatter myself that I can dress our master faster, and yet with more finesse, than any man alive. At present he is in Signor Feltrinelli's office reckoning the accounts of his estate, which is something he does about once in a month.'

'Then his private cabinet is vacant?'

'It was when I had occasion to go there, ten minutes ago. Why do you ask?'

'Because, my dear friend, I wish to go there.'

Insofar as a man may be said to blanch under a mask of dead-white paint, the valet did so. I felt his grip tighten about my shoulder before he loosed me altogether. In a confused whisper he said, 'What are you up to, man? I didn't take you for a thief!'

'I am not a thief,' I assured him. 'I desire only a moment's access and, on my honour, I shall take nothing.'

'And if we are discovered?'

'Then you shall say you caught me sneaking about the place and apprehended me.' I swallowed, appalled my own courage. 'You will be praised for your diligence and I shall accept the disgrace of any penalty.'

This proposal calmed Signor Alfonso, but he still looked at me narrowly. He said, 'Accepting what you say, Signor Ludovico, what advantage does your proposal have for me?'

And so we came to the crux of the matter in this corrupt world. Fortunately, Monsieur Arouet had provided me with some cogent means of persuasion. I withdrew two zecchini from my pocket, which proved a soothing sight for my friend. His eyes glittered with cupidity, but he whispered that I should put them away until we were out of the kitchen. 'Come, Signor Ludovico,' he said aloud. 'I have a compound of Hungary water which I bought recently from a Turk. I should be grateful for your opinion as to the merit of its scent.' He turned and treated his *inamorata* to a bow. 'I must leave you, my fair Chimaera, my Medusa, but I shall return when I have finished my business with this gentleman.' So saying, he led me from the kitchen and I gave him his money.

In the absence of the Contessa, the servants of the Ca' di Spagna had fallen into laxer ways and we were free to make our way through the chambers and corridors of the house without disturbing anyone except a single drudge who paid us no attention. This was as well since we made an absurd sight. My companion was so affected by nerves that he started at every creak of the stairs and would enter a room only by peering through the doorway like a spy. We proceeded so slowly in our caution that I wondered that Signor Morosini did not finish his conference with the factor and return to surprise us. At length we reached the door to our master's private cabinet, which I had visited only once: namely, when he received me following my arrest and release. It was the recollection of this recent event that had directed my attention hither.

We entered. I scanned the walls and furnishings. It was here that Signor Morosini kept those small works of art and *objets de vertu* that were most dear to him.

'What are you looking for?' enquired Signor Alfonso, watching me doubtfully, fearing still that I had theft in mind.

'I have no time to explain,' I answered, and I advanced on my goal which I had discerned affixed to the further wall. I would have accomplished my purpose except that, at that very point, there was a noise behind us and the door opened.

It was Signor Feltrinelli.

A Letter from a Brother to his—to Sister

Venice
19th February 17—

Dearest Sister,
   Your poor Brother writes in some Haste. Yet I shall try to give you a faithful account of recent Extraordinary Events which look likely to Overturn the World. It is a

Dangerous Time, for both the Innocent and the Guilty,
and I do not know what or if I shall be able to write to
you again.

What gives rise to this situation? It is this: that the
Murder, of which I have written to you and which was so
Mysterious in its nature, has been solved. The murderer is
Signor Morosini!

The Discovery was made within this last hour and
this was the manner of it. I was closeted with Signor
Morosini in my chamber, balancing the accounts of the
Estate and adjusting the payment of Specie between us.
For all his affected languor, my master has a keen Eye on
his Financial Affairs (especially since my predecessor was
dismissed) and we engage upon this reckoning regularly.

Our business finished, Signor Morosini went to attend
to some matter in his library. He asked me to bring him a
quizzing-glass from his private Cabinet (he does not admit
any defect of his eyesight). I went thither and opened the
door of the room, upon which I startled two Rogues who
were prying among my lord's effects like a pair of Thieves.

The two in question were Signor L——, an effeminate
Coxcomb and musician of sorts, and the Valet, who might
have had occasion to be there but whose guilty look made
clear that he was up to no good.

'Fie, Signori!' I exclaimed. 'What do I find here?'

Signor L——turned to me, composed himself rapidly,
bowed and said, 'La! Signor Feltrinelli, my friend, how
you have made my heart flutter. Please – I urge you – do
not take amiss what you see. Out of friendship and respect I
would have asked your permission, but the matter is urgent
and you were engaged otherwise. It touches upon the murder,
in which you have expressed such interest. Hear me out, I
beg you!'

The fellow's impertinence annoyed me, but I was

interested in anything he might say concerning the murder.
He has become intimate with Monsieur A———, of whom I
have told you. This Frenchman is a pretended Philosopher,
but, to my mind, a sharper and such another Charlatan as
Signor B——— the Magician. However, he shows a certain
mental agility with which he has turned Signor L——— into
his Creature. Together, they have been investigating the
crime. The poor Fool has no notion of the man he is dealing
with, or that in such an affair of Treachery and Illusion it
is as likely that Monsieur A——— is the Murderer as well
as anyone else – but that he now had a revelation for me. I
dismissed the valet before hearing it.

'Signor Feltrinelli,' lisped Signor L———, 'this is what
we have discovered. On the night of his Death, Signor
Molin ventured from his house for an appointment with his
Murderer, carrying with him a small Package, wrapped
in a Cloak. This Package was stolen by the Murderer and
we must suppose that it was upon that account that Signor
Molin was killed.'

I was anxious for further particulars as to how these
Discoveries were made, but Signor Morosini was waiting on
his quizzing glass. Signor L——— continued, 'When we visited
the Widow of the Deceased, my friend, Monsieur A———,
had occasion to notice that some of the Paintings in Signor
Molin's collection were Copies got up cleverly in the antique
manner. He has surmised that there has been a Commerce
in Paintings stolen from Signor Molin by an unknown
person and sold to someone equally unknown. It was such a
Painting that Signor Molin had about him on his Death
when he went to confront the Thief. Evidently he had
discovered the Imposture.'

Naturally, I was astonished at this Revelation! I asked
by what process of Reasoning these Discoveries led to Signor
Morosini's private cabinet.

He answered, 'Returning to the Palazzo Molin, we saw
that a particular Painting had been removed from the wall
and not replaced. It was of Our Lord and the Woman
Taken in Adultery. When I was earlier in this room I
noticed a small Picture, and although I am no Scholar,
it seems to me to be of the Subject in Question.' He pointed
at the Picture, and I believe he was right as to its Subject.
'How long has Signor Molin owned it?'

'About a month,' I answered truthfully. 'But I have
no Knowledge as to its previous owner or how our Master
acquired it.'

'Will you permit me?' asked Signor L——. I looked
cautiously at my watch and said (probably stiffly as you so
Reproach me, dear Sister) that he might proceed. He drew
out a Pin and stuck it in several places about the Picture-
frame, before offering it to me. 'Please,' he said, 'will you
please probe the Holes.' I obliged him and stuck the Pin
into the Holes where it entered only with Difficulty, as I
admitted when he examined me on the point. 'Then this
picture is the genuine one!' he pronounced. I asked why. He
gave an explanation about Wormholes which, like many
explanations of technique, made Sense at the time and is
now impossible to remember.

But consider! A Painting was stolen from Signor
Molin. It has now appeared in the Possession of Signor
Morosini. On the night of his Murder, Signor Molin set
forth to challenge the Thief. I said something in defence of
my Master, but the facts are incontrovertible. Nor can it
be denied that he had Opportunity to kill Signor Molin.
Though the Object of his Excursion on the night of the
Murder is not known (saving what we now know) the fact
of it is proven by the Testimony of his valet and, doubtless,
of other servants.

'Signore!' I protested. 'You overwhelm me. A man can

321

scarce take it in. But I must go to Signor Morosini, and you must leave Forthwith.'

This he did.

Thus my story. You will draw what Moral you wish. I will speak of my other affairs since they colour everything, even this account of the Murder and its Solution.

It has rankled in my Heart that you have considered me an unfeeling Brute. I have admitted that my manner is stiff and uncivil but have tried to explain to you my Passion for One who surpasses me in Virtue as much as in Rank. So be it. She has rejected me before I can even press my suit since what I offer is an absurdity as the World stands. I am left mute: before both my Mistress and the common Mob – indeed I can scarce express myself to you, dear Sister, and, if in these blunt words you hear some Pain of Feeling, I beg you to imagine that it is but a tenth part of what I feel in my Soul! I am racked in Torment. I feel my limbs torn and Knives enter my body. If I were wont to shed tears, I should shed them.

Yet, I feel no anger against her. She has not rejected anything; for it has not been openly offered. At worst she may be accused of Blindness. This Forgivingness on my part (and this is what surprises me and makes me wonder if I know myself) is not particular to her. Though hampered by my past habits, I seem (for all is seeming) to have become softer in my Nature. Why do I permit Signor L—— to call me 'dear friend'? Because, for all that he is a Nobody, he is good-natured; and the poor gelding is not responsible for his Condition. Whence comes this Forgivingness? I can only hazard. I believe I have loved truly and it is in the nature of authentic Love that it takes one out of one's-self; it is neither narrow nor self-regarding; rather it flows over the banks of any particular attachment and makes a Garden of all around it. Thus, even poor Signor L——, who to the

*World is an object of Contempt, is, within the perspective
of Love, an object of human Sympathy. I can say no more. I
embarrass myself. Love makes me Foolish.*

*But, dear Sister, it is too late. I am not redeemed by
Love. I have cast up my accounts and the balance weighs
heavily against me. If I had only* understood *that I loved
rather than laid claim to the Title without marking out
the wide bounds of that Estate! Instead, thinking that
Love was a small species of Property, I felt bitter when I
was denied and embroiled myself in deepest Sin. I cannot
speak of it.*

*I may have forgiven my Mistress for her Blindness, but I
have not forgiven the Class which inflicted that Blindness.
Each day in this City convinces me that there is nothing
to be hoped for from a Nobility whose notions of Public
Affairs (when they can be stirred from their Indolence to
consider these matters) are limited to the betterment of their
Fortunes and the increase of their Luxury and Prestige.
Instead of providing that service to the Commonwealth
which alone could justify their Rank, they reduce everyone
else to a Servile Condition; and those who possess some
useful Talent prostitute it as parasites on these greater
Parasites. As to Culture, they have None. Everything is
Fakement and Pretence. In the Arts, when they profess to
admire the Modern, they are satisfied with the Vapid and
Frivolous. When they admire the Antique, they mean a
sterile imitation of the Classics. The height of their Culture
is no more than a plausible Pastiche of what was once
living and true.*

*My Dearest, I am torn between the Virtues of
Love and the Rancour of Bitterness and Envy, and
I do not know how long I can continue being two
men. Surely one of them must attain Dominion over
the other? And I fear I know which it shall be,*

*for he has already essayed his Strength in terrible
exercises.*

*Thus, as I say, it stands with me. If anything should
miscarry you will find my affairs are in order. My papers
are lodged with the Notary Bartolomeo; and cash and bills
of exchange will be found with Cesare, the Goldsmith. A
Mass may be said for me, provided that you pay no more
than was paid for the Repose of our Mother's Soul.*

But why should things so miscarry?

*You must understand that the Discovery of Signor
Morosini's Guilt is not the end of the matter but the
beginning of the time of greatest Danger. There is Nothing
to which these people will not stoop to fix the Guilt upon
Another. Innocence is a qualification for Punishment, not
a Defence against it. Already an attempt has been made
to pin the Crime on one Fosca, a poor galley-slave but
uninvolved. Even Signor L—— was for a time imprisoned.
How, then, can you have confidence that it will fare any
better with your Brother?*

*With these thoughts in my mind, I returned to Signor
Morosini in the library, bearing his quizzing-glass. The
Murderer raised his head from his book, granted me his
condescending smile and, with his usual civility, dismissed
me to attend to my own affairs until I should wait on
his Pleasure at supper. I bowed and retired, knowing that
this man will have my Life if it is necessary to protect his
own — indeed, he would kill me to defend the least part of
his Fame or Property. Or, rather, would have me killed
somewhere off-stage and my death reported to him in the
manner of a French tragedy.*

*Signor L—— has provided evidence of my Master's
Guilt in the form of the Painting. Whether the entire
explanation consists of this vulgar tale of theft, I do not
know. As I write, Signor Morosini has left the house, and*

SCHERZO

I suppose him to be at this very moment in conclave with his fellow Conspirators, plotting who knows what Plot against Religion and the State.

Whatever may become of me, I beg you to trust in God. And if you should hear infamous reports of me, do not believe them. Think always Kindly on him who loves you, namely

Your poor and tortured Brother,

Giangiacomo

CHAPTER TWENTY-NINE

A True and Faithfull Account of the Egyptian Rite restored according to the System recovered by J. W. B. von Hymmen from Ancient Writings of that People

The True Egyptian Rite is called *Krata Repoa* signifying the Silence of God. Within it are seven grades, namely Pastophoros; Neokoros; the Gate of Death or Melanophorus; the Battle of the Shadows of Christophorus; Balahate; the Astronomer Before the Gate of the Gods; and Propheta or Saphenath Paneah.

Pastophorus is the title of the Candidate, though its more usual meaning is one who carries an image of the God or, according to Apuleius, a priest of Isis. The Candidate for the First Degree is prepared in a grotto and thence conducted to the Gate of Men by the Thesmophoros or dispenser of those laws which govern the Mystery. After the opening of the Gate and the putting of the questions, the Candidate wanders in the gloom of Birantha. He consents to the Constitutions of the Society and is led, blindfolded, to the Hierophant. Here is administered the Oath of Discretion and Fidelity, a sword being pointed at his throat. He is restored to the light. Placed between two pillars, the

Candidate ascends the ladder of seven steps to the vault with eight doors of entrance, which are open to him as a child of celestial researches and divine toils. The password is 'Amorm', meaning 'Be thou discreet'. He carries thenceforth as a talisman the Xylon.

Passing to the grade of Neokoros, the Candidate shall fast. On the day of his advancement he shall be served with choice meats and tempted to desire by virgins consecrated to Diana. Withstanding such temptation, he shall be questioned by the Thesmophorus and purified by the Stolistes. If he is chaste and prudent the guide shall cast a serpent before him and he shall be struck with terror as the Hall of Reception fills with serpents. Being courageous, he shall be taken before two pillars of great height, that of the East and that of the West, between which is a griffin driving a wheel in emblem of the Sun. He shall be invested with the Caduceus, which is the type of the Sun's motion along the plane of the ecliptic.

The worthy Candidate shall next pass to the Battle of Shadows. The Thesmophorus shall welcome him with sword and buckler. They shall travel through the Underworld, where the Candidate shall be attacked by dangers and a rope passed around his neck. When the bandage is removed from his eyes he shall behold the King, the Demiourgos, the Stolistes, the Hierostolistes, the Zacoris and the Komastis. To the Candidate shall be presented the Bitter Cup, the Kukeon, which he must drain to the dregs. Next he shall receive the shield of Minerva, the shoes of Anubis and the hooded mantle of Orcus. He shall be armed with a scimitar and commanded to behead a victim immured in a cavern. As he enters the cave he shall behold the living effigy of a beautiful woman and the assembly shall exclaim with one voice: 'Niobe! Behold the cave of the enemy!' The beheading done, the Candidate shall present the head to the King and Demiourgos. It is the head of Gorgon, spouse of Typhon who murdered Osiris.

The Candidate may demand the grade of Balahate. He shall be received in the Hall of Convocation and taken thence to a chamber to behold a pageant. There shall come forward Orus with other Balahates bearing torches. From the mouth of a cavern shall spout flames. The murderer, Typhon, is within. As Orus approaches with drawn sword, the monster raises his hundred heads and scaly body. Orus slays the murderer and cuts off his head. This is Typhon who symbolises fire, which is terrible yet without which nothing can be accomplished.

The Candidate, being a Balahate, shall be chained. The Gate of Death shall be filled with water on which the boat of Charon floats. He shall behold the sarcophagi containing the bodies of those who have betrayed the Order and be warned that it shall be likewise with him. Now is stripped from his eyes the vulgar belief in many gods. There is in truth but one God, transcending the comprehension of mankind. The Candidate shall be led to the Gate of the Gods and receive their full histories from the Demiourgos, nothing being concealed. He shall be taught the sacerdotal dance.

If all consent, the Candidate may become the Man Acquainted with the Mysteries. Following his reception there is a procession before the people and the Sacred Emblems are exposed. The adepti shall gather in a square house outside the town to communicate with the Manes, or Souls of the Dead. The Candidate shall drink a draught of wine and honey, for he has reached the term of his trials and may enjoy all the sweetness of knowledge. His badge is a cross, he is clothed in a white garment and his head is shaved. His title is Pannglach, meaning

Circumcision of the Tongue. Now is his tongue unloosed since he has acquired all the Sciences and may speak upon all.

Amorm! Monach Caronmini! Jas! Ibis! Adon!

CHAPTER THIRTY

Signor Ludovico's Narrative

I was at the same time elated and terrified by my discovery at the Ca' Molin (though the credit must go to Monsieur Arouet, who had anticipated it). Only the murderer would have had either motive or opportunity to remove the painting of Christ and the Woman Taken in Adultery from the body of Signor Molin. Indeed, only the murderer would have known that the deceased had the painting on his person. The fact, then, that the original of that work was now hanging in the private cabinet of Signor Morosini was incontrovertible proof that he had killed his former friend. Moreover, as I reflected on the matter, it was a solution wholly in keeping with my patron's character. As I said at the outset of my tale, he was a person capable of deep dissimulation. It suited him to affect the pose of an enlightened and civilised man, and to conduct himself so languidly and be so easy-going with his dependants that one might be misled into thinking he cared neither for the World's opinion nor for the management of his own affairs. But this was all upon the surface. In reality, he was vain as to his reputation and shrewd in financial matters. He fancied himself a connoisseur of the

Arts, and to possess a valuable painting at a fraction of its true worth would appeal to his vanity and his cupidity alike. The threat of disclosure, and ruin in the world's estimation, would have been ample reason for him to kill Signor Molin. So I concluded.

When I returned to Monsieur Arouet's lodgings I told him, with some elation, that his suspicions had proven justified.

He merely grunted and replied, 'Let us not get ahead of ourselves. What we have is merely another piece of information of which we must make such sense as we can.'

'But now you know the identity of the killer!' I protested.

'Ah, yes, the killer. I know his identity,' my friend answered and added, 'the poor devil. At least, so I believe. There remain some points of detail – suppositions I desire to verify. But in all substantial respects, I think I have the answer,' he concluded gloomily.

He seemed distracted. I saw that the progress of his packing was such that he might leave at any moment. I could have choked on my dismay, but what was I to do or say? Miserable creature that I was, I could not express my admiration or affection for my friend (which I assure you was of a purely spiritual character); nor propose any course for our future friendship, unless he would take me as his servant, which I doubted. From the true womanly feelings I had so surprisingly acquired, I wished to express all those tender concerns a woman might have for a man. Instead I was burdened by the limits of my outward form and could never appear other than a mincing, lisping eunuch.

Losing my concerns in his own, Monsieur Arouet broke from sorting his correspondence (which he had done throughout our conversation) and said, 'I hear the angelus sounding. We must shortly be about our business. Tell me, Ludovico, when you came here did you notice any ruffians loitering about this place?'

'I saw no-one,' I replied. This was not wholly true, for this quarter of the City was frequented by a riff-raff of seamen, Albanians, porters and the general mob whose presence signified nothing. 'Do you fear that you are spied upon?'

'I *know* that I am spied upon,' my friend answered sharply, then, softening, went on, 'Yet it is not to be helped.'

'Who spies upon you?' I asked, thinking of the Jesuit and his gang of pious cut-throats.

'The world in all its guises. The agents of the Serenissima, His Most Christian Majesty – or indeed the King of Bulgaria. I have had occasion to displease them all. A pox on them,' he muttered and regarded me slyly. 'We shall wrap up our present mystery, and then I shall turn my back on this city and my enemies may eat my farts.'

Again he gave a signal of his imminent departure and again my heart was torn with grief.

Night had fallen and a sullen rain was driving from the north-east when we issued from the house and took a gondola for the Ca' di Spagna. My spirits were oppressed by the weather of this mournful season, fear at what we should encounter when (as was our intention) we followed Signor Morosini and his fellows to the lair where they conducted their mysteries, and above all the sense that all things were coming to an end. For me there could be no triumph in the outcome of our efforts. If the murderer were indeed Signor Morosini, only danger would be our reward. If someone else, I did not doubt that all thanks and praise would go to others and I should be granted my usual portion of contempt. What interest of mine, I asked myself, had I been serving? It was surely no more than this: that I had hoped to earn the respect and affection of one who did not despise me – that, in short,

I had acted out of love. Unwittingly I had been seduced; but not by my carnal appetites: rather by a longing of my soul for someone who could see me in my divided nature and make me whole. Yet what an object I had chosen! A man whose nature was crabbed and cross-grained: vain, arrogant and sly. Ah! it seemed that there were to be no limits to my absurdity.

Thus my thoughts about my sad state as we steered the narrow canals to the hollow calls of gondoliers as they plied their craft in the darkness. I remember little of that journey, except that in some poor corner of the city a house had been quarantined for death or disease and smoked with bitter herbs to cleanse it of pestilence. These fumes I could smell above the stink of night-soil and the sluggish brine that lingers stale and putrid in the lagoon.

We sat, Monsieur Arouet and I, in our gondola in the deeper shadows within the shadow of night, watching the water-gate of the Ca' di Spagna. At our instruction our man had grudgingly doused his lantern. Mist formed around us. We did not speak, for it was as if there were no-one to speak to: such was the effect of the cloaks and masks that we wore.

How long we waited I cannot say. I doubt that it was very long, but it seemed an age, afflicted as I was by fear and uncertainty. Other boats came past, each one a tableau of light and noise that would appear briefly on the stage and then disappear into the darkness. I recall a vessel filled with Carnival revellers, some costumed as harlequins and punchinellos, others in Gothic disguise with horrible masks of black and silver. They arrived with a racket of tambours and fiddles but, seeing us motionless and dark in the water, fell silent and turned their hideous faces upon us. Doubtless there was no sinister intent behind this gesture, merely the careless curiosity of the idle; yet the effect was quite otherwise. As each pale visage with fixed grimace and sockets empty of eyes searched me out, I felt the object of some deep and cruel malice. My heart was chilled and I would have cried out, though it was but a momentary incident and without meaning except in the stirrings of my own guilty soul. Then, as suddenly as at the halting of their noise, the master of their revels gave a laugh and struck his tambour. The pale faces turned from me and the vessel glided away to the accompaniment of jolly music.

There came another gondola bearing two gentlemen in cloaks and masks as if on their way to a ridotto. A bell was tolling one o'clock by the angelus. The gondola stopped by the water-gate and one of the gentlemen rapped on the door with a silver-headed cane. It opened and a third man emerged from the Ca' di Spagna to join the others. The gondolier cast off his mooring and paddled away from us.

Monsieur Arouet signalled to our own man. 'Follow them.'

'Signori!' protested the fellow. 'It is dark. I shall damage my boat.'

'Steer by their lantern. I shall pay you for any injury.'

The man grumbled but did as he was bidden, and we slipped away into the darkness in pursuit of Signor Morosini (for I was sure that it was he).

Our way was not straight. No paths in Venice are. We wandered, keeping always to bywaters so dark that even the bridges manifested themselves merely as blacker shadows. Nor do I believe that we travelled directly. In our twists and turnings we seemed at times to come back upon ourselves, and although on occasion I could glimpse a church or other building I knew, they came upon me in no recognisable order, as if the map of the city had been recast and its monuments stood in new relations to each other. At the outset of my work I warned the Reader that my tale would take place in a Venice unfamiliar even to me; in which distances expanded or contracted outwith their usual bounds; in which nothing was seen whole but only in portion according to the flicker of lanterns; in which the proper juxtaposition of things which binds together reality was turned all to confusion. Truly on this night Venice was a vile place, like an old harlot who has set aside her finery and sits in the darkness of a filthy garret drooling over the memory of her vices.

My companion interrupted my brooding thoughts. 'We are followed,' he said.

I looked behind but could see little. We had passed few other craft and none had passed us.

'They show no lantern,' said Monsieur Arouet, 'but they row to a different rhythm and I hear them.'

'Have you seen them?'

'Just now, when we passed the priest with his link-boy I fancied I caught a glimpse of them by the Friulian's lantern. If my eyes did not deceive me, there were two in their company.'

It might be that they were others of Signor Morosini's party, coming in their own gondola: but why should they travel in darkness when my patron did not do so? I thought then of the Jesuit, Fra Angelo, and his acolyte, Signor Girolamo Molin. Whatever its justification, their enmity towards Signor Morosini and his friends was bitter, and, although the Jesuit had commissioned me to be his spy, it was not unlikely that he had further plans against the possibility that I should play him false. Was it indeed those two – or yet someone else?

'Ah, well,' sighed Monsieur Arouet, 'unless you wish to try conclusions with sword and pistol, we must rest content that they follow us.' I nodded. I had no desire to fight with anyone. I had only a small-sword by me and I doubt my friend had a pistol. Signor Girolamo, on the other hand, carried as many weapons as a Janissary and was a powerful beast to boot. Let him follow us if he wished, was my opinion: though the image of that monster and his efforts to kill me added to my gloom and foreboding.

At length we came to our destination. It was, so far as I could tell, the wreck of an ancient mansion, not wholly fallen into decrepitude but crazy and rotten with years of neglect and sinking slowly. This I got from the patches of light cast by the lantern borne by Signor Morosini's man, which gave me glimpses of escutcheons, arches springing from curiously carved corbels, and other sprigs of antique ornament, all worn and crumbling and melancholy. A door which formed the entrance from the canal into this relic of ancient pride was opened and the three gentlemen were admitted to the house. Their conveyance did not wait on them but was rowed away upon another errand, and Monsieur Arouet and I were left to contemplate our actions.

I am not a brave person: rather a faint heart who like many another christens his cowardice 'prudence' to bless the poor bastard with a reputable father. However, I am also so infirm of purpose that I can be encouraged into the imitation of virtue by the force of a stronger will. So, though I was frightened by the decayed solemnity of this place, which spoke of all manner of foul and hidden things, I was resolved that I would follow Monsieur Arouet wherever he might lead. And therefore, when he proposed to me, with a hint of strange gaiety in his voice, that we too should enter the mysterious house, I nodded gravely and answered that I was as willing as he. What did it matter if my bowels turned over and I felt a rush of bile to my throat?

My companion ordered our boatman to bring us alongside the water-gate. He had noted some peculiar pattern in the way those going before us had knocked upon the door which he now repeated. The door was opened by a ruffian bearing only a rush-light which showed little beyond a simian brow and a nose eaten by the pox.

'Are you the last?' the creature rasped.

'How many are we?' answered my friend.

'Thirteen, including your honours.'

'A veritable coven,' said Monsieur Arouet amiably. 'Yes, my good fellow, I believe we are the last.'

'Right – you'd better come in then, and I'll lock up.'

We entered. I could see nothing, but felt my shoes sliding upon some slimy paving and heard rats squeaking and scurrying. The Virgil who would guide us through this Netherworld barred the gate in case we had brought hope with us, saluted us with a belch, held up his taper so that it cast light upon his other hand, and, by the crooking of his forefinger, indicated that we should follow him.

'Very well, my good gossip,' assented my companion. 'Lead on through however many circles of Hell you may desire.' To me he observed, 'Have courage, Ludovico. Recall that it is in the nature of Hell that it has no substance, only a glamour and a seeming. God alone is truly real and He will not see you destroyed by an illusion.' This was the first firm intimation I had that my friend, despite his contempt of all priestcraft, placed his ultimate faith in the Almighty. And I confess that I was comforted. His reference to illusions was timely, for it had come to me that this house was like a darkened theatre in which all manner of horrible spectacles might be played out.

The Chthonian was eager to be at his supper or his bottle. 'Come on! Come on!' he urged us and scuttled away, leaving us to stumble in pursuit of his rush-light. We followed, two doubtfully wise men guided by an equally dubious star, making what we could of a way that meandered up and down stairs, through unknown chambers and galleries and round invisible obstacles. We were not wholly in darkness, for here and there we would come across strangers and servants, or in some great room find one corner lit, or catch a glimpse through a door into some other place. Always, however, our guide insisted that we should not linger; so that the scenes thus revealed were perceived only as fleeting impressions like the thoughts of a disordered mind.

We entered first what I took to be a kitchen. A table was laid with the remains of a sumptuous repast: the carcasses of fowl, the scraps from a joint of meat, great heaps of fruit, a dish of pastries, bottles of wines and spirits now empty. A single candle illuminated the table and little else; by it I saw the owner of this feast. A great fat man, whose flesh pressed beyond the limit of his clothes, he reclined in a chair in a stupor of repletion, his eyes glazed and his shirt soiled by a stream of vomit. To encompass the vastness of the meal he had loosed the ties on his breeches; his arse hung out and he had shat himself.

On and past an open door through which I glanced and saw a toothless old man in filthy clothes that would have shamed a beggar. This apparition sat at a table among a pile of papers. In front of him was a goldsmith's balance and around it lay heaps of gold coin which he was counting. When he spied us, the expression on his face changed to one of terror and he reached for a pistol among the papers. Gesturing with this, he slammed the door in my face and I was blind again.

'Come on! Come on!' cried our guide. But whither?

Past a nursery filled with broken toys. A man with a whip was flaying a naked child until its back bled. He saw me and returned my horrified stare with his own which said: This is me and mine and none of your business! I would have intervened, for the sake of the child, who was begging the monster to stop, but I felt Monsieur Arouet's hand upon my wrist. 'You must not!' he hissed. And so we went on, though I was both fearful and ashamed.

Now we entered a gallery, the far end of which was lit by a *torchière*. Two men were there, in the last extremities of a furious duel with sword and poniard. Their clothes were torn and I saw more blood from their wounds than I thought a man could hold. They fought without finesse but from sheer brutishness, striking blows that would dent an anvil, and gouging and biting each other when they came to close quarters. The clash of their weapons almost drowned their cries, but I heard one utter, 'She is mine! Confess it and I shall spare you!' This time it was our guide who seized me roughly and pushed me though a doorway and away from this infernal show.

My heart was pounding from these last two scenes of violence. The next was in some upper part of the house among the bedchambers, where I was permitted to stare into a small room. It was lit only by the last gutterings of a candle, but what I saw was a room fallen into decay where spiders had draped their webs over the last vestiges of furniture. A bed was there, obscured by its rotten hangings, but I saw lying in it a man with a yellow countenance and vacant eyes. Around him were the putrefying remnants of innumerable meals and the spills and stains of an overfilled piss-pot, and the stench was so overpoweringly foul that I wanted to retch. Yet I was not to be spared.

'Come on! Come on! Mustn't stay!' said the Chthonian angrily.

'Where are we going?'

'You will see! Ah, yes, you will see!'

He pushed me again, this time through the room and an adjacent dressing-room and through that into another bedchamber. This one was dark except for a candle burning on a chimney-piece over which hung a coat of arms with many quarterings. A man was on his knees in front of it in an attitude of idolatrous prayer. You may imagine with what relief I realised that this was all the room contained; for, although I suspected that it conveyed some message of malign import, it did not assail my senses and it was with a slight reprise of equilibrium that I followed Monsieur Arouet out of this chamber and into the final one.

Here two women lay upon the bed, one fat and one thin but both comely to look upon. The fat one lay with her legs spread wide and her organ of sex exposed and painted bright red. The thin woman was kneeling with her breasts hanging so that the other one could suckle on them. A crooked fellow with a painted face was behind the thin woman, taking her *au cul* with great thrusts and screams, and a trickle of blood ran down her leg. The room stank of stale bodies and spent seed.

'Enough!' I whimpered in a voice scarce audible even to myself. My shock can be imagined only if it is understood how I came upon these things: how, amidst blind and confused stumblings through the darkened byways of the house, each successive apparition surprised me in its vividness and yet was so fleeting that it was barely seen before it was gone. No reflection was possible – not even to consider whether what appeared to my eyes had any reality or was mere phantoms – for at every turn I was chivvied by the brute who had admitted us to this house of wonders. What, then, had I seen? By what name should I call it? Were these scenes mere accident: glimpses into an unnatural chaos that infected this ancient mansion? Or were they a contrivance, to be understood symbolically? I could not comprehend the manner of intelligence that could create such artifice or realise it with such conviction. How could the agony I had seen on the face of the whipped child be contrived? Had

I not seen the gaping wounds of the two duellists? Beyond any doubt the hunchbacked satyr who occupied the final chamber had buggered his mistress. No – it would not do to consider these things as reality or illusion, for they partook of both. Nor could they be understood as symbols alone, for the viciousness of the participants was unfeigned: and, though the mysterious owner of this palazzo might have put together the elements of his spectacle, he had composed it from materials that were to hand and not created them *ex nihilo*.

Hence my distress. My natural cowardice had compounded a very proper fear at entering this unknown place. Now to my mounting terror was added a burden of disgust and self-loathing. For was I not of the same corrupt species as these filthy and degraded creatures? Was I not affected by these scenes because they were comprehensible to my own nature?

'You are weeping,' said Monsieur Arouet tenderly, and he kissed me like a father upon the forehead.

'Are you not troubled by what you have seen?' I asked incredulously.

He answered, 'I expected, if not exactly this, then signs and wonders at least. Nor are they finished. Watch! Listen!'

Our guide had gone, unnoticed by me. We were some-where high up in the house, at the foot of a narrow flight of stairs and in perfect blackness. I could hear the sound of a flute and violin playing a sweet air somewhere above my head.

'This is our goal,' said Monsieur Arouet. 'You shall see what brings Signor Morosini and his friends here by night and what causes such fear and hatred in Fra Angelo and Signor Girolamo. You have seen nothing yet, dear Ludovico! Signs and wonders you shall have aplenty!'

*　　*　　*

And now I shall do what no story-teller should do and break the compact with my Reader. For have we not agreed (in pretence and by your good grace) that I shall be your faithful reporter? And, in pursuance of that obligation, have I not studied by whatever art I command to bring you to a peak of expectation, creating horrors and dark miracles only in preparation for what will happen next?

Here, then, is my crime. The signs and wonders *did* happen!

And I shall not tell you about them!

Well, perhaps I am not so cruel. I shall feed you something; but, like a toothless crone with memories of dining on meat, you must accustom yourself to a diet of pap again. I shall tell what I may tell, and – to remind you of my Prologue – it will contain no more lies and misdirections than the rest of my story. The difference is that now (because I have taught you to expect so much) the structure of my artifice is laid bare. You *know* (for I have told you so) that your narrator is a liar and that his message is, both within and without, as much as anything a tale of his follies and conceits. Let us proceed with it, then; and leave the truth as an unspoken dialogue between us.

Monsieur Arouet directed my attention to the narrow staircase which (as observation was to confirm) led to an attic or mansard in the form of a gallery along the length of the roof. It was thence that the music issued and thither that we mounted cautiously.

The staircase ended in a doorway. Monsieur Arouet rapped on it gently, using the pattern that had been effective below. The flautist interrupted his melody and the door opened. We entered not the gallery proper but a corner of it that had been curtained off. It was in this small enclosure that the two musicians, flute and violin, with a stool and a candle apiece, were playing. At their feet were plates containing a modest supper of bread and cheese on which they had evidently been dining at whatever intervals the music allowed. The flautist gave me a wink and bade us good evening in a low voice.

Monsieur Arouet was the first to peer beyond the curtain and, seeing nothing to alarm him, he passed through and I followed. We were now in the gallery proper, but, in so describing it and treating it as a single space organised by the normal rules of geometry, while I might be faithful to Euclid, I should not convey its essential nature. It was not *a* gallery, with all the singularity the term implies. Indeed, its quality as a gallery had no significance, and it contained within it one place or many places as it was lit now here and now there in the unfolding pageant of tableaux.

For reasons that will become apparent, I shall say little of these tableaux. Throughout them one thing was constant, namely the presence of the Hierophant or Master of these mysteries, who intoned hymns and parables in explanation of them. He stood in front of an altar formed of columns upon which were disposed certain vessels and holy instruments. Before him, in congregation, was a group of men, cloaked and masked like myself and my companion, but I could not be certain of their number since the light was dim and the nature of the rites in which they were engaged required that one or more should at be on his feet as cup-bearer or other servant to the Hierophant.

As to the Master himself, he wore a tall crimson hat, somewhat like a mitre in appearance, ornamented with ostrich plumes. His face was covered by a full mask in gold modelled so that the cheekbones were high, the nose pronounced and aquiline; and it contained within it some instrument for projecting the voice which gave his speech a *vibrato* character. For dress he wore a surtout of scarlet silk embroidered with emblems, together with breeches of an antique style, stuffed and slashed, and high-heeled buskins. Over the surtout was draped a form of cloak or chasuble, very long, black in colour and adorned with marvels worked in silver thread: such as unicorns, hippogriffs, chimaeras, hydras, manticores and cockatrices. These vestments, so I was to learn, were those which were worn anciently by the priests of Osiris (him that was slain by Typhon); and these ceremonies the same of which the great Alexander partook when he had conquered Egypt.

While Monsieur Arouet endeavoured to make sense of what we were witnessing, the flute and violin struck up with Egyptian music (it being similar to Gypsy music, the latter having formerly come from that country). It seemed inadvisable to stay by the curtain, where we were to some degree in view, and so, as opportunely as we could, we slipped behind the scenery which formed one of the tableaux. Though it was difficult to make out, it appeared to be a grotto of some kind with a pump or bellows that would cause a fountain of water to rise and then fall into a pool. I sensed we were not alone and I believe that, although the mysteries were being conducted for the benefit of the masked congregation, there lurked in the shadows a crew of rude mechanicals who whispered while working the engines that produced the miracles.

Of these there were enough. Although, as I have said, we were, so far as this sublunary world is concerned, in the attic of a ruinous Venetian palazzo, it was merely a stage from which we were to be lifted to higher spheres (to glimpse, perhaps, that sefirotic world to which the Kabbalist aspires); for I swear that, though the ancient tiles formed our roof, we could have been under the open sky of night or in the deep bowels of the earth. Lo! Now the stars shone! The firmament was streaked with lightning and rattled with thunder and it rained! Lo! Waters emerged from beneath the earth and it groaned as if aching to give birth.

Yes, it was done by mechanical art (who should know better than I how these things are contrived?). But, oh, it was sublimely done! Sight and smell, words and music – all was composed in such harmonious combination and all directed to elevate the spirit and understanding. What was understood? Those things beyond comprehension. This was the purpose of the ceremonies; and, *in fine*, what else is Art for, save to convey those truths that are beyond the precise formulations of Reason?

Or so I thought. But what did I know?

Monsieur Arouet and I haunted the rear of the various scenes as the Master took his congregation through the elaborate rites in which the symbolism of the tableaux was explained and the acolytes introduced to the mysteries. It was dark and uncomfortable, cluttered by the engines that operated the miracles, and the air was filled with the stink of spent gunpowder and the other explosive salts used to produce the effect of lightning. Also, here in close proximity to the engines, I was deafened by the peals of thunder and the various wails, gibbers and screams that accompanied the drama. Thinking to find my companion on my right-hand side, I found not him but one of the Hierophant's dwarfish minions who was operating the thunder maker. My shock at the sight of this goblin caused me to start, and I tripped over a piece of the apparatus. Unable to keep my balance, I went teetering from my hiding-place and stumbled onto a species of grotto where, as ill luck would have it, a flare or petard was exploded and I was left dazzled and in plain view of the assembly.

'A stranger is in our midst!' boomed the Master. 'Who is it that would profane our holy mysteries?'

A cry of 'Seize him!' went up, and, before I could escape,

half a dozen sword-points were at my throat and I was dragged by my heels to the centre of the floor, where I lay prostrate, entangled in my cloak. My mask was torn from my face.

'Who claims this creature?' enquired the Master.

A voice answered, 'It is Ludovico the Eunuch.'

'Does he come by the permission of any of our Brothers?'

'No!' was the reply.

The Master fixed his gaze on me. It seemed filled with unspeakable malice. 'What shall be done with him?' he asked.

'Kill him!' God help me, but I was certain that this last voice was that of my patron, Signor Morosini!

'No!' I cried in abject terror, and, like an insect exposed from beneath a stone, I tried to scuttle to safety but at every turn was blocked by a pair of boots and the point of a sword. 'In the name of the most holy, blessed Virgin,' I pleaded, 'spare me! Don't kill me!' Or, at least, I intended something to that effect. I was so unmanned that it may be that I uttered no more than sobs. I was convinced I was about to be slain, and I confess there was no more pitiable cowardly wretch than I as I begged for mercy. Nor did any tribunal appear more implacable than those ten men and the Hierophant whose faces were hidden from mine by their masks. If my terrified abasement had continued above another five seconds, I believe I should have voided both bladder and bowels, but, just as it seemed I would meet my Maker, a voice from some remote part of the gallery spoke a single word.

'*Amorm!*'

I had no notion what this signified, but it operated like a spell upon my assailants. The Hierophant brushed aside the threatening sword-points with his own blade and turned to the newcomer. They proceeded to exchange certain expressions which would mystify the Reader and which I may not repeat, except to say that they were directed at establishing the stranger's credentials with the Brotherhood.

In this he was successful, for the Master turned to his acolytes and said, 'We may not continue until this matter is clarified.' And he pronounced some words of dismissal.

Thereupon the various torches that illuminated the tableaux were extinguished and he ordered more candles to be lit upon the altar. The Brothers now resumed their seats. I was left cowering in a heap upon the floor.

Monsieur Arouet (for it was he) came forward and took the Master briefly by the hand.

The latter said, 'Our secrets have been exposed to the uninitiated. What do you propose we should do?'

'I suggest you swear him into the fraternity,' was my friend's reply.

I heard a hiss: 'Never! He is *evirato*!' Again I believe it was the voice of Signor Morosini.

'Peace,' said the Master, pleasantly. 'We cannot kill the poor capon. It would be against the spirit of our Order, and Signor Ludovico enjoys in some measure the protection of this gentleman, who, as you can see, is an adept.' He laughed. 'Nay, I fancy we have no choice but to admit him to the lowest degree in our mysteries.' To me he said, 'You are fortunate, Ludovico. Come, stand up. Let us proceed.'

Then I was admitted to the Brotherhood, and about that matter I shall say nothing further.

Amorm.

CHAPTER THIRTY-ONE

Signor Ludovico's Narrative

Upon the completion of my initiation into the Craft, my fellow-Brothers (as I suppose I may justly call them) slipped away. The lights had been extinguished save for those on the altar, and, in place of the recent wonders, we found ourselves in a dismal gallery in the attic of the house where only the dark shapes of the theatrical scenes and the reek of sulphur continued as testimony to that attempt to create miracles on this earth.

The Master removed his mitre and unfastened the strings that tied his mask. Taking off the latter, he revealed the handsome and cheerful face of young Signor Balsamo.

'Well? Was that not a fine show?' he asked in a tone that was blithe and mischievous. 'I doubt that your Grande Lodge has put on anything near so effective.'

'You may be assured of that,' Monsieur Arouet replied, mingling his admiration with amusement at the younger man's effrontery. 'I have never seen anything so thoroughly accomplished.'

'No, nor shall you. The cost is enormous (though how I shall recover it is my business, eh?). Still, I say that one owes it to the Mysteries that they should be *mysterious*. Before I arrived, Signor Morosini was putting on a very shabby performance, little more than incantations and a few oaths to frighten the children: in fact, not very inspiring at all. Of course, you recognised me?'

'Yes,' admitted my friend. 'You stand with a certain way of turning in your toes.'

'I do?'

'Your pomade is unusual and distinctive. Those things and other more circumstantial matters . . . Yes, I knew it was you.'

'Hey ho! Well, it does not signify. However, you took me aback when you pronounced the Word. I did not think it was common currency in the Craft.'

'Nor is it. But I recognised elements of your Egyptian rite and have made a study of the writings of von Köppen and von Hymmen. They were your source, were they not?'

'They and other things of my own invention. Now, I must change my dress, for I supper tonight at the Ca' di Spagna. But we may continue to talk.' He clapped his hands and from somewhere in the shadows came forth Ahmed the slave, bearing clothes, and his friend the simpering exquisite, whose painted face grinned over a tray that held liquor and some glasses.

'Good evening, Signori,' said the latter. 'How delightful it is that you should visit our house again. On the last occasion, did I tell you of the history of this gallery? It was constructed as a prison in which maidens of the most excellent families were incarcerated as playthings for the appetites of a certain Doge—'

'Enough!' interrupted his master. 'We have other matters to discuss. Pray go on, Monsieur Arouet, while I change.' With that he retired behind the altar and our conversation continued.

Monsieur Arouet asked, 'Why, when I arrived in this city, was I denied the usual signs that I was among Brothers in our Craft?'

'Ah, for that I apologise. It was my doing. I had my own projects which I wished to conduct without inter-ference. Though you may regard my remarks as a barbed compliment, I recognised in you a person who had the wit and sagacity to frustrate my operations among this society of boobies. Therefore I made certain suggestions to Signor Morosini which – I confess it – were unflattering as to your character. And, since I held that poor soul in thrall to my promises of admittance to the Hermetic Sciences, he was willing to comply with my request that you be excluded from our company.' To judge the effect of this revelation, Signor Balsamo stuck his face out from behind the altar and beamed at us. For my part, I could scarcely credit his brazen charlatanry, from which it was evident that his whole scheme of philosophy was directed at the purse of my patron and his friends. Nor did it seem to concern him in the slightest that he was exposing his villainy to Monsieur Arouet.

My friend ignored any insult in the other's speech and said, 'I understand you. However, your actions had the effect of confusing my enquiries into the murder of Signor Molin. That crime was imprinted with the hallmarks of our Craft, and yet I could find no-one who would admit to being a Brother. You, too, must have seen the signs: in particular, the mutilations on the corpse and the references in the coded message to the number Ten, which accords with the membership of Signor Morosini's lodge. Those facts were not coincidences. They were symbols and intended to be understood as such. Indeed, they were so understood. The whole purpose of arresting that miserable creature Fosca was to direct attention away from any involvement by our Brotherhood. Likewise, your purported decipherment of the code (for which I thank you: it was most entertaining) was a piece of misdirection so that I should pay attention to Jews and Kabbalists instead of looking closer to home.'

Signor Balsamo emerged, having changed into a suit of sage-green and a vest of the same colour embroidered with pimpernels. He was adjusting his cuffs and bands. He said, 'In your account of the connections between the murder and our Craft, you have not mentioned the second weapon.' He looked at me. 'Ah, Signor Ludovico, do I understand that this was a point you noticed?'

I admit that I regarded that discovery as my special contribution to our investigations and I was mildly disconcerted to find that another had made the same observation. This, I suppose, is a reflection of my vanity. Even a slight acquaintance with Signor Balsamo impressed one with his acuity.

'The weapon which killed Signor Molin was found embedded in the wound,' I replied. 'It follows that a second instrument was used to inflict the mutilations. I do not know what it was.'

'Monsieur Arouet knows,' came the answer – and Signor Balsamo then pronounced a word that I shall not repeat, for it referred to a certain ceremonial object to which I had been introduced only this night in the course of my initiation. I glanced at Monsieur Arouet, who nodded. And so the picture was complete: there was no doubt that Signor Molin had been murdered with an eye to the symbols of Freemasonry.

Signor Balsamo asked, 'Have you succeeded in deciphering the mysterious verse?'

'I have,' answered Monsieur Arouet, and he proceeded to explain his method briefly and that the content of the message was the Jesuit motto: *Ad maiorem Dei gloriam.*

'La! How simple and how clever! I confess that it escaped me,' replied the younger man. 'But it confirms me in my suspicion.'

'Which is?'

'That the murderer was *not* a Freemason.'

He gave his explanation. 'Although the murderer has contrived to give indications of the involvement of our Craft in the crime, he has but an imperfect knowledge of our rituals. The hanging of the body under the bridge and the mutilations of the corpse allude to the oaths taken by our Brothers and the penalties that await the oath-breaker. But consider them in detail: you, Monsieur, when you were admitted to the Grande Lodge; and you, Ludovico, upon your initiation tonight. The resemblances are superficial, but in detail they are wrong. Then consider the knife' – here he used the ritual word again. 'Have you reflected upon why the weapon was not left with the body? The answer is truly simple. Though the murderer was aware of the existence of such an item, he did not possess one. He could only hint at it, knowing the hint would be sufficient. The Jesuitical message but confirms his ignorance. He does not know the language of our Craft and therefore used whatever was available to him. Knowing the enmity the Jesuits bear towards us, he has sought to embroil both them and us in the appearance of a blood-feud. Surely, Monsieur, you above all people have noted these things?'

Did Monsieur Arouet know? He made no immediate reply but continued to study Signor Balsamo gravely – and, dare I say, speculatively? Here I touch upon my conclusions: those I drew from my association with my friend. And at the heart of these is that he was so full of contradiction that I cannot claim ever to have truly known him. Much of this came from well springs unknown to me – from a history which he was never willing to confide. But some was evident, such as the conflict between his philosophy and his vanity. I have remarked before that there was a strange *rapport* between this elderly Frenchman and Signor

Balsamo, and it was one in which the younger man seemed to have the advantage. If I had to hazard, I should say that my friend's arrogance always pressed his philosophy against the bounds of charlatanry and imposture, and it was this insight which Signor Balsamo so brazenly exploited. As for himself, where my friend was concerned Signor Balsamo was entirely careless in displaying his trickery. He was, so to speak, the complement of Monsieur Arouet: that is to say, that he pushed his villainy to the point of philosophy.

To return to my question (and Signor Balsamo's). Had Monsieur Arouet also deduced that the murderer was no Freemason? Signor Balsamo knew the answer. And I do not. For his part, Monsieur Arouet merely grunted, as if it were not a matter of importance.

His eyes broke off from their engagement with the young magician's and he said solemnly, 'I am always obliged to you for your thoughts on the matter of the murder. But – as yourself will allow – you have made every effort to distract me rather than take me into your sincere confidence. You will therefore grant me the liberty of drawing my own conclusions in this as in every other matter. I charge you with answering one question only: but, mark you, I seek an answer only to confirm what I already know. Moreover a man's life may depend upon it. *Do you understand me?*'

Signor Balsamo seemed to lose his self-assurance in the face of such forthrightness. He said, 'Test me with your question.'

'Very well. Upon your honour and oaths as a Brother, tell me this. Before the supper on that fateful evening, did Signor Morosini attend a meeting of his Lodge? Do you comprehend? If Signor Morosini attended his Lodge meeting in the usual way and then went directly to supper, he could not have killed Signor Alessandro Molin! Now, answer me!'

'On my honour, and as a Brother,' answered the other in a clear, slow voice, 'Signor Morosini attended his Lodge and thereafter went directly to supper.'

God help me, but I could not tell if he lied. Monsieur Arouet, however, appeared to take him at his word. For without any further words of explanation he said, 'We must return immediately to the Ca' di Spagna!'

'Why so?' I asked.

'Because Signor Feltrinelli is there, and he is a danger to the lives of his master and all his master's guests.'

There was a gondola in readiness for Signor Balsamo. The three of us took it and Monsieur Arouet urged our man to take us to the Ca' di Spagna with all possible speed. My mind was in a turmoil. Was I to understand that Signor Feltrinelli was the murderer? Although Monsieur Arouet and I had discussed the affair thoroughly, he had given me no information to lead me to this conclusion. Then, as I reflected upon our conversations, I realised that he had never been wholly frank with me. Had he not disguised everything he knew about the connections between the crime and the Brotherhood? Indeed, was not secrecy part of the pattern of his thinking, so that he might delight in surprising the World with his brilliance? I found it a bitter thought to acknowledge that I was no more than his catspaw and that his confiding in me was the measure not of our friendship but of his contempt. Perhaps I was unjust to him: who knows? Certainly it was a night for bitter thoughts. I had gone through trials of terror and mortal danger out of admiration for this man and, it seemed to me, I was basely repaid. Venice is a melancholy city and this was a melancholy night in tune with my reproachful sentiments. At all events, I cared nothing that Signor Feltrinelli was the murderer, and took no joy in our discovery.

Nor, to all appearances, did Monsieur Arouet. He concentrated only on urging our man to make more speed. His face was set grim, and so pale and hollow that it was as if he were dead and a demon had set up habitation in the shell. Of me I am convinced that he thought not at all. Instead, he was holding an interior conversation, calling himself a fool and saying aloud that he should have cautioned Signor Morosini against returning to the Ca' di Spagna with his guests.

'Why so?' I enquired.

He stared at me as though amazed that I existed. Then he granted me an answer. 'Think on what you have told me about your conversations with Signor Feltrinelli and your perusal of his papers. He is at war with this society for its vanities and baseness. The murder of Signor Molin, rightly understood, was not an isolated action but the opening of a campaign. It is only the derangement of his mind that has so far prevented the poor devil from understanding the true purpose of his mission. Once possessed of that knowledge of his own soul, and fearing that he must inevitably be detected, he will strike at his enemy's citadel.'

He fixed his gaze on me, willing me to follow the subtleties of his thought. But in bitterness and ignorance I could only protest, 'God help me, but I do not understand you, Monsieur! I have *never* understood you!'

'Then grasp this, you fool!' he retorted angrily. 'Tonight is the first occasion since the murder that Signor Morosini and his fellows have all been gathered together. It is the last opportunity for Feltrinelli to destroy those whom he hates before we hang the poor creature.'

We were approaching our goal, the Ca' di Spagna, when Signor Balsamo, who had been hitherto silent, said mildly, 'I fancy we are followed.'

I looked behind and glimpsed in the fugitive light of a

torch affixed to a building, an unlit gondola bearing two masked men.

'I believe it is Fra Angelo and Signor Girolamo,' I said.

The names meant nothing to our young companion, but Monsieur Arouet observed impatiently, 'Forget the miserable fools! They are nothing to us!'

I, however, could not forget that they had their own demented purposes and, driven by their fanatical lights, might commit some action of madness in pursuit of Divine goals. Monsieur Arouet saw no danger in them, but he had not faced them as I had. I was filled with terrible foreboding.

We arrived without incident at the Ca' di Spagna. The porter had instructions not to admit Monsieur Arouet, but he was persuaded otherwise by Signor Balsamo. As we entered my eyes fell immediately upon a clutter of baggage, which I had seen only the previous day when it was destined for the estate at San Cipriano. Catching sight of Signor Alfonso, I enquired of him what had happened to reverse the plan of exiling the Contessa and Angelica to the Terraferma.

'La! Dearest Signor Ludovico,' he answered with an elaborate bow, 'what upsets you have missed today! As you know, the Contessa was always opposed to the plan, which would have deprived her of society in Venice. She agreed only to oblige our master. Well, she and Signorina Angelica had gone only a little distance when our darling girl (who was even more opposed than the Contessa) overcame the latter with tears and arguments. So, instead of proceeding to San Cipriano, they went to the Palazzo Molin to take counsel from their dear friend Signora Molin (a most lovely lady, if I may say so without impropriety). Signora Molin agreed that our two ladies were being imposed upon and she offered them accommodation for last night, and promised her good offices to restore them in the favour of Signor Morosini after so openly flouting his will.'

'Good Lord!' I exclaimed.

The valet giggled. 'No, no, there is more! Signora Molin sent a note to Signor Morosini explaining the situation and asking for mercy on the miscreants. And, before any reply could be returned, the two ladies themselves followed the message to make a personal appeal. You may imagine the sequel! Our master, who is the most indulgent of men when approached with a humble petition, is quite otherwise when his authority is publicly repudiated and his natural pride affronted. How he stormed and roared! It was monstrous that his will should be denied! Was he not lord over his dependants? How should he maintain his authority over the servants when it was shamelessly disregarded by those who owed him the highest duty? In short, his family, the State, and everything under Heaven would be brought low if he acquiesced in this rebellion!'

'You are certain of this?' I asked in wonderment.

My interlocutor coughed behind his hand and murmured, 'Hm, hm – one hears things. They spoke in immoderate tones.' He continued brightly, 'But I have not told you the best! In their conversations at the Palazzo Molin, Signora Molin revealed to the Contessa, that she, too, lives under oppression: in her case from a gloomy and autocratic creature, namely her stepson, Signor Girolamo. He (so she says) daily afflicts her with the most indecent appeals that she should surrender her person to him. It is (she says) impossible for her to remain at the Palazzo Molin if she is to retain her character as a virtuous widow. Imagine!'

'What is the outcome?'

'She is here! Signora Molin is here! She has fled the Palazzo Molin and sought sanctuary with Signor Morosini. Which, I may add, poses him a dreadful conundrum. For, on the one hand, the Contessa and his daughter deny his authority. And, on the other, he feels he cannot deny the request of a beautiful widow, yet one who has fled the authority of her own master. His inclination to accede to Signora Molin's petition is strengthened by his dislike of Signor Girolamo. What a to-do!'

Trying to take in the import of this news, I asked, 'Where are they now?'

'Why, here of course,' said Signor Alfonso. 'They have retired to the Contessa's chamber and console themselves with tears and curses at the whole race of man. As for Signor Morosini, on his return from his usual excursion, he is in an evil temper and is dressing himself, having dismissed me from attending on him.'

So much for the valet's story; who was delighted at having someone to tell it to. Two points in his tale interested me. The first was that here, in part at least, was the explanation of Signor Morosini's enmity towards me as displayed in his enthusiasm for my death not an hour before. For was my appearance at the Masonic ceremony not also an act of rebellion? And, secondly, did not the presence of Signora Beatrice create an additional danger, given that the monstrous Signor Girolamo and his insane confederate had followed us here with some fell intention? My discomfort mounted.

I had forgotten Monsieur Arouet, but he was at my elbow and now spoke. His tone was wry. 'Well, well, forgive me, Ludovico, if I was impatient in getting here. Forgive me, too, if I have been . . . how shall I say? Rude? Come now, you are man enough to be generous!'

'I forgive you, Monsieur.'

'Grudgingly, alas. Still, let us not be offended. It seems we have anticipated Signor Feltrinelli. Perhaps I was too fevered in my imaginings. Or perhaps he feels safe and not yet forced to extremities. Let us hope so! Nevertheless, we must find the gentleman.'

Signor Alfonso raised an eyebrow at this intelligence, but I was not about to satisfy his gossiping curiosity. I gave him thanks for his information and led Monsieur Arouet and Signor Balsamo in the necessary direction. I confess that I felt a pang of guilt at violating Signor Feltrinelli's room where he had been kind enough to grant me shelter after my escape from the Leads.

We knocked on the door. When there was no reply, Monsieur Arouet drew his sword and Signor Balsamo and I did likewise. The door was locked on the key, which reflected no more than the factor's prudence and the confidentiality of his duties. However, my philosophical friend took this amiss and delivered a kick which shivered the woodwork and forced it open. I called for a servant to bring us a candle, since the room was in darkness.

'Where are those volumes you perused when you were here?' asked Monsieur Arouet.

I protested, 'Monsieur! I pray you: is this gentlemanly?'

'A fart for your delicate manners!' he snapped. 'I must be satisfied in every particular of this case!'

I pointed out the factor's commonplace book and his correspondence, which Monsieur Arouet seized upon eagerly. While he scanned these items, I waited outside the room, sword drawn lest Signor Feltrinelli return.

After a few moments of reading, Monsieur Arouet exclaimed, 'Ah! We have it!' He shook his head and said sadly, '"Vos, o patritius sanguis, quos vivere par est occipiti, caeco, posticae occurrite sannae."* You were right, Ludovico, but even you

* O ye men of patrician blood! You have no eyes in the back of your heads: beware of the faces that are pulled behind your back – *Persius.*

360

failed to convey the depth of Signor Feltrinelli's hatred and contempt for his patron and the whole class of patricians.' He turned a few more pages and expressed surprise. 'This you did not tell me. Our man is a victim of Cupid, the poor wretch. He has an *inamorata* who does not return his love: a lady who is much higher than he in her station. My dear fellow, this explains everything!'

I retorted, 'May God save us all, is Signor Feltrinelli to be denied even the secrets of his own heart?'

Monsieur Arouet chuckled, indifferent to my anger. 'Prettily said. Aye, very pretty.' He closed the volumes. 'I am finished. I think I understand the fellow well enough. Nay, Ludovico, do not look on me with such disgust. I am truly not without sympathy for this pitiful creature. But he is become a mad dog and we must put the beast down. Let us go to Signor Morosini.'

We found my patron and his guests in the chamber where they were wont to hold their suppers. In my interior turmoil it was strange to me to see these fine gentlemen quietly conversing or playing cards. Signor Morosini, as if in defiance of any challenge to his civilised world, was dressed in a suit of the finest ivory silk; he was powdered and patched, and so bespangled with silver brandenbourgs and pearl buttons that he positively shone. He greeted me with a pleasant smile and even acknowledged Monsieur Arouet with a bow that refused him nothing by way of courtesy.

'Signor Ludovico, you are a little late,' he said. He cast his eyes over the calm assembly of guests and continued, 'We are a little agitated this evening and long to have our spirits soothed by music. I have taken the liberty of placing by the instrument a trifle of my own composition, both words and music. Flatter your poor master by playing and singing it for him.'

No hint was given that we were now bound together by

the mutual oaths of our Brotherhood. I was Ludovico the castrato again, his creature. I took my accustomed place and, after a moment's study of the piece, began to play softly. It was about rustic swains in love with their maidens, and I sang it in a tremulous soprano as though my heart would break.

Monsieur Arouet intervened to break any silent appreciation of my efforts. 'I must beg your forgiveness, Signori, but I have news of utmost importance.'

Signor Morosini raised his quizzing-glass and observed the Frenchman with tolerant *ennui*. To me he said, 'No, no, Ludovico, do not stop. Play on.' And to Monsieur Arouet, 'Well, Monsieur, what have you for us? We are agog. Pray tell.' He smiled at his friends. 'Are we not agog?'

'I have discovered the murderer of Signor Alessandro Molin,' said Monsieur Arouet impatiently. 'It is your factor, Feltrinelli.'

I stopped playing. Signor Morosini waved at me to continue and then returned to Monsieur Arouet.

'Good Lord,' he said without the least emphasis or sign of disturbance to his equanimity. 'What a foul world it is. My own servant.'

'He must be taken up this instant,' intervened the Avogadore Dolfin, who was among those present.

'Yes, yes. He is somewhere about the house. I shall summon a man.' Signor Morosini tugged at the bell-pull and the whole company waited in silence except for the sound of my voice piping out of the shadows until at last even I was finished. Whereupon the supper-guests thanked me with some modest applause and my patron murmured, 'Very fine, Ludovico, most affecting. Now continue with something of your own choosing. But soothing, mark you, soothing.'

A lackey came into the room in response to the bell. Signor

Morosini told him, 'Bring Signor Feltrinelli. Tell him that I wish to see him. If he shows any reluctance or resistance, have him brought by force.' To Monsieur Arouet he said, 'See how I obey your wishes, mon cher Philosophe? It seems that you are master over all my servants, not merely Signor Ludovico, whose disobedience I forgive in accordance with the obligations that bind our Society. Well?'

'You are cool towards me, Signore, and I know not why,' replied Monsieur Arouet. And at this moment, which I knew to be his triumph, he looked tired and old and defeated. Indeed, he seemed worn out in the manner of a gambler who turns the last card in a game, knowing that it can make no difference, for success will not recompense his losses. I remembered then that he was packed to leave Venice and I regretted that I had harboured any bitter thoughts towards him.

When Signor Morosini next spoke, it was merely to say, 'Be that as it may. But, having intruded upon our supper, it is for you to explain yourself. Tell us, then, about the murder.'

CHAPTER THIRTY-TWO

Signor Ludovico's Narrative

It might be supposed that the laying bare of the mystery
would occasion pleasure, if not rejoicing: and therefore the
Reader may be puzzled that Monsieur Arouet's news was
received so coldly. However, a moment's reflection will recall
to you that any solution that implicated Signor Morosini's
factor was unlikely to redound to my patron's credit. As to
the others of our company, they took their tone from their
host; and, for myself, although I felt no especial friendship for
Signor Feltrinelli, as I had grown to know him these past few
days, so the warmth of my sentiments had increased: whereas
I cared not a fig for Signor Alessandro Molin. There was also
the fact that, for reasons I did not comprehend, Monsieur
Arouet's star was visibly on the wane, and he was now
listened to, as it were, on sufferance. If I had to characterise
the scene that followed his declaration, it would be in terms
of gloom and heaviness, both palpable and impalpable. For
the chamber, as I have described it, was dark, save for a few
sconces, and, moreover, damp and cold except in the vicinity
of the fire; and the mood was tense and secretive. Only your
narrator lightened this sombreness, which he did in the only

manner for which he was fitted: by playing the harpsichord, singing frivolous songs and, in general, acting the silly part for which Nature and Man had cut him out.

As a prelude, Avogadore Dolfin (whose nose had been once put out of joint in the matter of Fosca and who had some claim to apply the law to this crime) challenged my friend's credentials to expound on this matter. To this he received the dusty answer: '"Illiterati num minus nervi rigent?"'*

Monsieur Arouet then proceeded to describe his solution to the case, which, for want of skill, I now reproduce with minimal attempt to capture him exactly. Indeed I will eschew his language pretty much altogether, but, instead, endeavour to capture the spirit of it. That is to say, like a Philosopher, I shall set out the case in reasoned points, for you to accept if you can. In this I am sensible that, to a degree, I am violating the duty the Author owes to the Reader: namely, having introduced him to a mystery, to explain it with surprise, drama and *éclat*. But, if you have borne with me so far, you will appreciate that the solution to a mystery is like the goal of a journey, and that it is the journey not the destination which enlightens us. After all, does not the pilgrim who seeks to view the holy relics of St Peter find, at the end, merely a bag of bones in a jar? Thus, by frankness, may I turn a lack of skill to advantage by exposing the authorial tricks of which I am not master.

Here, then, is your bag of bones.

Point the First

There was once (said Monsieur Arouet) a sad and beautiful, lady who by force of circumstance was married to a man old enough to be her father. In itself such an arrangement is so common that it scarcely excites attention, but it is one which

---

* Men who cannot read do not find it harder to get an erection, do they? — *Horace*.

is unlikely to lead to happiness unless the husband is a man of exceptional parts and can encourage the affection of his young wife; or he has the sense to be complaisant provided that she act with discretion. Neither of these was the case with Signor Alessandro Molin. He was concerned with the preparation of his own soul for its final destination and had embraced narrow and fanatic religious opinions.

Point the Second

There was also (said Monsieur Arouet) a man of mature years and judgment, who had come from the country to seek his fortunes in Venice. He was of moderate education, rather more intelligent than was good for his health, and limited in his knowledge of the World by reason of his upbringing. What he saw of Venice appalled and disgusted him and caused him to conceive a mortal hatred of the patrician class from which none was exempted except one, and that was Signora Beatrice Molin. As that lady frequented the Ca' di Spagna from her friendship with the Contessa, and as Signor Feltrinelli saw her on those occasions when he had to visit the Palazzo Molin with regard to the necessary business of the Senate, his mind and affections were quite overthrown by the lady's loveliness, which was made more poignant by her melancholy circumstances. He fell head over heels in love with her. But, alas, the difference in their conditions meant that his love was unrequited, and, indeed, unexpressed except in his private correspondence and commonplace book.

Point the Third

To relieve her distress, Signora Molin began to frequent the Ridotto (introduced, no doubt, by the Contessa). Here she could forget the miseries of her existence in the excitement of card-play, and exchange the cold solitude of the Palazzo Molin for the gay company of sharpers and adventurers. How she escaped the vigilance of her husband

JIM WILLIAMS

is not known: it matters not, but, most probably, she acted under cover of supposed visits to her friend the Contessa. Since there was little other social intercourse between the two houses, the subterfuge was unlikely to be detected.

Point the Fourth

The visits to the Ridotto ended in their natural consequences: losses at cards and the prospect of disclosure and ruin. Yet, such was Signora Molin's distress that she could not abandon her reckless course but must needs find some source of further funds. She was not practised in these arts but required a confederate to act for her. Signor Feltrinelli was that confederate. From things seen or overheard, from the gossip of maids and the spying of valets, he learned of Signora Molin's desperate affairs and offered his services. ('He acted out of *love*, mark you!' said Monsieur Arouet out of charity to the miserable creature.)

Point the Fifth

Signor Alessandro Molin was the possessor of a fine and valuable collection of paintings, which, however, he ignored except in their character as an aid to his religious devotions. Signor Tomasso Morosini was a *cognoscento* of paintings. The two men were estranged, and neither could be supposed to know what works the other possessed. What could be better, then, than to sell the paintings of Signor Molin to Signor Morosini, provided that substitutions could be procured to disguise the theft? The monies so obtained would satisfy Signora Molin's demands, engage her good will towards her confederate, and the act itself would palliate Signor Feltrinelli's hatred against the patrician class. It was simple! It was perfect! Signor Feltrinelli even knew someone who could accomplish the task of forgery, a rogue called Pasticcio who had doubtless done work of cleaning and restoration for Signor Morosini. Thus the scheme!

Having completed his outline, Monsieur Arouet forgot his

system of numbered points, being more concerned to press on with his tale (and by the by display his own brilliance). I shall also forget them.

The scheme (continued my friend) was marvellous in its conception but ultimately flawed in its execution. Either Pasticcio became slap-dash in his work, or Signor Molin was more knowledgeable about his collection than was believed. *Christ and the Woman Taken in Adultery* (by Raphael or Andrea del Sarto, or neither – it does not signify) was a forgery. The imposture must have been done by someone within his household. It was altogether beyond the pilfering in which servants commonly engage. His suspicions fell upon his young wife and, from the suite, we must suppose that, when accused, she confessed to the crime.

Now (said Monsieur Arouet with relish) we come to the night of the murder. Signor Molin sent a message to the Ca' di Spagna, announcing his intention to visit and expose the infamy of his former friend. I have not found anyone at the Palazzo Molin who admits to carrying the message but a common porter would suffice. The billet may have been addressed to Signor Feltrinelli, but, more probably, it was sent to Signor Morosini and intercepted by the factor. The discovery promised to be fatal to the latter: he was burdened by the financial demands of his own relatives and faced with the prospect of the galleys and of an eternal parting from his beloved mistress. Only the death of Signor Molin would answer his purpose.

I suspect that Feltrinelli returned a reply in the name of his patron, asking Signor Molin to come discreetly, in view of the delicacy of the subject, and that Signor Molin felt under some obligation to respect the desire of a former friend to preserve his reputation. At all events, he set forth alone from the Palazzo Molin some time during that period between the angelus and the commencement of supper when (unknown to him) Signor Morosini was in conclave with his brothers in the Craft. This was a time when the servants would be about preparations for supper and when Signor Feltrinelli's ordinary work was done, and he could easily slip out of the palazzo when he was thought to be in his private chamber casting up accounts.

Signor Molin set out wearing his red senatorial gown and with the offending painting wrapped in another robe, this one being black. At some point he recalled his *incognito* and, the better to preserve it, exchanged garments. It was to no avail. Signor Feltrinelli was waiting for him by the Duodo bridge and slew him in the horrible manner of which you are aware. I may add that he was later to murder Pasticcio, his accomplice in the forgery, who, I do not doubt, thoroughly understood the meaning of Signor Molin's murder and intended to profit by it.

At last (said Monsieur Arouet – and I inform the Reader that his audience was so rapt in his story that the very dust could have been heard to settle if it had not been that your guide to these events, namely Ludovico il Tedesco, was still trilling like a bird since no-one had commanded him to cease) I come to the *manner* of the slaying and to the mystery of the encrypted verse.

Ah, how strange is the human soul! Did not prudence dictate that Signor Feltrinelli should kill his victim cleanly and simply, leaving the crime with every appearance of a common robbery such as that poor rogue Fosca might have committed? Yes, undoubtedly! Then why did he not do so? Because, at bottom Signor Feltrinelli's role in this matter of the paintings was just that: he was a thief! But to acknowledge that fact would be an admission his *amour propre* would not allow. What was a shabby act of dishonesty had to be refurbished so that in the murderer's own eyes it became an act imbued with far-reaching significance.

You must figure to yourself the mind of this humble factor. He was a proud man, vain of his achievements, which had lifted him from rustic ignorance, and of his little store of learning (which, by the way, was why he assisted me with hints to break his code so that the full extent of his cleverness might be known). He was aware of the existence of the Lodge founded by Signor Morosini and his friends, and it rankled him that his own station in life was too lowly for him to be admitted as a Brother; so that it became for him a symbol of that hated class which wasted its substance in luxury and immorality and refused to recognise true merit when it was patent to any intelligent observer. Thus we can understand the operations of his fevered brain as it copes with the knowledge that he is to become a murderer. The mutilation of the corpse and the writing of the cryptic verse are at the heart of the crime not because they point to the murderer: for they do not; they are a deceit and a misdirection. Their function is to transform the nature of the deed in the eyes of its perpetrator so that it becomes not a murder for gain, but an act of rebellion. Only in this way was it possible for Signor Feltrinelli to commit the crime and yet keep his good self-opinion – poor wretch.

With this last observation Monsieur Arouet paused to refresh himself with wine, which was the occasion for the company to do likewise. But there was no pleasure in the drinking: in truth there was little conversation. The Frenchman's exposure of how the world appeared in the eyes of an insignificant creature who had yet killed one of their number, was a sobering prospect for these lords of the Serenissima. I doubt not that it caused them to reflect disagreeably upon the obscure resentments nurtured in the bosoms of those disregarded menials who did their bidding: from the cook who prepared their wholesome food to the barber who held his razor to their elegant throats.

That such gloomy notions depressed their spirits was made evident when Signor Morosini snapped an order at me to continue singing, though I was hoarse from descanting about the amours of shepherds and similar nonsense. Yet it seemed I must sing, and therefore I decided to sing for myself. I began softly with Giacomelli's '*Sposa non mi cognosci,*' about which even now I can say little because, with the years, the recollection brings me to tears. Suffice it that I sang of the love of wives and children and of the loss of love, and that my heart ached at the barrenness which had been inflicted upon me. Suffice it, too, no more attention was paid to me than if I had been a performing monkey. I followed with a jolly song and they continued to talk of murder.

There was, it seemed to me, a void in Monsieur Arouet's discourse (one of which I was aware; for had he not instructed me in some rudiments of Philosophy?). It was this. While he had plausibly explained the facts as they were known and related them to Signor Feltrinelli, even explaining the mutilations and the cryptic verse which, on their surface, pointed rather away from the factor than to him; yet his explanation did not contain the element of necessity. That is to say that it identified Signor Feltrinelli as a possible murderer, *but not to the exclusion of any other*. This omission he now repaired once we had drunk our glass of wine and Signor Morosini had sent a further servant to locate his man of business.

In my deliberations (Monsieur Arouet resumed) I had to consider the situation of Signor Girolamo Molin. That gentleman harbours the same passion for his stepmother that she evokes in the breasts of all men who know her. He is also of a violent and intemperate nature. He spies upon Signora Molin and is aware of her visits to the Ridotto, and by the same token I do not doubt that he is aware of her debts and of the commerce in paintings between the lady and Signor Morosini. Now, therefore, consider this: if we are agreed that, following the discovery of the imposture, the reputation of Signora Beatrice was ruined in the eyes of her husband, is it not possible that Signor Girolamo killed his father in the deluded belief that he would earn the gratitude of his beloved as well as disposing of the obstacle to the gratification of his sensual desires? Certainly! Moreover, the mutilations to the corpse and the message within the cipher (which, by implicating the Jesuits, seems an egregious and incredible attempt to blacken them) – both of these facts, I say, bespeak a connection between the crime and our Craft. How delightful, then, for Signor Girolamo to commit the murder and lay it at the door of those persons whom he hates!

However, there is one insurmountable objection to this solution. The missing forgery! It was taken from the corpse by the assassin and has never been found; and I fancy it lies at the bottom of a canal. Why was it taken? Obviously, to hide the fact that it played a part in motivating the crime. But if this is so, why was the painting not restored to the walls of the Palazzo Molin, from where its brief disappearance was unlikely to be noticed? The answer is inescapable. The murderer needed to dispose of this item of evidence as soon as possible, *but he had no entry to the Palazzo Molin*! Therefore, the murderer was not Signor Girolamo.

So we turn to the Ca' di Spagna. If it is accepted that the paintings are at the root of the crime, and that the criminal was not in the deceased's own household, it follows that we must look to the household of Signor Morosini, where the stolen original now reposes in his most private cabinet. (Here Monsieur Arouet bowed to my patron and they exchanged glances, of triumph on the one part, and malevolence on the other.)

Whomever we suspect (declared Monsieur Arouet) must possess certain characteristics which are not shared by the generality of persons within the Ca' di Spagna. I speak of a man, since the violence and the manoeuvring of the body under the bridge do not allow of the murderer's being a woman. He must be instrumental in the theft of the paintings. And, furthermore, he must have sufficient education to devise the code. As it seems to me, only two people meet these conditions: namely, Signor Morosini and his man of business, Signor Feltrinelli. The problem is to distinguish between them.

(By way of digression: Signor Morosini intervened at this point. He had regained some of his composure, and, as if the suspicion of murder were the most elegant of compliments, he granted Monsieur Arouet a bow and announced, 'La! What a delight it is, to be accused of murder in one's own house and then exculpated by one's accuser!' The gentlemen enjoyed this rally and greeted it with laughter. Monsieur Arouet vouchsafed them a look of unspeakable contempt and continued.)

There are three reasons which convince me of Signor Morosini's innocence (he said), and which conversely must serve as proof to condemn the factor. Firstly, I have it on the word of you, my Brothers, that on the night of the murder Signor Morosini attended the meeting of the Lodge before supper and therefore could not have met and killed Signor Molin. Secondly, a prudent man, having taken and disposed of the forged painting, would have also disposed of the original so that no connection could be established. Signor Morosini did not do so because he was unaware that Signor Molin was carrying the forgery with him, and was therefore also ignorant of the connection. As to Signor Feltrinelli, he took no action in this regard because he did not feel endangered by a painting that was not in his possession, since it was not evidence against him: indeed for him to steal it would needlessly excite the suspicion of his master. And, thirdly – as I say, there is a thirdly – the evident Masonic trappings which ornamented the crime make no sense if they are attributed to Signor Morosini. On the one hand, they draw needless attention to the Craft which he is duty-bound to protect. And on the other, there are certain circumstances of detail which suggest that, whilst the murderer was familiar in outline with our proceedings, he was not fully acquainted with the particulars and could produce only a feeble pastiche. No, Signori (my friend concluded with a shake of the head), Signor Morosini will not serve as the murderer. And that leaves only Signor Feltrinelli. Now, where is that gentleman?

As Monsieur Arouet was finishing, to the murmured approbation of the company, two servants entered the room displaying every sign of alarm and distress. Signor Morosini turned to them, but, to his enquiry, they replied only in panic and terror, urging him to follow. He did not go alone, but the whole assembly followed him. We were taken through the byways of the house to a chamber which had been made ready to accommodate Signora Molin. We arrived to find the three women in the corridor outside: Angelica in a swoon, attended to by the Contessa, and Signora Molin herself, pale and as if in a waking nightmare. I swear by my God that I have never seen a countenance more expressive of tragedy, nor eyes that so eloquently implored that the agony of existence be taken from her.

Monsieur Arouet was the first to cross the threshold of that awful place. At first it was impossible to see clearly, since the candles had gone out; but, from those burning outside and the tapers we had brought with us, we gradually discerned the form of a man lying spread-eagled upon the bed. It was Signor Feltrinelli. His throat was cut from ear to ear and a razor lay on the floor. To all appearances he had not died immediately but had flung himself about the room with his head hanging half off and this circumstance accounted for the blood which had been splashed in great spurts everywhere, so much so that the place reeked of it. If this were not enough, we had had scarce opportunity to view this scene of carnage when a cry of 'Fire!' went up.

This was at first incomprehensible. We had seen nothing and smelled no smoke. Then of a sudden it seemed that all of the upper apartments were alight: a great billow of smoke rolled towards us and the half-darkness was relieved by a hellish glow. I heard a roar of flames and the sound of glass exploding. On this our company dissolved into chaos and panic, through which, though I could barely see him except by erratic flashes of flame, I heard the commanding voice of Monsieur Arouet ordering the women to be taken to safety, and water and brooms to be brought with which to fight the fire. However, the flames were beyond human force to master.

Where was the seat of the blaze? We could not tell. It was as though the fire had broken out simultaneously through all the upper part of the house. Moreover, and beyond reason, it seemed to be spreading downwards into parts which only a moment before had been safe. It was soon evident that we could do nothing, and our task was to save ourselves, which was no simple task for the building was filling with smoke and as we tried the several staircases new fires sprang up to threaten us.

I have commented on my want of courage, and this lack was as apparent now as on any occasion. I fancy I screamed and called upon our Saviour to intercede for my physical salvation. As I blundered in the maze of smoke and flame-filled chambers, holding the tail of Monsieur Arouet's coat, my prayers elicited a response, though not one I desired.

SCHERZO

My latest appeal to Our Lord earned a reply from a figure only dimly seen across a room, who informed me that, by Our Lord, Our Lady, St Peter and all the hosts of Heaven, I and all those within the Ca' di Spagna would die for our manifold blasphemies. I recognised the voice of Signor Girolamo Molin. He held a torch in one hand and a sword in the other. The Jesuit was with him, busily applying his own torch to any furnishings to hand and thereby spreading the fire. Signor Girolamo was not content with delivering us to divine wrath but proceeded to dash at us, roaring as loud as the fire and brandishing his blade.

I drew my small-sword and my companion did likewise, but Monsieur Arouet took the brunt of the first blow, which shivered his blade and knocked the hilt out of his hand. I yelled to him that he must save himself and thrust at my enemy but succeeded only in snagging an item of clothing. Signor Girolamo turned on me and rained upon me a series of strokes which, lacking in finesse, were easy to parry but by which he drove me backwards as if hammering in a nail. I retired with the usual fanfares of a coward: alternately defiance and begging for mercy. What possessed me to fight him at all remains a mystery to me except that perhaps one comes across valour in the same way that as one bows out of one room one enters backside-forwards into another. At all events, we coughed and spluttered in the smoke, scarcely seeing each other since the flames served only to cause the smoke to glow. When we determined that the shape before us was our enemy, we exchanged a few passes of the blade. For the rest we breathed in smoke enough to make our heads spin and I fancy the smoke would have done for me if two things had not happened. The first was that Monsieur Arouet reappeared and, seizing my arms to master the madness that had gripped me, dragged me towards a doorway and ultimately to safety. And the second was that a section of the coffered ceiling, seared by the heat, collapsed, raining a great mass of beams and plaster into the chamber. I caught a glimpse of Signor Girolamo pinned down by one of the beams. He was beyond effective help and, I believe, beyond wanting it. As Monsieur Arouet retreated before the smoke and flame, I heard the poor, mad devil ranting, 'God wills it so! God wills it so! God wills it so!'

CHAPTER THIRTY-THREE

Finale

It was a principle with Monsieur Arouet that nothing can be known with certainty in this sublunary world: bound as we are by ignorance, falsehood and illusion. Certainty lies only in the deluded eye of Faith. For the rest we must be content with probable explanations: probable truths. In this category, alas, must lie the solution to our mystery. Did Signor Feltrinelli indeed kill Signor Alessandro Molin?

Have I grounds for doubt? Who can say? For the evidence that persuades one man will leave another unconvinced. But let me be clear: I do believe that Signor Feltrinelli was the murderer. Yet I have not that necessary conviction which would justify taking a man's life – and be in no doubt that it was this affair of the murder that killed him, whether he slit his own throat or (as seems to me more likely) he was slain by that miserable creature Signor Girolamo Molin.

Consider the explanation propounded by Monsieur Arouet. As he himself admitted, the evidence for the most part led equally to the factor and to his master, Signor Morosini.

Indeed, there are other indications that would tend to reinforce the conclusion that it was my patron, and I instance only the fact that, over and above the matter of the paintings, there was an enmity between him and Signor Alessandro Molin born of ancient friendships betrayed and of the conflict between Religion and the Craft. Monsieur Arouet was dissuaded from accusing my patron only because of three points that had weight in his mind.

The first was that Signor Balsamo and the other members of the Lodge swore to the presence of Signor Morosini at a meeting of the Lodge at the time of the murder. Yet, as to Signor Balsamo, he was a person motivated solely by self-interest, who had every reason to preserve the life and property of the intended victim of his machinations. We may disregard his testimony. As to the others, they were bound to Signor Morosini by the interest of their class and by the most explicit oaths of mutual preservation which one Brother swears to another. Against these, what weight did the life or innocence of Signor Feltrinelli carry? Believe me: I make no positive accusation; but is one man to be exculpated and another condemned upon the evidence of such a tainted source?

Secondly, according to Monsieur Arouet, a prudent man, knowing that his connection to the murder was only via the paintings, having destroyed the forgery, would have destroyed the original. Yet the original was in Signor Morosini's private cabinet. Note how possession of the painting, which would otherwise have been damning proof of complicity now becomes proof of innocence! Yet the reasoning is sound *if* (and I take my terms from my teacher) the premises are also sound. For we are speaking not of a *prudent* man (who is a wholly abstract creature) but of Signor Morosini in the particular. In him the virtue of prudence was balanced by the vices of vanity and arrogance, and also by a covetousness in what concerned his collection of artistic objects. These defects alone might have overridden prudence. Moreover, did prudence itself absolutely demand the destruction of the painting? It is a matter of calculation. Think you how unlikely it was that Monsieur Arouet should deduce, from the colour of two robes, that Signor Molin had carried a parcel with him on the night of his death; or, from browsing and fiddling with the deceased's paintings, that the object in question was one of these. Prudence must be cautious and far-sighted to embrace such remote possibilities within her purview!

Finally, we must reflect upon the discrepancy between the Masonic trappings of the murder and the true rites of our Craft. These, in Monsieur Arouet's estimation, betokened an ignorance of the subject on the part of the assassin which could not be imputed to Signor Morosini. And, indeed, he is correct: nothing in the detail of the crime accurately reflects the penalties prescribed by the Grande Lodge, of which the Frenchman was an initiate, or the Egyptian Rite of Signor Balsamo. However, as the case of Signor Balsamo proves, our Craft is a tangled thicket; and, even after removing the myths and impostures that form its history, the Craft contains, as Our Lord promised, many mansions constructed by many builders under the eye of the Great Architect. And who is to say what rite Signor Morosini and his companions were following before their adoption of the Egyptian Rite? Might the mutilation of Signor Molin not have conformed to their ritual (even though perverted to an evil cause)? No. As Monsieur Arouet himself said, his explanation will not do!

Thus, turning my teacher's weapons against him, his 'proofs' will not suffice to acquit Signor Morosini, and therefore the latter stands with Signor Feltrinelli as a possible murderer of Signor Alessandro Molin.

Now consider this. May not the murderer be one Ludovico

il Tedesco, former subject of the Elector of Bavaria, pederast and eunuch? Is your narrator to be excused all suspicion because of the confidence between us? Let us review the case.

Firstly, I invite you to peruse this book. I assert that you will find herein no word of explanation as to where I was in the hours between the sounding of the angelus and the commencement of supper on the fateful night. In short, I have no alibi for the time of the crime.

Next, let us consider the characteristics of the murderer. He must have a connection with the house of Signor Morosini and enjoy sufficient standing with its master to be entrusted with the affair of the paintings. He must have some knowledge of Freemasonry. He must have sufficient learning to generate the ciphered verse.

As to my connection with Signor Morosini, you are aware of it. Granted that Signor Feltrinelli was my patron's confidant in matters of business and therefore more apt to handle the affair of the paintings: yet you should reflect upon the nature of that transaction. Which is more likely? That my master should use a man of whose uprightness and honour no word of complaint has been heard; or that he should use a degraded creature employed in a trade that offered neither respect nor security?

As to a knowledge of Freemasonry, it seems to me that Signor Feltrinelli and I are on an equal footing. At the time of the crime neither of us was admitted to the Craft but either could have scraped an acquaintance with its rites by spying and prying. There is nothing to choose between us.

With regard to learning, I would suggest that, again, there is nothing to choose between myself and the factor. I observe only that, while it may take skill to unravel a cypher, it takes no great wit to create one. The message itself was in Latin, a language in which, by virtue of my education in Rome, I could claim a greater fluency than Signor Feltrinelli. Not that the subject signifies, since the motto of the Jesuits is a commonplace which anyone may learn whether he knows Latin or no.

Allow then that, in point of opportunity and capacity, I am as qualified a murderer as Signor Feltrinelli. Are there any proofs which are conclusive against me? I offer you two.

The first is this. You will recall (and you may verify) I have said that I had never met Signora Beatrice Molin before my visit to her home, after the murder, in the company of Monsieur Arouet. Yet I have told you elsewhere that that sad lady was an intimate of both the Contessa and Signorina Angelica and a frequenter of the Ca' di Spagna. How, then, is it possible that I should have been unaware of her existence? In my defence I plead happenstance: that we visited the palazzo on different occasions and that chance never brought us together. But is this credible? Surely that same chance would have brought her name to my ear in the girlish conversations I held with Angelica? No! I *must* have known of her, and I have suppressed that innocent connection because the true connection was more culpable.

Secondly, I lay this before you. In what fashion has the content of the encrypted verse been explained to you? It said, *Ad maiorem Dei gloriam*, which is the motto of the Jesuits. Monsieur Arouet made no mention of it in his imputation of guilt against Signor Feltrinelli except by way of aside, when he intimated that this was one more proof of the factor's ignorance of the Craft which forced him to seek a message elsewhere. Let us allow this in principle. But why this particular message rather than another? In Signor Feltrinelli's letters and commonplace book, I read of his hatred for the class of nobles, but not one word did he say against Religion or the Church. Again no! It is speculation, not proof.

What, then, of Signor Morosini? Why should he deliver this message? To accuse the Jesuits of the crime? How? — when every other circumstance implicated himself and his Craft? To taunt his enemies? What taunt was it, when it would have gone unread had not Monsieur Arouet applied his skill? No. Always and again, no! It will not do.

Against these implausibilities you must have a mind to the following. Who, in this tale, possessed a smattering of intelligence and learning, yet was so disregarded and despised that he would wish to demonstrate his contempt for the World by paying it in its own coin? Who was emasculated in the name of Religion to sing the praises of God and thereby deprived of earthly joys and the hope of salvation, so that he should hate every root and branch of the Church and seek to damn it with his crime? Are these not motives more powerful than any that can be ascribed to Signor Feltrinelli and Signor Morosini?

Consider them, for I insist upon my guilt.

Dear Reader, I play games with you. I assure you that I am innocent of the crime. I have made my confession merely to reveal to you my own uncertainties in this matter and to convey to you how dependent you are for truth upon the account given to you by your narrator. Indeed, there is, for you, no message beyond your messenger, and he tells his tale for his own reasons and doubts that he knows even what they are.

Affected by the smoke, I was carried to my lodgings, where I lay in peril of my life for some two weeks. I was alternately cupped and blistered according to the whims of my physicians. Throughout this ordeal I was pampered by my dearest, loyal Tosello. In the first few days Monsieur Arouet called upon me several times and was all tenderness and concern, even to a feminine degree. But, if he had anything of import to say to me, I did not hear it. Then he disappeared and, upon my recovery, was not to be found anywhere within the city.

Rumours spread. Tosello came bounding into our room, clapped his hands together and pronounced, 'Oh, dearest! What can I say? We have had a *visitation*! Your friend, sweet and delicious Monsieur Arouet, is none other than the famous philosopher Monsieur Voltaire!' He elaborated this account by explaining that the philosopher had visited Venice under a *nom de guerre* in order to see to the printing of a certain work that had been forbidden by the edict of His Most Christian Majesty. I did not know what to make of this intelligence, since one's friends are one's friends and we all piss in the same pot; and, no matter how singular their parts may be, we do not hold them in the same awe as strangers of equivalent reputation: indeed, it is almost as if they are two persons; one who sends his suit of clothes into the World to receive its plaudits; while we and the other drink a bottle together and sniff on our sociable farts.

I had scarce taken in that news when other rumours came to my ear. Monsieur Arouet had fled the city, taking with him a deal of gold placed with him by various merchants and patricians by way of subscriptions for his fictitious book and investments in the *Rentes* and other bubbles. A letter had been received by Signor Morosini from the Duc de Richelieu, friend and patron of Monsieur Voltaire, in which he denounced Monsieur Arouet's letter of recommendation as a forgery and condemned the latter as an imposter and scoundrel. Thus it was that I learned the cause of the respect initially shown to my friend.

Until now I have obliged my Readers by adhering to the dramatic unities of time and place, but I must beg your indulgence, for within a short space of my recovery I began those peregrinations throughout the continent of Europe that have led to my present situation, writing this memoir; and it was only after some two years that I learned anything more of relevance to the present account. In the intervening period two things occurred. I parted from my dearest Tosello. As to the causes of this event, certain things are beyond even my lies, and my obligations to him exceed any conceivable fault on his part. So, in this matter, the Reader must remain for ever ignorant. Secondly, I left Venice. The city had become for me the embodiment of corruption and confusion, and, despite all its loveliness, every waking moment had become a doubt as to whether I was looking upon substance or illusion. More to the point, every contact with the house of Signor Morosini had become poison to me. I could not look upon his pale and powdered face, the patch on his cheek, the curl of his rouged lips, his fine silks or elegant calves, without wondering if I were looking at a murderer.

In due course I wrote to Monsieur Voltaire.

Letter from Monsieur François-Marie Arouet de Voltaire to Monsieur Louis L'Allemand

Ferney
17th September 17—

Dear Monsieur Louis,

Believe not those who say that there is no new thing under the Sun; for, truly, even if the parts are familiar to us (being begged, borrowed or stolen), still they can be put together in new combinations that have the capacity to surprise us and thus qualify as Original. Therefore, though you have told me a tale of Forgery and Imposture, verily you astonish me! What am I to make of it? Is it fact or fiction? If fact, then I caution you that all the World will steal it and give you no credit. If fiction, you should take care lest your Expectations may be above your Deserts; for, in valuing his work, even a blind man sees by a truer light than an Author. However, I shall give credit to your pretensions and answer them in the character of fact since you so present them.

Let us come to the nub. Do I know Monsieur Arouet?

I do — for I am certain we speak of the same person: the Trickster, the Charlatan, the Hypocrite, the False Philosopher; the Windbag full of Metaphysical Nonsense, trite morality and every species of Meretricious Argument that man ever knew; who convinces his victims with a show of Insubstantial Cleverness and deadens their brains with Bludgeons of hot air; who represents every manner of Fake Wisdom; who, in his personal attractions, without our knowing it, insinuates himself into our thinking such that person and argument are inextricably confused. Ah, yes! I know the Villain!

Believe me, Monsieur Louis, I have lived with him these forty years. There is not a day that I sit at my desk without finding him at my elbow; nor can I kneel at my Prayers without he prays beside me: nay, I cannot love a woman unless he intervenes, like an Adulterer, to invite her to love a man who is not me though he follows every particular of my features. You cannot comprehend the Struggle I have had with Monsieur Arouet, who is like a Leech on my existence: for he knows me to the very core, kernel, centre, essence, quiddity and hypostasis. He is me and more than me: for, while I am an inconstant creature of moods and changes, Monsieur Arouet is a reliable fellow in those matters that concern him, always as full of Opinions and Nostrums as a Pox-doctor's clerk. But do

not mistake me. He is not a selfish fellow. He attends to
my Soul. He is my Confidant, Confessor and Friend. Nor
in these parts is he necessarily a Flatterer. Oh, yes! To the
World, of course, he says I am a fine fellow! But to me
he can be angry, unreasonably condemning, unreasonably
forgiving, maudlin and possessed of immoderate Appetites.
He has a poor eye for paintings, has no ear for music and
often buys my clothes.

If Monsieur Arouet has attached himself to you, I wish
you well of his Friendship. I wait eagerly for news of him,
and until then remain
>   *Your servant, etc.*

Despite the ambiguity and sombre playfulness of Monsieur
Voltaire's letter, it was clear that I was to understand that
he did not know Monsieur Arouet as the corporeal reality to
whom I had committed my trust and my affections. Who,
then, was my Monsieur Arouet? A secretary, valet or steward
to Monsieur Voltaire – a wretched lackey, who, possessed of
a little learning and intelligence, had broken into the House
of Philosophy and stolen the silver spoons? And I, poor fool,
had bought those items thinking that I was acquiring the
entire treasure!

I cannot describe the bitterness I felt towards Monsieur
Arouet, which was in measure as I had earlier admired him.
It was in this mood that I picked apart his reasoning as to
the murder of Signor Alessandro Molin and reached those
doubts of which I have advised the Reader. In the same vein
I acquired, when I could, the works of Monsieur Voltaire and
compared the clarity and reasonableness of his thought with
that of my former friend. What did the latter possess? Was
not his philosophy mere commonplaces dressed up in fine
language, and his learning mere cleverness that a shrewd
man might get from skimming a book? In everything he

had told me, I found, on searching, that it contained no substance; and thus, after ploughing my field, he had sowed only barren seed. My heart became dead to him.

Thus it was for some years, until even anger wore out through disuse. Then, reflecting upon my time in Venice and those events that had been strange to the point of wondrousness, I was struck by an idea so bizarre that I thought my mind was overturned. It was simply this. Hitherto I had thought that the mystery was who had murdered Signor Alessandro Molin. Certainly the World thought so, and all our activities had seemed directed to this end: to answer that question. Yet what did I care? What were Signor Molin and Signor Feltrinelli to me? Why had I put my life in danger and thrown my emotions into turmoil? No, this explanation would not do! I had laboured under a misconception.

What then? Why had I acted as I did? What was the true mystery that I had tried to solve by pursuing the false? It was this. I wished to know who Monsieur Arouet was. There had never been anything else. I wished to know his name, his history, his thoughts, his moods, his waking and sleeping anxieties – in short, his soul. I did not wish to possess him as the evil-minded might think, but to know him so that I might know myself better. Is this so perverse?

Ah, Reader, what is this book? Is it mystery or comedy or love story? The proper subject of my tale is Monsieur Arouet, but I have told you more about myself. Yet how can I tell you about him with any hope of creating a true likeness, when in every point of philosophy, wisdom, eloquence, generosity and kindness he overreached me? How should the ignorant describe knowledge? How should the dumb speak eloquently? Granted that my friend was made not of true metal but of inferior stuff, no more than an imitation or pastiche, who plundered others for his reputation; yet, was he wholly without value? Has mediocrity no share in wisdom? No share in beauty? No share in love because its passions are of the quiet, middling sort? Are the realms of this world to belong entirely to Signor Morosini and the realms of the spirit to Monsieur Voltaire; and are Monsieur Arouet and I to live beggared of both gold and wisdom?

Truly I cannot answer. I do not know what wisdom is: still less whether I possess it. I buy my knowledge, like my fish, in cheap markets with a whiff about it. I cannot tell true diamonds from imitations. But is this not a small share of wisdom: that I can tell fake diamonds from real pebbles?

So, after my years of bitterness, I return to Monsieur Arouet. For did he not teach me about that very difference? Through him I have been lifted above baseness and ignorance and shown, if not the glory of Art and true Philosophy, at least the glitter of the Pastiche and the Second-Rate. I say this not in mockery, but because I could not have attained even those lowly objects by my own efforts. Thus I have learned, and the Lord knows it is little enough. To you, dear Reader, I can offer only my lies, my illusions and my ignorance. And it is for you to sort them through and discover: how much is Wisdom and how much is merely a Joke?

Scherzo was the next step in a writing career that had developed initially in the fields of spy thrillers and historical romances. Having written *The Hitler Diaries*, *Last Judgement*, *Farewell to Russia* and *Conspiracy of Mirrors* under the pseudonym Richard Hugo and *Lara's Child* as Alexander Mollin, I finally owned up to being Jim Williams for *Scherzo*, my first murder mystery.

The novel began to take shape in the form of the fictional character Ludovico, whom I first came across in a radio broadcast on the subject of *castrati*. My original idea was to create a novelty detective as the basis for a series of novels, but on reflection it became clear to me that this was an old fashioned notion and that, for the book to succeed, it must do so at the level of form and subtext. In many ways my initial difficulties lay in gaining confidence to break out of the conventions of the genre and subvert it to suit my purpose.

Scherzo playfully explores the parameters of our understanding of great art and thought. Whilst we cannot necessarily understand them (almost by definition they are beyond us) we still seek beauty and wisdom, and so, through imitation, create mediocre art and philosophy.

It was my desire to unify form and content which led to my approach to character and plot in *Scherzo*. Ludovico is an imitation of a woman, Monsieur Arouet is a fraudulent philosopher, Signor Giacomo (Casanova) is a hypocrite in his pretensions to honour, Pasticcio is a painter of fake pictures; Balsamo is a bogus magician. Indeed, the stolen painting, which is central to the solution, exists both as an original and a copy, and the original itself (though attributed to Raphael) may only be a copy. So too, the historical chronology is quite impossible and most of the references in the footnotes are phoney. The style throughout is a pastiche of classic eighteenth century English literature.

In the final chapter containing Ludovico's reflections, I outline some sort of resolution. Ludovico compares Monsieur Arouet with Voltaire and realises that the former is merely a fraudster (though he may indeed be Voltaire, for it can be argued that all prophets are to some degree charlatans). From that comparison he understands that, no matter if the source is second rate, he has drawn at least some wisdom from it.

In terms of writing, the crucial transformation occurs if the process of imitation creates something original which has value in its own right. To find beauty in, and construct meaning from, the unoriginal, the superficial and the second rate, is to invent a new world of reference, discourse and people.

The comedy in *Scherzo* derives from three sources; my own temperament (I laughed throughout at my own conceit) the identity of the central character and the choice of setting in a frivolous city and time.

Scherzo is my first novel under my real name. This is perhaps an ironic twist, since as I return to my own identity as the author I depart from the confines of writing in a voice that is uniquely mine. It is this playful contrast of the humble self against the extraordinary past masters that informs my writing and thinking. In the final sentence I leave it to the reader to determine how much is wisdom and how much is merely a joke. I'm damned if I know.

Jim Williams